THE CAPTIVE HEART

Glas Lib ¯in the 1920s is a time of hard adjustment
to   for
the   ers.
Bu   ble
faç

Lir   has
bro   eve
fro   e's
mo   for
Lir   the
sar   to
mo   om
the   eet
by   ho
ma

Me   nd
loy   der
Ge   dle
old   at
hap   ite
on   nal
inv

THE APPLE HEART

Glasgow in the 1920s is a time of hard inducement in a harsh new world. World War I ended well for the Franklins, prosperous Clydeside shipbuilders. But trouble is brewing behind their respectable facade.

Lindsay Franklin McCulloch's brother-in-law has brought his rebellious teenage daughter Maeve from Ireland to stay with the Franklins. Maeve's mother caused nothing but grief and heartache for Lindsay and it seems that Maeve may do the same. Lindsay's husband, Forbes, is struggling to modernise the shipyard in spite of resistance from the rest of the family. But he is swept off his feet by wealthy and manipulative Stella Pickering who may, or may not, hold the key to his future.

Meanwhile, Lindsay is torn between love and loyalty when handsome Lieutenant-Commander Geoffrey Paget walks back into her life to rekindle old flames and offer her a second chance at happiness. As the slump of the 1920s begins to bite on Clydeside, troubles both financial and personal invade all their lives.

THE CAPTIVE HEART

Jessica Stirling

**WINDSOR
PARAGON**

First published 2004
by
Hodder and Stoughton
This Large Print edition published 2004
by
BBC Audiobooks Ltd
by arrangement with
Hodder Headline Limited

ISBN 0 7540 9538 X (Windsor Hardcover)
ISBN 0 7540 9424 3   (Paragon Softcover)

British Library Cataloguing in Publication Data available

Printed and bound in Great Britain by
Antony Rowe Ltd., Chippenham, Wiltshire

Contents

PART ONE

CHAPTER ONE

The Velvet Glove

It was typical of her husband to pretend to fall asleep in the big leather armchair in the piano parlour. Lindsay knew that he wasn't really asleep, of course. When he slept his features sagged and his mouth popped open and he would snore, not loudly but with a soft rhythmic gurgle at the back of his throat. This afternoon, though, he was silence personified, his hands folded neatly over his stomach, legs stretched out, lips pursed.

The feathery little moustache that he had cultivated over the course of the winter fluttered not all and when she moved from behind the armchair and her shadow marred the light from the window, she noticed that his eyeballs flickered under the lids and realised that he was not nearly as relaxed as he would have her believe. Feigning sleep was simply another small act of self-containment, one of many ways Forbes had devised for shutting her out, but no one, not even Owen Forbes McCulloch, could possibly be so calm when within the hour he would be obliged to greet a brother whom he hadn't seen in fifteen years and meet for the very first time a girl who might, or might not, be his daughter.

Lindsay wandered to the window and looked down on the road that ringed Brunswick Park. The park wasn't much to write home about at the best of times and half past three o'clock on a drizzling afternoon in early March was certainly not the best

3

of times.

Snowdrops and crocuses had come and gone and the daffodils, three or four sad little clumps, were still on strike against the weather. The shrubs, mainly laurel, were dry and dusty-looking even under rain and the elms stubbornly refused to unfurl their quota of spring leaves. Of the shipyards that flanked the Clyde, the great bristling frieze of commerce and industry that propped up the line of the Renfrewshire hills, there was no sign at all, for rain, Glasgow's blight and bane, absorbed every sight and sound and robbed the city of its density.

It had been raining the last time she'd clapped eyes on her brother-in-law, just before he'd run off to Dublin with Forbes's mistress who was carrying Forbes's child. Sylvie Calder was a pathetic little child-woman in sore need of a man to take care of her. By all accounts Gowry had done just that. He had married her and raised the child as his own. Now he was returning to Glasgow and bringing the girl with him.

'When's the boat due to dock?' Lindsay enquired.

Forbes opened one eye. 'Is that them? Have they arrived?'

'No,' Lindsay said. 'I asked when the boat—'

'I heard you the first time.'

Forbes let his head drop back against the upholstery and bridged his hands over his stomach once more.

Lindsay said, 'You should have driven down to meet them yourself. Despatching a driver to pick up your own brother is a bit thick even for you.'

'I didn't invite him,' Forbes said. 'He didn't write to me. You were always in cahoots, you and Gowry,

4

and by the smell of it not much has changed.'

Forbes had developed the habit of reworking the past to suit himself. Facts had nothing to do with it. Forbes believed what he wanted to believe, and that was that. Their relationship was marked by indifference now, not animosity. For fifteen years they had lived almost separate lives while the fortunes of the Franklin family had waxed and waned. And Europe had been torn apart by the Great War and half a million young men, including her cousin Johnny, had sacrificed their lives for a patriotic ideal.

Lindsay found it hard to believe that she had reached her fortieth year and had two grown-up sons and that the portly, moon-faced man slumped in the armchair was the same raffish, brown-eyed Irish charmer whom she'd first met in her grandfather's house on Harper's Hill in the spring of 1898. She found it even harder to believe that she was still married to Forbes McCulloch and that he still referred to her, without a trace of irony, as his dearly beloved wife.

'Did it not occur to you, Forbes,' she said, 'that your brother's being diplomatic?'

'Diplomatic? Gowry doesn't know the meaning of the word.' He sat up. 'I wonder what sort of white lies my mother's been telling that would lead Gowry to suppose you'd make him welcome when he knows I won't.'

Forbes had cut himself off from his family in Dublin. Only his mother's visit had kept him in touch with Irish events over the years. Now that Kay McCulloch was widowed and living in Glasgow even that trickle of information had dried up. He tugged at his moustache and looked down at his shoes. He had arrived home from the office an hour before lunch to change into clothes that stated loudly and clearly that he was the only one of the McCulloch clan who had made something of himself. No drab twill or Italian cloth suits for Owen Forbes McCulloch but his increasing girth made even a silk-lined jacket, double-breasted waistcoat and striped trousers seem stuffy and Victorian.

Lindsay said, 'Are you worried about meeting the girl?'

Forbes said, 'Why would I be worried about meeting a girl I've absolutely no connection with?'

'She's . . .' Lindsay changed her mind. 'She's Gowry's daughter.'

'I'm not willing to take in every Irish tink who's looking for a fresh start.'

'Pappy took you in, did he not?'

'Ah!' Forbes said. 'So you think that providing Gowry's daughter with board and lodging is a means of paying off my debt, do you?'

Lindsay shrugged. 'Blood's thicker than water, Forbes, and a little generosity on your part, a measure of forgiveness—'

'Forgiveness,' Forbes interrupted. 'What have I to forgive Gowry for?'

'True,' Lindsay said. 'Really, I suppose Gowry did you a favour all those years ago by taking Sylvie Calder off your hands.'

She stood by the window, watching the rain.

Forbes said, 'The beggar didn't even have the decency to turn up for Dada's funeral.'

'He sent a wreath.'

'A wreath! Three withered leaves and a bit of black crape,' Forbes said. 'If Gowry's so desperate

6

to get his daughter out of Dublin why did he ask us and not Tom Calder? Have you told Calder she's coming?'

'Not yet.'

'For God's sake, why not?'

'I'm keeping it as a surprise.'

'No you're not. You're afraid Calder won't want anything to do with her or that his dear wife won't be as accommodating as you expect me to be.'

'I don't expect you to be anything,' Lindsay said, adding, 'except polite. Do you think you could manage that, Forbes, just for a day or two?'

She looked from the window. The brand-new Lanchester, her husband's pride and joy, was visible through the leafless trees. She watched the motor-car swing into Brunswick Crescent and halt below the house. The driver opened the passenger door and a man hauled himself stiffly on to the pavement. He was clad in a grubby overcoat and a beret that had once been blue. It took Lindsay a moment to realise that she was looking at Gowry McCulloch and that the years, and the war, had not been kind to him.

The girl was tall, dark-haired and pretty. She wore a tightly belted coat, a pleated skirt and a hat that was more like a trilby than a bonnet. Her leather gloves, gauntlet-style, reminded Lindsay of Gowry's uniform in the days when he'd chauffeured for the Franklins.

Gowry offered her his arm but she batted it away. Plainly exasperated, he caught her by the shoulder and turned her to face the steps. Miss Runciman, the housekeeper, limped down the steps and the girl drew back as if she intended to dive into the Lanchester and hide there. Gowry

7

snared her by the waist and for a split second they grappled on the pavement like wrestlers, then, surrendering, the girl planted her hands on her hips, snapped out a response to poor Miss Runciman's no doubt innocent question and with Gowry close behind her, marched up the steep stone steps into the hallway.

'Forbes,' Lindsay said, sweetly, 'I do believe they've arrived.'

*　　　*　　　*

Maeve had no intention of letting her father see how much the handsome terraced house impressed her. The front was ornamented with pediments and wrought-iron railings, the doorway topped by an electrical lamp, already lit. There was a huge oak outer door with brass handles and, below the level of the pavement, steps going down to the basement. She recognised posh when she saw it and this crescent was posh in the same way Harcourt Street in Dublin was posh, about as far a cry as you could get from the tenement in Endicott Street where Mam and she had lived since the British soldiers had blown up the Shamrock Hotel at the time of the Easter Rising.

She had sailed from the North Wall with her heart breaking and had every excuse for shedding tears. Grieving for Turk Trotter hadn't dented her appetite, however, and Daddy had coaxed her down to the saloon with him for a bite of supper. Then they had gone up again to sleep on the chairs on the deck. When she had wakened, shivering in the half light, she had nagged him to buy her breakfast, as if it were his fault that she was cold

8

and famished, which, in a way, it was. Although Daddy had driven for Flanagan's Motoring Company and she was well used to motor-cars, the Lanchester her uncle had sent to collect them at the quay was very powerful, more powerful than the rusting rattle-traps that Turk drove or even the Hudson that Fran Hagarty and her uncles had flashed about in when they were all much younger —and all still alive.

In spite of the grand motor-car and the warm welcome she was still fizzing because Daddy had brought her to Scotland in the first place; fizzing because she wasn't old enough to elope with Turk Trotter and become a renegade's wife. What was going on inside her head, let alone her heart, however, was nobody's business, for she was beginning to realise that she couldn't hold on to Turk as easily as all that. She wasn't giving in, though. Oh no, she told herself, she certainly wasn't giving in without a fight.

The hallway was long, like the hall of the Shamrock in its glory days, though it didn't smell of boiled cod and disinfectant. A marble-topped table supported a telephone and a silver tray and on the walls were many photographs of ships. She squinted up a staircase coated with turkey-red Axminster and, craning her neck, at a beautifully moulded ceiling and four-globe chandelier.

A woman emerged from a door at the end of the hallway. Maeve was aware that the housekeeper and the woman were waiting for her to make the first move. Daddy was taking the bags from the driver and would probably tip the chap sixpence just to show what an important man he was, all appearances to the contrary. She took a deep

9

breath, pulled off her gloves and offered her hand.

'Hello,' she said. 'I'm Maeve McCulloch. I believe you're expectin' me.'

'Of course we are,' her aunt said.

There was something wrong with the housekeeper. She walked with a limp and her hands were gnarled. Daddy and she would get on well, Maeve thought cynically, him with his wooden hand and her with her twisted fingers. Her aunt was very poised and stylish and wore a dress of pale blue silk velvet lightly trimmed with lace. She had small, cold fingers that rested like feathers in Maeve's rough palm.

'I'm Lindsay,' the woman said. 'I'd prefer you to call me Lindsay rather than Auntie.' She spoke like Mam only with more emphasis on the vowels. 'I'd like to introduce you to Miss Runciman, our housekeeper. She looks after us—and does it very well.'

'Miss Runciman,' said Maeve, chastely. She had been rude to the woman on the doorstep when she'd still entertained the silly notion that if she kicked up a fuss Daddy might take her back to Dublin with him. 'I think you asked if I'd had a pleasant journey. Well, Miss Runciman, the answer is, I did have a pleasant journey. Thank you for enquirin'.' Her father grunted approval and Maeve heard herself say, 'This is my father, Gowry McCulloch.' But the words were hardly out of her mouth before she realised how stupid it was of her to introduce a man who had worked for the Franklins and who had once lived in this very house.

'Good to see you again, Gowry,' Aunt Lindsay said.

10

'What's left of me, you mean.'

'I confess you do look somewhat the worse for wear.'

'You've hardly changed at all,' her father said. 'Where are the boys?'

'At school.'

'Boarding?'

'No, at the Academy. They'll be home shortly.'

'And himself, his lordship?'

Aunt Lindsay's answer was a curiously weary little nod in the direction of a door at the end of the hallway. 'He's in there.'

'Fuming?' her daddy said.

'Posing more like,' said Lindsay.

'That's what I'm afraid of,' her daddy said and, nudging Maeve before him, followed Aunt Lindsay along the hallway into an airy, well-lighted room.

*   *   *

Forbes McCulloch stood by the fireplace and did, indeed, seem to be posing. If Maeve hadn't been so nervous she might have laughed. One foot was planted on the brass fender, one elbow on the mantelshelf, his chin lifted to show off his profile, which might have been quite daunting if her uncle had been a matinée idol like Richard Barthelmess or Clive Brook. As it was, he was not very tall, not very distinguished and had too much tummy. Still, he might just have managed to pull off the lord of the manor act, Maeve thought, if it hadn't been for the squiggly little moustache on his upper lip.

'Gowry.'

'Forbes.'

Her uncle's tone was as flat and hard as a

11

ship's biscuit.

'Smooth passage?' he said.

'Smooth enough.'

'Came up on the morning tide, did you?'

'Aye, we lay off Greenock for a time.'

'Always do. Pilot's never punctual. What line?'

'Burns Laird.'

'Have a cabin?'

'Too expensive.'

'How much?'

'Thirty-five shillings.'

'I always have a cabin,' Uncle Forbes said. 'Drink?'

Uncle Forbes was the man who was never spoken of at home, the Great Unmentionable. Whenever she had quizzed Mam about him Mam had changed the subject. Only Grandma McCulloch had been free with information but it was so obvious that Forbes was the apple of Gran's eye that her opinion was worthless.

'What have you got?' her father asked.

'Whisky, gin—sherry.'

'I think I'd prefer tea.'

'What about the girl? What will she drink?' Uncle Forbes said.

Maeve heard herself say, 'She'll drink tea too, thank you very much.'

He studied her for the first time and seemed surprised that she had spoken a language he could understand.

'Are you Maeve?' he asked.

'I was when I left Dublin,' Maeve answered.

'You're not what I expected.'

'What did you expect? Two heads?'

Until recently she had been in company where

12

the line between forthrightness and insolence had never been made clear. She spoke to her uncle as she would have spoken to Turk or Breen Trotter, to Pauline, Breen's wife, or to any of the crowd who lived in Wexford or mustered in the back room of McKinstry's public house.

'I thought you might be more like—like . . .'

Maeve's cynicism had not yet hardened into cruelty. She had sense enough not to utter the first words that leaped into her mind: 'Like my mother, you mean?'

'Maeve,' Aunt Lindsay put in, 'perhaps you'd like to inspect your room.'

She felt her father's hand on her back, the wooden hand. 'I could be doin' with a pee,' she said, 'if you happen to have a facility handy.'

Miss Runciman said, 'I believe we have a lavatory somewhere on the premises. Come with me. I'll show you.' And Maeve followed Miss Runciman and Aunt Lindsay out of the parlour, leaving Daddy and her uncle alone.

*　　　*　　　*

'What the devil do you mean dumping her on us?' Forbes said.

'I had to get her out of Dublin.'

'Had to? Why?'

'Don't you read the newspapers?'

'Well, as far as I can make out Ireland's just the same old madhouse,' said Forbes. 'My God, you haven't turned into a Republican, have you?'

'My daughter has.'

'Maeve is your daughter, isn't she?' Forbes said. 'You're not trying to foist her off on me, I hope?

13

Did Sylvie put you up to this?' He lowered his voice. 'How is Sylvie, by the way? Is she well?'

'As well as any of us in Dublin these days.'

'Mother tells me she had another child, a boy.'

'She had.'

'A child not of your making,' Forbes said. 'I can't understand why you stick by her.' He seated himself on the high brass fender at the fire. 'She was damned attractive in her own daft fashion when she was young but—let's be honest, Gowry— she was always a bit of a tart.'

'You're talking about my wife, Forbes,' Gowry reminded him.

'Yes, well, she didn't exactly remain steadfast and true when you were off fighting for king and country, did she?'

'She was told I'd been killed in action.'

'That's not what I heard,' Forbes said. 'I heard that our Sylvie was having a busy little fling with some gun-runner long before you enlisted.'

Gowry eased himself on to the arm of a chair and stuck the wooden hand between his knees. He wasn't the same chap who had walked out on Forbes fifteen years ago, who had shouldered the burden of Forbes's indiscretions and who, after a fashion, had saved Forbes's marriage. He was scarred inside as well as out, but he still cared enough for Sylvie to defend her.

He picked his words with care. 'The boy isn't mine, no.'

'You're a better man than I am, old chap. I'd have left her to stew in her own juice if she'd put the horns on me. I suppose you're going to tell me you stayed for the girl's sake?'

'I stayed for my own sake,' Gowry said. 'I had

14

nowhere else to go.'

'Oh that's sad, so sad,' said Forbes, without a trace of compassion.

'If it had been left to me I'd have asked Tom Calder to look after Maeve.'

'Why does anyone have to look after her?' Forbes said.

'Because I've brought her here to get her away from the troubles,' said Gowry, testily. 'She's been associated with rebels, our brothers, Peter and Charlie, among them since she was old enough to walk and you can't escape their influence. In other words, she's more than halfway to becoming a militant Nationalist.'

'Nationalism's a worthy cause.'

'Maybe it is,' Gowry said, 'but the British don't seem to agree with you. It isn't safe to walk the streets in broad daylight any longer, especially if you're Daniel McCulloch's granddaughter and Peter McCulloch's niece.'

'Don't tell me our Peter's blowing up railway trains and shooting at soldiers,' Forbes said.

'That's exactly what he's doing,' Gowry said.

'Dear God!'

'Peter's right-hand man's a feller named Turk Trotter. Maeve's been soft on Trotter since she was ten years old. He's a decent enough bloke in his way an' he's always been fond of Maeve but now she's grown up, or nearly so, she expects him to marry her. We're not goin' to stand for that.'

Forbes nodded. 'I see your problem.'

'You don't seem to realise how much hatred there is in the old country. Pure hatred. The hatred's more infectious than the patriotism. Don't think the military authorities don't know who

15

Maeve is or that because she's a girl no harm will come to her. If Maeve does rush into marriage with Turk Trotter she'll be a fugitive with a price on her head.'

'If she's genuinely infatuated with this Trotter character . . .'

'She is, she is. She's furious at me for draggin' her away from him.'

'Perhaps it's her destiny to marry Trotter,' Forbes said, shrugging.

Gowry reached out with his artificial hand, a clumsy contraption wrapped in withered leather with only the thumb, his flesh, exposed. He grabbed his brother by the shoulder. *'Don't say that. Don't ever say that.'* He thrust his face down. 'I don't know whose daughter Maeve is. Even Sylvie doesn't know for sure. Let's just say she's *our* daughter and I'm not willin' to write her off in the name of destiny, or any other bloody thing.'

Gowry drew his hand away and pressed his thumb back into place as if it, not the fingers, were hinged.

Forbes said, 'Does Sylvie really not know whose daughter Maeve is?'

'No,' Gowry said. 'After all these years, Forbes, does it matter?'

'I suppose not,' Forbes said. 'May I get up now?'

'Will you look after her for a while?'

'I really could do with a drink.'

'Forbes, damn it, man: will you look after her?'

'Of course I will,' Forbes said. 'What'll you have?'

'Brandy,' Gowry answered just as Maeve and Lindsay returned and, a moment later, the boys burst into the room.

16

If there was one thing that Lindsay admired about her sons it was their candour. At times she found it hard to believe that they were Forbes's children, for honesty had never been a McCulloch trait. Harry, the elder, reminded her of her grandfather Owen, for he already exhibited all the best Franklin characteristics of drive and determination. She was too modest to admit that her influence upon him had been considerable or that openness and enthusiasm had once been features of her character too and that if she had not met and married Forbes McCulloch, might have remained so.

At the dining table that evening, the boys were on their best behaviour; showing off, of course. Lindsay could hardly blame them. Maeve was a very pretty young woman and Gowry had the battered visage of a warrior in the heroic mould. Her sons were probably bursting with questions about the circumstances that had brought Maeve and Gowry to Scotland but they were too well-mannered to ask pointed questions.

Twenty-three years ago, almost to the month, Lindsay had been seated at a crowded dining table in her grandfather's house trying desperately not to appear forward in the presence of her Irish cousin, Forbes. He had seemed no less attractive, no less a curiosity to her than Maeve McCulloch must seem to her sons. Her cousin Cissie and she had competed for his attention with a fervour that had been nothing short of gauche.

Maeve appeared to be indifferent to the boys'

attentions. She was comfortable with the array of knives and forks that Enid had set out and ate with the same rapidity as Forbes, as if consumption was being measured against the clock. She wore an off-the-peg woollen day-dress that had seen better days. If she stays, Lindsay promised herself, we'll have to see what we can do about smartening her up. She felt a surge of pleasure at the prospect, for however much she adored her sons they could not share her interests and enthusiasms.

She watched the girl slice pie with a dessert fork and operate upon it with her spoon, dab her lips with her napkin and let out a sigh that seemed to signify that she was satisfied at last.

Twenty years ago the family would have retired to the parlour and gathered round the piano for a jolly musical evening. None of that nonsense in Brunswick Park these days; Forbes wasn't partial to music and her father had long ago given up trying to persuade him to invite the cousins round for a good old-fashioned sing-song.

'Do you sing, Maeve?' Lindsay asked.

The girl seemed startled by the question.

'Do I what?'

'Do you sing?' said Lindsay, gently. 'Are you musical?'

'I can carry a tune.' Maeve glared at her father, daring him to contradict. 'You're not expectin' me to sing, are you?'

'No, no,' Lindsay reassured her. 'We don't expect you to do anything you don't want to do.'

'That's just as well,' said Maeve, ' 'cause I don't reckon I'll be stayin'.'

'Oh!' Philip exclaimed. 'I thought you—'

Harry administered a kick under cover of

the tablecloth.

Lindsay glanced towards the door and beckoned to Enid to clear away the pudding plates and asked her to serve coffee here in the dining-room.

She looked across at Miss Runciman who ate with the family and not downstairs with the maid and the cook. Miss Runciman raised one thin eyebrow, and said, 'I trust you won't be running off too soon, young lady, certainly not before you've had an opportunity to meet the rest of your relatives. They're exceedingly anxious to meet you.'

'Oh!' Maeve said. 'Why?'

'Because you're one of us,' said Philip.

He was smaller than his brother and slightly built. He had his father's long eyelashes and dark eyes but didn't really resemble Forbes, Lindsay assured herself, though other folk said that he did.

'I am not,' Maeve said.

'You're a McCulloch, aren't you?' said Harry.

'What if I am?' said Maeve.

'With the exception of Miss Runciman,' Harry said, 'we're all McCullochs here.'

'Aye, well, we might share a name,' said Maeve, 'but I'm not one o' you an' never will be.'

'Unfair,' Harry said. 'You hardly know us.'

'An' you don't know me at all.'

'You're tired, Maeve,' Gowry said. 'Maybe you should go to your room.'

'I'm not tired.'

'Of course you're not tired,' Lindsay said. 'It's far too early to think of going to bed. Enid will serve coffee in a minute.'

She was tempted to reach across the table and pat the girl's hand, to demonstrate affinity. Miss Runciman, it seemed, had much the same thought.

19

She covered Maeve's hand and gave it two or three little taps with her fingertips.

'Do you know what that means?' Eleanor Runciman asked.

'What what means?' said Maeve, frowning.

Miss Runciman tapped again. 'That?'

'Nope,' Maeve admitted, 'I don't know what it means.'

Harry laughed and exchanged a knowing look with his brother.

'It's code, Miss—Maeve,' he said. 'Morse code. She used to do it all the time when Phil and I were young. It's SOS, Miss Runciman, isn't it?'

'Well, I don't need my soul savin',' Maeve said. 'I'm not in distress.'

Forbes spoke up. 'It's a family joke,' he said. 'I, however, never did see the point of it.'

'That's because you're a fuddy-duddy, Forbes,' Lindsay said and, turning, asked Gowry, 'How did you lose your hand?'

Gowry peered at the artificial hand. 'Jerry shell.'

'The Somme, was it, sir?' Philip asked.

'Guillemont,' Gowry said. 'The raid on Guillemont.'

'With the Irish Rifles, sir?' said Harry. 'Did you fight on our side?'

'Aye, he fought on your side,' said Maeve. 'He should've been fightin' on our side but he joined the British instead.'

'Are you a Republican?' Harry asked.

'I'm Irish,' Maeve answered, ' 'course I'm a Republican.'

'Dad's Irish,' said Philip, 'and he's not a Republican.'

'More fool him, then,' said Maeve.

20

'Enough!' said Gowry, sharply this time.

The girl was not distressed, not even angry. She was a prickly Dubliner, Lindsay guessed, who loved nothing better than an argument. It had been years since the dining-room in Brunswick Crescent had rung to the sound of raised voices, for her father, Arthur Franklin, and her husband had reached an agreement that any shouting that had to be done would be done at the office and not at home. She wished that Papa was here but he had gone to Norway with Martin to chase contracts and would not be back until Monday or Tuesday.

'I suppose I may as well tell you,' Maeve said. 'I'm only here 'cause my mam and dad are frightened I'll wind up in jail.'

'Jail?' said Philip. 'Have you—I mean, have you been in jail?'

'Not yet,' said Maeve. 'I'm not scared o' servin' hard labour, though.'

Lindsay had anticipated a certain degree of adolescent anguish in the girl but not this challenging attitude. She was pleased with herself was Miss Maeve McCulloch, and clearly felt superior to her cousins.

Harry said, 'Are you a member of the Volunteer Army, Miss—Maeve?'

'Oh, you've heard of the Volunteers, have you?'

'Grandma subscribes to all the Irish newspapers,' Philip said. 'Are you on the wanted list?'

'My man is,' Maeve answered. 'My man has a price on his head.'

'How much?' said Philip.

'Five hundred pounds.'

Philip whistled admiringly. 'What did he do?'

21

'If you think I'm goin' to tell you that, think again,' said Maeve.

'At least tell us his name,' said Philip.

'Turk Trotter's his name. He fought in the Rising and served a stretch in Frongoch, that's a Welsh prison, in case you didn't know.'

'Is he really your sweetheart?' said Philip.

'Sweetheart! He's my man.'

'What does that mean,' said Philip, 'exactly?'

'It means,' said Lindsay, 'you've had your share of questions, Philip. Let someone else get a word in, if you please.'

'Oh!' He nodded. 'Right!'

Harry took up where his brother had left off. 'Are you staying with us because you're on the run?'

'I might be,' Maeve said, 'but I'm not.'

Gowry said, 'Maeve an' me don't see eye to eye on unification policy. I brought her here to keep her out of harm's way.'

'Huh!' Maeve said. 'Harm's way, is it? Why don't you tell them how the British are tryin' to crush our spirit by murderin' anybody they don't like the look of.' Her voice rose. 'Tell them how they murdered Mr Hagarty and how they blew up our hotel while you were off fightin' the Germans.'

'Stop it, Maeve,' Gowry said. 'This isn't the place for one of your rants.'

Forbes leaned both elbows on the table. He had shed his lethargy and his eyes glittered with interest. 'No,' he said. 'Let her have her say.'

Sanction from her uncle was so unexpected that Maeve fell silent.

'My daddy's right,' she said, at length. 'I'm bein' rude. Sorry.'

22

'No, you're not. You're only defending what you believe in,' Forbes said.

In all the time she'd known him, Lindsay thought, Forbes had given allegiance to no other cause than his own advancement. He had mocked his brothers for pursuing impossible ideals and condemned his father for running the McCulloch's profitable little brewery into the ground for the sake of the Irish Brotherhood, though Kay McCulloch said it was a fondness for whiskey and three-legged horses that had really done Daniel in.

'All right then,' Maeve said, 'I believe I should rightfully be in Ireland, shoulder to shoulder wi' my man.'

'Good,' Forbes said. 'But I would like to point out that the cause you're fighting for isn't just about blowing up police stations and shooting soldiers; it's as much about economic oppression as anything else. And that, young lady, is the sort of war you can fight whether you're in Paris, Dublin or Glasgow.'

'What are you drivin' at?' said Maeve.

'Tell you what,' Forbes said, 'whatever money you earn for the cause between now and the day you turn eighteen, I'll double. No, I'll treble. I'll even buy you a steamer ticket to get you back to Dublin, back into the fight.'

'Is this your way of getting rid of me?' Maeve said.

'On the contrary,' Forbes said. 'Unless I miss my guess you're not the sort of girl who'll be happy mooching about the house all day long. I'm offering you an incentive to go out and find employment and do something for the cause in which you believe.'

23

'What's the catch?'

'No catch,' said Forbes. 'I'm trying to keep you out of mischief while soothing my own conscience at the same time.'

'*Your* conscience, Forbes?' said Gowry.

'I haven't done much to aid the Irish cause,' Forbes said, 'but now Peter and Charlie are in the thick of it, I feel I have to do something.' He turned to Lindsay. 'Aren't you always reminding me that blood's thicker than water?'

'Three times what I earn?' Maeve said. 'You'll donate that to the cause?'

'My word is my bond,' said Forbes. 'Do we have a deal, young lady?'

'I'm not afraid o' hard work,' Maeve said. 'Aye, it's a deal.'

Forbes reached across the table and clasped Maeve's hand.

And Lindsay, somewhat shaken, signalled to Enid to bring in the coffee.

*   *   *

The room at the top of the house had once been the nursery. Stencilled on the walls were a bunny rabbit, a goose wearing a bonnet and a fish with a smile on its face, the friendly little figures almost invisible in the glow of the electrical lamp. There was a curtained window, a bed, a chest of drawers, several miniature chairs and a table so low that Maeve had to hunch over it to write to her mother and to print a large-letter greeting to her brother, Sean, who had just learned to read. Sean could be annoying at times. He was so greedy for attention that he would follow her around, tug at her skirts and demand to be played with. Only Daddy could really cope with Sean, for Daddy had the patience of Job and spent a lot of time with the boy, a lot more time, Maeve thought, than he had ever spent with her when she was Sean's age.

Things had not been right since Turk had been released from Frongoch prison and had charged down the gangplank of the Liverpool steam packet and swept her into his arms. She had been a few weeks short of her thirteenth birthday then but already madly in love with him.

She had seen little of him in the next year and a half, though.

Turk had been busy organising the brotherhood down in Wexford, and she'd been stuck in school. Then Pauline, Breen Trotter's wife, had persuaded Mam to let Maeve visit the Trotters' farmhouse in Wexford during the summer holiday and she had spent a week touring horse fairs and cattle marts with Breen and Turk's father and going to meetings in the evenings in public halls or secret houses out in the countryside. Soon after she'd left Wexford, five of Turk's men had ambushed a load of gelignite that was being carted to a quarry under police escort. Two policemen had been shot, Turk's boys had got clean away with the gelly and a five hundred pound reward had been offered by the government for information leading to the arrest of the ambushers.

That December her Uncle Peter had shown up at the tenement in Endicott Street and asked for sanctuary. Daddy had taken him in but he was furious at the risk involved and had telephoned the Trotters and Turk had appeared on the day after Christmas and had persuaded Peter to move on.

25

That night Turk had kissed her for the first time. He had stuck one hand under her coat and squeezed her breast, then, with a bellow like a bull-calf, had shoved her away and gone loping off down Endicott Street to find someone to take in Peter and hide him for a week or two.

Turk had kissed her often after that but had never touched her breast again. He had taken her to meetings in McKinstry's pub or to a basement under the old O'Connell Halls where the best of the Dublin boys gathered. It could only be a matter of time, Maeve thought, until she was old enough to become Turk's wife and join the fight proper. Then, late one night, she'd told Daddy what was on the cards and Daddy had flown into a rage and before she could draw breath she'd been whisked out of school and put to work in the biscuit factory where, if Daddy had only known it, there was more plotting going on than in the chambers of the Dáil. She had written to Pauline asking her to tell Turk she was ready to run away with him, but she had received no answer. She had written to Pauline again and when Pauline failed to reply for a second time had written to Charlie and when he didn't answer either, had written to old man Trotter; not one of them had deigned to reply.

Then, late one winter afternoon, a Sunday, she had been grabbed by two peelers and hustled down an alley at the back of Mrs Cafferty's boarding-house. They had pushed her against the wall, stuck a revolver to her head and told her that if she didn't tell them where Turk Trotter was hiding they would shoot her. She told them it would make more sense if *they* told *her* where Turk was hiding because she had no bloody idea and it was high

26

time he turned up and kept his promise to marry her. The peeler with the gun had laughed and stuffed the gun back in its holster and told her that marriage was the last thing on Trotter's mind, for he was having far too good a time of it poking all the young girls in the houses that were daft enough to give him shelter. She had laughed at that whopper and said, 'Sure and you're not going to get round me with that bloody lie' and one of the peelers had put a hand round her throat and rammed his other hand up her skirts and felt her belly under her drawers and told her that Turk didn't know what he was missing. Then they had gone away.

She had been too upset not to tell Mam, and Mam had told Daddy. Within a week Daddy had had her on the boat for Glasgow—and she still hadn't heard a word from Pauline, Charlie or from Turk himself.

She peered at the goose, the bunny, the grinning fish, licked her pencil and smoothed the surface of the notepaper. She wanted to write 'Dear Turk,' or 'My Dearest Darling,' but the memory of what the peeler had told her lingered, together with the memory of Turk's hand on her breast and the stranger's hand groping her drawers. She sighed and instead of writing about her uncle's offer and asking how she could transfer the money to those in Ireland who needed it most, she drew a heart, a big heart, and, as she had done once before, long ago, printed beneath it:

Maeve & Turk.
One True Love.

though she wasn't quite sure what true love meant any longer.

A knock on the nursery door startled her. She had almost forgotten that she was in Glasgow now and had nothing to fear.

'Who is it?'

'Lindsay. May I come in?'

'Sure an' I can't stop you.'

Her aunt was dressed as she had been at the dinner table but seemed softer, and younger, in the shallow light from the lamp.

'I'm not intruding, am I?'

'Nope,' Maeve said. 'See, I haven't run away.'

'I thought you might be in bed.'

Maeve covered the notepad with both hands. 'Just goin'.'

'Do you have everything you need?'

'Yes, thank you.'

'Then I'll leave you to your letter-writing,' Lindsay said. 'Breakfast is at seven forty-five but Cook will make you something later if you decide to lie in.'

'I'll be up.' Maeve managed a smile. 'Where's Daddy?'

'One floor down,' her aunt said. 'Goodnight, Maeve.'

'Goodnight,' Maeve said and as soon as her aunt had gone, tore up her silly drawing and flushed the pieces down the pan in the lavatory next door.

*   *   *

For many years it had been Miss Runciman's task to shut the big oak door, lock the inner door and switch out all the lights except the one little bulb

28

that burned throughout the night. The door had become too heavy for Miss Runciman to cope with, though, and Arthur Franklin had taken over the chore, for Lindsay's father still regarded himself as head of the household.

When Lindsay came downstairs from the nursery she was surprised to find both inner and outer doors lying wide open and a cool, damp breeze filtering through the hall.

'Forbes?' she said, tentatively. 'Is that you, Forbes?'

'No, it's me.'

She stepped outside and saw Gowry outlined against the glow from the lamp-standard, cigar smoke swirling around him like cream in a coffee cup.

'What on earth are you doing out here?' she asked.

'Grabbing a breath of air.'

'Where's Forbes?'

'Gone to bed. I said I'd lock up.'

Lindsay looked out over the misty suburbs towards the river. The flash and flare of a late-shift welding crew showed against the belly of the cloud. She wondered if it reminded Gowry of his days in the trenches, if that, multiplied a thousandfold, was what an artillery barrage looked like. She had never cared for Gowry. He had been too much Forbes's man, too alien and Irish for her taste back in 1906 when she'd been fighting her own domestic wars. She felt sorry for him now, though, so battered and torn and mournful.

'You can smoke indoors, you know,' she said.

Gowry plucked the cigar from his mouth. 'Not these smelly things,' he said. 'Sylvie won't let me light up inside. I go out in the street or into the back yard when I want to smoke. They are pretty foul, I suppose.'

'Not as bad as Donald's pipe. Do you remember it?'

'Aye,' Gowry chuckled, 'it reeked like a tug-boat's funnel.'

'Donald retired soon after the Armistice. Lilias and he live down the coast now, in Largs.'

'One o' the boys was killed, wasn't he?' Gowry said.

'Yes, Johnny went down with the *Vengeance*, torpedoed in the Baltic. There were very few survivors.'

They were both silent for a moment, thinking of the dead and of days that were gone; then Gowry flicked his cigar away and they watched together the curving arc of the coal in the air and the little splash of sparks when it struck the wet pavement. 'It's late,' Gowry said. 'I'd best be getting to bed.'

'No,' Lindsay said. 'Wait.'

He glanced at her quizzically. He seemed very tall out there in the half darkness, almost grotesquely so. She could smell cigar smoke on him and another faint, not unpleasant odour, like cinnamon.

'What is it, Lindsay?' he said. 'Don't you like my daughter?'

'Yes, I like her. She's been hurt, though, hasn't she?'

'We've all been hurt one way or another,' Gowry said. 'She's young enough to get over it.'

'Is it the man, the soldier?'

'Trotter's an agitator, not a soldier.'

'I gather you don't approve of him.'

30

'It doesn't matter whether I approve, or not,' Gowry said. 'Trotter won't marry her and if he did, she'd be widowed within a year.'

'What Forbes said at the dinner table, his offer, will it help or hinder?'

'He's a smarmy bastard, my brother,' Gowry said. 'He knows what the promise of money for the cause means to Maeve.'

'At least he's given her a reason to stay in Glasgow.'

'The velvet glove,' said Gowry.

'It may be more effective than the iron hand,' said Lindsay. 'We'll take good care of her, I promise.'

'I'll miss her,' Gowry said. 'By God, I'll miss her,' then he stepped quickly back into the house and left it to Lindsay to close the big oak door.

CHAPTER TWO

Coming Up For Air

In the absence of his cousin, Martin, Forbes took the chair at Franklin's weekly management meeting. As a rule it was Forbes who went in pursuit of new business but he had no fondness for Norwegians or their climate and had foisted that trip on to Martin and Arthur Franklin.

Naval contracts and the restocking of merchant fleets in the immediate aftermath of the war had resulted, until now, in a full order book.

Martin had been content to take on everything that came their way, everything, that is, that did not

31

involve capital investment. Forbes, on the other hand, was an advocate of modernisation.

Currently on the stocks were four ships in various stages of construction, including two half-built S-class destroyers, Franklin's share of an Admiralty order for sixteen such vessels, but three building berths were empty.

Forbes was keen to move on, to move, as he put it, into the future. The future as he saw it lay not in warships or general cargo vessels but in bulk oil-tankers, a specialised form of construction that would mean altering the layout of the yard and impose a considerable strain on lying capital. His reasoning, Lindsay agreed, was sound, but his methods of persuasion left a lot to be desired.

Although she held more shares than her husband and, strictly speaking, had more say, Lindsay had drawn back from interfering in the running of the yard and rarely attended the weekly meetings. She had come to Aydon Road today for one reason only—to invite Tom Calder to lunch.

From her chair at the boardroom table, Lindsay could make out the roof of the testing tank, another of Forbes's innovations, and behind it, rearing up against the grey sky, the stern portion of one of the cargo ships with carpenters clambering all over the scaffolding.

'What's this item here?' Forbes held up a sheet of graph paper attached to a typed letter under the Admiralty crest. 'Has Martin dealt with it?'

'No,' said Archie Robb, frowning. 'He hasn't seen it yet.'

'What is it, precisely?'

'Specification changes,' said Tom Calder. 'We offered Portland cement for all areas and that was nodded through. Now the Navy Board has changed its tune and requires bituminous materials for lining the engine and boiler rooms, bilges and decks.'

'Good God!' Forbes said. 'Have Swann Hunter and Barclay Curle received similar notification?'

'Yes,' Archie Robb answered. 'It's a general change in specifications.'

Forbes held the graph paper up to the light and squinted at it. He was, Lindsay knew, primarily a 'bottom line' man, not a trained engineer.

Archie Robb sat up very straight. He was a small man, pinch-faced, with reading glasses perched halfway down his nose. Tom Calder rested his chin on his palm. Forbes flapped the graph paper down on the table and pressed it flat, as if he were squashing a fly.

'I assume,' he said, 'that the navy realise bituminous materials cost more than basic Portland and will require more man hours to apply?'

'Of course they do,' Tom Calder said, sighing.

'Do they expect us to absorb the additional costs?'

'That's about the size of it,' said Archie Robb.

'The theory,' Tom said, 'is that deadweight will be lightened and speed at sea increased accordingly. They haven't used bituminous materials in destroyers up until now so I can only assume some bright spark of a constructor-commander thought it was time he earned his next promotion.'

'How much will it cost per vessel?' Forbes said.

'Difficult to say,' Tom answered. 'Cold state application at an approximate rate of one hundredweight of material per sixteen square feet ...'

'Oh,' Forbes groaned, 'do it, just do it. Do we

33

have enough material on hand? If not, order it in and adjust the costing accordingly.'

'I wonder what Mr Martin'll have to say about that?' said Archie Robb.

'I've approved it, haven't I? Isn't that good enough for you?'

Forbes handed the graph and letter to his personal secretary, Mrs Connors, and instructed her to type out a standard letter of compliance to which he would add a paragraph or two.

Mrs Connors, a dumpy widow in her mid-thirties, placed the letter into her folder and made a shorthand note on her pad. She was no less efficient than any of the men in the room but nobody had ever been able to wheedle out of Meg Connors what she really thought of Mr Forbes or Mr Martin, or any of the other partners. She worked with her files and typewriter in a room that had once belonged to Johnny Franklin and kept her door, literally and figuratively, closed at all times.

Lindsay listened with half an ear to a lacklustre discussion on the benefits of installing mobile lavatories for the workforce and just how much trouble the proposal would cause with the trade unions.

She had heard it all before. Indeed, she seemed to have been listening to the same discussion in one form or another since she was a little girl playing on the carpet in Grandfather Owen's drawing-room, and was just as bored by the rumble of serious male voices now as she had been then. She listened to the *tock-tick* of the big wall clock, hammering from the yard and the jovial *whoop-whoop-whoop* of a sanitation department tug rolling downriver with a string of barges behind it. She was as bored as Tom Calder, more so in fact, for Tom didn't know what lay in store for him when the meeting ended.

Lindsay had arranged with Miss Runciman to bring Maeve to the Central Hotel at twelve thirty. Now, of course, all she had to do was prevent Forbes spoiling the surprise by blurting out that the girl was in Glasgow.

'. . . stop the damned apprentices pissing into the tea cans,' she heard Robb say. 'Sorry, Mrs McCulloch.'

'Sorry for what, Archie?'

'The—er—the language.'

'I'm well aware that apprentices have unruly bladders,' Lindsay said with a smile. 'However, if this meeting is going to continue along such indelicate lines perhaps it would be less inhibiting if I took my leave.'

'You don't have to go, Linnet,' Forbes said.

Lindsay was already on her feet. The managers, gentlemen all, scrambled to rise but Lindsay motioned them to remain where they were.

'Tom, if I might have a word with you,' she said. 'Outside.'

'If you don't need me, Forbes . . .' Tom said.

Forbes opened his mouth to protest then closed it again with an odd little snap that spread into a sly grin. 'No, we don't need you. We're almost through here. Go, by all means. I think my dear wife is taking you to lunch.'

'Is she?' Tom said, surprised.

'Just make sure she foots the bill,' Forbes said and, with a dismissive wave of the hand, returned to talking about toilets.

As soon as they had settled into the back seat of
the taxi-cab, Tom said, 'Now, Lindsay, what's this
all about?'

'Don't look so harassed. I'm only taking you to
lunch.'

'Where—the Ashton?'

'No, the Central.'

'Really!' Tom said.

The Central Hotel was situated in the heart of
the city next to the railway station but shipbuilders
and industrialists preferred the more rough-hewn
surroundings of the Ashton.

'How's Cissie?' Lindsay said.

'Blooming, as well you know.'

'And the children?'

Tom had been a widower when he had fallen for
Cissie or, more accurately, when she had fallen for
him. She was a plain girl, excitable, and it had come
as a vast relief to Donald and Lilias when Tom
Calder had straightened out his tangled domestic
affairs and finally popped the question.

He wasn't quite the bleak, cadaverous figure that
he had been at the turn of the century, marriage
and good cooking had fleshed him out a little, but
he still had the hollow cheeks and haggard lines of
a man who could not shake off the worry habit. He
was also, now, very short of hair and rather
sensitive about it, a fact that his daughters, Dorothy
and Katy, did not take into account when they
patted his bald spot by way of showing affection.
Tom's son, Ewan, was a pupil at the Academy, a
dour, very clever boy, who only really came out of

his shell when his cousins were there to lead him on—or so his parents believed.

'The children are well enough,' Tom answered. 'Blessed if I know what to do with the girls, though. It can't be much fun having a father who's almost sixty and can't keep up with them.'

'Come now, Tom, you're not sixty, you're only fifty-seven. You don't have one foot in the grave just yet.'

Tom shrugged and looked out of the window at the traffic. 'If you intend to interrogate me about Forbes's plans for a bulk oil-tanker, I should warn you I've been sworn to secrecy.'

'It can't be much of a secret,' Lindsay said, 'if we'll have a model in the testing tank come summer. Are there problems with the design?'

'Endless problems,' Tom admitted. 'The main problem, though, is that we don't have a buyer. Designing, let alone building ships on spec is a highly risky business that makes everyone nervous —including me.'

'Forbes wouldn't go ahead without a firm order, would he?'

'No, probably not.'

'In any case,' Lindsay said, 'we can't start laying down a keel until the destroyers have been delivered.' She paused. 'How profitable would building an oil-tanker be?'

'Profitable,' Tom said. 'Very profitable.'

'Enough to justify the capital outlay?'

'I imagine so, yes,' Tom said. 'Look, I thought I was just out for a pleasant lunch, not a grilling.'

'All right,' said Lindsay. 'No more shop talk, I promise.'

The cab turned from Argyll Street into the

37

bottom end of Hope Street where, even at that hour, traffic congestion was considerable. Lindsay's excitement became tinged with panic at the thought that Maeve might not co-operate with Miss Runciman, might refuse to enter the Central Hotel, might flounce off to explore the city on her own, and that her surprise would be spoiled.

'Pay the driver, Tom,' Lindsay said. 'We'll walk from here.'

'What's the rush?'

Lindsay opened the cab door and stepped on to the pavement. She peered up Hope Street towards the hotel. Locked in by horse-drawn carts and a clutter of tramcars, the taxi-cab remained at the kerb.

Tom joined her on the pavement.

She turned to him and, on impulse, reached up and straightened his necktie and dusted the lapels of his overcoat, then took his arm and hurried him towards the hotel door.

'We're meeting someone, Lindsay, aren't we?'

'I'm hungry, that's all.'

'Is this another of Forbes's nasty little tricks?' said Tom, suspiciously.

'No,' Lindsay answered, 'it's one of mine.'

*   *   *

They had left the house in Brunswick Crescent shortly after eleven o'clock. Maeve had slept like a top and had stuffed away an enormous breakfast and felt more cheerful than she had done last night. She had been relieved when her cousins had galloped off to school, though, for she found their eagerness to please wearing. She had not been

38

particularly surprised when Uncle Forbes had hurried off to the shipyard and, a short while later, Aunt Lindsay had followed suit. Even her father seemed to have things to do.

'Are you going to visit Gran?' Maeve asked.

'I might,' Daddy answered.

'Do you want me to come with you?'

'Do you want to?'

'Not especially.'

'I'd better drop in on her, I suppose,' Daddy said, with a sigh, 'though all she'll do is complain because I didn't come over for the old man's funeral.'

'She should have brought him home for burial. I mean, he should have been put down into the earth in Ireland, then everybody would have shown up.'

'I think,' Daddy said, 'that's what your gran was trying to avoid.'

'What are you goin' to tell Gran about Peter and Charlie?'

'As little as possible,' said Daddy.

Then it was settled that the housekeeper would take her down town to see the sights—which, Maeve hoped, meant window-shopping—and they would join Aunt Lindsay for lunch at half past twelve.

They rode along Dumbarton Road in a two-decker tramcar, seated upstairs in the front compartment above the driver.

Maeve had the impression that riding upstairs in a tramcar was an unusual experience for Miss Runciman and not one that the woman particularly enjoyed. There were lots of things she wanted to ask about Uncle Forbes and Aunt Lindsay but Maeve guessed that Miss Runciman would be too loyal to her aunt and uncle to tell her what she really wanted to know.

She had expected Glasgow to be much the same as Dublin but it was not. Everything about it was different: the shapes and colours of the tenements, the ornate style of the civic buildings, its green parks and long hills and all along the riverside a densely packed mass of warehouses and towering cranes far taller and far more impressive than anything she'd seen on the Liffey. There were more motor-cars, fewer horses. Small shops and pubs bore different signs and the big shops, the departmental stores, were vast. And, of course, there were no soldiers on the street corners, no armoured cars, no barracks or barricades.

They got off the tram in Sauchiehall Street and went directly into a huge department store and up in a lift to the third-floor tea-room and had a cup of tea. After that, Miss Runciman went to the ladies' cloakroom and Maeve wandered among the glittering display cases and inhaled the aroma of very expensive, very desirable clothes, which made her only too aware of her own shabby outfit.

She walked down the carpeted stairs, one floor at a time, and found Miss Runciman resting on a chair by a display case filled with powder compacts and vanity cases while a young woman in a tight-fitting black wool dress was doing her best to persuade her to buy an indelible lipstick.

'How much?' Maeve asked.

'Pardon?' the assistant said.

'The lipstick, how much?'

'Twenty-three shillings.'

'Twenty-three shillings!' said Maeve. 'Is that all?'

'It's Dorothy Gray, you know.'

'Looks more like Scarlet Woman to me,' Maeve said and, extending her hand, assisted Miss Runciman to her feet. 'Shall we be goin' now? It's almost time for our next appointment.'

Miss Runciman, poker-faced, said, 'Tréron's or Rowan's?'

'Oh, Tréron's, by all means,' said Maeve, who had no idea what or where Tréron's was. Linking arms with Miss Runciman, she accompanied the woman out of the main doors into the street where the housekeeper paused and uttered a strange barking laugh.

'What?' Maeve said. 'What is it?'

'Scarlet Woman,' Miss Runciman said, shaking her head. 'My, my, my!' Then, still holding on to Maeve's arm, steered a course into Wellington Street and down the long steep hill towards the Central Hotel.

*   *   *

He was taller than Daddy, taller even than Turk. He was skinny, though, and had stooped shoulders. When he took off his hat she saw that he was almost bald. Nobody had to tell her who he was, or why she had been brought to this swank hotel for a lunch she didn't feel like eating.

She knew only the bare bones of her grandfather's history: he was a draughtsman and worked for the Franklins, had married one of the Franklin girls and had three children, though it was hard to imagine that this tall, stooped pole of a man had daughters younger than she was. She watched his faded grey eyes widen, then, to her horror, he swung away and, like a music-hall comic

41

pretending to be bashful, covered his face with his hat.

'Tom,' she heard Aunt Lindsay say. 'Oh, Tom!'

He mumbled into the lining of his hat for a second or two, then straightened his shoulders and turned. Maeve could not believe that the sight of her standing by a potted cheese-plant in a hotel lobby clad in a patched overcoat and a second-hand bonnet could affect anyone so much.

Miss Runciman gripped her arm.

'Give him a moment, dear,' she whispered, 'just give him a moment.'

He crossed the thick rose-coloured carpet in four strides.

'Maeve?' A light voice, not guttural.

'Aye.'

'You're—you're not what I expected.'

'You're not the first person to tell me that,' Maeve said. 'I'm sorry if you're disappointed.'

'No,' he said. 'I mean, you're not—is Sylvie—is your mother with you?'

'She had to stay in Dublin to look after my brother.' Maeve experienced none of the anger that she was supposed to feel on her mother's behalf. She sucked her bottom lip, then said, 'Sure an' I'm thinkin' Aunt Lindsay has put one over on the both of us. Am I really not what you expected?'

'I thought of you still as a child.'

'I'm not a child any longer.'

'No, you're certainly not,' her grandfather said. 'Time and tide—the years just fly by, don't they? To tell you the truth you remind me very much of my first wife, Sylvie's mother.'

'She died young, didn't she?'

'She did,' Tom Calder said. 'I haven't thought of

42

her in years.'

'Is it a shock me lookin' like her?' Maeve asked.

'It is.'

'Well,' Maeve said, 'I can't help that either.'

'Of course you can't. I'm just glad you don't look like me,' Tom Calder said, then, with a glance at Aunt Lindsay, offered Maeve his arm. 'I think we're expected to go in and eat lunch now. Are you hungry?'

'Famished,' Maeve said, and let him lead her away.

*　　　*　　　*

Gowry caught a tram to St George's Cross only to discover that Kirby's infamous drinking den had been replaced by a massive sandstone office block.

Disappointed, he walked north into Maryhill Road, along which he had once driven Forbes's first motor-car all tricked up in a fine green uniform, peaked cap and leather gloves. He had looked a treat in that uniform. It had suited him better than anything Flanagan had pulled from the closet or the quartermaster of the Sperryhead Rifles had issued in the barracks at Fermoy when he'd become an Irish soldier fighting for the British, which had been more than enough to put him beyond the pale as far as his brothers were concerned. The rest of the sorry story—Sylvie's affair with a gun-runner, the birth of a son, a love of his own in France—could not be discarded, though here in Glasgow he felt, at long last, as if he might be coming up for air.

He walked, as he always did, in march step.

He tucked his artificial hand into the pocket of

43

his overcoat and bit down on the vulcanised rubber wedge with which the army doctors had replaced his missing teeth.

What the army doctors had been unable to replace were the lost years, and the lost love, and he certainly wasn't going to find them on the streets of Glasgow. Back in Dublin he had a job, a wife, an adopted son; that was his future, pretty well all of it—all except Maeve. Maeve was only thing left that gave his life dimension. He had brought her to Glasgow in the hope that she might stumble on the path that he had lost. If finding it meant that she became more Franklin than McCulloch, so be it. His greatest fear was that she would rush home again as soon as she could, lured back by her infatuation with Turk Trotter and her belief in a united Ireland.

Pubs were opening for the dinner-time trade.

Gowry picked one at random and went in. The interior stank of beer, sawdust and sweat. The fire in the iron grate had not been raked and the coals smouldered and smoked. One naked light bulb burned above the counter. The rest of the room was in deep brown shadow. In one dark corner two old women were sipping stout. Huddled on a chair by the fireplace a young man, missing a leg and an arm, nursed a nip of whisky.

Gowry ordered a pint of heavy beer and paid for it.

The barman was small and unshaven. He wore an army greatcoat draped over his shoulders like a cape. He eyed Gowry guardedly.

Gowry looked round. He half expected to find Albert Hartnell, Sylvie's foster-father, crammed into one of the alcoves, but, of course, the old

44

rogue was no longer in Glasgow. Nobody knew where he was. He might be dead for all anyone cared.

'Is yon a haun?' the barman said.

'Sorry?'

'Yur haun, is yon a haun?'

'My hand?' Gowry lifted the wooden fist. 'Aye, it's a hand.'

'They give you thon?'

'They did.'

'Ah gotta fit. Wid.'

'A wooden foot,' said Gowry, 'yes. Is it comfortable?'

'Naw.'

Gowry nodded. 'Where did you lose your foot?'

'Arras.'

'Who were you with?'

'The Argylls,' the barman said. 'Lucky, eh?'

'Aye,' said Gowry. 'Lucky.'

The barman gestured. 'See him.'

Gowry had been through this sort of thing many times before, but in Dublin there was less camaraderie, less rapport and a lot more caution, for where you'd left a piece of yourself marked the sort of man you were. He no longer wanted to talk about the war, about death and dismemberment, to compare wounds and experiences and bemoan the fact that the dead were honoured and the living all but ignored.

'I see him,' Gowry said.

'Nae wurk fur him.'

'No,' Gowry said. 'I imagine it must be difficult.'

'Three weans an' a wife,' the barman said, 'an' nae wurk. Terrible, eh?'

'Terrible,' Gowry agreed.

45

He was irked by the barman and the sadness that the conversation stirred within him, a thin broth of sentiment that contained no nourishment at all.

He finished his beer in two long swallows and clumped the glass down on the counter. It was time to leave, time to leave not just the pub but Glasgow, to return home to Dublin, to Sylvie and Sean.

He swung away from the counter, saying nothing.

The young man by the fire glanced up. His face was gaunt and his skin flaking. He balanced himself awkwardly on the chair, his leg stuck out at an angle. The empty sleeve of his jacket was pinned tight to his shoulder. He braced the shoulder against the edge of the fireplace where a wooden crutch was propped. There was not one ounce of camaraderie in his glance. His eyes smouldered like the coals in a fire that no one had raked yet.

Gowry slipped a hand into his trouser pocket, fished out a ten shilling note and crumpled it into his palm. Ten shillings was a fair slice of the cash he'd saved to buy food and drink on the homeward voyage. He didn't have to go hungry, though. He could do what he had promised himself he would not do—ask Lindsay to help him out, or borrow from Forbes.

He crossed to the fireplace and dropped the note into the young man's lap. He didn't stop, didn't even pause. He carried on towards the door without looking round but just as he reached it a voice behind him shouted, 'Bastard! You fuckin' bastard!'

Gowry, cheeks aflame, hurried out into the grey late-morning air and set off on the long march back to Brunswick Park.

*   *   *

In Forbes's humble opinion the working habits of most shipbuilding magnates left a lot to be desired. Cousin Martin was disposed to follow the general trend and put in the sort of day that Forbes considered not only unnecessary but just this side of lunacy.

Martin would arrive at Aydon Road on the dot of half past eight. First he would deal with his letters, then he would don his badge of authority, the ubiquitous bowler hat, and would tour the yard to inspect the progress of the jobs on hand. Prompt at twelve thirty he would repair to the boardroom where a light, strictly temperate lunch would be served.

By one thirty he would be back at his desk, interviewing accountants, managers, union officials, salesmen, or apprentices who had strayed from the straight and narrow and needed a good talking to. Late in the afternoon he would dictate memoranda, bring his personal log up to date and, at a quarter past six precisely, would head off home to Harper's Hill.

Martin, like the fool he was, believed that his presence in Aydon Road had a galvanic effect on the employees. Forbes, on the other hand, didn't give a tinker's curse about the employees. Men worked because they had to, not because they wanted to. He paid for their labour, not their respect. Unlike Martin, he chose to remain invisible, to be here, there, and nowhere at all. Even the conscientious Mrs Connors, who had charge of his diary, knew not where he was to be found much of the time, or what he was up to.

What Forbes was up to that March afternoon was lunching with a lady friend in the dining-room of the Cardross Arms some twenty miles downriver from Aydon Road. The lady friend went by the not inappropriate name of Hussey and was, of course, married.

She was the latest in a string of women with whom Forbes had enjoyed intimate relations. He was always exceedingly careful when it came to selecting his companions and cannily refused to surrender to the blandishments of young war widows, however attractive or wealthy, for he was leery of creating a scandal that would give Lindsay an excuse for dragging him into the divorce court and picking his bones clean.

He had no fear that Marjorie Hussey would betray him, however. If anything, she was more cautious than he was and she had no intention of sacrificing the benefits that her husband's fortune accorded her for a few extra hours of passion in a seaside hotel or in the bed in the little apartment that Forbes had leased in Flowerhill Drive.

Marjorie and he had been together for almost two years. The affair had lost its original intensity and had become almost matrimonial. Lunch was no longer a prelude to love-making, dinner no longer an excuse for bending the mattress in the flat in Flowerhill Drive. They met two or three times a month, often in the elegant little inn overlooking the river and spent more time discussing how they could safely be together than they did locked in each other's arms. Impulse had given way to intrigue, passion to planning and now that his curiosity had been satisfied Forbes was beginning to find the relationship, and Marjorie's chatter, just a wee bit dreary.

'He wants me to go sailing with him this summer.'

'Does he?' Forbes said. 'Cowes?'

'No, in the Med, in the *Corona.*'

'There are worse ways to spent the summer, you know.'

'It's so hot in the Med, though. I wilt, I positively wilt in the heat.'

'Yes, the Med can be the devil in high summer,' Forbes agreed.

He looked out at the river. Rushes and scrub alder screened the shore. It was a calm afternoon, the Clyde like grey silk. A paddle-steamer cutting over from Greenock to Craigendoran hardly seemed to be moving. He wondered if Maeve might enjoy a trip on one of the paddle-wheelers and if he could put up with the smell of greasy food, beer and the ineffable jollity of the common herd on holiday.

'You're not listening, Forbes.'

'What? Yes, darling, of course I am.'

'If Mitchell insists . . .'

'You'll have to go, of course.'

He pushed aside the cutlery and took her hand.

'Will you miss me, Forbes?'

'Terribly,' he said. 'How long will you be gone?'

'Mitchell says six or seven weeks.'

'Good God! An eternity.'

'I know. Oh, I know,' Marjorie sighed.

She was a pretty little woman, if rather vapid. In spite of the fact that she was two years on the wrong side of forty and had given birth to three

49

children, she still had a girlish air about her that reminded Forbes of Sylvie as she had been all that time ago when he was a brash and brazen boy and Sylvie no older than her daughter was now.

Blue eyes, a slim figure, blonde hair in bubbling little curls; in bed little Mrs Hussey was more inhibited, less accommodating, than she was out of it, more expert at flirting than love-making. Even so, he found her passivity, her reluctance to experiment, exciting, and blamed himself, not Marjorie, for his cooling ardour. He had a great deal on his mind these days and Marjorie Hussey was not the sort of woman to acknowledge that business must always come before pleasure.

Mitchell Hussey was in his early sixties. He had made a fortune from processed meats and owned canning factories in several large towns. Marjorie knew nothing of stocks, shares, market fluctuations or the fact that, on the eve of war, Hussey had secured a contract to supply the British army with field rations, a coup that had paid for the motor yacht and the Victorian pile in three thousand acres of deer forest in remote Sutherland to which Hussey hoped to retire when the steam went out of his boilers. If Marjorie knew little about food processing, she knew even less about shipbuilding, a state of ignorance that Forbes had found refreshing at first but, as time wore on, left him somewhat short of conversational topics.

He continued to fondle her fingers, and wished they'd hurry up and bring in the fish. He watched ice melt on the lip of the wine bucket and was just on the point of reaching for the bottle when a male voice behind him boomed, 'Why, Marjorie, what a pleasant surprise!'

50

Forbes released the lady's hand as if it were a live grenade.

He thrust back his chair and rose, rocking the table and almost overturning the wine bucket. His heart rushed into his gullet on a tide of mock turtle soup and all his aplomb, all his guile deserted him. Sealed letters, anonymous telephone calls, a knock on the door late at night were trivial compared to the hearty male voice that boomed in his ear.

'Forbes, isn't it? Forbes McCulloch?' A hand on his shoulder pressed him down into his chair. 'Please, don't get up.'

Forbes looked up, squinting and smiling, smiling so hard that he felt as if his lips might split like a banana skin. He didn't dare look at Marjorie. He wondered how long the couple had been in the dining-room, if they were leaving or arriving, and what possible excuse he could offer for holding hands with another man's wife.

'It is McCulloch, isn't it?'

'Why yes,' Forbes heard himself say, 'yes, it is.'

'I thought I recognised you. Stella spotted Marjorie at once.'

Pickering: bloody Pickering, bloody Sir Andrew Pickering, former president of the National Shipowners' Association, chairman of Far East Oil, a shipping magnate on the grand scale. For years Pickering had drifted past him at banquets and dinners and meetings of this institute and that association without so much as a nod of recognition. Now, at a quarter past two on a drab Wednesday afternoon in the dining-room of the Cardross Arms, the bloody man was smarming all over him as if they were bosom pals.

Forbes forced himself to his feet.

51

Pickering looked more like an Irish navvy than a knight of the realm. He had broad, coarse features and a beetle-brow. Forbes had heard that Pickering had come up the hard way. However humble his origins he had shed his plebeian accent and spoke in a loud, rich, rumbling voice that could be heard all over the room. 'Not one of our usual haunts. Popped in for a spot of refreshment. Been to a funeral. Nobody awfully important. Company clerk. Dashed cold in church, though. Wasn't it cold in church, Stella?'

Pickering's wife wore black. Black fur trimmed her coat and on a silk cord about her neck hung, of all things, a black fur muff. Black suited her. She was a pure ash-blonde with a complexion like Devon cream. Her eyes were emerald green with long curling lashes, so pale that they were almost invisible.

'Freezing,' the woman said. 'God, but I need a drink.'

'Patience, my dear, patience,' Andrew Pickering said.

The woman look straight at Forbes, brows arched.

'You're Franklin's, aren't you? I don't believe we've met.'

'He's Martin's cousin,' Pickering said.

'Ah! I see.'

She did not offer her hand.

'Marjorie,' the woman said, 'what an astonishing coincidence bumping into you here.' She glanced round, casually not ostentatiously. 'I don't believe we've ever been here before. Do they serve a decent lunch?'

'Quite decent, actually,' Marjorie managed to

52

reply. 'We're having fish.'

She had gone an odd colour, Forbes noticed, and was picking away at her table napkin as if she intended to tear it to sheds.

'So,' Pickering said, 'the fish is worth having, is it?'

Marjorie said, 'Yes. Usually.'

'Isn't Mitchell with you?' Stella Pickering asked.

She had a wide mouth accentuated by too much lipstick. When she smiled there was more mischief than malice to it and the little fan of laughter lines at the corners of her eyes deepened.

'No, he . . . No, I . . .'

Forbes drew in breath.

'I can recommend the soup,' he said. 'Very decent soup. Very warming.'

'I'm sure it is,' Stella Pickering said. 'What I really want is a brandy.'

'You shall have one, my dear.' Her husband took her arm and aimed her at a corner of the bar. 'We will lunch thereafter at a table around the corner and leave Mrs Hussey and her friend to enjoy their fish in peace.'

'Of course we will,' said Stella Pickering.

The couple moved away.

Forbes watched them go.

Stella Pickering clung to her husband's arm as she were already slightly tipsy and, after a moment, rested her forehead against his shoulder.

Marjorie leaned forward, her face chalk-white except for a spot of colour on each cheekbone. 'What she's doing? Oh, Forbes, what is she doing?'

'Laughing, I think,' said Forbes.

CHAPTER THREE

A Kiss and a Promise

Craddock Street lay on the edge of Partick, not quite high enough uphill to be considered 'posh' and not far enough down to be deemed a slum. The tenement close sported no tile facings, the gas mantels were not encased in glass and the stairs clambered up between distempered walls sticky with condensation to a landing lit only by a back court window.

Gowry was surprised that Forbes hadn't found a better home for their mother. He remembered the airy kitchen in the cottage adjoining the brewery at Towers, its windows looking out on trees and fields, the smell of the sea rising up on the breeze; recalled how he, his sisters and brothers would congregate round the roaring stove on stormy nights to hear the old man tell tales about Irish heroes, not Fintan, Cormac or Cuchulainn but Michael Davitt, Wolfe Tone and the martyred Robert Emmet, and how the girls, even fat Winn, would be moved to tears and he and his brothers to anger and defiance.

How odd, Gowry thought, that his mother had been reduced to living in a Partick tenement, dropped down to what the Franklins had been three generations ago, before old Owen pulled himself up by his bootstraps and made them all wealthy.

Gowry tapped a horseshoe knocker that had been brought over from the cottage at Towers and, out of habit, took off his faded blue beret and held it down by his side. He had no time to button his coat before the door was tugged open and there was his dear old mother, peering up at him.

'Oh, it's you, is it?' she said. 'Have you had your dinner?'

'Aye, I've had my dinner.'

'Well, you'd better come in.'

She was undeniably old now but in spite of all the hardships that his father's waywardness had piled upon her, she had always been smart. Even now she had twenty or thirty pounds worth of tweed and wool on her back, but Gowry noticed that the expensive hand-lasted half-boots she'd worn indoors and out had been replaced by soft flannel slippers that slapped on the polished linoleum as she led him into the kitchen.

'Are you staying for your supper?'

'No,' Gowry said. 'I can't.'

'I don't have much in the larder.'

'Ma, Ma,' Gowry said. 'I'm not here for a free meal.'

'You'll be staying with Forbes?'

'Yes.'

'She'll be feeding you, I suppose.'

'Yes.'

'It's not her does the cooking, you know.'

'I know,' Gowry said.

He watched her fill a kettle at the sink beneath the window and place it carefully on the gas stove that occupied the lower half of the pantry. She had lost weight. She had never been all that buxom to begin with but she had been strong. He noticed that she used two hands to lift the half-filled kettle and that her hand shook as she held a match to the gas.

'Are you all right, Ma?'

She studied him for several seconds without answering, then said, 'You look terrible, Gowry. Is your wife not taking care of you?'

'Sylvie take cares of me fine.'

'You haven't left her then?'

'Of course I haven't left her.'

'What are you doing in Glasgow?'

'I brought Maeve over for a bit of a holiday.'

She planted teacups and saucers on the table. The table was covered with a linen cloth that had been preserved in paper in a drawer of the sideboard in the cottage in Towers. Perhaps, Gowry thought, she's given up keeping things good for tomorrow. The room was furnished with three chairs, a dresser, a table and an iron fireplace with a tall wooden over-mantel. There were only a few small ornaments on the mantelshelf, and no photographs.

'Well, that's not the whole truth,' Gowry went on. 'I brought Maeve over to get her away from the troubles.'

'Is Trotter still making sheep's eyes at her?'

'Sure an' it's the other way round, I think,' said Gowry.

'Has he got her in trouble, is that what you're telling me?'

'Trouble?' For Gowry the word had other connotations. 'No, not exactly trouble, Ma. He's taken her to meetin's at McKinstry's a few times and she's stayed in Wexford with his family, but lately he's kept away.'

'Has he been inside her?'

'Pardon?'

56

'Is she carrying Trotter's baby?'

'Mother! For God's sake! She's only a baby herself.'

'That she's not,' his mother said. 'She was never a baby, that one. She was conceived in sin, with more than her fair share of—'

'That's enough, Ma!'

Kay McCulloch shuffled to the pantry and brought out a milk jug, poured sugar into a cut-glass dish and set jug and dish on the table. She perched herself on the armchair by the fire, not the big, wooden-backed armchair in which his father had napped after supper but a little piece from the parlour, an old nursing chair, low and sagging, with a new brocade cushion propped upon it to hide its stains.

'You didn't come to the funeral,' his mother said.

'I didn't know Da was dead until it was too late.'

'Didn't Winn tell you?'

'I haven't heard a word from either Winn or Blossom in years. I did hear from Peter, though,' Gowry said. 'He was fair annoyed at you. He wanted the old man to be buried in Glasnevin in the shadow of Parnell's tomb with the brotherhood on parade, and a piper and a twenty-one-gun salute.'

'Reason enough,' his mother said, 'for having the funeral in Scotland.'

'Where's the grave, exactly?'

'In the Western Necropolis.'

'I take it there's a monument?'

'Forbes paid for a stone, yes.'

Gowry nodded. It mattered not to him where his father had been laid to rest. Out on the plains of Flanders were a hundred thousand graves without

57

mark or monument. It might have been different if the McCullochs had been Catholics, then Charlie would have found a priest eager to perform the service. The Royal Irish Constabulary would have been out in force, the army too perhaps, and there would have been bloodshed somewhere along the route. He wondered if his mother realised just how much the situation in Dublin had changed now that sectarianism had entered the picture. Long ago, when his father had first joined the brotherhood there had been few divisions along religious lines; everyone, whatever their creed, had been persecuted equally.

'Have you heard from Charlie?' Gowry asked.

'He's too busy to write letters.'

'What about Peter?'

Forbes had always been her favourite but Peter, surly and spoiled, was her pet lamb. He had been badly wounded in the Rising and had suffered much in prison where his surliness had hardened into hatred. The last time Gowry had seen him, two Christmases back, he had been shocked by Peter's fanaticism and felt sure it would only be a matter of time before Peter died in a hail of bullets.

'I've heard nothing from Peter,' Kay McCulloch said.

She looked down bleakly at her slippers.

The kettle steamed on the stove.

He waited for his mother to get up and make tea but she sat where she was in the armchair, looking down at her feet. He was tempted to kneel before her, take her hand and assure her that everything would work out all right, but he knew she wouldn't believe him.

'Will you bring Maeve to see me?' his mother

said.

'I can't,' he said. 'I'm going back home first thing tomorrow. Forbes will bring her down and if he won't then I'm sure Arthur will.'

'Arthur!' She pressed her lips together in disapproval.

Gowry had never understood the disharmony between his mother and her brothers. Arthur and Donald had always treated her with more respect than she deserved. She had been the black sheep of the family, of course, running off with an Irish brewer. What had drawn Dada and Ma together, what magnetism had Dada possessed that Ma had found irresistible? It was a question none of them, not even Winn, had ever dared ask.

'What's Arthur done to offend you?' Gowry said.

'Nothing.'

'Is it this place? Don't you care for it?'

'This place suits me fine.'

'Why didn't Forbes take you in?'

'No room.'

'Rubbish! There's plenty of room.'

'I don't want to be a burden.'

'What about Donald?'

'What about him?'

'Have you fallen out with Donald, too?'

'I haven't fallen out with anyone,' his mother said. 'Donald sends his motor-car for me and I go down there for weekends when the weather's up to it.'

'I see,' said Gowry. 'So you are bein' looked after.'

'I'm still able to look after myself,' his mother said, 'no thanks to you.'

'Me? What have I done?'

'You should never have married that girl.'

'Mother, for God's sake! I've been married to Sylvie for the thick end o' sixteen years. If I hadn't married her . . .' He bit off the sentence. He still couldn't bring himself to tell her about Sylvie and her affair with Forbes.

He was beginning to understand why Forbes had put the old lady out to pasture. She had always been a bit of a scrounger and had even fewer scruples than Forbes when it came to getting her own way. This, he saw, was exactly what she wanted: the martyrdom of age and widowhood without any of its discomforts or inconveniences. If there was one person in the wide world he didn't need to worry about it was his dear old darling ma.

He grinned and said, 'If I hadn't married that girl, Ma, then you wouldn't have a granddaughter like Maeve, would you now?'

'She won't want anything to do with an old body like me.'

'Oh, but she will, Ma,' Gowry said. 'Once she finds out where you live wild horses won't keep her away.'

She jerked her head and glowered up at him. He felt a certain satisfaction at having caught her out. He knew that she was keen to see Maeve again.

He got up briskly and said, 'Here, let me make the tea.'

His mother rose too. 'No, I'll do it.'

'Don't you even trust me to make a pot o' tea?'

'No, Gowry, I don't.'

'Why not?'

'Because you never do anything right,' his mother said and shuffled behind the door of the pantry to hide her sullen tears.

Maeve had barely managed to survive lunch with her grandfather without making a fool of herself and wanted nothing more than to slip off her shoes, unbutton her bodice, lie back on the parlour sofa and put her feet up. That, she supposed, was asking too much of Aunt Lindsay's tolerance and instead she had to be satisfied with collapsing into a chair before the fire and letting her daft boy cousins dance attendance on her.

Tea came in a dented enamel pot, milk in an earthenware jug. The muffins, already buttered, were heaped on an oval plate. There were no cups or saucers, just three tall beakers and three tea-plates that Enid laid out on a knee-high table protected by pages from *The Times*, a precaution that proved sensible when her cousins began spreading jam.

'Tea?'

'Yes, please.'

'Sugar?'

'Please.'

'How many?'

'Three.'

'Harry takes four.'

'Harry's bigger than me.'

'Miss Runciman says his teeth will rot.'

'My mam—my mother says the same thing.'

'Grandee says we need energy because we're still growing.'

'Grandee?'

'Grandfather,' Harry told her.

'He's not my grandfather,' Maeve pointed out.

'No,' Philip said. 'I'm not sure what you'll call him. That's the trouble when cousins get married. Everything becomes rather confused.'

'To put it mildly.' Harry handed Maeve a beaker of sweet tea and offered her a buttered muffin. 'Did you meet Tom today?'

'Yes, we had lunch in a hotel in town.'

'Tom *is* your grandfather,' Harry said.

'He's our uncle, sort of,' said Philip. 'He's married to my mother's cousin, actually. We call her Aunt Cissie, though that isn't strictly accurate.'

'However, we don't call Tom "Uncle" Tom,' Harry informed her.

Maeve licked butter from the rim of the muffin. 'Why not?'

'Mum says it makes him sound like a negro minstrel.'

'What's wrong with that?' Maeve asked.

'Apparently it isn't polite,' Philip answered. 'Grandee says if he could play the banjo like most negro minstrels he wouldn't give tuppence what you called him.'

'That's just Grandee being controversial,' said Harry.

'Grandee can be very controversial, actually,' Philip said. 'You'll like Grandee. Everyone does. Everyone except Dad.'

'Be that as it may'—Harry frowned at his brother—'tell me, Miss—Maeve, when will you be introduced to your sisters and brother?'

'Half,' said Philip.

'Yes, half-sisters and half-brother,' said Harry, tolerantly.

'No, wait,' Philip said. 'That isn't right. If Cissie is Mother's cousin and Tom is Maeve's grandfather then Tom and Cissie's children will be—'

'Stow it, Phil, for heaven's sake,' said Harry. 'You're nit-picking.'

Maeve bit into the muffin, caught a trickle of melted butter on her knuckle and said, 'I had nits once.'

The boys stared at her.

'Nits?' said Philip.

'She means head lice,' said Harry. 'You haven't got them now, have you?'

Maeve laughed. 'God, no! Half our class had them. An infestation they called it. We all knew where they came from, who brought them in.'

'Some boy from a poor family, I expect,' said Philip.

'We were all poor families in my school,' said Maeve.

'The—the things,' said Philip, 'how did you get rid of them?'

'Lye soap an' a bone comb. Three washings a day, an' comb like mad.'

'Ugh!' Philip pulled a face. 'Didn't it itch?'

'Didn't it just,' said Maeve.

'What else have you had?' Philip asked.

'Phil, that's enough,' said Harry, sounding remarkably like his mother.

'Dad had shingles when he came back from Brazil,' Philip went on. 'They drove him crazy for weeks.'

'What was he doin' in Brazil?'

'Selling ships,' said Philip. 'Only he didn't.'

'The order fell through,' said Harry.

'Is that what you plan to do when you leave school?' Maeve said. 'I mean, are you both goin' to work in the shipbuilding?'

'Possibly,' said Harry, defensively.

'Harry wants to be a painter, like our Uncle Ross,' Philip said.

'What—ceilings an' walls?' said Maeve.

'No, real painting,' said Philip, rolling his eyes. 'Art, you know.'

'I wish you'd shut up, Phil,' said Harry.

'Grandee says Harry only wants to be a painter because ladies will have to pose for him without their clothes on.'

Philip was too nimble to be caught by his brother's attack. The boys wrestled on the rug for a few seconds then parted, Philip grinning, Harry scowling. Maeve looked down her nose at them, feigning disapproval, though for two pins she might have forgotten that she was a modest young lady and have thrown herself into the fray. Harry sat back on his heels. He brushed a lock of hair from his brow with his wrist. His school tie was askew, his shirt rumpled. He was a burly chap, Maeve realised. When he matured a little more he would probably be quite handsome. She reached for the teapot.

'More tea?' she said. 'Tea's awful good for cooling you down.'

'Yes, sorry,' Harry said. 'This little twerp can be very—'

'Not so much of the twerp,' said Philip.

Maeve poured tea into the beakers. She kneeled too, skirt tucked under her, all three of them on the carpet now in a little circle, like Boy Scouts round a campfire. 'Is it true?' she said. 'Do you really want to be a painter?'

'Oh, it's just a pipe dream,' Harry said. 'Dad's set on me reading law at university so I expect that's where I'll wind up.'

'You don't have to do what your dada tells you,' Maeve said.

Philip opened his mouth to point out the paradox in his cousin's last remark but a soft roar from Harry, a clearing of the throat, dissuaded him.

He said, 'Never mind us, what about you?'

'Me?' said Maeve. 'What about me?'

'What are you going to do?' Philip said.

'I don't—I mean, I haven't had a chance to think about it.'

'Dad meant what he said, you know,' Harry told her. 'He can be quite generous when it suits him, and he always keeps his promises.'

'Go on the stage,' said Philip, suddenly.

'What?'

'Go on the stage and become a star,' Philip went on. 'Then when you've made an enormous pile of money, it'll cost Dad a fortune to triple it.'

'Pay no attention to him,' said Harry. 'He's talking drivel as usual.'

She looked directly into her cousin's eyes for the first time.

'Not,' Harry went on, 'that you aren't pretty enough to go on the stage.'

'Really?' said Maeve. 'Is that what you think?'

'Yes,' Harry said, quietly. 'That's what I think.'

'Me too,' said Philip.

'I don't suppose,' Harry said, 'that you've had any theatrical experience.'

'I worked in a biscuit factory, scrubbin' out the tubs,' Maeve said. 'Is that theatrical enough for you?'

'I doubt if would cut much ice with the management,' said Harry.

Maeve propped her beaker on the fender and leaned back on her elbows. 'You're right, though. I'm goin' to have to do somethin'. I can't lounge about here all day. We used to run a hotel in Dublin before the soldiers blew it up. Perhaps I could find work in a hotel, or a pub.'

'A barmaid,' said Harry. 'I doubt if Father would stand for that.'

'He's not my father,' Maeve said. 'I'm not at his beck an' call.'

'That's true, Maeve,' said Harry, 'but Dad's bound to have some say in the matter while you're staying under our roof.'

She gave a little sigh. 'Aye, I suppose you're right.'

'Don't worry,' Harry said, 'when it comes to finding suitable employment Grandee will have something up his sleeve.'

'Will he?' Maeve said.

And Philip, grinning, said, 'You bet.'

*   *   *

During dinner her dad asked Uncle Forbes, rather pointedly, what he meant by sticking Gran McCulloch in a tenement flat and Uncle Forbes answered, rather curtly, that that was what the old besom wanted and that if he, Gowry, didn't approve then why didn't he take Gran back to Dublin with him.

Soon after, Uncle Forbes asked to be excused, took himself off into the hall to make a telephone call, and did not return.

Shortly after ten o'clock Maeve asked if she might be permitted to go to bed. She went upstairs

66

to the nursery, threw herself down on the bed, stuffed her face into the pillow, and had a real good noisy cry.

She was still lying on the bed when someone knocked on the door.

Maeve sat up. 'Aunt Lindsay?'

'It's me,' Daddy said.

She wiped her eyes and swung her legs round so that she was seated, not lying, upon the bed. 'What is it?'

'I'd like a word, Maeve, if you're decent.'

'I'm decent.'

Since she had grown up her daddy was conscious of her need for privacy and respectful of her modesty. He never barged about the house in Endicott Street half clad, never entered her bedroom without an invitation. He had always been more of a gentleman than she had ever given him credit for. She couldn't really blame him for being wary of Turk and the Wexford gang or for keeping Charlie and Peter at a distance. Her dad had always been conservative and consistent in his views and had put up with a lot from Mam and her.

He said, 'Have you been cryin'?'

'Sure an' I have not.'

He said, 'I'm sorry I have to do this, Maeve.'

'Do what?'

'Leave you here.'

'You should have thought of that before you brought me.'

'Is it not all right?'

'No, it's . . .' she said. 'It's all right. I'll be all right.'

'It's not quite up to the standards of Frongoch prison camp or a cell in Dublin Castle, I know, but

I think you'll be comfortable enough. If you need anything, anything at all, just ask your aunt for it.'

'I don't like askin' for things.'

'No, of course you don't, but . . .'

'Is it a debt?'

Her father nodded. 'Nothing's grudged, dearest, let me put it that way.'

'He didn't want me here, did he?' she said. 'Uncle Forbes, I mean.'

'No, but I think he's changed his mind,' her father said. 'He bought me a cabin ticket for the boat tomorrow and he's drivin' me down to the quay himself. Perhaps he just wants to be sure I've gone.'

'I don't want you to go,' Maeve said.

'No,' her father said. 'I know.'

He came to the bed, sat beside her, put an arm about her and let her rest her head against his shoulder.

'Two things,' he said, softly. 'First, I'd like you to go down the road an' visit Gran McCulloch some time soon. She's anxious to see you again an' have news of what's goin' on with Charlie an' Peter.'

'How much will I tell her?'

'Not it all.'

'No,' Maeve said. 'Definitely not it all.'

He gave her a little pat with the wooden hand and went on, 'Second, I want you to write to your mam as often as you can, at least once in the week.'

'I'll do that too,' said Maeve. 'What else?'

'That's it.'

'Will you come back soon?'

'In the summer, if I can.'

'With Mam an' Sean?'

'Your mother will never come back to Scotland.'

'But you will. Promise me, you will.'

'If I can,' Daddy said. 'I promise, if I can.'

He took his arm away and got up. She waited, tense now, grieving not for Turk but for Mam and Sean, for Daddy and home. If she hadn't cried already she would have cried now. She remembered how on the night before he had gone off to join the army he had slipped into her room and kissed her brow and whispered that he loved her more than anything in the world. She hadn't been alarmed, hadn't even been aware that he was going away, only that she was loved and that, come what may, her daddy would look after her.

He leaned forward and kissed her brow.

'Behave yourself now,' he said.

'Of course I will,' said Maeve, and only just managed to hold back another flood of tears until after he had closed the door.

*   *   *

Lindsay, without knocking, opened the door of her husband's bedroom. He was seated on the side of the bed wearing a fleecy vest and pyjama trousers. He was staring at the pool of lamplight on the carpet. If she hadn't known him as well as she did she might have supposed that he was praying. The moment he caught sight of her he leaped to his feet.

'What?' he said, shrilly. 'What's wrong?'

'Nothing's wrong,' said Lindsay. 'Calm yourself, Forbes.'

'Has someone called?'

'No one called. What's the matter with you?'

He plumped down on the bed, then immediately shot to his feet again.

69

Lindsay was used to his fluctuating moods, to sulks, tantrums and outbursts of restless energy, but she had seldom seen him so nervous.

Now and then she wondered if her refusal to sleep with him was cruel hypocrisy, but she could not forgive him for what he had done to her. She was well aware that he had other women. She couldn't blame him. And she was far too sensible to blame herself. He had set the pattern for their loveless marriage. She had merely embellished it. They had not been intimate in almost fifteen years. She had her own bedroom on the second floor. Forbes slept in the big bedroom on the first floor, next door to her father.

'I—I thought someone may have . . . Has Gowry gone to bed?'

'Long since,' Lindsay answered.

'I sent out to the shipping office and bought him a cabin ticket for the trip home. Did he tell you?'

'Yes.'

'I thought he might get on his high horse and refuse to accept it.'

'He's too polite to do that,' Lindsay said.

She pulled out a captain's chair from the walnut desk within which many of Forbes's secrets were locked away. She swung the chair on its castors closer to the bed and seated herself.

'What are you doing?'

'Taking the weight off me plates,' said Lindsay. 'Put something on, Forbes. I don't want you catching cold.'

'I'm fine as I am.' He clutched his pyjamas to his groin in a manner that suggested alarm rather than modesty. 'Are you staying?'

'Not for long.'

'Are you going to wring my ear because I left the dinner table before Enid dished out pudding? I had a telephone call to make, an important call to—to Graham Dobbs.'

Lindsay had no notion who Graham Dobbs was or what sort of business Forbes was conducting at half past nine at night. She fancied that the 'important call' might be to one of his sundry lady friends but she was too tired, and too indifferent, to challenge him.

She said, 'What do you make of her?'

He was still distracted, still anxious. 'Who?'

'Maeve, of course.'

'Oh yes, yes. She's seems very civilised.'

'What did you expect?'

'I don't know,' Forbes said. 'Someone less couth.'

'The question is—what are we going to do with her?'

'Do with her?'

'Have you been drinking again?'

'No,' Forbes said. 'I just don't understand the question.'

'Employment.'

'Ah!'

'Obviously we can't send her to college. I doubt if she'd be interested in furthering her education,' Lindsay said. 'Tom suggested she might care to train as a tracer in our drawing-office.'

'Absolutely not,' Forbes snapped.

'We employ girls, lots of them.'

'Good God, Lindsay, she's my niece. It wouldn't look right.'

'If she were a boy you'd expect her to start at the bottom.'

'Different, quite different.'

Forbes was on his feet, pacing up and down. He looked faintly ridiculous in full managerial flow with his vest riding up over his stomach and his pyjamas sagging at the rear. He clutched the drawstring with one hand and waved the other hand about as if he were conducting an orchestra.

'Apart from anything else,' Forbes went on, 'we may not be employing any women at all in six months' time. We may not be employing anyone.'

'Surely you're exaggerating.'

'Perhaps I am, but only a little,' Forbes said. 'Sooner or later—and I reckon it'll be sooner—reparation demands, delays in the repair yards and congestion in the ports will be cleared and we'll discover we have a massive tonnage surplus on our hands. I don't just mean Franklin's; I mean universally. When that happens we'll plunge into a slump so quickly it'll take your breath away.'

'What does that have to do with Maeve?'

'I'm not wasting time and money training a tracer who might not be with us very long.'

'You're the one who offered her money to stay.'

'Oh that! Just a bit of fun, really. Give her something to think about.'

'Are we really facing the possibility of a slump?' Lindsay asked.

'If you listened, Linnet, if you paid more attention . . .' He sighed. 'One and a half million gross tons a quarter being launched, and replacement demand shrinking. An end to the boom is inevitable.'

'Don't we have any new orders lined up?'

'No, and we're sitting on three empty berths as it is.'

'Is that what's got you so het up, Forbes?'

72

He seated himself on the bed and paused before he answered.

'Yes.'

'Is that all?'

'Dear God, isn't that enough?'

'I take it Martin's aware of the situation?'

'Martin's a bloody ostrich. Sticks his head in the sand and hopes all our problems will vanish.'

'He's not that much of a fool.'

'Matter of opinion,' Forbes said. 'The future for shipbuilding's in long-haul vessels, tankers and the like. In four or five years the trade base will be global and the only yards that will prosper will be those that have looked far enough ahead and planned for it.'

It hadn't occurred to Lindsay that Forbes might be burdened by concerns that weren't entirely selfish. She had become complacent of late, too mentally slack. She said, 'If things are that difficult perhaps we should find someone else to look after Maeve.'

'Can't do that,' said Forbes. 'I've given Gowry my word.'

'Tom would look after her,' Lindsay said. 'He was absolutely delighted to meet her and they seemed to hit it off together from the start.'

'Lunch is one thing,' Forbes said, 'lodging another. Cissie wouldn't take kindly to having a total stranger landing on her doorstep.'

'Your mother might . . .'

He threw back his head and uttered a little bray of derision.

'Now you really are being daft.'

'Yes, I suppose I am,' Lindsay admitted.

'Maeve is far too young to set up in a place of

73

her own, so here she'll have to stay,' Forbes said. 'She's a lively young thing and a bit of female chit-chat will do the boys no harm. I assume *they* don't mind having a girl in the house.'

'I'm sure they don't,' Lindsay said.

'Well then'—Forbes reclined against the bolster —'why don't you take her into town, buy her some new clothes and smarten her up. You'll enjoy doing that, won't you?'

'I expect I might.'

'No rush in finding her something to do. We can afford to feed and clothe her. We're not in queer street just yet.'

'Are we going to be in queer street, Forbes?'

He smiled, the same sly, silky smile that she remembered from years ago when he had challenged and defied Grandfather Owen and, sweeping her father's protests aside, had convinced her that he loved her and that they would make an ideal couple.

'Not if I can help it,' he said. 'Meanwhile, will you take charge of Maeve?'

'Of course,' Lindsay said.

She rose from the chair and pushed it into the knee-hole in the desk. When she turned, she saw that Forbes had stripped off his under-vest and slipped into bed. He had left the blankets turned down, though, and, leaning back against the pillow, patted the sheet beside him.

'Won't you join me, Linnet,' he said, 'just for old times' sake?'

'Don't be ridiculous, Forbes,' Lindsay said and left the bedroom to answer the telephone that apparently only she could hear ringing faintly but persistently in the darkened hallway below.

74

CHAPTER FOUR

Pickering's Party

'Cocktails?' Forbes said. 'Who on earth would call at half past eleven at night to invite us to a cocktail party? Why didn't I hear the telephone?'

'Perhaps you were asleep?' said Lindsay.

'Of course I wasn't asleep. You know I wasn't asleep.'

'In any case,' Lindsay said, 'a printed invitation arrived by the afternoon post so apparently it isn't a hoax.'

'What made you think it might be a hoax?'

'The woman sounded—well, not quite sober.'

'Why didn't you mention it at breakfast?' Forbes asked.

'Our social life, such as it is,' Lindsay said, 'didn't seem terribly important at breakfast this morning.'

'Yes, Maeve in tears surprised me too. I had the impression that Gowry and she didn't rub along too well and that she'd be glad to see the back of him.'

'Which shows just how little you know about girls.'

'Where is she, by the way?'

'Downstairs, talking to Cook and Enid.'

'Talking to the servants? About what?'

'How do I know?'

'Maeve doesn't belong downstairs.'

'Eleanor's with her,' said Lindsay, 'so she won't come to much harm.'

'Is that sarcasm?'

'Of course it is,' Lindsay said.

'Where's this invitation?'

'I put it on your desk.'

'The woman who telephoned in dead of night—I don't—I mean, I really have no idea who she is.'

'She's Sir Andrew Pickering's wife,' Lindsay said.

'I mean—what I mean is, I've only met her once. Briefly.'

'You obviously made a good impression.'

'This cocktail thing, where is it, and when?'

'It's all on the invitation.'

'Lindsay!'

'Merriam House, half past six o'clock, Monday.'

'Merriam House? Where the devil's that?'

'Dalmuir.'

'Dalmuir! Nobody with any sense lives in Dalmuir,' Forbes said. 'I thought Pickering had a place in Kelvindale.'

'We don't have to go, you know,' Lindsay said.

'We can't just ignore it.'

'Why not?' said Lindsay. 'We ignore most other invitations.'

'Pickering,' Forbes said, 'isn't the sort of chap you cross. He's a director of Far East Oil, you know.'

'I know.'

'I wonder what he wants with us?'

'Perhaps he's just being sociable,' Lindsay said.

'And I wonder why she called you in the middle of the night,' Forbes said.

'I told you; I think she was tipsy.'

'She didn't—I mean, she didn't ask for me, did she?'

'No.'

'What exactly did she say?'

'Just that Drew—she obviously doesn't stand on

76

ceremony—that Drew and she were giving a little cocktail party on Monday evening and she wanted to make absolutely sure we'd be there.'

'Absolutely sure? Did she say that?'

'In effect, yes.'

'Odd.' Forbes tweaked his moustache. 'Damned odd, given that "Drew" hasn't exchanged two civil words with me until now.'

'Perhaps he's heard that we have an oil-tanker for sale.'

'For sale? Well, hardly!' Forbes said. 'He knows Martin, though, and he may have heard that Martin's in Norway, so he invited us instead.'

'Sounds plausible,' said Lindsay. 'Are we going?'

'I think we'd better,' Forbes said, 'don't you?'

'I do indeed,' said Lindsay.

*　　　　*　　　　*

When the Lanchester vanished behind the trees Maeve was tempted to race after it, wailing like one of the women in a Greek play Mam had taken her to see.

Fortunately the boys had been hustled off to school and the Great Unmentionable had gone to collect the Lanchester from the garage around the corner before she had dissolved in tears. They weren't crocodile tears either. She wasn't putting on a show to make her dad feel guilty.

Daddy had edged her towards Aunt Lindsay who had hugged and restrained her at one and the same time. And as soon as the Lanchester had disappeared she had been helped back into the dining-room and made to drink a cup of hot tea. Then Aunt Lindsay had told her to put on her coat

77

and hat and had taken her by taxi-cab to Rowan's in Buchanan Street where she, Aunt Lindsay, had shopped for a cocktail dress, and, almost in passing, had bought Maeve a new blouse and several pairs of stockings.

They had returned to Brunswick Crescent for lunch. By that time Maeve had felt better, a bit drained, a bit shaken but, on the whole, better. She had dozed on the sofa in the parlour for half an hour before Miss Runciman invited her downstairs to meet the cook. Enid had been there too and it was impossible to be depressed in Enid's company for she chattered on nineteen to the dozen and told hilarious stories about her brothers and sisters. Maeve would have happily remained in the cosy kitchen for the rest of the afternoon but Harry was sent down to inform her that Cissie Calder, her daughters and son had arrived and were eager to meet her. Reluctantly, Maeve dragged herself upstairs to the drawing-room to be inspected by yet more members of the clan.

The boy and the girls were seated side by side on a long divan. The boy was tall but very thin and pallid. When Maeve shook his hand he didn't look at her, not so much as a glance, but the girls were curious about their quaint new relative and couldn't stop staring at her. Family, Maeve thought: they are my family even if I can't quite calculate how we're related to each other. Cissie Calder was plain and plump. She reminded Maeve of a farmer's wife. She didn't dress like a farmer's wife, though. She wore a French-style jacket and a pleated skirt in scarlet and pink that seemed too startling for afternoon visiting.

After the initial introductions were over

conversation spluttered and died. Maeve felt like yelling out, 'Where is everybody then and where's the bloody tea?' Instead she seated herself demurely on an upright chair while the three females stared at her, tongue-tied.

'Am I not what you expected?' Maeve said, at length.

The girls' heads swivelled. The boy let his chest sag towards his knees, as if he were falling asleep. Cissie Calder cleared her throat.

'What—what makes you ask that?'

'Everyone tells me I'm not what they expected.'

'I'm not—I didn't . . .'

'Did you not know about me, is that it?'

'Oh yes, we knew about you,' the boy said, still sagging. 'Dad told us about you. You didn't come as a complete surprise.'

He might be shy but at least he was willing to communicate.

She focused her attention on the boy.

'What did your dad tell you?' she asked.

'That you're his granddaughter and we've to be nice to you,' Ewan said.

'You don't have to be nice to me,' Maeve said, 'if you don't feel like it.'

'Your mother is my half-sister,' Ewan said, 'and, to tell you the truth, I find that very disconcerting.'

'I find it disconcertin' too,' Maeve said, 'but there's not a blessed thing I can do about it.'

'Oh no,' Ewan Calder said. 'There's nothing anyone can do about it.'

Cissie spoke up. 'How—how is your mother?'

'Fine, she's fine,' said Maeve. 'She has her hands full lookin' after my baby brother,' an answer that brought a little sniff from one of the girls.

I dawned on Maeve that Mam was really the object of their disapproval. If they were still tutting over a bit of hanky-panky from twenty years ago what would they have to say about all the things that had happened to her in Dublin? Well, it isn't my place to enlighten them, she thought, but wondered what Grandpa Calder's son and daughters would make of her dad if he came slouching into the drawing-room right now, if they would avert their eyes from the sight of his faded blue beret, false teeth and wooden hand.

She said, ' 'Course, Sean's only my half-brother. I mean, my father's not his father. His father was shot in cold blood by the English pigs.'

The boy's blue eyes held no trace of deference.

He said, 'He was a gun-runner, wasn't he?'

'How did you know that?'

'I've read his poems.'

'His poems? I didn't know Fran wrote poems.'

'Published in the *London Review*, some of them,' Ewan Calder told her. 'My father showed them to me. They're rather good, if a little polemical.'

'Polemical, what's that?'

'Biased,' Ewan Calder said. 'I have the clippings somewhere, if you're interested. Hagarty was a victim of history. He wasn't the only one. Lots of promising poets died in the war.'

He wasn't showing off, like Harry and Philip. He was simply informing her that the connection between them was stronger than she had anticipated.

She stared at the boy, waiting for him to say more.

He shrugged and shrank back into his shell.

'Where,' Cissie said, 'did you get that lovely

blouse?'

'What?' said Maeve. 'This? From Rowan's.'

'Did Aunt Lindsay buy it for you?' one of the girls—Dorothy—asked.

'Yes, she did.'

'Lovely,' said the other girl, Katy.

'Aunt Lindsay has very good taste,' said Dorothy.

'She has a personal account in Rowan's,' said Katy.

'We don't,' said Dorothy. 'Dad won't allow us to open one.'

'He says he can't afford it,' Katy said.

'Of course he can afford it,' said Dorothy.

'He's just being mean,' said Katy. 'He says money doesn't grow on trees.'

'I wish it did,' said Dorothy. 'Don't you, Maeve?'

Now that their brother had broken the ice, the girls obviously felt it was safe to talk to her. They weren't hostile after all, just younger and less experienced than Maeve had given them credit for.

She smiled at Dorothy. 'If every raindrop was a silver sixpence, how happy we would be.'

'Oh, that's lovely,' said Katy.

'And so true,' said Dorothy. 'Did you just make that up?'

'No, it's a song,' Maeve said.

Then, to her relief, Harry and Philip crashed into the drawing-room, followed by Aunt Lindsay and Uncle Forbes and, a moment later, by Enid pushing the tea-trolley. Maeve was soon swept up in family gossip and Dublin and Fran Hagarty were forgotten.

* * *

81

The problem with maintaining a love-nest in Flowerhill Drive was that his cousin Ross Franklin had recently moved into a house at the far end of the street. Ross was a creature of habit and notoriously disinclined to take exercise. Forbes reckoned that the chances of bumping into him on the pavement were very slim. Even so, he might have been tempted to relinquish the lease on the top-floor flat if he hadn't gone to so much trouble to secure it in the first place.

The three-storey terraced house had been built sixty-odd years ago and was so conservative in design that it might have been a warehouse. Over the years it had sheltered a fair number of kept women and erstwhile lovers and Marjorie Hussey was by no means the first married lady to grace one of its gloomy bedrooms. Before her, in no particular order, Forbes had entertained the wife of a school teacher, the wife of a metal broker, the wife of a marine insurer, and the wife—now a widow—of a lieutenant in the British Army Service Corps.

The lieutenant's widow might have been his sweetheart still if her hubby hadn't had the misfortune to be blown sky-high in the Macedonian campaign.

Forbes still thought wistfully of the merry little widow—who hadn't been a widow then, of course—and all the uninhibited things that she had been willing to do to please him, things that Marjorie wouldn't dream of doing. Marjorie's primness was both maddening and enticing but lately he had grown tired of her pointless modesty. Not today though. Today he could muster so little interest in 'doing it' that his performance was almost perfunctory.

Marjorie lay motionless beside him while he lit a cigarette.

'I'll have to go,' she said.

'To the bathroom?'

'No, home.'

'Is Mitchell expecting you for lunch?'

'He's in Sheffield.'

'Where are the boys?'

'I have no idea.'

'Well,' Forbes said, blowing smoke, 'I can't linger either.'

He had promised Philip that he would bring Maeve to the Academy ground where Philip was playing in an inter-house rugby football match. Forbes had no interest in sport and rarely watched his boys play. Maeve, however, had been surprisingly keen, even after he had pointed out that Philip's team was composed of skinny little wretches few of whom would ever represent the school when victory, not mere participation, was demanded of them.

'What are we going to do?' Marjorie asked, dolefully. 'I mean about Monday?'

'The best we can,' Forbes said.

He propped himself on an elbow, holding the cigarette away from her.

'Why did she call? Why did she call both of us?' Marjorie said. 'She's going to tell everyone. I know it. She's just the sort of woman who'll take pleasure in ruining my marriage.'

'What sort of woman is she?' Forbes said.

'She has so much money,' Marjorie said. 'So much money . . .'

'You mean, she thinks she can do what

she likes?'

'She drinks a great deal, so I've heard.'

Forbes sighed and rolled away.

He extricated himself from beneath the musty bedclothes and was tempted to leap to his feet, dress and leave her there, moaning about her misfortune. Marjorie had told him that she'd never had an affair before, and he believed her. If she'd ever had an affair before she would have known how to behave when the cat popped its nose out of the bag.

'How well do you know Stella Pickering?' Forbes asked.

'Mitchell knows Drew quite well, I think.'

'You think?'

'We've dined with them once or twice; not alone, in company.'

'At this place in Dalmuir?'

'Oh no, that's brand new. They only moved in last month. It's frightfully grand and modern, so I've heard. Wonderful views.'

'Tell Mitchell you don't want to go to this cocktail thing.'

'If I do, he'll suspect something's wrong.'

'Something is wrong,' Forbes said. 'I just can't work out what the Pickering woman is up to.'

He crushed the cigarette into an ashtray then slid his feet to the floor. He rested his elbows on his knees and contemplated the pile of clothing on the linoleum. He had been so eager to get the tryst over with that he hadn't taken off his socks and suspenders. Marjorie hadn't noticed.

Holding the quilt to her throat, she sat up.

'Oh, Forbes, what'll we do?'

'Brazen it out,' Forbes said and, scooping up his

clothes, hurried into the bathroom to press on with the rest of the day.

*　　*　　*

'Are you tired, Uncle Forbes?' Maeve asked.

'No, I'm starving.'

'Didn't you have lunch?'

'Hadn't time,' he said. 'Delayed at the yard.'

Maeve paused to yell at a massive young man who had just hurled Philip to the ground. The fact that she knew nothing about the rules of rugby football did not deter her from voicing her opinion.

A handful of spectators lined the pitch, brothers, fathers, one or two teachers. Maeve was the only female. Harry had given her his scarf to wave when Philis's team put the ball over the end line. So far Philis's team hadn't put the ball anywhere near the end line. There was no logic to the game, none that she could see. Most of the boys were small and skinny and so camouflaged by mud that she could barely distinguish one from the other. Still, she was glad to be out in the fresh air and grateful to her uncle for bringing her.

'I think I noticed a pie shop down at the gate,' Maeve said. 'Would you like me to fetch you somethin' to keep you goin', Uncle Forbes?'

'That's jolly decent of you, Maeve. Tell you what, though, I'll trot down myself since you seem to be more caught up in the game than I am.' He peered across the field to the gate where the Lanchester was parked. 'Back in a tick.' Hands in his overcoat pockets, he jogged across the damp grass and vanished through the gate beneath the bare-branched elms.

The game had bogged down in mid-field. Maeve could see nothing of the ball, only a pile of legs, arms and heads. She felt rather self-conscious now that the Great Unmentionable was no longer with her. She really must stop thinking of him as the Great Unmentionable. He was quite a decent chap, really, not the ogre that Mam made him out to be.

'It's not awfully stimulating, is it?'

Ewan Calder crept up behind her. His chin was tucked into his collar, a long scarf wrapped round his neck.

Maeve took a step towards him. He stepped back.

'No,' she said, truthfully, 'it isn't, really.'

'Do they play rugby football in Ireland?'

'Sure an' they do,' said Maeve. 'Hurley's the game, though. Now that is exciting, especially when they started bashin' each other with the sticks.'

'Hurley,' Ewan Calder said, pedantically, 'is a cross between field hockey and lacrosse, not unlike shinty, I believe.'

'Aye, probably,' Maeve said. 'Why aren't you playin' today?'

He shrugged. 'Weak chest.'

Maeve sidled closer. This time he did not back away.

'Consumption?' Maeve said.

'No, I had asthma as a child. Fortunately, I appear to be growing out of it. It bothers my mother more than it bothers me.'

'I see,' said Maeve. 'She fusses, your mother?'

'She does.'

The chin inched up out of the scarf. She was beginning to find his shyness irksome. She wondered if he was only pretending to be shy to

86

make people feel sorry for him. He was obviously brainy, too brainy by half. She was less cautious about offending him than she might otherwise have been.

She said, 'I don't think your mother likes me.'

'She's not entirely unsympathetic to your situation.'

'What does that mean,' Maeve said, 'in plain English?'

'She thinks you might be a bell-wether. Do you know what that is?'

'A kind o' sheep,' said Maeve.

'Mother thinks you've been sent to Scotland to lead the flock.'

'Flock? What flock?'

'Your mother, father, brothers . . .'

'One brother,' said Maeve, 'just one.'

'She's frightened of you,' Ewan Calder said, 'or, more accurately, frightened of your mother.'

'What's my mam got to do with it?'

'My father's not as young as he used to be.'

'He's not ailing, is he?'

'Oh no, just—not young.'

'I understand,' Maeve said. 'Your mam's frightened my mam will come over to Glasgow and lay claim to what's rightfully yours.'

'Rightfully,' Ewan said, 'but not necessarily legally.'

'God, money never crossed my mind, nor my mam's neither.'

'Yes,' said Ewan, 'but you're not a Franklin.'

Maeve paused. 'Are you makin' all this up?'

'No, I know how their minds work.'

She found it hard to believe that he could be so perceptive and wondered if it was acuity or imagination that had led him to such cynical conclusions. 'Got it all sized up, haven't you?'

'One does try.'

He's a prig, she thought, a pretentious prig, just trying to impress me with all this nonsense. She tossed Harry's scarf about her neck and adjusted her beret. Out of the corner of her eye she saw Uncle Forbes returning, a cup in one hand and something wrapped in paper in the other.

She said, 'What does one make of my Uncle Forbes, then?'

Ewan nodded approvingly. 'He's one to watch out for.'

'Is he?'

'My dad says he won't be happy until he owns everything.'

'Everything?' said Maeve. 'What's everything?'

Ewan had spotted Forbes too and was already inching away.

'Hello, young Master Calder,' Forbes said. 'Flirting with my lovely niece, are you? Can't say I blame you. Don't let me chase you away.'

'Sir,' Ewan mumbled and cut across a corner of the touchline and took to his heels.

'Creepy young devil, isn't he?' Forbes said. 'I shouldn't be so critical, I suppose. You may like chaps like that?'

'Not,' Maeve said, 'in a month of Sundays. What've you got there?'

'Bovril,' her uncle informed her. 'Bovril and a mutton pie.'

'Ugh!'

'Don't be so disparaging, Maeve,' Forbes said. 'When needs must, you can't beat the simple pleasures of the poor. Who's winning?'

'No idea,' said Maeve.

'Haven't you been watching the game?'

'Nope, I've been listenin' to that boy tellin' tales.'

'And what tales would those be?' Forbes asked, through a mouthful of pie crust. 'Tales about us?'

'He thinks I'm a gold-digger,' Maeve said.

'Hah!' her uncle exclaimed. 'He would! He's a nasty piece of work, is our Ewan. He's always trying to stir up trouble.'

'But why?' said Maeve.

'He's jealous of Harry and Philip,' Uncle Forbes told her. 'In fact, he's jealous of everyone. He thinks he's superior to us in the brains department and can't understand why we don't like him.'

'He has asthma.'

'Uh-huh,' Forbes said. 'That's always been his excuse.'

'I'm not a gold-digger, Uncle Forbes, am I?'

'Of course you're not,' Forbes told her. 'But if you were, sweetheart, you'd be a dashed good one.'

'I hope that's intended as a compliment,' Maeve said.

'In my book it is,' Forbes told her and, smiling, tossed back the dregs of the beef tea, and threw the cup away.

*　　　*　　　*

On Sunday morning everyone went to church, everyone except Forbes, who elected to stay in bed. Miss Runciman, Cook and Enid came too, trailing uphill from Brunswick Crescent then down again to St Anne's on the corner of Crow Road and Madison Street.

Tom and Cissie Calder and the girls were seated

in front of the McCullochs and on the pavement afterwards there was a great deal of cheerful chatter. Ewan, Maeve gathered, had taken himself off to the First Church of Christ Scientist at Charing Cross, a 'conversion' to Christian Science that Cissie considered too embarrassing to discuss but that Harry and Philip found hilarious, though Miss Runciman warned them not to mock something they did not understand.

After lunch, Harry and Philip were pressed into taking Maeve to visit Gran McCulloch and the cousins spent a depressing couple of hours listening to Gran complain about everyone and everything, from Eamon de Valera's penchant for spending time in America to the irregularity of deliveries by her local coal merchant. Maeve found herself being treated like one of Gran's contemporaries and could not make the old woman understand that she couldn't possibly have known Augie O'Rouke or Mr MacManus from East Tyrone or that she hadn't even been born when Thomas Clarke was released from an English jail in 1898. It was after five o'clock before the cousins managed to effect an escape and ran, literally, out of the close mouth, whooping quietly with joy at being free again.

That evening Maeve retired to write to Mam again. She had lots to tell and the words flew from her pen. The letter became very long and when it was finally finished Maeve found that she was too tired to write to Turk.

She sank into bed, exhausted.

She had barely closed her eyes when she heard a telephone ringing down in the hallway and, a moment later, raised voices. She sat up in the nursery bed, wondering what the ruckus was about.

The disturbance was over almost before it began, however. Silence descended on the household once more and Maeve, with a contented little sigh, fell asleep.

*   *   *

'For God's sake, Linnet, will you get a move on,' Forbes shouted. 'If there's one thing I don't want to be, it's late.'

Lindsay paid no attention to her husband's irate cry and continued to apply make-up as if she had all the time in the world. Forbes was pacing up and down in the hall below, decked out in a smart lounge suit. In a couple of minutes, Lindsay predicted, he would march outside to the motor-car, start the engine and tamp the horn, then come stamping into the house once more.

'*Are* you going to be late?' Maeve asked.

'Of course not,' Lindsay replied. 'These things never start on time.'

'Will it be a very grand affair?'

'Probably.'

'What is it, anyway? Uncle Forbes seems . . .' Maeve shrugged.

'Nervous? Yes, he is. According to the invitation it's a cocktail party, a sort of house-warming. We don't know the Pickerings—at least, I don't—but your uncle seems to regard an invite from Sir Andrew as the equivalent of a royal command.'

'*Sir* Andrew,' Maeve said. 'How posh! Is he a shipbuilder?'

'He's a ship-owner. He doesn't build ships, he buys them.'

'Maybe Uncle Forbes is hoping to sell him

some ships.'

'Some ships?' Lindsay laughed. 'One would be quite enough.'

Outside, the motor-car horn sounded.

Maeve grinned. 'You were right, Auntie.'

Lindsay removed the linen bib that protected her dress. Maeve and she had visited a hairdresser that afternoon and her hair had been delicately coiffed, Maeve's trimmed and back-combed in a suitably 'modern' style.

Lindsay turned and held her hands above her head.

'What do you think, Maeve?'

'You look lovely,' Maeve said. 'Just like a film star.'

'Hardly,' Lindsay said, though the flattery pleased her.

She put on her hat and coat and lifted her purse.

From below: 'If you're not down here in one minute, Lindsay, I'm leaving without you.'

'Good luck,' Maeve said.

'Thank you,' Lindsay said. 'I may need it,' then unhurriedly left the bedroom and, thirty seconds later, roared off into the night.

*   *   *

Merriam House, like its owner, was violently exhibitionist. Even Forbes, no die-hard traditionalist, was taken aback by its ultra-modern design. It occupied one of the airiest sites in the county, with views to the distant Cowal Hills and the peaks of Arran. The river wound away towards the firth, its banks crowded with tenements, factories and shipyards. Even in gathering dusk the view was enough to take your breath away.

More than three acres of land surrounded Merriam House, much of it already landscaped with laurel and pine and seeded for lawns and flowerbeds. The boundary wall was white stucco inset with narrow apertures that reminded Lindsay of a Moorish castle, an impression enhanced by the massive arched entrance-way and wrought-iron gates.

Motor-cars of every shape and size were parked along the gravel drive and ladies and gentlemen, many in evening dress, were drifting towards the brilliant oblongs of the house. Somewhere within, a band was ripping out a ragtime tune.

Forbes nosed the Lanchester into a space beneath an ornate lamppost, applied the brake and cut the engine. He leaned on the steering wheel and peered, scowling, at the house.

'What the hell is that?' he growled.

'Splendid,' said Lindsay. 'Quite splendid, and very daring.'

'Daring? It looks like a bloody ice-cream factory.'

'It's the future, Forbes.'

'The future—in bloody Dalmuir!'

'What is wrong with you?' Lindsay said. 'You haven't seen the place properly yet. This, I think, is just the kitchen yard.'

He turned and glared at her, then, shaking his head, chuckled grudgingly.

'So it is, Linnet,' he said. 'So it is. They must have locked up the hens for the night. Are you fit for the fray, dearest?'

'As fit as I'll ever be,' said Lindsay.

'All right then,' Frobes said. 'Let's get it over with.'

The enormous living-room was floored with polished wood, like a dance-hall. There were no potted plants, no rugs, no antiques, only a series of bays formed by tubular steel sofas and glass-topped tables. The jazz band was tucked away in a corner, penned in by a baby grand piano. The bar was long and top-lit, its shelves glistening with bottles and glasses. Three male bartenders in crisp white jackets served drink to the throng. Beyond the bar a great plate-glass window opened on to a balcony gilded by the rays of the westering sun.

'Think Pickering ordered up the sunset too?' Forbes whispered.

'I wouldn't be surprised,' said Lindsay.

'*Forbes! Forbes, how wonderful!*' Stella Pickering shouted to make herself heard above the strains of 'When My Baby Smiles at Me'.

She balanced a champagne flute in one hand and a highball glass in the other and drank first from one and then the other as she slithered through the crowd, smiling the wide, red-lipped smile that Forbes remembered only too well from his first and only encounter with the woman.

'Lady—Mrs Pickering,' he got out, 'I don't believe you've met my wife.'

'Stella,' she said. 'I'm Stella.' To Forbes's consternation, she proceeded to kiss Lindsay on the cheek. 'I'm Stella, and I'm afraid I'm really rather pickled.'

'Are you?' said Lindsay, cool as a cucumber. 'Point us to the bar, Stella, and we'll soon catch you up.'

'Oh, I like her. I do. Name again?'

'Lindsay.'

'Lindsay, pleased, as they say, to meetcha.'

She wore an evening gown in silvery-grey satin and had silver-tinted her beautiful ash-blonde hair. Her headband sported a silver ornament, like a pineal eye, that winked when she tossed her head.

'His highness is around here somewhere,' she said. 'He'll catch up with you eventually. Who else? Marjorie? You know Marjorie, don't you, Forbes? I mean, you *are* acquainted with the Husseys?'

'The Husseys? I don't believe . . .'

'Oh, haven't you had the pleasure? Funny, I was sure you'd had the pleasure. Now'—she spun round, swaying—'where has Marjorie put herself? Perhaps she's hiding on the balcony.'

'There's Sneddon,' Forbes yelped. 'I do know Sneddon.'

'Charlie? Boring chap, boring. Wife is even worse. Baptists, I believe.' Stella nudged Lindsay. 'I say, you're not a Baptist, are you?'

Lindsay, smiling, shook her head. 'Boring Church of Scotland.'

'I really must find the Husseys. Mitchell's so eager to meet you, Forbes.'

'Look,' Forbes said, 'why don't we sample one of those delicious-looking cocktails first.'

'To the bar then,' Stella said and, discarding the champagne flute, took his arm and led him off, leaving Lindsay to fend for herself.

*   *   *

Lindsay sucked an onion from a cocktail stick and crunched it between her teeth.

'The Husseys?' she said. 'Who are the Husseys and why is Mrs Pickering so anxious for us to meet them?'

'I've no idea,' Forbes said. 'The woman's obviously deranged.'

'Or pickled,' Lindsay said. 'Who are all these people?'

'Sneddon's in steel,' said Forbes. 'She's right: he really is a dreadful bore. Over there—Oliver Hutchinson. He's on the board of Far East Oil. The three bully-boys propping up the end of the bar are big cheeses in the Shipowners' Association. There's Braun from Dundee. Wonder what he's doing here?'

'Where's Pickering?'

'Haven't a clue,' said Forbes.

'You're not going to do much business here, Forbes.'

'Not with this infernal racket going on, no.'

'Take me outside,' said Lindsay.

'Outside?'

'Out there, on to the balcony.'

'What for?'

'To watch the sun go down,' Lindsay said, 'or perhaps you'd prefer to wait for Stella coming back from the toilet.'

'All right, all right,' Forbes said. 'Come on.'

He deposited the noxious blue cocktail that Stella had ordered for him on the bar, took Lindsay's arm and steered her through the crowd and out by a sliding glass door on to the balcony.

With no visible pillars or struts to support it, the balcony seemed to float in space. Lindsay felt as if she were suspended on a haze of smoke from the chimney-pots of old Clydebank. The rays of the

96

setting sun lit the breast of the hills so vividly that she could pick out sheep grazing on the moor and farm cots nestling in the folds. The river channel was fiery red, shored by velvet shadow. Streetlamps patterned the townships, big yards and big ships brooded under towering cranes and she could hear the beat of hammers and the thump of presses clear as church bells on a frosty morning.

Leaning on the rail, Lindsay gazed out at the panorama.

'If we were rich, Forbes,' she said, 'if we were really rich, I'd love to build a house here, a house like this.'

'It's too big, too inconvenient.'

Forbes eyed the guests who, like passengers on an ocean liner, were crowded against the rail, cocktail glasses and cigarettes in hand. Watching the sun set over the valley of the Clyde should have been a humbling experience but Pickering's friends were too busy trying to impress each other to be aware of it.

'Who are you looking for?' Lindsay said. 'The Husseys?'

'Of course not.'

'Perhaps they're avoiding you.'

'Why would they be avoiding me when they don't even know me?'

Ragtime had given way to 'Look for the Silver Lining'. Couples were dancing. His back to the rail, Forbes studied the dancers. 'Perhaps,' he said, 'just to be civil, I should go and have a word with Charlie Sneddon.'

'Charlie Sneddon?' Lindsay said. 'Why not?'

'Wait here,' Forbes said. 'I shan't be long,' and went back into the living-room through the sliding

97

glass door.

Lindsay watched him edge between the dancers. She wondered if the Hussey woman was, or was about to become, another of Forbes's conquests. On tiptoe, she endeavoured, vainly, to keep Forbes in view.

She was just about to turn away when she noticed a man dressed in a navy-blue blazer and grey flannels at the far end of the balcony. She looked away, then back again. There was something appealing about him, something familiar. He lifted his hand—a wave, a little salute.

Age had blunted Geoffrey Paget's features and his hair line had receded but he was undoubtedly still handsome. All that had happened in the years between suddenly fell away and for an instant Lindsay suffered again all the longing and regret that she'd felt that morning long ago when Lieutenant-Commander Paget had told her that he loved her and had asked her to go off with him.

She matched his little salute with one of her own.

He came to her, walking with the relaxed gait of a sea-going sailor.

At one time he had served with the Admiralty and had been sent north to supervise the building of a special type of submarine. Forbes had assumed that the Admiralty would dole out more orders for sub-sea vessels but in-fighting in Whitehall had directed the contracts elsewhere. Forbes had blamed her, blamed Geoffrey, blamed the affair that never was. She had kept in touch with Geoffrey for several years but the paper friendship had lapsed with the coming of war. She had heard that he had gone back to sea as a submarine commander but beyond that—nothing.

She put an arm about him, lightly.

'Geoffrey,' she said, 'what a fantastic surprise.'

He returned her little one-armed hug, then stepped back.

'Did you know I'd be here?' Lindsay asked.

'I thought you might be.'

'Are you still a serving officer?'

'Yes, for a year or two longer.'

'Are you stationed in Scotland?'

'I'm back at the Admiralty, in London.'

'Then what are you doing at Pickering's party?'

'I came to look for you,' he said.

*　　　*　　　*

'For God's sake, Marjorie,' Forbes hissed. 'Why did you come?'

'Why did *you* come, Forbes?'

'I couldn't talk her—my wife—I couldn't talk her out of it.'

'I don't think you tried very hard.'

'She's up to something, you know.'

'Who, your wife?'

'No, damn it—Stella.'

'It's Stella now, is it?'

Marjorie held a cocktail glass to her breast and pressed her shoulders against the wall as if he were about to molest her. He had gripped her arm so tightly that she would probably have a bruise and had hustled her out of the crowd and into a quiet corridor before she could gather her wits or—her first instinct—call out for her husband to save her.

By moving her eyes a little she could see the dancers and the bar, Mitchell with his back to her,

99

laughing at something someone had said. If Mitchell turned around and spotted her crushed against the wall by Forbes McCulloch, how would she explain it? How would she convince her husband that it was just an innocent encounter? She was no good at telling lies to Mitchell, though heaven knows she'd had enough practice. She had lasted this long with Forbes only because Mitchell hadn't got wind of it. She blamed him, blamed Mitchell for being so trusting. Yes, it was really all Mitchell's fault.

Forbes's cheeks were flushed, his moustache spiky.

'For you information,' Forbes went on, 'she's hell-bent on *my* wife meeting *your* husband.'

'Face to face?'

'Yes, face to face. Of course face to bloody face.'

'But—but why?'

'Because she's a bitch,' Forbes said.

He glanced at the oblong of activity visible from the corridor. He had no idea where the corridor went, for there were no doors leading from it and only a soft sort of darkness at the nether end. He had a horrible feeling that at any moment Stella Pickering might come sailing out of the darkness with a glass in each hand, yelling for everyone to look, look at what she had found, at the nasty little secret she'd uncovered.

'I—I can't do this any more, Forbes.' Marjorie was close to tears. 'Let me go. Please, let me go.'

'He doesn't want to meet me, does he?'

'Who?'

'Mitchell, your husband.'

'He doesn't even know who you are.'

'All right, all right,' Forbes said. 'Pull yourself

100

together, Marjorie, and we'll try to keep them apart.'

'Stella won't—'

'Stella will,' Forbes said, 'given half a chance. What's this damned party in aid of, anyway?'

'House—house-warming.'

'Bloody show-off,' Forbes said. 'I must get back to Lindsay.'

'Forbes, what—what are we going to do?'

'Keep circulating,' Forbes told her, 'just keep circulating,' and went back into the living-room to scrounge a glass of something civilised to drink.

*   *   *

Geoffrey had always been straightforward. Lindsay had no reason to suppose that he had changed. He had fallen in love with her without wishing to and had made no attempt to push her into bed. It wasn't that he hadn't wanted her, of that she was sure, but he was a gentleman through and through and had treated her with the respect due to another man's wife. Sometimes she wished that he had been more forceful, more selfish and had persuaded her to throw up her responsibilities, abandon the boys, Forbes and the family and run off with him.

'So you came all the way to Scotland just to look for me?'

'Yes.'

'But why?'

'Old friends,' Geoffrey said, 'are the best friends.'

That, Lindsay thought, sounded just a tiny bit glib.

Perhaps she'd been too quick to form an opinion of his character. Perhaps he had changed—or perhaps her interpretation of that almost affair sixteen years ago had been naïve and Geoffrey had been more calculating than she'd realised at the time. He had been a cadet at Dartmouth College, a career officer from the word 'go'; an affair with a married woman would have ruined his chances of promotion.

'Are you still a lieutenant-commander,' she asked, 'or have you risen to dizzy heights?'

'No dizzy heights, I'm afraid.'

'You haven't been appointed First Sea Lord, then?'

'I think you might have heard if I had been,' Geoffrey said. 'I'm still an L-C, stuck with that rank for good, I imagine. When Jellicoe took over from Fisher he got shot of the gin-and-bitters crowd and brought in lots of young Turks from the Grand Fleet to fill posts on Naval Staff, and I was left rather high and dry behind my old desk at the Admiralty.'

'You were never one of the gin-and-bitters crowd, Geoffrey.'

'No, that's why when the war started I applied for sea duty.'

'Admiral Fisher let you go? I am surprised.'

'Old Jackie Fisher saw the writing on the wall, I think. Besides, he badly needed experienced commanders in the submarine branch.'

'Where were you based?'

'Devonport.'

'And where did you fight?'

'Started in the North Sea but wound up patrolling the Dardanelles.'

'And survived,' said Lindsay, 'obviously.'

'Yes, and survived.'

'You still haven't told me what you're doing here?'

'Stella invited me.'

'Stella? Do you know Stella Pickering well, then?'

'Rather too well,' Geoffrey said. 'She used to be my sister-in-law.'

'You're married?'

'I used to be,' Geoffrey said. 'It didn't last long.'

'Do you have children?'

'No, no children.'

'I'm sorry,' Lindsay said.

'For what?'

'That your marriage wasn't a happy one.'

'What is it they say? Marry in haste . . .'

'Repent at leisure,' Lindsay said.

'True in my case,' Geoffrey said.

'Did she sweep you off your feet?'

'In a manner of speaking,' Geoffrey said. 'I thought I was in love with her but it was just—I don't know—infatuation.'

'And she wasn't in love with you?'

'Not for long, not long enough.'

'What was her name?'

'Jo—Josephine. The oldest of the three famous Proctor sisters.'

'Famous?' said Lindsay. 'I can't say I've ever heard of them.'

'Glasgow's a long way from Mayfair.'

They were together now, close at last, drawn back from the rest of the crowd on the balcony. The sun had rimmed the hills and long velvet shadows consumed the last of the light on the water.

'How—how long will you be in Glasgow?' Lindsay asked.

'Until tomorrow.'

'Is that all?'

'It's long enough, don't you think?' said Geoffrey.

*   *   *

A tap on the shoulder; Forbes almost choked on the brandy that he had coaxed from one of the snooty barmen. He swung round.

She had shed the flute and the highball glass and no longer seemed tipsy.

'I want to dance,' she said.

The band were playing something vaguely like a waltz. The piano-player was crooning into a microphone that added timbre to his mellow voice.

Forbes downed the rest of the brandy.

'Dance,' Stella said again.

'I'm not sure I can manage . . .'

She attached herself to him and spun him away from the bar. The tubular sofas had been pushed back and fifteen or twenty couples had laid claim to the floor. Mostly the younger set, Forbes noticed, sons, daughters, sweethearts, with only the odd elder statesman and dowdy wife rotating cautiously among them.

He had never learned to dance properly. He couldn't remember the last time he had tried to dance with Lindsay. He shuffled awkwardly to find steps to match the rhythm. A trumpet blared, a saxophone wailed, the drum sounded like Struther's steam hammer gone daft. Stella

104

Pickering pulled him closer. Her breasts crushed his lapels. He inhaled the heady essence of alcohol and perfume—and encouraged her to lead.

'I don't know what you see in her,' she said.

'Who? Lindsay—my—my . . .'

'Marjorie Hussey.'

She whirled him around effortlessly.

'It isn't what you think,' Forbes said.

'Oh, but it is.' Stella smiled broadly. 'I'm sure it is.'

She had perfect teeth, Forbes noted, lots and lots of perfect teeth.

She said, 'You can do better than Marjorie Hussey.'

'Can I?' Forbes said. 'I don't know what you mean.'

'She's not your type.'

'What is my type?'

'Someone with more experience.'

'Experience of what?'

'Life.'

The sun had slipped below the level of the hills and he could no longer see the balcony through the window. He wondered if Lindsay was still out there, obediently awaiting his return. The air would be chilly now and she had no wrap. He felt an unusual concern for his wife's welfare while Stella whirled him round and round and round.

He said, 'I haven't seen hilt nor hide of your husband. Is he actually here or did he duck out at the last minute?'

'He's here,' Stella said. 'Somewhere.'

Forbes was conscious of her body under the material of the dress. She wore no corset, no boning of any sort and moved with a suppleness that put him to shame. She guided him with a subtle nudge here, a tug there.

She said, 'Does it matter where Drew is?'

'I just thought it might be nice to have a word with him.'

'What sort of word?'

'To thank him for inviting us,' Forbes said, 'and to congratulate him on building such a magnificent house.'

'Oh,' Stella said. 'How disappointing! I thought you were going to drag me into the corridor.'

'Where does the corridor go?'

'Out to the servants' wing.'

'Wing?'

'Of course,' Stella said. 'Don't you have a wing for servants?'

'Only a basement,' Forbes admitted.

'Poor boy,' she said. 'Poor boy,' and the moment the music stopped, released him.

*   *   *

'There you are,' Forbes said. 'I've been looking everywhere for you.'

'Have you?' Lindsay said. 'I've been here for ages.'

The buffet was situated in a long L-shaped section of the living-room, hidden by the bar; colds meats, spring salads, caviar, fowl of various species, and a brace of snotty servants in white bum-freezers to attend to your every whim. Forbes had no appetite but Lindsay was eating heartily enough from a large white china plate decorated with painted palm trees.

'Have some,' Lindsay said. 'The pheasant is

delicious.'

'No thanks,' Forbes said. 'As soon as you've finished what's on your plate, we're leaving.'

'Are we? Why?'

'I told you, Linnet, cocktail parties are not my cup of tea.'

There was something different about her, but he was too distracted by his encounter with Stella Pickering to pinpoint it exactly. She seemed lighter, more alert, more alive. She said, 'I've been chatting to Charlie Sneddon.'

'Have you really?'

'He's not as boring as you made him out to be.'

'What were you chatting about?'

'This and that,' said Lindsay. 'Baptism mostly. Did I see you dancing with our hostess?'

'Yes.'

'That must have been a dreadful strain.'

'It was, believe me,' Forbes said. 'Have you seen anything of Pickering?'

'He's in the library, I believe, entertaining some *very* important people.'

'Like who?'

'Navy people.'

'Navy people? What does Pickering want with navy people?'

Lindsay popped a fragment of cold roast pheasant into her mouth and chewed thoughtfully, as if she were dreaming up an answer.

'No idea,' she said, at length. 'Are you sure you won't eat something?'

'Not this cold muck,' Forbes said. 'Let's go home, dear, please.'

'Don't you want to say goodbye to Stella?'

'She won't even know we've gone.'

'Are you sure?' Lindsay said.

'Yes, damn it, I'm sure.'

'All right, I'll fetch my coat from the cloakroom.'

'I'll wait outside by the car,' said Forbes.

*　　　*　　　*

The night was cool now, almost cold. The last of the cloud had dispersed with the setting of the sun and the sky was crystal clear and sprinkled with stars. She glimpsed the moon too, a perfect crescent, before Forbes turned the Lanchester on to the steep, rutted track that led down to the outskirts of Clydebank. She sat back against the leather, her collar turned up, and tried to sort out her feelings as best she could.

Forbes was muttering, 'Navy people, for God's sake! What's Pickering doing, sucking up to the navy? Fuel contracts, I suppose. Royal Dutch Shell and the Anglo-Persian Oil Company have been at each other's throats for years. Maybe the government's planning on pumping more public funds into APO and Pickering's trying to pick up some subsidiary profit for Far East Oil.'

Lindsay knew of the bitter rivalry that existed between the major oil companies but tonight, especially tonight, she had no desire to listen to one of Forbes's dreary lectures on the subject.

He went on, 'Rumours abound about a merger in the making. The Admiralty's opposed to it, apparently. The party thing was probably just an excuse for a bit of informal lobbying. What do you think, Linnet?'

'Hmm?'

'You haven't heard a word I've been saying,

108

have you?'

'Oil, what about oil?'

'Never mind,' Forbes said. 'Go back to sleep.'

'I wasn't asleep,' Lindsay said. 'I was thinking.'

'About what?'

'Why we never got to meet the Husseys,' she said and snuggled down to look for the moon again and dream of tomorrow when she would meet Geoffrey in the Central Hotel where, not by coincidence, they had kissed and said goodbye sixteen short years ago.

CHAPTER FIVE

Two Hands in Harmony

Blue sky over the rooftops, white clouds, like soap suds, scudding overhead, the wind strong and steady and not at all cold: a perfect drying day, in other words.

Mounds of dirty clothes were heaped in baskets in the laundry room outside the kitchen door and a colorful array of garments flapped on the lines that crossed the sloping lawn. Maeve had offered to help but Miss Runciman would have none of it. Unwritten laws governed what 'upstairs' could and could not do, and laundry work was considered too menial for a niece of the master of the house. Maeve was peeved. She had been even more peeved when Aunt Lindsay had hurried off to keep an appointment in Glasgow and, rather curtly, had refused to take her along.

The morning post had brought a letter from

Mam. Maeve had scanned it at the breakfast table and had waited for homesick tears to trickle down her cheeks. She had slipped the letter back into its envelope to read in her room, anticipating that she would cry buckets at the news from home, but she had remained calm and dry-eyed; Dublin was still Dublin, Mam was still Mam and life in Endicott Street was dithering on quite placidly without her.

Puzzled by her lack of sentiment and still annoyed because Aunt Lindsay had gone to town without her, Maeve sat by the window and watched poor Enid struggle with clothes-pegs and sheets while Miss Runciman hobbled about in the windy sunshine issuing instructions. By half past ten, she was thoroughly bored. She thought of catching a tram into the city or going for a walk round Brunswick Park, anything to get out of the house. She had already decided that she wasn't cut out to be a lady of leisure and lay tummy-down on the bed and wondered what she could possibly do to occupy her time.

Certain jobs were bound to be deemed unsuitable; barmaid, waitress, shop assistant, factory hand, for instance. She had assumed that Aunt Lindsay would come up with something but so far nothing had materialised. Perhaps she was just being impatient, because she was bored. The house was uncannily quiet. She could hear nothing except the wind whistling along the eaves.

Then, suddenly, a chord of music resonated up from below.

Maeve sat up.

Another chord, and another.

Someone was playing the piano in the parlour.

Maeve rolled from the bed and hurried

110

downstairs.

The pianist was into the swing of it by now. Music flowed through the house like a warm draught, a gay, light-hearted melody that Maeve thought might be a Strauss waltz. She pushed open the parlour door.

He was elderly, no doubt of that, but not lacking in energy. He looked, Maeve thought, like a robin redbreast, all perky and alert. His eyes were bright and smiling when he glanced up at her. He still wore his overcoat. A black Homburg had been tossed on top of the piano and two scuffed leather suitcases dumped on the carpet just behind the door.

'Do you know what it is?' he called out.

'I think it's by Strauss.'

'Ah-hah, but which one?'

Maeve shook her head.

The old man said, 'Johann the First. "*Morgenblätter*." "Morning Leaves". Leaves meaning newspapers. The piece was written for a society of journalists. Do you play?'

'No.'

'You could learn.'

'Bit too late for me, I think.'

'Nonsense.'

'Are you Harry's grandfather?'

'Guilty as charged,' Arthur Franklin said.

He played softly now, working the pedal with a polished toe.

'I'm Maeve, from Dublin.'

'I guessed as much,' Arthur said.

'I don't know what to call you.'

'Arthur will do nicely. The boys refer to me as Grandee, which was all well and good when they

111

were children but sounds rather too regal now. In any case, I'm not your grandfather. Tom Calder's your grandfather. Met him yet, have you?'

'We had lunch last week. Aunt Lindsay arranged it.'

'Talking of which,' Arthur said, 'where is Lindsay?'

'She's gone into Glasgow. Uncle Forbes is at work an' Miss Runciman is out on the green showing Enid how to hang out washing,' Maeve said. 'I don't think anyone expected you back this morning.'

'Fair winds down the Oslo Fjord and a reasonably calm crossing meant that we docked early,' Arthur said.

'I shouldn't ask,' Maeve said, 'but did you make a contract with the Norwegians?'

'Why shouldn't you ask?'

'It isn't any of my business.'

'Of course it is,' said Arthur. 'We're not a secret society. The answer is, no, we didn't wangle an order out of the Norwegians. The chill wind of caution has already begun to blow and shipping agents and owners are pulling in their horns—even in Norway.'

'I see.'

'Do you?' said Arthur.

'Well, actually no, not really.'

'I'll explain it to you when we have more time.' He stopped playing, got up from the stool and rubbed his hands together. 'By George, I needed that,' he said. 'Norway might be the home of Grieg and Christiania might have a wonderful musical society but it's dashed difficult to find a piano properly tuned. Something to do with climate,

112

I expect.'

He took off his overcoat, tossed it over the piano stool and before Maeve could back away, gave her a brisk hug. Then he pushed her out to arm's length and studied her, head on one side, exactly like a robin redbreast.

'I never met your mother. Do you look like her?'

'No,' Maeve said. 'More like my dad, I think.'

'Good,' Arthur Franklin said. 'Now, I wonder if I might impose on you to trot downstairs and tell Miss Runciman that the wanderer has returned and will require a spot of lunch about half past twelve o'clock. I take it you've no objection to joining me—for lunch, I mean?'

'I'd love to,' Maeve said.

'No fish,' Arthur said. 'Tell Cook—anything but fish.'

And Maeve, no longer bored, laughed and headed for the stairs.

*   *   *

Forbes had been in his office for the best part of an hour before the telephone call came through. He had dictated letters to Mrs Connors and tidied up three or four matters of business that had been lying on his desk since Martin went away.

However much he might despise his cousin, Forbes was forced to admit that Martin ran a tight ship and was, in several respects, a better manager than he would ever be. Martin's obsessive attention to detail and his sympathy for 'the men' blinded him to the big picture, however, and he had more or less ignored the rumours of an impending slump that had been circulating throughout the industry for the past half year or so.

The telephone rang.

Forbes lifted the receiver, growled his name.

A shiver went through him at the sound of her voice.

'Forbes, I'm delighted to find you hard at work at this early hour.'

She sounded tipsy. Come to think of it, perhaps she *was* tipsy. Tipsy or not, he couldn't deny that Stella Pickering's voice was seductive.

'Mrs—Lady Pickering, what a sur . . . how unexpected.'

'I missed you last night.'

'Pardon?'

'Naughty boy, you slipped away without saying goodbye.'

'Yes—sorry—wife—headache.'

'Drew was looking for you.'

'Was he?' said Forbes.

The office door was closed but he could hear footsteps in the corridor and nurtured an irrational fear that Mrs Connors was eavesdropping. He swivelled his chair to face the wall and lowered his voice by half an octave.

'What did he want with me?'

'I'll let him tell you that himself.'

'He's *there*?'

She laughed, huskily. 'Of course he isn't here.'

'Where is—I mean, yes.' Forbes adopted a cool, objective tone. 'I would like to take this opportunity to thank you for inviting us to your beautiful home. My wife will be writing to you in due course to express our gratitude.'

'Forbes,' Stella Pickering said, 'I'm not your stenographer.'

'Oh! Sorry! Yes. Quite!'

'Come to the house.'

'Now?'

'This afternoon, after lunch.'

'I'm not sure we can . . .'

'We?'

'Oh, I see,' Forbes said. 'It's not—uh—formal?'

'No, not formal,' Stella Pickering said. 'About three?'

He sucked in a deep breath.

'Yes,' he said. 'Fine. I'll be there. Are you . . .'

Stella had already hung up.

*   *   *

It was flattering to be told that she hadn't changed a bit but Lindsay was well aware that she wasn't the same girl who had sat at a table in the Central Hotel's cavernous dining-room all those years ago, nursing a broken heart.

Powder, paint and vanishing cream couldn't disguise the furrows on her brow or the sagging muscles under her jaw. As a rule she spent very little time at her dressing-table. This morning, though, she'd chased Maeve out of her bedroom and had devoted a good half-hour to fussing with creams and lotions. Although she had put on weight she was still slim enough to wear the latest boyish fashions without seeming ridiculous. Short hair and neatly tailored suits helped, but come summer it might be more difficult to pretend that her figure still ran straight up and down.

Geoffrey's features had softened and slackened but Lindsay still felt her heart flutter in a strange, unsophisticated way when she looked at him. He

115

wore naval uniform; lunch was a treat stolen from a busy schedule and he would have to leave soon after two o'clock to catch a train to Newcastle.

Lindsay had more sense than to enquire what business he might have on Tyneside or, for that matter, what business he had with Andrew Pickering. Six or eight men had been summoned to the private meeting in the library of Merriam House. Geoffrey had spent only a few minutes with her on the balcony before hurrying back to join them. If Forbes had spotted Geoffrey she would have been shipped off to lunch with orders to find out all she could about Pickering's involvement with the Admiralty.

And that would have ruined everything.

She ordered clear soup and a veal cutlet and said nothing while a waiter touched Geoffrey's glass with white burgundy and filled her glass to the brim.

She rarely drank at lunchtime but when Geoffrey held his glass out, she *tinked* the rim and sipped. Wine increased her exhilaration. When Geoffrey solemnly reached for her hand she felt like giggling.

'I have missed you, you know,' he said.

'Why did you stop writing?'

'Marriage.'

'Yes,' Lindsay said. 'Tell me about this unfortunate marriage.'

'Not much to tell, really.' Geoffrey said. 'It was something of a rush job. I was dazzled by Jo Proctor. You've met Stella. Well, Stella is nothing compared to her sister.'

'Was she—is she beautiful?'

'Stunning,' Geoffrey said, grimly.

'How long did it last?'

'Not long. Months, really.'

'No cottage in the country then, no roses round the door?'

'God, no!'

'Is that what you expected, what you wanted?'

'I don't know what I wanted—or expected,' Geoffrey said.

'How long ago did all this take place?'

'Nine years.'

'So it wasn't a wartime romance?'

'It had nothing whatsoever to do with the war. I was still on Fisher's staff at the time, still working for the Admiralty. No, Lindsay, I have no excuses to offer.' He slipped his hand away and raised his glass again, as if one reunion toast wasn't enough for him. 'I didn't belong with Jo Proctor and she certainly didn't belong with me. Jo wanted things I couldn't possibly give her. Once the gilt had gone off the gingerbread it didn't take her long to find someone more interesting.'

'I see,' Lindsay said.

She had a feeling that Geoffrey had rehearsed the account of his failed marriage, for the story seemed too familiar, too pat to ring quite true.

'What about you?' he said. 'You're still with Forbes, I see.'

'Yes.'

'Loyal to the bitter end.'

'To my family—yes.'

She wondered what Stella Pickering had told him; the shipping fraternity was swamped by gossip and misinformation. It crossed her mind that Stella Pickering might have engineered her meeting with Geoffrey and that the unexpected invitation had been to lure her, not Forbes, to Merriam House.

'Your boys must be grown up by now?' Geoffrey said.

'Almost.'

'Are they set on becoming engineers?'

'Harry, I think, will read law.'

'And the other?'

'Philip—we haven't decided yet.'

'And you, Lindsay, are you still an active partner in Franklin's?'

She was sure he knew the answer before he put the question.

'Yes,' she said. 'I still hold stock.'

'Seat on the board?'

'I leave all the important policy decisions to Martin and Forbes.'

'You're not in touch then?'

'In touch with what?'

'What's happening in the world at large.'

It was the sort of thoughtless remark she might have expected from a rating who knew no better, not from Geoffrey Paget. She wondered if war had coarsened him or if, perhaps, she had enlarged her brief unfulfilled affair into something it had never been.

'Geoffrey,' she said, 'why didn't you come back for me?'

'I don't know.'

'Did you write me off as a lost cause?'

'Good God, no!' he said. 'The job—duty if you like—carried me off in other directions. You didn't honestly expect me to come back, did you?'

She shook her head. 'I suppose not.'

'We did remain friends.'

'For a while.'

'Are we not still friends?'

'Yes,' she conceded. 'Old friends.'

'I should have told you about my marriage. I don't know why I didn't.'

Lindsay said, 'I'd no claim on you, Geoffrey, no right to disapprove of anything you did, especially finding a wife.'

'Yes, and what a wife Jo Proctor turned out to be.'

'Business—navy business—will it bring you back to Scotland?'

Forbes would have applauded her deviousness.

Geoffrey hesitated. 'Possibly.'

'How soon?'

'That depends on the Secretary of the Navy.'

'Is that who you're working for?' Lindsay said.

'Only in the broadest terms,' said Geoffrey.

'I thought perhaps you were involved in negotiations about overseas defence,' Lindsay said. 'After all, if the Americans persuade the League of Nations to curtail naval rearmament the effect on the Anglo-Japanese alliance and Far Eastern and Pacific affairs will be far-reaching. It's not just navy yards that will suffer; we'll all feel the pinch. In fact, we're feeling the pinch already.'

There was nothing arcane about knowing what was going on in Washington and Tokyo, let alone London. President Harding's proposals to the American Congress were just as relevant to Franklin's future as the price of steel or the latest round of wage demands. In spite of their pact not to discuss business at home, her father and her husband often talked about international affairs at the dinner table.

'Well, well, well!' Geoffrey said. He leaned

119

forward. 'You told Forbes you were meeting me today, didn't you, Lindsay?'

'No, I did not.'

'Why then are you fishing?'

'Am I fishing?'

'Certainly you are.'

'Perhaps it's just habit, a bad habit, but a habit nonetheless.'

'I can't tell you what I'm doing in Scotland,' Geoffrey said.

'I thought you said you came to find me?'

'Oh yes, that's certainly true.'

'Well, now you've found me . . .' Lindsay began.

'I'm not going to let you go again,' he said.

'Have I no say in the matter?'

And Geoffrey answered, 'None.'

*   *   *

Men had always liked her. She certainly liked men—which was probably just as well for here in Glasgow she was surrounded by them; Tom and Ewan Calder, Harry, Philip, Uncle Forbes, and now Mr Arthur.

He reminded her of the street traders in Wexford market towns, all bounce and bubble, with a shrewd streak underneath. During lunch she found herself telling him far more about herself than she had intended, prattling on about all the nasty things that had happened to Mam and her as a result of the Easter Rising. She even told him about Peter and Turk, and things she hadn't mentioned to anyone else, so far.

Mr Arthur did not appear to be prying. His questions were delivered casually, with a lift of the

120

eyebrow or a tilt of the head, as if he were surprised to find himself asking questions at all.

Enid was still occupied with laundry and lunch was served by Miss Runciman. The housekeeper's pleasure at having Mr Arthur back in the fold was obvious. It was all she could do, Maeve thought, not to stroke the old chap's fluffy white hair when she leaned over him to remove the dirty plates.

'Everything all right below decks, Eleanor?'

'Tickety-boo, Mr Arthur, tickety-boo.'

'This Irish lassie isn't giving you any trouble, is she?'

'No trouble at all,' said Eleanor Runciman and, smiling fondly, went off to serve coffee in the parlour.

Taking coffee in Brunswick Crescent was a far cry from sitting on the step outside the tenement in Endicott Street sipping black tea from a tin mug and sharing a ciggie with whoever happened to have one to spare.

Arthur seated himself on the sofa.

He seemed pleased with himself, pleased with her too.

'So, Maeve,' he said, 'what do you intend to do with yourself until your parents admit you've a mind of your own and let you marry this chap from Wexford?'

'Turk.'

'Yes, Turk.'

Maeve told him about Uncle Forbes's offer.

Arthur's brows rose. 'Do you like Forbes?'

'Aye, I do.'

'And why not?' Arthur said. 'He can be quite charming when it suits him. However—yes, it's a generous offer and I've no doubt he'll stick to his

121

end of the bargain. If I know my son-in-law, though, he'll make it difficult for you to find a job; nothing will turn out to be suitable for you, or for him.'

'That's what Harry told me.'

'Good for Harry.'

'I thought I might apply for work in the shipyard.'

'I can't quite see you as a riveter, Maeve.'

'I'm thinking more of the drawing-office. Could I not train to be a draughtsman?'

'Precious few female draughtsmen,' Arthur said. 'Tracers, yes, but it's not well paid. If we paid you more than the going rate we'd be in trouble.'

'Sure an' I wouldn't be expectin' any special favours,' Maeve said. 'What else do girls do in shipyards?'

'Office staff, clerks,' Arthur said. 'French polishing.'

'I could polish,' Maeve said, 'if I had to.'

'Have you talked to Lindsay about the matter of employment?'

'She says she'll give it some thought.'

'My daughter probably doesn't want you to work at all. She'll have fun taking you out and about. Shopping, matinées, showing you off to her friends, that sort of thing.'

'I don't want to be shown off, thanks all the same.'

'I don't imagine you do,' Arthur said. 'On the other hand, you may as well take advantage of what we have to offer while the going's good.'

'I'm not a sponger, Mr Franklin.'

'It didn't cross my mind that you were,' said Arthur. 'However, one of the harsh facts of life in an industrial society is that the longer and harder you labour the lower your rate of pay.'

'Is that true?' said Maeve.

'True enough to pass as a generalisation,' Arthur told her. 'Candidly, Lindsay won't want you traipsing off at half past seven every morning and trudging back here at half past six worn to a frazzle. And Forbes won't allow you to take any sort of job that will damage his reputation.'

'That's not ladylike, you mean?'

'That's exactly what I mean.'

'Aye, Mr Arthur, but I'm no lady.'

'I disagree,' said Arthur. 'You are every inch a lady. Coat of varnish and a bit of French polish and you could pass muster in any company.'

'Shop assistant?'

'I doubt it,' Arthur said. 'Indulge me for a moment, will you? Stand up and walk to the window.'

'What for?'

'Please.'

Puzzled, Maeve got to her feet and, acutely conscious of Mr Arthur's scrutiny, strolled to the window.

'What?' she said.

'Turn around.'

Maeve turned around.

Arthur nodded. 'All right,' he said. 'You may sit down again.'

Maeve plumped herself back into the armchair and planted her hands on her knees. 'What?' she said. 'What is it?'

'I have an idea,' said Arthur. 'It's not something your Uncle Forbes will approve of, but—well, let me make a telephone call and we'll see how the land lies in that direction.'

123

'What direction?' said Maeve, intrigued.

Mr Arthur bounced to his feet and headed for the door.

'Back in a jiffy,' he said. 'Don't go away,' and vanished out into the hall.

Maeve was too tense to sit still. She got up and walked to the window and peered down at the gardens, hoping that Aunt Lindsay would step out of a taxi-cab in time to protect her from whatever the old chap had in mind. She wondered if he was teasing or if he really had thought of a job that would suit her situation. She had a faint notion that Mr Arthur didn't exactly dote on his son-in-law and if Miss Runciman had come in to clear away the coffee cups she might have asked the housekeeper to tell her what to expect. Miss Runciman did not appear, however, and within a couple of minutes Mr Arthur returned.

'Yes,' he said, grinning. 'We're on. Well, no time like the present. Pop upstairs and put on your titfer and we'll toddle round there right now.'

'Round where?' said Maeve.

'You'll see,' said Mr Arthur. 'Very soon, you'll see.'

*   *   *

Tom Calder had just come out of the lavatory in the corridor that linked the main block to the drawing-office when Martin Franklin appeared at the top of the stairs.

'Dear God!' Tom said. 'What are you doing here? You look awful.'

'I feel awful,' Martin said. 'I can't hold anything down.'

'Rough crossing, was it?'

'You know what a rotten sailor I am.' Martin leaned his shoulders against the corridor wall, and shivered inside his heavy Chesterfield. His hat was pulled down so that the brim shielded his eyes from the quiet light from the stairwell window. 'The crossing was smooth enough. I think it's something I ate.'

'Chill, maybe,' Tom said, not unsympathetically. 'When did you dock?'

'This morning.'

'Haven't you been home yet?'

'Yes, I rested for a couple of hours but felt I had to come in.' Martin pushed himself away from the wall and turned unsteadily to face the corridor. Tom put his arm about the younger man's waist and supported him. 'Where's Forbes?'

'In his office, I assume,' Tom said.

'Not in the yard?'

'He's never in the yard,' Tom said. They lurched forward. 'Did you scratch up any orders in Christiana?'

'Nary a one,' said Martin. 'The trade's as dead as a dodo.'

'Did you talk to Petter Lund?'

'Nothing doing there, alas.'

'What about Stenberg's?'

'Stenberg's have just placed an order with an American yard.'

'An order for what?'

'Two tankers.'

'Did you tell them that we—'

'Yes, yes, yes, yes,' said Martin, irritably. 'I can't understand it, Tom. The doors appear to be closing on us with no prior warning. I'm beginning to think

Forbes is right and that we are heading for a slump.'

'You'd be better at home, tucked up in bed.'

'Not—not until I speak with Forbes.'

'What's the urgency?'

'Make my report.'

'Your report can wait until you're feeling better.'

'No. Now,' Martin said.

Tom pushed open the door of Mrs Connors's little cubicle. The woman was seated on a stool before a huge filing cabinet, her knees splayed. She had a pile of folders in the lap of her skirt and was slotting them into the cabinet one at a time, in precise alphabetical order.

'Mr Forbes?' Tom asked, respectfully. 'Is he in his office?'

'No, he's gone out, sir.'

'Out? Out where?'

'Beardmore's, I think, sir,' Mrs Connors said, with a sharp little sniff, as if to indicate that while her answer might not encompass the whole truth it was the only one they were going to get.

*   *   *

Beach pyjamas! My God, Forbes thought, she's wearing beach pyjamas!

In an outfit more suited to the Côte d'Azur in mid-summer than Dalmuir in early spring, Stella Pickering posed on one of the low leather sofas in the ultramodern living-room, her long legs drawn up, a pastel-tinted shoe dangling from one bare foot. She was smoking a cigarette and drinking a cocktail.

All Forbes could do was gape.

'Thank you, Ronnie,' she said to the male servant who had admitted Forbes to the house. 'That will be all.'

Ronnie? Forbes thought. She calls her butler Ronnie? Ronnie, of course, was not in proper butler's uniform, or anything like it. He wore a collarless shirt and a pair of white ducks, had bare arms, a mop of curly black hair and the battered features of a fairground pugilist. Forbes was relieved when the fellow grunted and retired, closing the door behind him.

Stella placed the cocktail glass on the floor and extended an arm.

'Forbes, how wonderful to see you again.'

'Uh-ah! Yes,' Forbes said. 'Kind of you to . . .'

'Come here.' Forbes remained rooted. 'Come along, come along, don't be so shy. I'm not going to eat you.'

Clumsy as a milkman's horse, Forbes propelled himself across the polished acres, and took her hand. She swung her legs and placed her feet on the floor. The pastel-tinted sandal slipped neatly on to her foot. Still holding his hand, she stood up. Against the passive afternoon light her figure was displayed to full advantage.

Forbes tried not to stare, not to look at her at all.

'Is—I thought—Sir Andrew . . . ?'

'All business, you men! Come.'

She led him the full length of the room and into the corridor where he had conducted his hasty little interview with Marjorie Hussey less than twenty-four hours ago. For a split second he wondered if Stella might be going to press *him* against the wall and give him a piece of *her* mind.

She guided him on to a wooden staircase with

brushed steel handrails and down it to a half-landing with four panelled doors leading off it. It dawned on Forbes then that Merriam House had more apartments tucked within its walls than any of the grand old mansions on Harper's Hill and that, modern or not, Pickering's palace was sumptuous.

'Why is it called Merriam House?' he heard himself ask.

'The ground was once part of the Merriam estates,' Stella told him. 'Two or three hundred years ago the family seat stood on this very spot, but raiders from the Highland glens burned it down and slaughtered the last of the heirs.'

'Why?'

'Envy, perhaps, or greed,' Stella told him. 'All very historical.'

'Is there nothing of the old building left?'

'A few stones, one wall, at the bottom of the hill.'

'How interesting!'

'Not,' Stella said, 'terribly.'

She ushered him into a large well-lighted room heated, like the rest of the house, by hot-air vents. Forbes had a vision of some sweaty stoker down in the bowels of the building shovelling through great piles of coke just to keep the lady Pickering comfortably warm.

The window presented a view of chimney-pots and steeples, veiled by the branches of an ancient oak. Forbes hardly noticed the window, or the view. The shelves around the room were crammed with books of all shapes and sizes, a lovely Victorian clutter of reading material that seemed eccentrically out of place at the heart of a twentieth century folly.

On Pickering's desk—teak and steel, of course—

were three wireless sets, two telephones, and an electrical coffee percolator the size of a small cathedral.

'Drew's room,' Stella explained. 'Drew's lair.'

At that moment Forbes felt a peculiar affinity with Andrew Pickering; this was indeed a man's room and, in spite of fresh plaster and new paint, there was a pleasant hint of coffee, cigar smoke and whisky in the air.

He forced himself to face her.

She was full-breasted, with a narrow waist, rounded hips and long legs. She didn't look like a woman who had borne two children. She seemed too insular in her appeal, glazed by a glamour so sexually pernicious that Forbes could not relate to it at first. He pulled himself together. He, after all, was Owen Forbes McCulloch, a full partner in Franklin's, not some wide-eyed apprentice who had never been alone with a good-looking woman before.

'What do you want with me?'

'Your advice,' Stella Pickering said. 'Your expert advice.'

'What sort of advice would that be?'

'I want to buy a boat.'

'Franklin's don't build motor launches.'

'No, I mean a boat, a real boat,' Stella Pickering said.

'What sort of boat?'

She rested her bottom on the edge of her husband's desk and smiled her wide red smile. 'An oil-tanker.'

Forbes said, 'For Far East Oil, you mean?'

'No,' Stella Pickering told him, 'for me, just for me.'

'An oil-tanker?' Forbes said, trying not to smirk.
'Of my very, very own,' said Stella.

* * *

The studio occupied the upper floor of a detached sandstone house at the nether end of Flowerhill Drive, a huge room with north-facing windows backed by a bedroom, a closet-sized parlour, a simple kitchen and bathroom.

Before he had purchased the property, Ross had lodged with his parents and brother Martin in the rambling family mansion on Harper's Hill. After Donald and Lilias had gone to live by the sea, however, Martin had politely suggested that since Ross wasn't short of a shilling or two he might care to find a place of his own. Ross certainly wasn't short of a shilling or two. A few years before the war he had sold his shares in Franklin's and taken himself off to Paris to become a painter.

Donald and Lilias had been shocked by their son's descent into Bohemianism, though anyone less Bohemian than Ross was hard to imagine. He had avoided the Paris night life and spurned the company of dissolute artists who seemed to do precious little but talk. He'd spent his days not idling at café tables but with an eighty-six-year-old drawing master in a cold attic on the old Rue du Bac learning everything he possibly could about perspective and pictorial form. Artistically, his relationship with the old man was a marriage made in heaven, for his teacher wanted no truck with Fauves or Cubists and even managed to convince Ross that the last truly great painting produced in France was Delacroix's *Liberty Guiding the People*.

In due course Ross returned to Scotland and set about establishing himself by producing stiff set-piece paintings based on scenes from Scottish history that soon found a ready market among industrialists with more money than sense. To the Scottish cultural elite, though, Ross Franklin remained an upstart and an outsider, his work tainted by the fact that his canvases sold for large sums of money and that his dealer had enough commissions to keep Ross busy with his brushes for a decade or more.

The painting in hand, three parts complete, was propped on a huge custom-built easel. It depicted a mass of foliage, a distant mountain and in the foreground a couple of sheep so real, Maeve thought, you could almost hear them bleat. At the centre of the picture, however, was a gigantic white hole.

'What's it meant to be?' Maeve said.

Ross had a palette stuck to his thumb, a pipe stuck in his mouth. He wore thick stockings and thick-soled boots, his stance solid, as if, like the easel, he had been custom-built. Though his trim beard was already flecked with silver, Maeve took him to be about Forbes's age.

'I assume,' Ross said in a rumbling baritone, 'that you are not familiar with the works of Fiona McWhirter.'

'Can't say I am,' Maeve confessed.

'The female Scott,' said Ross.

'Scot?'

'Scott,' said Ross, 'as in Sir Walter.'

'Oh, I've heard of him,' said Maeve. '*Ivanhoe*, an' that.'

'Well,' Ross went on, 'Fiona McWhirter

advanced upon the literary scene somewhat later than Sir Walter. She died only a couple of years ago.'

'I'm sorry to hear it,' said Maeve.

'Aged eighty-seven,' said Ross. 'She enjoyed a long career as a lady of letters, had two hundred and eighteen novels published, a universal following . . .'

'And a heck of a lot of money in the bank,' Arthur chimed in.

'Quite!' said Ross. 'Her daughter, Lady Mary Faid, asked me to select a favourite scene from one of her mother's novels and—well, paint it.'

'And this is the result?' said Maeve.

'It is,' Ross said. 'It's from the opening chapter of *When the Bloom is on the Heather*, one of the best-loved of all Fiona McWhirter's novels. Young Hamish, a rude shepherd boy, stumbles on Catriona Elphinstone drowsing under a dog-rose bush and instantly—'

'Fancies her?' said Maeve.

'Loses his heart to her,' Ross rumbled, 'is the phrase I had in mind.'

'Does he get away with her in the end?' Maeve asked.

'The book closes on their wedding day.'

'Books like that usually do. I take it he's not really a rude shepherd boy an' she comes out of it a lot better off than when she went in?'

'More or less,' said Ross.

'Why is there a gap in the middle of the picture?'

Arthur lay on a brown leather chaise-longue, head resting on his hand. On hearing Maeve's question, he chuckled. 'You may as well tell her, Ross.'

'If you must know,' Ross said, 'I'm stuck.'

'Tell her why you're stuck.'

'I can't find a suitable model for the girl.'

'Which, Maeve,' said Arthur, 'is where you come in.'

'Now, now, Uncle,' Ross said, 'I'm making no promises.'

'Look at her,' Arthur said. 'She's everything you said you required, a raven-haired, dark-eyed beauty exactly the same age as Catriona What's-her-name. Since you insisted I read the dashed novel, the least you can do in return is give the girl the once-over.'

'I'm not taking my clothes off,' said Maeve.

'I do not paint nudes,' said Ross, curtly. 'I've done my stint at drawing from the figure and I've no wish to repeat the experience.'

'Come along, Ross,' said Arthur. 'Out with the old sketch pad and do your stuff, otherwise you could be staring at that hole in your painting long after it's due for delivery.'

'That, alas,' Ross said, 'is something I can't deny.'

He lumbered to a cabinet in a corner of the studio and, with some difficulty, detached the palette from his thumb. He set it down on top of the cabinet, opened a drawer and brought out six or eight sheets of graph paper and a tray of pencils. He carried the paper carefully across his arm like a bridal dress and fastened it to a drawing board that he had unearthed from the attic in Harper's Hill. He cranked a handle at the side of the board, adjusted height and rake, smoothed the surface sheet with both hands, balanced the tray of pencils on the ledge of the board and instructed Maeve to perch herself on the chaise.

She did so, primly, knees together, hands clasped in her lap.

'This do?'

Ross was already intent on drawing. 'Hmm.'

Arthur got up and quietly moved away.

*   *   *

Forbes seated himself behind Pickering's desk and immediately felt more in control. He had been taken aback when the woman had started blathering about 'buying' an oil-tanker, as if she were ordering up a hat or a pair of shoes.

'A tanker,' he said. 'Precisely what size of tanker did you have in mind, Mrs Pickering?'

'A big one.'

'Uh-huh,' Forbes said. 'May I ask why you think that I can deliver such a vessel?'

'You build ships, don't you?'

'Oh, yes, absolutely,' Forbes said. 'We've built fighting ships, cargo ships and ships designed to sail on all the major rivers of the world. We've even built a submarine in our time, but we have not, not until now, designed and built an oil-tanker, so, Mrs Pickering—'

'I do wish you'd call me Stella.'

'So, Stella, I'm afraid I can't provide you with an off-the-shelf price. Cost estimating is not an exact science, especially when it comes to specialised carriers. For instance, what capacity you would require in this tanker of yours? What sort of propulsion machinery? Designers don't just work with pens and tee-squares, you know. They use equations and deadweight-displacement coefficients and all sorts of mathematical formulae that are quite beyond me.'

'You can't sell me a ship, is that what you're saying?'

'I may not be able to sell you a ship, Stella, but I can build you a ship, or, rather, have one built. "Big" isn't good enough, however. We'll need a great deal more information before we can begin to lay out a design.'

'How long will the process take?'

Forbes thought quickly. 'Approximately three years.'

'Three years!' she exclaimed, and pulled a face.

At that moment Forbes realised that she was testing him. Stella Pickering wasn't *that* stupid. He got up from behind the desk and walked around it. She backed away, one step, then two, no longer acting a part. He placed a hand on her shoulder, a strong, soft, rounded shoulder, and held her at arm's length.

'Cut it out, Stella,' he said. 'I didn't come up the Clyde on a kipper boat, and neither did you. I don't know what you want from me but it certainly isn't to buy yourself an oil-tanker to play with in the bath. Did your husband put you up to this and, if so, what's his game?'

'It isn't his game,' Stella said. 'It's my game.' Forbes watched her succulent red lips form the word, '*Mimosa.*'

'What about the *Mimosa*?'

'Torpedoed in mid-Atlantic in November 1915,' Stella told him. 'She went down with all hands.'

'Did you lose someone you loved on the *Mimosa*?'

She laughed, softly. 'That's a wonderfully romantic notion, Forbes McCulloch, but also

135

rather silly. Do you really think I'd spend upwards of a hundred thousand pounds on a memorial to a dead lover?'

'Then it's the ship,' Forbes said. 'You owned the ship.'

'Partly true,' Stella said. 'Half true.'

'Where was she registered?'

'Panama,' Stella said. 'We lost the crew, the ship, and the cargo.'

'And Lloyd's wouldn't fully cover an act of war?'

'She wasn't insured with Lloyd's.'

'I gather we're not talking about Far East Oil,' Forbes said, 'and that your husband knows nothing of this?'

'Drew wouldn't be where he is today if it wasn't for me,' Stella explained. 'He had nothing when he married me, not one penny to call his own. I financed him, or at least my father did. But my father didn't trust him, not entirely, and I was given a little wedding gift that no one ever knew about, not even my husband.'

'Shares?'

'Yes, in Gideon Rowe and Spellman.'

'Never heard of them,' Forbes said. 'Where's head office?'

'Rabat.'

'Rabat!'

'In Morocco.'

'I know where Rabat is,' Forbes said. 'I'm just wondering how you managed to keep it secret from your husband for all those years and why you're asking me, asking Franklin's, to build a tanker to replace the *Mimosa*?'

'Only bigger and faster.'

'Why the pretence?'

'I wasn't sure I could trust you.'

'What made you change your mind?' Forbes asked.

'This,' she said and, parting her red lips, kissed him full on the mouth.

CHAPTER SIX

The Captive Heart

The plotters gathered in Arthur's bedroom about half past ten o'clock. Swaddled in a dressing-gown, Arthur lay on top of the covers, a mug of cocoa clasped in both hands. Lindsay too wore a dressing-gown over a nightdress and only Miss Runciman was still fully clad. Lindsay seated herself on one side of the bed, Miss Runciman on the other.

'All right, Papa,' Lindsay said. 'Out with it.'

'I took the girl round to see Ross this afternoon.'

'Ross? Why Ross?' Lindsay said.

'He's looking for a model.'

'Oh, God!'

'He pays five shillings and sixpence an hour.'

Lindsay reached over the cocoa mug and poked a forefinger into the fine white chest hair that showed beneath the folds of her father's dressing-gown.

'You,' she said, 'are a wicked old devil. You know what Forbes will say about this, don't you?'

'I imagine he won't be too pleased,' said Arthur.

'He'll be livid,' said Miss Runciman.

'He'll just have to be livid, then,' Arthur said. 'It's not Forbes I worry about. It's you, dearest.

137

What do you think?'

'What does Maeve think?' said Miss Runciman.

'Once she realised that she wouldn't have to take her clothes off . . .'

'She's all for it, in other words?' said Lindsay.

'She is, she is,' said Arthur.

'Then it's a *fait accompli*,' said Miss Runciman.

'It is, it is,' said Arthur. 'Unless, of course, either of you object.'

'I assume,' said Lindsay, 'this is another of those great empty paintings that some idiot has commissioned to hang above their mantelpiece.'

Arthur nodded, sipped cocoa and left a milky brown moustache across his upper lip. Eleanor Runciman wiped it off with a corner of her handkerchief.

Arthur said, 'The painting's entitled *The Captive Heart*, and illustrates a scene from a novel by Fiona McWhirter.'

'Oh, God!' Lindsay groaned again.

'Two figures and several sheep romping about in the heather.'

'Romping?' said Eleanor Runciman.

'Lying down, actually.'

'Lying down?'

'The girl is, the boy—well, I'm not sure what the boy's doing.'

'One hardly dare imagine,' said Eleanor.

'Why are you telling me this?' said Lindsay. 'Oh, I see, you want me to soften Forbes up, do you? Papa, you really are the giddy limit.'

'If it comes from me he'll reject the whole idea outright.'

'In addition to convincing Forbes that modelling for a painter, even if he is family, is perfectly respectable,' Lindsay said, 'someone's going to have to tell Maeve's mother, though she can hardly object on moral grounds, can she? By the time she was Maeve's age she was already playing fast and loose with boys.'

'Ross isn't interested in boys, or girls either, for that matter,' Arthur said.

'Tom won't like it,' Lindsay said.

Arthur drank the remains of the cocoa and handed the mug to Eleanor Runciman. 'When a picture of his granddaughter hangs in the Royal Scottish Academy I'm sure Tom will be just as proud as the rest of us.'

'Ross has never had a painting accepted by the Academy,' said Lindsay. 'Unless he changes his tune, he never will have either.'

'Maeve's a very pretty girl,' said Eleanor. 'If I were an artist with an eye for beauty I think I'd be paying more than five and six an hour to have her sit for me. I doubt if Forbes will see it that way, however.'

'Which,' said Arthur, 'is why I'm keeping out of it.'

'What a coward you are, Papa. When's her first sitting?'

'Tomorrow afternoon.'

'I'll go with her,' Lindsay said. 'I'll talk to Ross.'

'And Forbes?' said Arthur Franklin, innocently.

'Yes,' Lindsay sighed, 'and Forbes.'

*   *   *

One of the few places in Aydon Road where Forbes felt comfortable was the drawing-office. Removed from fires, fumes, freezing winds, deafening

139

noises and the thousand-and-one harsh realities of shipyard life, the drawing-office provided sanctuary.

Skylights trapped an early blink of sunshine and the room was already warm. Several draughtsmen had removed their jackets and rolled up their shirt sleeves. Tom Calder had his own cubicle but was more often to be found on the floor explaining an equation to a junior or arguing a point of design with a journeyman. He was firm but fair and rarely lost his temper, not even with Mr Lightbody, leader of the local organising committee of the Association of Engineering and Shipbuilding Draughtsmen, a thorn in the flesh of the management.

'Tom?' Forbes spoke in a hushed tone. 'Might I have a word with you?'

The tow-headed boy with whom Tom was talking scowled at Forbes as if he couldn't bear to be interrupted, even by one of the partners. He swivelled an inch one way then an inch the other on the stool. On his board was an elevation of a propeller flange, as delicate as a leaf or a flower petal.

'All right, Bobby.' Tom patted the lad's shoulder. 'Check the calculation, see if you can track down the flaw.'

'Aye, Mr Calder.'

Hostile slate-grey eyes fixed Forbes for a moment then the young man returned to his board and Tom and Forbes headed for Tom's cubby.

'What's wrong with him?' Forbes asked.

'Not a thing,' said Tom.

'Is there a problem?'

'Nothing out of the ordinary. You've talked with

Martin, I take it?'

'Not yet.' They entered the cubicle and seated themselves, Tom on a stool, Forbes in a wooden-armed chair. 'Martin can wait.' He put a hand on Tom's thigh. 'I've something I need to discuss with you, but only on the strict understanding that it goes no further than these four walls.'

Tom nodded. 'I gather you weren't ordering machinery at Beardmore's yesterday afternoon?'

'No, I was down in Dalmuir at Pickering's house, on the receiving end of one of the most outlandish proposals I've heard in a long time.'

'Pickering? Um, any proposal from Pickering isn't to be sneezed at.'

'The proposal didn't come from Pickering; it came from his wife.'

'His wife!' Tom exclaimed. 'Are you sure you should be telling me this?'

'She wants to lay an order for a ship.'

'Does she, by Jove!'

'A bulk oil-carrier.' Forbes went on to tell Tom Calder much, though not all, of what had transpired during his meeting with Stella Pickering. He concluded, 'Now do you see why I need to keep this dark?'

'What's the name of the shipping line she claims to represent?'

'Gideon Rowe and Spellman.'

'Where are their offices?'

'Would you believe Rabat?'

'Do they actually exist?'

'They're not listed in *Brassey's Annual*,' Forbes said.

'Well'—Tom pulled a hefty tome from the shelf above his desk—'they might be in the *International*

141

Directory of Ship Owners and Agents. If they owned the *Mimosa* and she went down in the middle of the war then it's safe to assume they've been operating for some time.' He opened the volume, riffled the pages. 'Yes, here they are. The entry's not awfully informative, but at least we know they're *bona fide*.' He turned the book towards Forbes who bent forward to read. 'Must be quite handy being the only shipping company with head offices in Morocco.'

'Why do you say that?' Forbes asked.

'Because,' Tom answered, 'there are no fuel oil stations along the North African coast, nothing between Lisbon and Las Palmas, in fact.'

'Dear God, how you remember these things?'

Tom shrugged. 'With more and more trading vessels converting to oil any ship-owner who supplies fuel oil on the African coast is on to a good thing. Oil is definitely the fuel of the future. It's cleaner and cheaper than coal, gives a higher average speed in the seaways and involves no stand-by losses. Besides, diesel engines are becoming more efficient all the time.'

'Wouldn't it be interesting to find out who's constructing storage tanks at Rabat?' Forbes said.

'The French?' Tom suggested.

'God, I hope not.'

'The French won't dole out licences to British or American construction companies,' Tom said. 'However, the company your Mrs Pickering represents are ship-owners, so provided they have certificates of seaworthiness and are properly registered . . .'

'In Panama,' Forbes put in.

'Oh!' Tom paused. 'Well, many a good ship has

been registered in Panama. If the lady isn't spinning a yarn for her own amusement and Gideon Rowe and Spellman do want to put a tanker into service why are they approaching Franklin's to build it for them? We aren't tanker specialists. To accommodate a ship of that size we'd have to alter the slipways and go in for a deal of retooling and retraining. Look what happened last time we moved further than our capabilities: the submarine.'

'The submarine wasn't my responsibility.'

'I'm not blaming you, Forbes,' Tom said. 'I'm only advising caution. We'll need a great deal of concrete information before we can contemplate accepting the commission—and we'll have to see the colour of their money.'

'I'm not an idiot, Tom, not entirely,' Forbes said. 'Fishy though the whole story sounds there's just enough weight behind it to make it worth pursuing, don't you think?'

'Well, we do have preliminary designs in hand,' Tom said. 'Quite advanced designs, though I say so myself. Have you any idea why this woman picked us to build her a ship?'

'I think,' Forbes said, 'she wants to play it close to the chest, not let her husband know what's she's up to.'

'Then why not have the dashed ship built in Osaka or New Jersey, not right on her own doorstep? Does she imagine we can build a large oil tanker in Aydon Road without anyone noticing?'

'Perhaps she's hoping we'll bring it in at a competitive price.'

Tom hesitated. 'Forbes, is your relationship with

143

this woman purely professional?'

'Of course it is,' Forbes retorted. 'What the devil do you take me for?' Flushing, he said, 'If we do decide to accept the commission, rest assured I'll keep Stella Pickering at arm's length.'

'And will proceed with caution?'

'With all caution, yes.'

'Then,' Tom Calder said, 'I see no reason not to fire ahead.'

*   *   *

Now and then over the years awareness of time passing had caused Lindsay to consider embarking on an affair—not with anyone in particular, certainly not with one of the conceited fools who chanced their arm with every woman they bumped up against, but with some vague ideal of manliness, a chap who would be both sexually fulfilling and at the same time tender and loving. Geoff Paget's appearance at Pickering's party had swept her off her feet. Lunching with him the following afternoon, however, had brought her down to earth again and left her wondering if there hadn't been more contrivance than romance in their sunset encounter on the dizzy heights of Dalmuir.

She had long since given up confiding in her husband. She said nothing to Forbes about her meeting with Geoffrey, nothing about Arthur's plan to keep Maeve, as it were, off the streets.

She followed Maeve up the steep stone steps to Ross Franklin's lofty studio and watched the girl thump the doorbell with the heel of her hand.

'Do you think he knows we're here?' Maeve asked.

144

'I think he just might,' Lindsay answered.

'All right, all right. I'm not deaf, you know,' Ross grumbled, and pulled open the door. He stood to one side, sucked in his stomach, and allowed Maeve to pass into the cloakroom. He let his stomach out again, winked at Lindsay and said, 'You've a handful there, old thing. What are you doing here?'

'I'm the chaperone,' Lindsay told him.

He ushered Lindsay into the studio. 'For her protection, or mine?'

She had seen little of her cousin since he had returned from Paris on the eve of the Great War. In the spring of 1915 he had enlisted as a private in the Royal Army Medical Corps but for some reason known only to God and the War Office, he had been posted to Bramwell military hospital in Wiltshire to help tend cases of shell shock. Hidden in the bedroom in Flowerhill Drive was a portfolio of drawings from his time at Bramwell. They were less mannered, more spontaneous than anything he had produced since but no one, not even Arthur, had ever been shown them.

'You haven't been here before, have you, Lindsay?'

'Haven't been invited.'

'I'm not much of a one for entertaining,' Ross said.

Maeve had already thrown off her overcoat and was peering intently at the painting on the easel. 'You haven't added anything.'

'No,' Ross admitted, 'not a single stroke.'

'Why not?'

'All right, Miss Nosy,' Ross said, 'if you must know, I have to position the figures with a high

145

degree of accuracy.'

'How many figures?'

'Two.'

'Me an' who else?'

'Aren't you getting a little ahead of yourself?' Ross said. 'I haven't decided to employ you yet.'

'Aye, you have,' Maeve told him. 'You told Mr Arthur—'

'I said I'd have to make sure you were suitable.'

'What's not suitable about me then?'

'You fidget.'

'I do not.'

'Fidget, fidget. Prattle, prattle.'

'Prattle?' said Maeve, indignantly. 'Me, prattle?'

'How long can you hold a pose?'

'Hours,' Maeve said.

'On one leg?'

'You never said anything about one leg.'

'He's teasing,' Lindsay put in. 'At least I think he is. Are you, Ross?'

'Not me,' Ross answered. 'Modelling is a deadly serious business.'

'Am I supposed to be modelling today?' Maeve asked.

'Absolutely,' Ross said.

'I'm not taking my clothes off.'

'For God's sake, girl! I don't want you to take your clothes off. In fact, I want you to put clothes on. Pop into the bathroom where you'll find a long skirt, a baggy blouse, and a plaidie.'

'A what?'

'A plaidie is a cross between a blanket and a shawl,' Ross informed her. 'Stick that lot on and we'll see if you look anything like a timid Highland lassie.'

146

'I'm Irish,' Maeve reminded him.

'And I'm making a painting, not a gramophone record.'

'True,' Maeve admitted, ruefully. 'Where's the lavatory?'

'The bathroom,' Ross said, 'is just there.'

Maeve vanished into the bathroom and closed the door.

Lindsay seated herself on the chaise. She watched her cousin clip a sheet of paper to a drawing board and check the sharpness of his pencils with the ball of his thumb. She liked his trim beard and country-style suit. He looked, she thought, more like a landed gentleman than a wild and woolly artist.

She said, 'I don't recognise the landscape.'

'I worked it up from sketches. The hill is part of the ridge of the Campsies. I found the sheep wandering about in a field near Lennoxtown.'

'And the trees?'

'Kelvingrove Park.'

'So you fit all the pieces together like a jigsaw puzzle, do you?'

'I do indeed.'

'That's very clever.'

'Not really,' Ross said, with a shrug.

He rolled a dais from behind the easel and trundled it across the floorboards into the window bay.

'Tell me a little more about the girl,' he said.

'She's Forbes's niece, as you know. She was raised in Dublin in the family boarding-house until the British shelled it in the Easter rebellion. Gowry McCulloch's her father. I don't expect you remember Gowry.'

'I remember the scandal,' Ross said. 'I remember my parents whispering in corners and those interminable family meetings behind closed doors. I'm not that much younger than you are, Lindsay, but I was busy with other things at the time. It *was* a scandal, though, wasn't it? Something to do with Forbes and Tom Calder's daughter by his first marriage?'

'Tom Calder's daughter is Maeve's mother.'

Ross stroked his beard with a large hand. 'I'd forgotten that.'

'Gowry brought the girl over here to get her away from the troubles.'

'She seems remarkably mature for her age.'

'She hasn't had an easy life, I gather. Can you make use of her?'

'Oh yes, I imagine so,' Ross said.

Maeve emerged from the bathroom wearing an ankle-length skirt with a ragged hem and a bulky linen blouse, the plaidie thrown about her shoulders.

She planted her hands on her hips and hid her embarrassment by striking a jaunty pose. *'Voy-la!'*

Ross nodded approvingly, led her to the dais and seated her upon it, turned a little so that the light fell on her.

'Short hair?' he said.

'It's the fashion,' Lindsay said.

'Maeve, pull the plaidie up until it covers your hair.'

'And hides my face?'

'No, just your hair.' He lowered the shawl over her head and arranged the folds to his liking. 'Hold this pose for me, please?'

'And smile?'

148

'No, no smiles, no frowns.'

He walked to the board, took up a pencil and began to draw.

Lindsay had seen men draw before, many times, but only in the engineering style, never freehand. Ross concentrated on accuracy of line and recorded what he saw before him with a precision that seemed, at least at first, almost mathematical.

'May I talk?' Maeve said.

'No.'

She sat where he had placed her and said not a word until Ross unclipped the top sheet of paper from the board, furled it up and laid it behind him. He told Maeve to walk about a bit, then he repositioned her, lying back, elbow on a cloth cushion, the plaid draped about her shoulders.

'May I see what you've done?' Maeve asked.

'Certainly not,' Ross told her, and immediately returned to work.

*   *   *

Forbes had not been himself since the evening of Pickering's party. Lindsay hoped that he would be distracted enough to agree to her proposal without kicking up a fuss. She should have known better.

As soon as dinner was over, she chased Arthur and the children into the parlour and requested a moment or two of Forbes's time, alone. He was immediately suspicious and prickly but remained seated while Miss Runciman helped Enid clear away the pudding plates.

Across the hall in the parlour Arthur vainly tried to pretend that nothing untoward was happening by striking chords on the piano for the instruction

149

of his grandson Philip, who was much more interested in what Maeve was whispering to Harry.

'Phil, old son,' said Arthur, 'do try to pay attention.'

'Yes, Grandee,' Philip said, and flapped his lugs all the harder.

Maeve was practically sitting on Harry's lap, her cheek pressed against his neck. Philip was on the point of calling out, 'What, what is it?' when from across the hallway, his father's voice rose in a thunderous shout.

'Over my dead body!'

Maeve threw herself away from Harry and sat bolt upright.

'Oh, God!' she said. 'Oh, God, it's started.'

'What?' Phil said. 'What's started?'

'Never you mind,' Arthur said.

'No niece of mine is going to strut about like a tart for some so-called bloody painter to ogle at and paw.'

Maeve collapsed against the cushions and covered her ears.

'I don't care if he is a bloody relative . . .'

'Uncle Ross?' Philip asked.

Harry nodded.

'. . . she's not flaunting herself in a state of nature in front of any man.'

'Sure an' I knew there'd be trouble,' Maeve groaned.

'Paying her? Paying her HOW much?'

'How much?' Harry echoed.

'Five and sixpence the hour,' Maeve told him.

'She'd make more on the bloody streets.'

'Dad's not taking it very well, is he?' Harry said.

'Me, you want me to tell her, Lindsay? Don't think I won't.'

'Uh-oh,' Philip said. 'Here he comes.'

Arthur closed the lid of the piano and drew his grandson to him as Forbes burst into the room. 'Ah, Forbes, there you are,' he said.

'You put her up to this, didn't you, Arthur? Well, by God, I'm still master in this house and I'm not going to stand for it.'

'Mr Arthur isn't to blame,' Maeve said, bravely. 'It was all my idea.'

'Don't lie to me, Maeve.'

'You just don't want me to earn any money, do you?'

'It's not the blasted money.'

'What is it then?'

'First it'll be Ross then it'll be some other lecherous . . .'

'Calm yourself, Forbes.' Lindsay touched his arm.

Forbes thrust her away. 'If you're so desperate for work, Maeve, I'll find you a job at the shipyard.'

'Tracing?' Maeve said. 'No thank you. I have a job.'

'Modelling isn't a job. It's—it's . . .'

Maeve reached a hand under the sofa, fished out a roll of paper and, shaking it, unfurled the delicate pencil drawings.

She advanced on her uncle, holding the drawings before her.

'They're lovely, that's what they are,' she said, 'plain lovely.'

Maeve pushed the drawings at him, holding down the springy paper as she might hold down her skirts in a high wind.

Forbes had seen Ross Franklin's paintings. He recalled one in particular, propped in an art

151

dealer's window and priced at three hundred pounds; nymphs, or angels, in scanty veils prancing round the body of a soldier with a spear sticking out of his chest. He hadn't been impressed then and refused to be impressed now.

Maeve waved the drawings in his face.

Perhaps it was her flushed cheeks or the fire in her dark eyes, a reflection of Sylvie's passionate nature or, perhaps, his own conceit that brought about his sudden change of heart. He closed his mouth and took the drawings from her.

The top drawing was so detailed and complete, so much a finished thing, and so like her, that he was moved by it. He rubbed a hand over his moustache. He wasn't used to giving in to women but now, with the girl and the likeness of the girl staring him in the face, he capitulated.

'Is that you?' he asked, huskily.

'Who else would it be?' said Maeve. 'Don't you like it?'

'It—yes, it's very nice,' said Forbes. 'I didn't realise . . .'

'What?' said Harry. 'That Uncle Ross is such a good artist?'

'No, that . . . no.' Forbes sighed. 'All right, Maeve, provided you promise not to pose for anyone but Ross, you have my . . .' He spread his hands helplessly.

'Blessing, do you mean?' said Lindsay.

And Forbes, sighing once more, said, 'Yes.'

*   *   *

The weather had turned nasty. The boys huddled on the veranda at the rear of the school tuck shop.

152

In spite of the rain the proprietor was doing a roaring trade in ginger pop and sticky buns but most of his customers had trailed back to the common room in the main building carrying their comforts with them.

Ewan Calder professed to enjoy the rain. He had dragged his Franklin cousins around the corner of the shop where they leaned disconsolately against the wall, watching water spill from the eaves, and chewing their walnut toffees.

Ewan swigged ginger beer from a dumpy brown bottle.

'Well, have you seen them yet?' he said.

'Seen what?' said Harry.

'Her bubbies.'

'Her what?' said Philip.

'Breasts,' said Ewan Calder, with a little hiss.

'Don't be an idiot, Ewan,' Harry said. 'Of course not.'

'Wouldn't you like to?'

'Haven't thought about it.'

'Bet you have.' Ewan swilled a mouthful of ginger beer in his cheek and spat it over the rail of the veranda. 'Bet you think about it all the time.'

'We're not all girl mad, like you,' said Harry.

'Bubbies that big,' Ewan went on, 'I'd want a look at them.'

'Oh, for God's sake!' Harry said and, rain or no rain, made to step down from the veranda. 'I don't have to listen to this.'

Ewan caught his arm, the movement so uncharacteristically forceful that it stopped Harry in his tracks.

'No harm in looking,' Ewan said. 'I've looked often enough.'

153

'What? At Maeve's—Maeve's chest?' said Philip.

'Not hers, not yet,' said Ewan.

'Whose then?' Harry said, challengingly.

'My secret,' Ewan said. 'Thing is, this uncle of yours, he'll have her out of her dress before—'

'I should never have told you,' Harry said.

'I'd have found out sooner or later. Aren't you going along to watch?'

Harry said, 'Maeve wouldn't stand for it.'

'You know the fellow well enough.' Ewan swigged from the bottle. 'We could just show up unannounced, couldn't we?'

'We?' Philip said. 'All three of us?'

'Catch her naked, if we're lucky,' Ewan Calder said.

'I'm beginning to find this conversation offensive,' Harry said. 'Maeve's a guest in our house. I wouldn't dream of taking advantage of her.'

'Fancy her, do you?' Ewan asked.

'I like her, yes,' Harry answered.

'Well, you'd better not get *too* fond of her,' Ewan said.

'What's *that* supposed to mean?' said Harry.

Ewan smiled slyly. 'I know something about her that you don't.'

'Oh really?' said Harry, angrily. 'Like what?'

'Something my mother told my sisters.'

'And your sisters promptly told you, did they?' said Harry.

'The girls share all their secrets with me,' Ewan said. 'Take me along to your uncle's studio and I'll tell you what I know about Maeve McCulloch.'

'No, Ewan,' Harry said. 'It's just not on.'

Ewan Calder shrugged. 'Suit yourself.'

'I will,' Harry said. 'And in future please keep your nasty suggestions to yourself. Come on, Phil, time we were back in class.' He vaulted the wooden rail and set off towards the school buildings.

'Bubbies?' Phil said. 'Whose bubbies?'

'PHILIP.'

'All right, I'm coming,' Philip shouted and scuttled down the steps to join his brother, leaving his solemn question hanging unanswered in the air.

* * *

Ross was mixing colours on an old marble-topped table he had redeemed from the attic in Harper's Hill. Mixing colours gave him great satisfaction. He worked with jacket off, sleeves rolled up, pipe clenched in his teeth, humming an aria from Gounod's *Faust*, an opera that Arthur, in frivolous mood, had once referred to as 'Gonads First'; a good smoking-room joke that Ross had shared with several patients at Bramwell in an attempt to cheer them up. Most of the poor devils were beyond cheering up, though, and would simply roll their red-rimmed eyes and pull down their mouths as if they had never heard of Gounod, let alone Faust.

A tint for the girl's flesh, thin paint in a series of delicate glazes to build up tone. He would do well by the girl, do her justice. Arthur had been right to bring her along. She was lovely, quite stunning, in fact; not, thank God, the shallow beauty of a primping brunette or a vacuous champagne blonde but a substantial sort of beauty that reflected a depth of character very rare in one so young. He added a drop of walnut oil and smoothed the mixture on the marble with his brush. He preferred

155

to mix colours in natural light but he was fired up tonight. He lifted a clean brush, charged it with paint and was just about to test the tint on a strip of canvas when the doorbell rang.

Ross growled into his beard.

It couldn't be his 'daily'. Mrs Ormond refused to venture this far west after dark and would probably be snugly ensconced in her local pub by now. He laid down pipe and brush and, still growling, stalked across the studio to open the front door.

'Forbes?' he said. 'What an unexpected pleasure.'

He hadn't clapped eyes on Forbes McCulloch for almost a year.

Forbes wore a flapping raincoat and a slouch hat and, Ross thought, looked more like a gangster than a shipbuilder. No prizes for guessing why Lindsay's husband had turned up tonight. He led Forbes through the studio into the parlour where the fire in the grate had all but burned itself out and the remains of his supper lay on the table for Mrs Ormond to clear away in the morning.

'Whisky?'

'No,' Forbes said. 'Thanks all the same. I'm pressed for time so I'll come straight to the point, if you don't mind.'

'I don't mind in the slightest,' Ross said. 'Indeed, I think I'd prefer it.'

'The girl, Maeve, my niece . . .' Forbes removed his hat and held it across his chest as if he were swearing an oath. 'Are you employing her as a model?'

'Come now,' Ross said, 'you know I am.'

'For how long?'

'How long? Well, I dunno, really—a month,

156

six weeks.'

'For this painting, this *Captive Heart* thing?'

'Do you object?'

Forbes shook his head. His hair was thinning. Ross wondered if the fluffy little moustache was some sort of compensation.

'How much do you intend to pay her?' Forbes asked.

'Five and six the hour.'

'What do you charge for a painting?'

'That depends,' said Ross, cagily.

'Say four by six, with a stout gilt frame.'

'Complete with water-cooled boilers and cargo pumps, perhaps?'

'Not funny,' Forbes told him. 'If I commissioned a painting, how much would it set me back?'

'If you need a little decoration for the boardroom, might I suggest you try McNiven or Gordon Taylor. I really do have a full order book right now.'

'I'm thinking of a portrait of my niece.'

'Are you, indeed?' said Ross.

'I'll pay you to do it properly,' Forbes said, 'but I don't want anyone, especially Maeve, to know I'm buying it.'

'May I ask what you intend to do with it?'

'Give it to my wife,' Forbes said. 'It'll make a nice surprise for Lindsay's Christmas. Can you run something up by Christmas?'

'Oh, yes,' Ross said. 'I reckon I can knock something off in eight months, but, as I've just told you, my order book's already chock-a-block.'

'Couldn't you possibly fit it in—as a favour to me?'

'I take it you've seen my drawings?'

157

'Yes, and I admit I'm impressed.'

'Must be,' Ross said, 'to have you haring round here.'

Forbes put his hat on and tugged at the brim. 'You've got her here,' he said, 'and whether I approve or not isn't the issue. It would be very easy for you to paint her portrait without telling her I'm paying for it.'

'It would,' Ross agreed.

'Will you do it, then?'

'I don't come cheap,' Ross said.

Forbes nodded, obviously at ease negotiating terms.

'What sort of sum are we talking about?' he asked.

'I can't quote you a figure off hand,' Ross said. 'What sort of portrait do you require: head and shoulders, half-length, full figure?'

'Figure?' Forbes said, alarmed. 'No, I don't want her figure.'

'Full length,' said Ross, patiently, 'in a pretty dress then? I'll show you some postcards of famous paintings and explain what half-length and full-length actually mean. You'll have to leave the final pose to me, though.'

'I don't want her lying dead on a heap of straw.'

Ross had never had much affinity with his brothers, none at all with his Irish cousin. He felt a little wave of pity for Lindsay who had to put up with this philistine day after day. He stroked his beard, and said, 'No spears, no rustic bowers, I promise. That isn't the way I see her.'

'How do you see her?'

'In a floral dress and summer hat, looking back over her shoulder.'

158

Once, an eternity ago, on a family picnic on Grandfather Owen's estate in Perthshire, he had caught Lindsay in that pose. The image had lodged in a corner of his mind and he had summoned it up many times during the darkest days at Bramwell, bringing Lindsay, as it were, to his rescue.

'Working on that basis,' Forbes said, 'how much?'

'Three hundred.'

'Pounds?'

'Guineas.'

'Framed?'

'Materials included,' Ross said. 'Frame extra.'

'On that preliminary quote,' Forbes said, 'do we have a deal?'

'Well, it seems,' Ross said, 'that we do.'

*   *   *

Arthur was playing cards with the children. They were wagering peppermint sweets in lieu of coins and having an uproariously good time.

Lindsay recalled the rowdy games that had taken place in this very room when the Franklins had crouched on the carpet and wagered florins and half-crowns on the turn of the cards. She was pleased that Grandee was handing on the tradition to a younger generation who, it seemed, had somehow lost the knack of enjoying itself. Seated on the sofa, Miss Runciman was darning stockings. Lindsay was perched on the piano stool, sipping a gin and tonic. If Forbes had been at home the game would never have started but, not unusually, her husband had failed to show up for dinner.

Lindsay enjoyed watching her sons when they

were off guard. The presence of the girl brought out the best in them. It seemed right to have a girl in the house, a lovely, lively young lady. She sometimes wished that her marriage hadn't foundered on the rock of Forbes's infidelity, that she had borne more children, a girl to be her ally when, as must inevitably happen, Miss Runciman and her father passed away. She did have the boys, of course, and the boys were her salvation, but in time they would take wives and father children of their own and she would be left to rattle about here with only Forbes for company.

An ace appeared. Maeve shrieked in delight. Philip fell back clutching his heart. Arthur, an arm about Harry's shoulder, moaned in mock horror.

The din all but drowned out the ringing of the telephone.

Lindsay said, 'It's probably Forbes. I'll take it.'

Carrying her glass, she went out of the parlour and into the hall. It was in her mind that Gowry had received her letter and had been angry enough to invest in the expense of a telephone call. She wasn't sure what she would do if Gowry objected to his daughter posing for an artist.

She unhooked the telephone receiver and held it to her ear.

'Lindsay, are you alone?'

The question sounded so theatrical that Lindsay almost giggled.

'Geoffrey?'

'Yes, *are* you alone?'

'No, as a matter of fact. Why do you ask?'

'I thought Forbes might be . . .'

'Forbes is finishing his dinner.' The lie came easily. 'Where are you?'

'Not far away.'

'What does that mean? Newcastle?'

'I'm in a telephone box at the corner of Madison Street.'

She should have known by the tinny echo that he had found one of the few public telephone boxes. She heard the clink of coins and, for an instant, lost the connection. 'Geoffrey, Geoffrey, are you still there?'

'Yes, I'm here—in front of the church.'

'St Anne's?'

'Yes.'

'Do you want to call round?'

'Can't you come here?'

'Geoffrey . . .'

'Make some excuse. Take the dog for a walk.'

'We don't have a dog.'

'Please, just for half an hour.'

'Why all this secrecy?' Lindsay said.

'I have to see you again.'

'We could lunch tomorrow.'

'I may not be here tomorrow. Come now.'

He spoke in the clipped tone of a man used to giving orders.

Lindsay sipped from the glass and tasted gin on the back of her throat. She was more amused than flattered now by the naval officer's attentions. After years of separation, he could hardly be suffering from a broken heart or, for that matter, infatuation.

She said, 'Is it raining?'

'Beg pardon?'

'Is it still raining?'

'No, it appears to have gone off.'

'All right,' she said. 'I'll see what I can do.'

161

'Lindsay . . .'

Gently, she replaced the receiver, finished the gin and tonic and took the empty glass back into the parlour where the card game was still in full swing.

Her father glanced up. 'Forbes?'

'Minnie Escourt.' She could have told him it was Charlie Chaplin and got away with it so absorbed was he in the game. Casually, she said, 'I'm just going out for a stroll. Shan't be long.'

'A stroll,' Miss Runciman said. 'At this hour.'

'It's early,' said Lindsay. 'I have a little bit of a headache.'

'Take your umbrella, Mum,' Philip advised.

'Yes, dear, I will,' said Lindsay.

*　　　*　　　*

It was well after nine o'clock before the taxi swung into Flowerhill Drive and drew up at the kerb. It sat there for an interminable time before Marjorie got out and the taxi drove away. Forbes watched her fuss with her scarf and, hands on her hips, wriggle as if she were adjusting her underwear.

He stepped from the doorway and said, 'You're late.'

'Mitchell took so long over dinner, I thought he wasn't going to his lodge meeting after all. What do you want with me, Forbes?'

'You know what I want with you, darling,' Forbes said.

'I thought we weren't—I mean, it's so soon. After Stella's party you said it was too dangerous to go on meeting.'

'No more dangerous than it was before,'

162

Forbes said.

He steered her into the deserted hallway and up the staircase to the flat.

She'd been nervous the first time he'd brought her here. He'd had to coax her into the bedroom and on to the bed. She was a typical example of a female whose unwillingness to be made love to was at odds with her need to be loved. There would be tears tonight, though, buckets of tears when he told her they would be going their separate ways, but behind her tears would be relief that she had escaped from the affair unscathed.

He bolted the flat's outer door, caught Marjorie by the waist, pulled her close, slipped his hands between her knees and raised the layers of clothing that covered her belly and thighs.

She wriggled, resisting yet not resisting, yielding yet not yielding. Buckles, tapes, buttons, ribbons, cami-knickers under a petal skirt, the plump stomach. Dark in the hallway, faint light from the street lamps seeping across the linoleum but dark enough to pretend she was someone else, someone other.

'Forbes, you're hurting me.'

'Am I?' he said. 'Sorry.'

He found her with his fingers.

'Forbes . . . !'

He tucked her skirts around her waist and tugged the tiny pearl buttons that held her knickers together. He pushed his hand firmly against her, felt her rise on tip toe and then, almost lazily, sink down on to his fingers.

'Not here,' she complained in a squeaky voice. 'Not like this.'

'Hold still, Marge,' he told her.

163

He took himself out of his trousers, raincoat floating out behind him, hat tottering on the back of his hat. He was very hard. One stroke was enough to bring him up. Cupping her hips, he jerked her forward and went in. She sagged, bent her knees, uttered a weird little bray, then fell against him, her head resting on his shoulder, her hat-pin scratching his ear.

Carefully, very carefully, Forbes withdrew.

'No,' she said, 'no, not—no, it's not . . .'

'Enough?'

'No, no. No.'

He doubted if she'd ever had it like this before, upright against a wall, like one of the tarts that hung around the Gallowgate. He had finally managed to shake her out of her complacency, that prissy, repressed, ladylike need to yield only on her own terms.

He shucked off the raincoat and tossed it to the floor, hurried into the bedroom and switched on the electrical lamp, ran down the blind and closed the curtain. He stripped the quilt from the bed, flung off his jacket, unbuttoned his waistcoat, unbuttoned himself all the way down. The front of his shirt stuck out stiff and white, like quality wrapping paper.

Marjorie loitered in the doorway, hat askew.

'I must go home, Forbes, before Mitchell . . .'

'Take your clothes off.'

'What?'

'All of them, everything.'

'Aren't you finished?'

'I haven't even started yet,' Forbes said.

She backed into the shadowy hall. He caught her, pulled her into the bedroom and slammed the

164

door with his heel. 'Be a good girl, Marge,' he said, 'take your damned clothes off and let me look at you.'

'I—I can't. I won't.'

'Then I will.'

'No, Forbes, please.'

Impatiently, he threw her across the bed and straddled her. She spread her arms like a supplicant while he unbuttoned her coat, blouse and bodice and exposed her breasts. He rubbed himself against her breasts while he laboriously hauled off her coat. He pulled down her pleated skirt and knickers, leaving her belly framed by straps and stocking tops.

'For God's sake, Marjorie, give me a hand, will you?'

Then, in abject horror at what he was doing, he saw the tears trickling down her cheeks and, being less of a man than he supposed himself to be, covered her hastily with the quilt and rolled away, defeated.

*   *   *

The kiss was more than a friendly greeting. His lips were cold, his chin smooth. He smelled of spice and talcum powder. The nap of his overcoat was dewed with moisture for it had begun to rain again. He held his hat by his side and looped an arm about her waist as if he intended to dance with her on the wet pavement under the high, hazy streetlamps.

She had forgotten how tall he was, how small she was. She lifted herself on tiptoe to kiss his cold lips. She was sure she wasn't in love with Geoffrey Paget but she loved kissing him and, at that moment, found the pretence of love more satisfying than love itself.

'Are you well, Lindsay?'

'I'm perfectly well, thank you.'

He kissed her once more, almost as if he could not help himself.

She felt light as thistledown, ready to float away.

'Is Forbes at home?' he asked.

'Snug as a bug,' Lindsay answered.

'Shall we walk for a little while?'

'We shall.'

He reached for her hand and they walked round the broad corner by St Anne's on to the sweeping curve that led back to Brunswick Park.

There were lots of folk about, girls and boys, families, picture-goers, a staggering drunk or two, dog-walkers, dour and pedestrian. Forbes was out there too, on the loose. Lindsay didn't care. She strolled hand-in-hand with Geoffrey, pretending that this was love again.

'I missed you,' he said.

'And I missed you.'

Fibbing seemed to strengthen the bond between them.

'I had to see you again,' he said. 'You know that, I think.'

'Yes,' she said. 'I know.'

In a splash of shadow shaken from a plane tree, they kissed once more.

Lindsay sighed. 'I thought you might have gone back to your wife.'

'I don't have a wife,' Geoff said. 'But you do have a husband.'

'Aren't we rather getting ahead of ourselves?'

'I suppose we are, rather.'

'Are you sorry you let me go, Geoffrey?'

'Did I let you go?'

'Well, perhaps not,' Lindsay conceded. 'Perhaps you just allowed me too much room to manoeuvre.'

'Yes,' he said, 'yes, that's probably it.'

'Are you putting up at the Central?' she asked.

'Yes.'

'For how long?'

'Not long enough, I'm afraid.'

'Long enough for what?'

'To take you there.'

'To lunch?'

He looked down at her, smiling. 'Yes—to lunch.'

'Will you take me next time you're in town?' Lindsay said.

'If you'll come.'

'I'll probably have to be coaxed.'

'Consider it done,' said Geoffrey.

*　　　*　　　*

She had been gone for less than an hour but when she returned she found that the card game had been disbanded and Forbes was lurking in the hallway, wearing a sour and suspicious scowl.

'Where the devil have you been?' he demanded.

She felt very calm, almost serene.

'Out walking,' Lindsay said, 'with my lover in the rain.'

Forbes hesitated, then laughed; then, with a little wave of the hand to acknowledge the joke, he turned and went upstairs to bed.

CHAPTER SEVEN

Payment in Kind

Tom Calder did not automatically assume that all artists were wicked through and through or that creative people were more libertarian than caulkers or welders, or, for that matter, doctors, lawyers and architects.

If he was at all upset that his granddaughter was to become an artist's model he gave no sign of it. He told Cissie and the girls quite matter-of-factly, though he knew that Cissie would be scandalised. The girls, dutifully following their mother's lead, expressed disgust that any decent self-respecting girl would be so immodest as to pose for a man she hardly knew. The girls were just as hypocritical as Cissie, though, and far from despising Maeve were full of admiration for her boldness.

'Dad?'

'Yes, son.'

'Do you believe in original sin?'

Tom hesitated before answering, 'No.'

'Neither do I,' Ewan said. 'How about the Divine Mind?'

'Christian Science?'

'Yes,' Ewan said. 'I'm not so sure about the Divine Mind.'

'What aren't you sure about?' Tom said. 'The existence of the Divine Mind, or the application of it?'

'The application.'

Tom swung round in his chair and held his

fountain pen away from the desk; the carpet around the desk was already sprinkled with ink stains. Ewan lolled in the armchair by the fire where he often sprawled and read or chatted while Tom wrestled with problems of stress-bearing beams or the precise dimensions of split-pin washers.

'Have you spoken to Dr Bradley about it?' Tom asked. 'He may not be a Christian Scientist, but he is a doctor of theology.'

'Conducting a flute band and drinking whisky at an Orange lodge aren't my idea of theology,' Ewan said.

'I take it you've had a disagreement with Dr Bradley?'

'Sort of,' Ewan admitted. 'He told me that Christian Science was almost as bad as Roman Catholicism, and advised me to go away and pray.'

Although he had a great deal of work to do, Tom braced himself to endure another of Ewan's rambling, soul-searching harangues.

Then Ewan said, 'Can cousins marry?'

'Pardon?'

'Can cousins marry—legally I mean?'

'Of course they can. Your Aunt Lindsay and Uncle Forbes are cousins.'

Ewan pondered. 'And they're married?'

'What a daft question! Of course they are.'

'So, theoretically, Harry could marry Maeve McCulloch.'

Tom said, 'Theoretically, yes, I suppose he could.'

'But if she's your granddaughter . . .'

'I'm not related to the Franklins.'

'Mum is.'

'Has Harry said anything to lead you to suppose that he might *want* to marry Maeve one day?'

'I think he's smitten.'

'I see.' Tom rolled the fountain pen between finger and thumb. 'You're not smitten by Maeve too, by any chance, are you, son?'

'That would be incest, wouldn't it?'

'Only if—yes, yes it would,' Tom said. 'No harm in *liking* her, of course.'

'She isn't my type,' Ewan said. 'What would be the legal position if Harry's father was Maeve's father?'

'Harry would be in breach of the law if he married her, or if he—'

'Cohabited?'

'Yes, cohabited. Maeve is Harry's cousin, however, not his sister, so the point's entirely moot.' Tom put the pen down. 'Why are you asking me these questions, Ewan?'

For a young man who was not athletically inclined, Ewan could be incredibly nimble at times. He rose from the armchair in one fluid movement.

'Just curious,' he said and sauntered out of the study, leaving his father not just puzzled but thoroughly perplexed.

*　　　*　　　*

Strange, Forbes thought, how things trail you from place to place. The horseshoe knocker that adorned the door of his mother's room-and-kitchen had once been attached to the back door of the cottage in Towers in which he'd been born and raised and was an object redolent of childhood innocence, or what passed for innocence in the

170

McCulloch family.

He rapped on the door.

Waited.

Knocked again, using the horseshoe this time.

No response from within.

He wondered if the old bat was lying dead on the lino. Unlikely, he thought, since Ma wasn't the sort to pass on without a maximum of fuss.

He put his ear to the door, heard scuffling.

Whispers.

His mother's voice, hardly more than a croak: 'Who's there?'

'Friend,' said Forbes, dryly. 'Open the bloody door, Mother, will you?'

She opened it an inch, and glowered out at him.

'What do *you* want?'

'We haven't seen anything of you for weeks,' Forbes said. 'I popped round to see if you're all right, and to invite you to supper.' She was so stooped, so shrunken that he had to peer to make her out. 'What's going on?'

'I'm busy.'

'Busy? You!'

'Come back tomorrow, Forbes.'

'Are you entertaining a man in there?'

'Maeve's not with you, is she?' Kay McCulloch asked.

'No.'

'Well then, I suppose it's all right for you to come in.'

She allowed him to push open the door and ushered him into the kitchen.

It was grey dark in the kitchen without any gaslight.

The man was over by the pantry door, near

171

the sink.

'Is this your boy, Kay?' he said.

The buttery accent that Forbes hadn't heard in years brought back memories of men gathered in the kitchen in the cottage at Towers, Charlie and he peeking through the doorway till Da shooed them away.

'Aye,' Kay McCulloch said. 'This is Forbes.'

'Now you know who I am,' Forbes said, 'who the hell are you?'

'The name's of no consequence,' the man said. 'I'll shake your hand, though, since it's you has brought me here.'

'Me!' Forbes exclaimed.

The man was about sixty, tall and stout. He wore a frieze coat and leggings and might, Forbes thought, have been a farmer or an officer of the Irish Liberation Army, or both. The leggings were a give-away but Forbes had been out of Ireland too long to interpret the clues properly.

The stranger said, 'Will you not be shakin' my hand then?'

Forbes stepped forward. 'Of course, yes, why not?'

The man's grasp was powerful, his fingers calloused.

'Been in Glasgow long, have you?' Forbes asked.

'Not long, not long at all.'

Forbes pulled out a chair and seated himself.

'All right,' he said. 'Let's cut the cackle. What gives you the impression that I brought you here?'

'This fine staunch woman here is the impression.'

'Are you still in touch with the brotherhood, Ma?' Forbes said.

'Sure an' she is, an' why would she not be?' the man said.

He too seated himself at the table.

Kay McCulloch went into the cupboard where the stove was. Forbes heard the scratch of a match, the plop of a gas ring and saw a faint halo of light reflected in the window. The stranger had ample cheeks and a dewlap. He wore a smart-respectable suit under the frieze overcoat, striped trousers tucked into the leggings, boots polished to a high shine.

'Are you a soldier?' Forbes enquired.

'That I am—after a fashion.'

'All right,' Forbes said. 'Since you seem to be labouring under the misapprehension that I've something to offer the brotherhood, perhaps you'd be good enough to tell me what it is.'

'It's money, son,' Kay McCulloch said. 'He's here for the money.'

'Money, what money?'

'The money you're giving Maeve for our Peter.'

'Eh?'

'This gentleman is here to make sure it finds its way to the right people.'

'Whoa!' Forbes said. 'Hold your horses. My arrangement with Maeve has nothing to do with you, or the brotherhood.'

'That's not what the girl wrote her ma,' the man said.

'Dear God!' Forbes exploded. 'Will Sylvie never learn! Look, you—whatever your name is—I'm sorry you've been dragged over here but there's no money for you to collect. I told Maeve I'd treble any sum she earned just to keep her out of mischief, not to fund your damned war with

173

the English.'

'Has Maeve found employment yet?' his mother said.

'Yes,' Forbes said, 'she's modelling for an artist.'

'Ross?'

'Yes—Ross.'

'Who put her up to that—you?'

Before Forbes could answer, the man said, 'Aye, Kay, an' there's worse things a girl could be doing for the cause, is there not now?'

'Your name's not Trotter, by any chance?' Forbes asked

'Turk? Nay, not me. I'm somebody else.'

'Maeve's not interested in the brotherhood,' Forbes said, 'only in this Trotter chap.'

' 'Course she's interested in the brotherhood,' the stranger said. 'She's Dan McCulloch's flesh and blood, is she not?'

'I don't care tuppence who her grandfather was—my father, I might point out—the girl doesn't know what she's doing.'

'But you do, don't you?' the man said.

'I'm not funding any organisation,' Forbes said. 'My hands are clean.'

'And are not our hands clean?'

'Clean or not—it's no business of mine.'

'Make it your business, Forbes,' his mother urged.

'For God's sake, Ma! I thought you despised the brotherhood. You always said you despised the brotherhood for what it did—or didn't do—for Da. Have you been sending money to Charlie and Peter?'

'What if I have?' his mother said. 'How else can I keep the memory of your father burning bright?'

174

'So that's why you're living like a bloody anchorite, is it? You're funding the rebels with the money I give you.'

'I don't want my lovely boys to starve.'

'Now you'—Forbes turned to the stranger—'you think you can finagle more money out of me, do you? Well, you can't. I told you—'

'The girl,' the man interrupted. 'You care for the girl, do you not?'

'Of course I bloody do.'

'Show him,' Kay McCulloch said. 'Go on, show him.'

'Show me what?'

The stranger opened his overcoat and dug into his pocket. He pulled out a sheet of paper and handed it to Forbes.

Forbes said, 'If I'm expected to read this rubbish, Mother, maybe you could spare me some light, eh?'

She lit the gas mantel and turned up the flame.

Forbes smoothed the paper on the table top and with a little shock, like a blow to the heart, scanned the typewritten message:

AN EYE FOR AN EYE, A TOOTH FOR A TOOTH, THEREFORE A LIFE FOR A LIFE

'What the hell does that mean?'

'Just what it says,' the man told him. 'It's a death notice.'

'Is it meant for me, to scare me?'

'It's not intended for you.'

'Who is it intended for, then?' Forbes asked.

'It was sent to Maeve,' his mother said.

175

'Where?'

'In Dublin,' the man said. 'Endicott Street. Sylvie opened it.'

'She didn't tell anyone, not even Gowry. She went straight to Charlie with it,' Kay McCulloch put in. 'He told Mr Coffey—'

'Coffey? Is that your name?' Forbes said.

'Charlie told this gentleman and sent him over here to warn us.'

'I don't believe a bloody word of it,' Forbes said. 'You're trying to scare me into parting with cash. What do you need it for—bullets, dynamite, pistols? Not food for your starving kiddies, I'll be bound.'

'Ay-hay, but that's harsh,' Mr Coffey said. 'Sure an' that's harsh.'

Forbes scanned the letter again. Anyone could have typed the message, anyone. Did they think he was entirely stupid? All this because he'd made a gesture of good faith to keep his brother's child happy? He experienced a flash of rage, crumpled the letter and tossed it at Coffey, shouting, 'Who sent it, if you didn't send it? If Charlie didn't send it, who did? Tell me that.'

'Some bravo in English Intelligence,' Coffey answered. 'The streets of every county town in Ireland are littered with murder notices. It's not your girl they're after, it's Turk Trotter.'

'Why threaten Maeve?'

'To shame Trotter into giving himself up.'

'Does Maeve know about the death threat?'

'No, not yet.'

'Don't tell her,' said Forbes.

'It's our obligation to tell her.'

'Come on,' Forbes said, 'the English aren't

unscrupulous enough to down a young girl in cold blood. They might just have gall enough to do it in Dublin but not here on the mainland.' Coffey retrieved the crumpled sheet from the floor and put it back into his pocket. 'All right,' Forbes went on, 'I'll give you fifty pounds for that thing along with your solemn promise you won't breathe a word about any of this to Maeve.'

'She's in danger,' Kay said.

'She's not in danger,' Forbes said. 'Damn it, Ma, do you think I'm as gullible as my old man? I know you're taking me for a walk in the park and all you really want is some hard cash. Mr Coffey, am I not right?'

'Hard cash is always useful.'

'Fifty pounds.'

'Make it a hundred.'

'Buggered if I will.'

'Eighty.'

'Eighty then—and I get the letter,' Forbes said. He threw a hand in the air, despairingly. 'No, bugger it to hell, never mind the letter. You could have another one typed up in five minutes.' He got to his feet. 'By God, Mother, I never thought you'd stoop so low as to blackmail your own son, never mind your granddaughter.' He leaned on the table and thrust his face up close to Coffey's. 'And if I ever see your ugly mug again, Mr Coffey, I'll shop you. Don't think I won't. And if I learn from Maeve you've leaked word of this so-called death threat, Ma, I'll set the coppers on you too.' He pushed himself away from the table and rammed on his hat. 'I assume you won't accept a banker's draft?'

Mr Coffey smiled. 'Cash preferred.'

'I'll have someone bring it round tomorrow

morning.'

'Will you be requirin' a receipt?' Mr Coffey asked.

'No receipt,' said Forbes and, with one last withering glance at his mother, stalked out of the tenement flat, and headed for the nearest pub.

*   *   *

Lindsay and Eleanor Runciman were in the drawing-room when Forbes arrived home. He put his head round the door, and snapped, 'Where's Maeve?'

'In her room.'

'What's she doing in her room?'

'I imagine she's gone to bed,' Lindsay said. 'What's wrong with you?'

'Nothing.'

She followed her husband into the hall cloakroom and watched him hang up his overcoat and hat. 'Have you been drinking?'

'I had a brandy, that's all. One damned brandy.'

'No need to bite my head off.'

'Was there post today, a letter for Maeve?'

'Not that I know of,' said Lindsay. 'What's wrong?'

'I told you—nothing. I'm tired, that's all.'

He pushed past her and went upstairs.

She was tempted to follow him but instead returned to the drawing-room. Miss Runciman raised her brows in enquiry. Lindsay shook her head. If he hadn't asked about Maeve she might have supposed that Forbes had found out about her late-night promenade with Geoffrey Paget. Sooner or later he *would* find out about Geoffrey.

She rather looked forward to that day. She lingered by the drawing-room door, listening to the creak of the stairs, and wondered what Forbes could possibly want with Maeve at this late hour.

* * *

'Who is it?'

'Uncle Forbes. May I come in?'

'Just a minute.'

She put on a dressing-gown—one of Harry's— over her nightdress. She hadn't been asleep. She had been sitting up in bed studying a book of engravings by a Dutch chap called Vermeer that Mr Arthur had dug out of the library. The engravings weren't like real paintings but even without colour they looked very cool and calm. She wondered if Ross would like to paint her at a piano or standing at the window of his kitchen pouring milk from a jug.

The dressing-gown was brown with a silk cord. It swept about her feet like a princess's train as she hurried to the door.

'Something wrong?' she asked.

Forbes's smile was colourless, like a steel engraving.

'Absolutely not a thing,' he said. 'I just came to wish you goodnight.'

She didn't know if it would be right for him to come into her bedroom. She wouldn't ask Harry or even Philip to come in when she was in her nightclothes, though it would probably be all right with Mr Arthur, for he was old.

She hesitated, holding the door with both hands.

Her uncle said, 'Have you heard anything from

home, lately?'

'I had a letter on Saturday,' Maeve said.

'From your mother?'

'Aye, she was asking about you.'

'Was she, indeed?' her uncle said. 'Saturday—nothing since?'

'What?' Maeve said in alarm. 'Has something bad happened in Dublin?'

'No, God no.' Forbes shook his head. 'Nothing like that, sweetheart. Next time you write, do give your mother my regards.'

Still frowning, Maeve said, 'I will.'

The material of Harry's dressing-gown sagged away from her chest. She could feel her breasts within its folds. She removed a hand from the door and closed the collar of the dressing-gown, just in case her uncle thought she was flirting with him.

'What about your feller, have you heard from him?' Forbes said.

'My feller? Oh, you mean Turk. Nope, not a word.'

'Perhaps he's not the sort of chap who likes writing letters.'

'Aye well, he certainly doesn't like answerin' mine.'

'Of course, if he's on the run . . .'

'He knows where I am.'

'Did you tell him you were coming here? Give him our address?'

'Sure an' I did.'

'Well . . .'—that odd, counterfeit smile again—'perhaps he'll turn up one of these days and surprise us.'

'Perhaps he will,' Maeve said, 'but I doubt it. Goodnight, then.'

And rather more abruptly than intended, she closed the bedroom door.

*　　*　　*

On Saturday afternoon, about half past one, Lindsay dropped Maeve off at Ross's studio and, excusing herself, caught a tramcar down town.

She presented herself at the reception desk of the Central Hotel and asked the clerk to inform Lieutenant-Commander Paget that she had arrived. The pompous young clerk hunted through the register for several minutes then, without an apology, scooted off to find a manager.

'Paget?' the manager said. 'A naval gentleman?'

'Lieutenant-Commander, actually,' said Lindsay, with all the patience she could muster. 'I have an appointment.'

The manager eyed her as if she had wandered in off the street.

'There is no Lieutenant Paget on our register.'

'There must be some mistake,' Lindsay said.

'Madam, there is no mistake. Is the gentleman your husband?'

'Certainly not.'

'In that case . . .'

The manager's gesture was patronisingly dismissive. Lindsay moved closer to the mahogany counter and in a confiding tone, said, 'I am Mrs Forbes McCulloch of Franklin's Shipbuilding. I am here at the request of the Navy Board, on behalf of my husband. Lieutenant-Commander Paget was resident in your hotel early this week and if he has been called back to duty then I'm sure he's left a forwarding address.'

181

The manager clicked his fingers to summon up the clerk. He whispered in the young man's ear. The young man disappeared and returned a few moments later with a card folder. He placed the folder on the counter. Lindsay watched the manager's podgy little fingers flick over the pages. At length, he looked up.

'Paget,' he said, 'spelled with a P—as in "Pomegranate"?'

'Yes.'

'No one of that name has registered this month.' He could not resist delivering a sniff of triumph. 'Therefore, madam, if the gentleman after whom you enquire did not check in to our accommodations, the gentleman after whom you enquire could not have checked out. I can only suggest that you telephone the Navy Board who may have information concerning the officer's whereabouts.'

'Thank you,' Lindsay said, 'I will.'

And walked out.

*   *   *

The smell of paint was strong. By the easel was a tea-trolley with little brass wheels upon which umpteen small pots and a dozen or so fat tubes of oil paint were neatly arranged, together with sable brushes, three round porcelain plates, perfectly clean and virginal, and a bottle filled with spirit.

'Oh,' Maeve said. 'Are we finally getting started?'

The drawing board had been wheeled away, the dais moved closer to the easel, though it was still within the window bay.

'When Bobby turns up,' Ross told her.

182

'Bobby? Who's Bobby?'

'Your ardent swain.'

'Swine?'

'Swain.'

Maeve walked to the easel, studied the white space in the centre of the canvas and saw that it was no longer blank. Fine pencil lines mapped out the position of the figures, her figure and the figure of a young man.

'Bobby,' she said, 'presumably?'

'Yes.'

'When did you draw him?'

'Several weeks ago.'

'Why haven't I seen him here?'

'His time is limited.'

'Why?'

'Because,' Ross said, 'he isn't a professional model.'

'I'm not either. Don't you use professional models?'

'Very infrequently.'

'Too expensive?'

'Too flighty,' said Ross.

'When Bobby isn't pretending to be an ardent swain,' Maeve said, 'what does he do for a living?'

'He works for the Franklins.'

'Really? What—in the shipyard?'

Maeve guessed that Ross was feeling loose-endish now that everything was in place and he was ready to begin. Perhaps painting made him nervous, though she couldn't imagine him ever being nervous about anything. He fished a curved pipe from the pocket of his tweed jacket, and a box of matches, lit the pipe, puffed, blew smoke, and said, 'He's draughtsman.'

183

'Really!' Maeve said again. 'I wonder if he knows my grandfather.'

'I'm sure he does,' Ross said.

'How did you discover him?'

'Arthur found him for me.'

'Mr Arthur seems to have a knack for that sort of thing.'

'He knows my requirements pretty well.' Ross wandered to the window and looked down into Flowerhill Drive. 'He can also be very persuasive.'

'What do you mean?'

'Initially young Mr Shannon was exceedingly reluctant to come within a mile of an artist's studio.'

'Did he think you might be up to some funny business?'

'Hmm! Probably,' Ross said. 'Also, he knows he'd be a laughing stock in the shipyard if it ever got out what he does at weekends.'

'Why does he do it then?' Maeve said.

'Partly because Arthur's a big cheese,' Ross said, 'but mainly because he needs extra cash.'

'How much do you pay him?'

'Same as I pay you.'

'I don't suppose draughtsmen earn much.'

'The salary scale is fixed,' Ross said. 'But no, it's no fortune, particularly when you're only twenty-one years old.'

'Twenty-one?' Maeve peered again at the pencil outline. 'He looks older.'

Ross laughed, a deep, chesty chuckle. 'How can you tell?'

'He's scowling.'

'He's not scowling,' Ross said. 'He's lusting.'

'Lusting?'

184

'I mean, he's just fallen madly in love with you.'

'Not me,' Maeve said, quickly. 'You mean with the girl in the painting.'

'Yes, you're right, of course.' Ross clenched the pipe between his teeth and fished a watch from his vest pocket. 'Well, Bobby won't be falling in love with anyone if he doesn't show up soon.'

Maeve crossed to the window by Ross's side.

'Because of the light?' she said.

'Yes.'

'Vermeer preferred a north light for his interiors,' Maeve said.

Ross glanced at her, a bushy eyebrow raised. 'Did he, indeed?'

'Didn't you know that?'

'I think I have heard something to that effect, yes.'

'Don't you like Vermeer?'

'Do you?' Ross said.

'Yes, I think he's lovely.'

'De Hooch and Jan Steen,' Ross said. 'Have a look at those if you ever get a chance. More my cup of tea.'

'Why?'

'The girls are much prettier,' Ross said, then, 'Ah, here's our Bobby now.'

*   *   *

Forbes parked the Lanchester at the bottom of the hill and walked up the track to Merriam House. He was out of breath by the time he reached the gate. In afternoon sunlight Pickering's palace looked more American than ever, and a lot less like an ice-cream factory. There was no sign of Ronnie, the

185

bare-armed butler, but Stella was waiting for him at the door.

'Drew's gone off to a rugby football match,' she told him, as if she had read his mind. 'In Edinburgh.'

'Does he still play rugby?' Forbes asked.

'No,' Stella answered. 'He never did. Drew was a boxer.'

To his disappointment she wasn't wearing beach pyjamas. She had on a belted jacket and finely pleated skirt and sharp little heels that, he thought, would do the parquet flooring not one bit of good.

She led him into the living-room. A long glass-topped table was positioned close to the French doors. Stella went around behind the table, brusque today, all business. 'I assume you have something to show me,' she said, 'or you wouldn't have requested a meeting?'

'Requested a meeting?' Forbes said. 'You make it sound very official.'

'Why did your secretary call? Why didn't you call yourself?'

'And risk having your husband answer?' Forbes said.

'I don't like being snubbed.'

'Snubbed?'

'Fobbed off.'

'That,' Forbes said, 'was certainly not my intention.'

'What would you have said if Drew *had* answered?'

'I wouldn't have said anything,' Forbes told her. 'Mrs Connors, my secretary, would have asked for the date of the next association meeting.'

'April 25th, a Monday.'

'Ah, I see you keep tabs on your husband's engagements,' Forbes said.

'I prefer to know where Drew is,' Stella said, 'at all times.'

'Understandable,' Forbes said, 'when you're trying to run a profitable business on the q.t.'

'I take it you've done your homework?'

'On Gideon Rowe and Spellman? Of course.'

'Are you satisfied?'

'Not quite,' Forbes said. 'I'd like to find out who's supplying the licences for the new fuel storage tanks at Rabat.'

Surprised, Stella paused before answering, 'The French.'

'To a company registered in Panama?'

'Only the ships are Panamanian.'

'Even so, aren't you—I mean the company— setting up a string of bunkering stations on the North African coast?' Forbes said.

'We're exploring the possibility.'

'If Gideon Rowe and Spellman are investing in tank facilities in North Africa will they be able to borrow sufficient capital to put out on a new tanker?'

'How shrewd you are.' Stella Pickering said. 'But I'm not Rowe and Spellman's only silent partner. How do you imagine we obtained sites in French territories, let alone building and trading licences?'

'Other partners? You mean foreign partners?'

'*Mais oui.*'

'Ah!' Forbes nodded. 'I begin to get the picture.'

'I doubt it,' Stella said. 'However, if I were to put down eight per cent of Franklin's estimated cost before you even lay keel would that allay your fears?'

'It would go a long way towards doing so,' Forbes admitted.

'Let's agree on that as a working principle.'

'Suits me,' Forbes said.

'Very well then,' Stella Pickering said. 'Show me what you have.'

*   *   *

In the beginning she didn't take to him. He seemed too aware of himself, too bumptious. He was tow-headed, grey-eyed, square-faced, with a dent in the centre of his chin and, though not much taller than she was, managed to give the impression that he was looking down his nose at her. She had seldom encountered such pugnacity in a young man before, not even in her Uncle Peter who would pick a fight with anyone at the drop of a hat. Then he grinned. And when he grinned Maeve realised that his belligerence was only skin deep and that he had just been sizing her up.

She wondered if she should have presented herself to young Mr Shannon lying on a cushion on the dais, if he would have been more impressed by her in a prone position. No, a snap judgement suggested that perhaps Bobby Shannon wasn't the sort of chap you lie down to and that it was better to be meeting him with both your feet on the ground.

He did not offer his hand. He gave her a nod instead.

When he nodded a lock of soft fair hair tumbled over his brow. He swept it back impatiently and gave it a pat—more of a slap, actually—to keep it in place and then, grinning again, nodded again.

'Miss McCulloch?'

'The same,' Maeve said.

She had a terrible impulse to drop a curtsey but settled for a nod instead.

There they were, nodding away at each other like a couple of seaside donkeys while Ross watched with a twinkle of amusement in his eye. It *was* funny, she supposed, the boy and she sniffing at each other like a tom and a tabby, not knowing what to do next, except nod and grin.

'Bobby,' the young man said, at length. 'Bobby Shannon.'

'Maeve,' she said. 'Maeve McCulloch.'

They nodded again, pathetically.

'Well, now that's over and done with,' Ross said, 'and you have established who you are, perhaps we can get on with it, what!'

'Dress?' Maeve said.

'Yes,' said Ross. 'One at a time, please.'

'Ladies first, then,' said Bobby, gallantly.

Maeve headed for the bathroom.

*　　　*　　　*

Stella came round the table and stood by him. However formal her suit might be she acted on his senses as few other woman had ever done. He stretched out the drawings he'd removed from his briefcase and pinned them down with the lead washers he'd brought along for the purpose.

Stella leaned over the drawings, hands behind her back.

'Big,' she said. 'She certainly is a big baby.'

'Four-four-five feet between the perpendiculars,' Forbes informed her. 'Deadweight capacity ten thousand three hundred tons. Summer draught of twenty-six feet. She isn't to scale. This isn't much more than a preliminary sketch but we can move pretty quickly if this is what you're after.'

'Propulsion?'

'Four-cylinder piston diesel, we reckon.'

'Quite advanced.'

'I know,' Forbes said. 'With that engine she'll develop about three thousand horse power and provide a service speed of thirteen knots.'

'Good, very good.'

He traced the lines of Tom Calder's design with his forefinger. 'Here's where it gets really clever,' he said. 'Cargo space is divided by longitudinal and transverse bulkheads into twenty-seven separate compartments.'

'How many pump-rooms?'

'Two, feeding eight independent pumps.'

'Good,' Stella Pickering said again. 'Very good.'

'Which means she can carry all grades of oil. We'll install a system of high-velocity jets to clean the tanks between loadings.'

'Accommodation?'

'Standard,' Forbes said. 'Captain, officers and wireless operator housed forward of amidships; engineers, crew and mess-room aft.'

Stella put an arm about his shoulder and leaned against him, her breast crushed against the muscle of his upper arm.

He said, thickly, 'Problems?'

'No, no problems. She really is huge, though.'

'I thought that's what you wanted.'

'Oh it is, it is.'

'Candidly, Stella, she's well ahead of her time.'

He drew her round to face him. He was never

190

more sincere than at the beginning of a seduction and, knowing that Tom Calder's design had already impressed her, pushed his advantage. Hand cupped on the swell of her hip, he looked directly into her pale green eyes and felt himself going down into her like an anchor into the sea.

'Yes, Stella,' he said, softly. 'Franklin's can build her.'

'Promise.'

'I promise,' said Forbes.

* * *

The pose was a good deal less comfortable than Maeve had supposed it would be. Lying motionless for half an hour was a strain. Worse for Bobby Shannon, though. Positioned above her, weight on his left knee, right leg pulled back, he looked more like a chap jumping a hurdle than someone who had been newly struck down by love.

Ross had marked the dais with strips of gummed paper—a buttock here, an elbow there—and had adjusted the platform precisely before he stalked to the easel and plucked a brush from the jar. All Maeve could see of him now was a tweedy elbow and glimpses of his hairy face when he popped his head around the edge of the stretcher to have another squint.

After ten minutes she was beginning to stiffen. After a quarter of an hour cramp set in. Although she was supposed to be asleep, she could peep through her lashes at Bobby Shannon, at a torso covered by a transparent garment that looked more like a shroud than a shirt. His skin—pink—showed through the material and if she raised her head a

191

tiny bit she could see his bare knees protruding from under the folds of his kilt.

For twenty minutes Maeve managed to hold her tongue.

Behind the easel, Ross too was silent.

She could hear the creak of floorboards and the occasional crack of a match as he relit his pipe. Silence, she knew, meant concentration. Bobby Shannon was concentrating too, eyes open, his grey eyes unnerving in their fixity.

'Shannon,' she whispered, 'is that an Irish name?'

'Nup.'

'The Shannon's a big river in—'

'Ssshhh!' Bobby warned.

Her bum had gone numb now. Cramp wormed its way into the small of her back. She longed to squirm and change position but she did not dare. She had a feeling that if she so much as twitched all Mr Ross's efforts would be wasted, like a photograph when somebody moves before the shutter closes.

She fluttered her eyelashes and peeked at the boy again.

How did he do it, she wondered, how did he hold that unnatural position without collapsing? He appeared relaxed, not frozen, not stiff, not aching the way she was; yet when she looked more closely she noticed sweat on his brow and realised that Bobby too was earning his fee the hard way.

A drop of perspiration slid from his brow and landed, warmly, on her cheek. 'Sorry, hen,' Bobby whispered, his lips, like a ventriloquist's, not moving.

Maeve braced herself to receive more droplets

of moist male sweat.

Then Bobby called out, 'Rest, Mr Franklin, please.'

The painter's head appeared, horizontal to the edge of the canvas. Shreds of tobacco ash spouted from his pipe together with a gout of blue smoke.

'Rest?' Ross said. 'Already?'

'Aye, Mr Franklin.'

Ross stepped from behind the easel, a brush in his right hand. He gripped it, Maeve noticed, very lightly, the way a violinist grips a bow.

'Is that a half-hour gone already?' he asked.

'It is, sir,' Bobby answered.

'All right,' Ross said. 'By all means rest.'

Before Maeve could swing her feet to the floor, young Mr Shannon pressed down on her. He shook the sleeve of his shirt across his hand, poked a finger into the material and gently dabbed away the trace of sweat that had fallen on Maeve's cheek.

'There,' he said. 'Is that better?'

Maeve drew her knees to her chin, bowed her back and tried to stand up. The studio spun round dizzily. Bobby looped an arm about her.

'A wee bit peerie-heided, like?' he asked.

'What?'

'Is your head spinning?'

'Yes, a bit.'

'It's the blood supply. You'll get used to it,' Bobby said, and released her.

Maeve didn't want to be released just yet. She wanted to hang on to him for as long as possible. But the dizzy spell soon passed and all her aches and pains with it. Now she was up and moving, she felt better.

Ross was at the tea-trolley, carefully cleaning

paint from the sable. She went around the easel to see what had been accomplished in the long half-hour.

'My God!' she exclaimed, indignantly. 'Is that all?'

No underpainting, no groundwork, just the glaring white space with its tracery of pencil lines, and there, on the rim of the foliage, one toe, perfectly rendered down to the first joint.

'It's a good afternoon's work for him,' Bobby murmured. 'Lovely wee toe, though, if you don't mind me sayin' so.'

'My toe,' Maeve reminded him, with more than a trace of pride.

And somewhere on the far side of the easel, Ross laughed.

CHAPTER EIGHT

A Snake in the Grass

Forbes could not be sure whether it was the taste of Stella Pickering's lips or the smell of her money that blinded him to what was really going on. At first it seemed like just another seduction, though quite who was seducing who was a matter for debate. He was rather taken aback when she suggested meeting at the Cardross Arms Hotel, a choice of venue that seemed tactless, or teasing or, perhaps, a little bit of both.

Wednesday, Stella said: no other day would do.

Forbes had the devil's own job sneaking off on Wednesday.

Bob Lightbody of the Draughtsmen's Association and Jack Burgoyne of the Amalgamated Society of Engineers had called a meeting for Wednesday afternoon and Martin was in a panic about it. Forbes felt guilty about deserting his post when, by nightfall, Franklin's might have ground to a halt.

He also fretted about the Irishman, Coffey. He had withdrawn eighty pounds from his personal account and found a dim-witted tea-boy to deliver it to Craddock Street. What worried him now wasn't the 'death threat' to Maeve but the fact that his mother was still in close touch with the brotherhood.

The sight of the river broadening into the firth cheered him somewhat. He wondered what sort of mood Mrs Pickering would be in today. Would she be brusque and businesslike, or frilly, feminine and all kissy-kissy? He suspected there were faces that she hadn't shown him yet, facets of her character that, with luck and perseverance, would soon be revealed as he plunged down into those very mysterious, very English depths.

He whisked the Lanchester through the curves of the road and brought it down by a tree-lined lane to the back of the Cardross Arms. He was up for it now, chipper and almost worry-free, and strolled into the bar with a swagger as if he, not she, were leading the dance.

Pearl earrings, a loose ankle-length dress, a tight-fitting cloche hat that made her look like an aviatrix; Stella leaned against the bar, smoking a cigarette and sipping beer from a tall glass.

Forbes sauntered up, planted an elbow on the counter and informed the barmaid that he would have what the lady was having. He looked up at

Stella. She looked down at him. He asked what sort of a journey she'd had. She told him she'd come down by train. He asked if she would care to join him for a spot of lunch. Parting her beautiful red lips and blowing a plume of cigarette smoke over his head, she told him she would give it her consideration. He asked how long it would take her to make up her mind. She told him that she was not a creature of impulse.

'Are you sure about that?' Forbes said.

She smiled widely. 'Well, perhaps I am.'

Forbes grinned. 'I'm told the soup here is very good, very warming.'

'Mock turtle?' Stella said.

'How did you guess?' said Forbes and, carrying his glass, followed her to the table by the window that he had reserved in advance.

*   *   *

Lindsay hadn't been in London in years. When her grandfather had been alive her cousins and she had been brought up to the capital en route to the annual naval review at Devonport. But all that seemed very far away now and she had only a hazy memory of the Admiralty buildings that loomed over the Mall.

The Admiralty had changed a great deal. A warren of offices had sprung up to accommodate a confusing number of new departments. She had no idea which department Geoffrey was attached to or which of the Sea Lords he worked under. She seemed to recall that he had mentioned the Navy Board. She telephoned the Board's main office, and drew the first of several blanks.

She tried the office of the Third Sea Lord next, and drew another blank. And when she finally spoke to a minion in the department of the Permanent Secretary she was treated so high-handedly that she had to pause for coffee and a cigarette to cool down before she embarked on another round of calls.

Maeve had gone into Glasgow with Miss Runciman to spend some of her weekend earnings on new clothes, her promise to save every penny to assist the Irish cause forgotten, at least for the time being. Lindsay had the house to herself, apart from Cook and Enid.

By half past eleven she was on the telephone again, and after another hour of fruitless conversation with clerks and secretaries found herself talking to a person of indeterminate rank in the Department of Contracts and Commissions. Reluctantly, he informed her that Lieutenant-Commander Geoffrey Paget was presently on shore leave. Her enquiry as to when Lieutenant-Commander Paget might be expected to return was deftly turned aside—at which point Lindsay gave up in disgust.

She went into the parlour, drank more coffee, smoked another cigarette and wondered not only where Geoffrey was hiding but why he had bothered to come back to Scotland at all. The answer was so obvious that she almost overlooked it. However much Geoffrey might decry his ex-wife, it was all too apparent that he remained on good terms with his sister-in-law.

Cup in hand, Lindsay wandered to the window and looked down into the little park. It was just an ordinary sort of day, except for the blustery wind that shook the branches of the trees and bent the columns of smoke that rose from the tall chimneys along Clydeside. How often had she stood at this window looking out at this scene? How often had her mind idled along, like a tug with a defunct engine, bumping into this thought, that wish, nudging the soft uncompromising shoals of longing and regret? However devious, however banal, Geoffrey Paget's urgent courtship had awakened the realisation that being a good mother and a dutiful wife were no longer enough, that she was no longer taking revenge on Forbes but on herself.

She set the cup down on the window ledge, went out into the hall and seated herself on an upright chair by the telephone.

She read the number from a card, dialled carefully, heard it ring.

After almost half a minute a voice spoke into her ear, a deep voice, curt and cautious. 'Yes?'

'I'd like to speak with Mrs Stella Pickering, please,' Lindsay said.

'Mrs Pickering is not at home. May I ask who's calling?'

'Lindsay McCulloch.'

And the voice, Sir Andrew's voice, said, 'Ah!'

*   *   *

Stella Pickering proved to be a much better conversationalist than Marjorie Hussey. Fuelled by gossip, politics and a fair quantity of wine, lunch ticked along most satisfactorily.

Forbes had never had much of a head for drink. He was still haunted by the spectre of his old man, who had boozed himself out of a small fortune and

198

had come very close to ruining all their lives. He didn't know whether to be dismayed by or admiring of Stella Pickering's capacity for alcohol and, with something approaching envy, watched her pour down not one but two glasses of brandy on top of dessert.

He passed on brandy and drank his coffee black.

He was enthralled by her worldliness. He didn't have to flatter her to disguise his desire. He was careful to say nothing about the tanker, though; not to push too hard.

Stella asked about his wife, his children—and Marjorie. He told her about his wife, his children—and Marjorie; informed her wistfully that it was all over with Marjorie, that the friendship had run its course. Stella offered sympathy and spoke in turn of a long-ago friendship of her own that had ended in tears.

She asked about Franklin's and he talked at length about the ships Franklin's had built, including the submarine the navy had commissioned back in 1906. He even told Stella about Maeve, his lovely, dark-eyed Irish niece, and how fond he had become of the girl in a short space of time; then, after a pause, he returned to discussing the American proposals for arms limitation.

At half past four o'clock, Stella said she really must leave to catch a train back to Dalmuir. Forbes rose and paid the bill.

It was very quiet and peaceful in the empty dining-room as he waited for Stella to return from the cloakroom. He would drive her home, of course, at least as far as Dalmuir. He wondered where the afternoon had gone and why he had spared no thought for Lightbody and Burgoyne, for his mother and vengeful brothers, or any of the problems that had harassed him earlier in the day.

He heard the thud of the cloakroom door, and looked up.

Framed against the wooden panels, arms raised to fit on the cloche, she looked, he thought, utterly and incredibly beautiful.

She caught sight of him watching her, smiled the wide red smile, came to him and with an effortless little twirl locked her arm with his.

'Do you have a motor-car?' she whispered.

'It's outside, out back.'

'Come then,' she said. 'Drive me home.'

*   *   *

Failure to contact Geoffrey Paget at the Admiralty and a foolish telephone call to the Pickerings had brought nothing but embarrassment. Maeve and Eleanor hadn't returned from shopping and it would be another couple of hours at least before Forbes came home, for there was more than a whiff of union agitation at the yard and a shop stewards' meeting had been called for that afternoon.

Lindsay understood the mechanics of labour disputes only too well. Hardly a week went by without one or other of the trade unions demanding better terms. Only skilful negotiation on her father's part, and Martin's willingness to capitulate, had kept Franklin's free of costly strikes. But without future orders soon there would have to be pay-offs, and clashes between men and management would be inevitable. She wondered if Donald had seen the writing on the wall, if there had been more to his abrupt retirement soon after

200

the Armistice than grief at poor Johnny's death.

She ate a solitary lunch, dozed in an armchair in the parlour for a half-hour then wandered about the parlour, her brain numbed by the pointlessness of trying to manage a household that already ran like clockwork. She drooped by the window in a state of lethargy so perilously close to torpor that she found she had been staring at the person in the park below for a good three or four minutes before she recognised him.

She straightened, frowning.

'Ross?' she said aloud. 'Dear God! It's Ross.'

She bustled into the hallway, snatched an overcoat from the cloakroom, ran down the steps, across the pavement and on to the path that ringed the sad little oval of grass.

Ross was seated on the park's one and only bench, holding down a sketch pad with his forearm and drawing upon it with a stick of red chalk. He wore a short, quilted topcoat and a deerstalker hat and, with the briar pipe stuck in his mouth, resembled an unlikely cross between Augustus John and Sherlock Holmes.

The setting was very painterly, tinted clouds riding over the lofty terrace, patches of sunlight and swift shadow moving among the trees; painterly but surely not static enough, Lindsay thought, to inspire her mathematical cousin to work out of doors.

'Ah-hah!' Lindsay said. 'Caught you breathing fresh air at last.'

'Need a house,' Ross said. 'Thought yours might do.'

'A house? For what?'

'Book illustration.'

'You—an illustrator?'

He puffed on the pipe and continued to sketch, his big hand sliding across the paper. The wind ruffled the sheet. He pressed down on it firmly and seemed, just for a moment, to be tracing the shape of his own fingers, the way a child might do.

'Earning a crust,' he said, 'just earning a crust, dear.'

'Would you like me to leave you in peace?'

He glanced up, glowering. 'Heavens no.'

Lindsay seated herself at the end of the bench. She made no attempt to peep at the drawing. She squinted up at the terrace and the vault of the sky; blue, umpteen shades of blue, fading back and back into depthless infinity.

She wished that she were a painter and had the hand as well as the eye to do what Ross was doing.

'Red chalk?' she said.

'The subject requires a bold line.'

'What's the book?'

'Something about Victorian cities. Black's are putting it out.'

'How many illustrations are you submitting?'

'Six. I've already done George Square, the art gallery and the university. The Botanical Gardens next, probably.' He peeped along the length of the bench. 'Meanwhile, Brunswick Crescent; a lovely subtle curve made up of straight frontages. Something a little out of the ordinary for a change.'

'Harper's Hill too, perhaps?'

'It crossed my mind,' Ross said, 'but it's too close to home.'

Lindsay was quiet for a time.

Then she said, 'You're not hoping to bump into Maeve, by any chance?'

'Why would I want to bump into Maeve?'

'I don't know.' Lindsay shrugged. 'I just thought . . .'

'Not Maeve, no,' Ross said.

'Who then? Me?'

'A lovely subtle curve made up of straight frontages?' Ross said.

'Point taken.' Lindsay laughed. 'Its too late to offer you tea, I suppose?'

'Yes, and too early for supper,' Ross said. 'Besides, I've work to do.'

Lindsay moved closer, edging along the bench.

Ross crooked an arm about the pad to protect it. He leaned over the drawing, pipe at an angle, and seemed to be scribbling his signature over and over again. He fanned away a cloud of chalk dust.

'Is that all you ever think about, Ross?' Lindsay said. 'Work?'

'Pretty much,' he admitted. 'To tell you the truth, it's the only thing that gets me out of bed of a morning.'

'Oh, sad, that's sad.'

'What gets you out of bed of a morning?' he asked.

'I have to attend to my family, see them fed.'

'Really? Can't they find their mouths without your help?'

'You know what I mean,' Lindsay said. 'Lilias did the same for you.'

'That's true,' Ross said. 'Spoiled we were, spoiled something awful.'

He removed the pipe from his mouth and placed it on the gravel, fished in the pocket of his coat and brought out a small, oblong block of sandpaper. He filed the chalk stick with it, bevelling the edge, blew away dust and applied himself to drawing

203

once more.

'What are you doing now?' Lindsay asked.

'Adding detail.'

'Where the devil lies?'

'Absolutely.'

'Is painting really the only thing that makes you happy?'

'Hmm,' he murmured. 'I suppose it is.'

'Why have you never married?'

'Never had time.'

'Excuses won't do, Ross.'

'I like working,' he said. 'I like painting.'

'Love painting?'

'Yes, I suppose that's true.' He sighed. 'Don't you have anything better to do than tease a poor hard-working artist with awkward questions?'

Lindsay sat very still, prim, like Maeve on the podium, knees together, hands folded in her lap, pretending to be an awfully good girl.

Ross dug a stubby wax crayon from his pocket and added ten or a dozen strong vertical lines to the drawing. He swung the pad on his knee and, to Lindsay's surprise, proceeded to jot down a series of notes, linking them to parts of the finished drawing with arrows and circles and, in the process, ruining it.

'Watercolour,' Ross explained. 'I'll tart it up in the studio, later.'

'So this is only a blueprint?'

He nodded, completed his task, swung the pad round and secured it with a stiff tissue overleaf and three broad rubber bands.

'Aren't you going to let me see it?' Lindsay asked.

'No.'

'Why not?'

'You may not approve.'

'Would that matter?' she asked.

'It would to me,' Ross answered.

'I'm no critic,' Lindsay said. 'I'm only your big cousin.'

'Older cousin,' Ross said.

'Ancient, you mean?'

He didn't laugh, or even smile. He stooped, lifted the pipe from the gravel, wiped it on his sleeve and put it into his pocket. He buttoned his topcoat, adjusted the deerstalker and tucked the sketch pad under his arm.

Lindsay, looking up, watched him make ready to leave.

He didn't seem sullen or sad or even self-absorbed. He was his own man, very much his own man, and she respected him for it. He stood before her, large, compact and all of a piece, the sketch pad held securely beneath his arm, the way a gamekeeper might hold a shotgun.

'Lindsay,' he said, without warning, 'would you sit for me?'

'Don't you have enough sheep to be going on with?'

'Seriously,' he said.

'I'm no romantic McWhirter heroine.'

'You and Maeve together.'

'With Maeve? Both of us?'

'Yes, a double portrait.'

She gave a stuttering little laugh, flattered, embarrassed and intrigued all at once. 'Who on earth would want to buy . . . I say, are you hoping I'll commission . . .' It was quite the wrong thing to say. She realised it before the words were out of her mouth. She leaped to her feet and laid her hand against his chest. 'Oh, Ross, dear Ross, I'm sorry. How crass of me.'

'No, you're right,' he said. 'Absolutely right.'

'I didn't mean to imply that you were mercenary.'

'I am, though.'

'I know you have a living to earn and . . . Maeve, yes, of course, but why would you waste precious time painting an old hag like me?'

'Because I want to,' he said. 'Will you do it?'

'Yes,' Lindsay said. 'Of course I will. When will the sittings begin?'

'In the summertime,' said Ross.

'When all the trees are green-o?' Lindsay said.

And Ross, with a whiskery smile, said, 'Quite.'

*   *   *

Ronnie, the butler, wore a spotless white bum-freezer, a clean shirt and a nifty little dickey-bow and had a bar towel draped over his shoulder. He gave Stella a grunt by way of greeting, relieved her of her overcoat and hat then padded back into the living-room and stationed himself behind the bar.

There were two men with her husband and, by the look of it, they had kept Ronnie busy for most of the afternoon.

Geoff Paget was definitely well oiled. He had unbuttoned his uniform and lay back against the leather of the long sofa, scratching his chest like a tramp with fleas. Mitchell Hussey was laughing, his small, tonsured head thrown back, mouth wide open, a whisky tumbler clutched in both hands.

Drew had stripped off his jacket and removed his cuff-links and, with shirt sleeves rolled up, looked more like a dock labourer than a knight of the realm. He was drinking beer, bottled beer at that, and, Stella reckoned, was a good deal less sloshed than he appeared to be.

She had interrupted him in the middle of some long-winded anecdote, no doubt filthy, and waited obediently for him to finish it before she made her entrance. He knew she was there, of course, but chose to ignore her. He might, she thought, have been somewhat less neglectful if he had known that she was still moist down below, that Forbes McCulloch's kisses had roused her and that, roiling about in the broad back seat of the Lanchester, she had given Forbes an inch of liberty that had somehow extended into a mile.

It had been several years since anyone had made love to her in the back seat of a motor-car in broad daylight. However much of a fool McCulloch might be, he was very adept at love-making. She wished, in fact, that there had been more time, that they had arranged to meet for dinner, not lunch, and could have driven out to some country lane or by-way and, under cover of darkness, have finished what they'd started.

Drew speared his little audience with the sting in the tail of the joke.

Stella heard Geoff's *yaw-yaw-yaw* and Mitchell Hussey's whinny in the hollow spaces of the room, then she went forward, smiling and swaying her hips.

'Stella, darling, so you've returned from the wars?' Drew said, not rising.

Geoff made a vain attempt to tuck his long legs under him but, locked in the clutches of the sofa, gave up, while Mitchell Hussey rose, staggered slightly, lifted her hand and kissed it, a courtly gesture he wouldn't have dreamed of making if he'd been sober.

'Decent lunch?' Drew enquired.

'Tedious, awfully tedious.'

'Took long enough,' Drew said. 'Drive you back, did he?'

'Drove me to distraction,' Stella said.

'His wife telephoned this morning.'

Stella felt hot and unusually bothered by the eyes of the men upon her. She wondered if excitement had left its mark. She smoothed her hands down the front of her dress. 'Hold the fort, chaps,' she said. 'I really must bathe and change before dinner.'

Drew caught her arm, dragged her down and pulled her against him.

'Drink first,' he said. 'News first.'

'Is he on the hook, Stella?' Geoff said, sitting up.

'Did he swallow it?' said Mitchell Hussey.

'Do we have him?' her husband asked.

She flopped back against the leather, draped an arm about Drew's shoulder and made them wait for an answer.

'Gentlemen,' she said, at length, 'he is, he did, and we do.'

'Bloody good show!' Mitchell Hussey cried and, with all the anger of a patient man, punched the air with his fist. 'Now all we have to do—'

'Is reel him in,' said Geoffrey.

PART TWO

CHAPTER NINE

Painting on Glass

The love letters had no undertone of desperation;
that, at least, was Lindsay's interpretation, for she
had almost gone off the notion of giving herself to
Lieutenant-Commander Paget. Back in March she
had fallen in love with the notion of being in love
but the emotions that Geoffrey had inspired in her
then were the very emotions that acted against him
now.

If Geoffrey had been camped out at his sister-in-
law's house in Dalmuir he certainly wasn't camped
there now. The letters were postmarked from all
over the place, from Portsmouth, Southampton,
Newcastle, Cardiff and Barrow-in-Furness, as well
as London. If she had really been in love with
Geoffrey she would have charted his travels on a
map and stored his letters in a velvet-lined box. She
was too rueful, too sensible to indulge in that sort
of nonsense, however, and, at first, just burned
them.

As March gave way to April and April to May,
though, and Forbes still refused to remark on the
fact that she was receiving letters from a person
unknown, she became deliberately careless.

Maeve, Arthur and the boys were more
observant.

'Is that another one?' Arthur asked.

'It is.'

'Who's it from this time?'

'A friend, just a friend.'

'Does this friend not have a name?'

'Of course my friend has a name.'

'Aren't you going to tell us, Mum?'

'No, I am not.'

'Is it a sweetheart?' Maeve asked.

Lindsay had rehearsed a light laugh that hinted at much but gave nothing away. 'Married ladies don't have sweethearts.'

'A secret admirer, then?'

'Mum?' said Philip, troubled. 'It's not, is it?'

'It's not a "secret" anything, darling.'

Standing morosely by the window or lolling half asleep in the armchair, Forbes paid no attention.

'How many is that, all told?' Arthur asked.

Miss Runciman raised three gnarled fingers. 'Three this week.'

'Oh, I'm being spied on, am I?' Lindsay said.

'Hardly spied on, dearest,' Arthur said. 'Given that you're flaunting the dashed things in our faces.'

She would rise then, wave Geoff's latest letter in the air as if to dry the ink on the page, and carry it out of the room with her. Forbes would open one eye, or swing round from the window, but refused to rise to the bait.

'It's the sailor man, isn't it?' Eleanor Runciman said.

'Sailor man? What sailor man?' said Lindsay.

Lindsay and Eleanor were alone in the dining-room after breakfast.

Forbes and Arthur had left for the shipyard, the boys had gone haring off to school and Maeve had dashed out to post a letter to Dublin.

'The chap you used to be in love with—Paget.'

Lindsay tossed the letter on to the tablecloth.

212

'Yes, they're from Geoffrey.'

'What does he want with you?'

'To take me to bed.'

The housekeeper's weary features registered no surprise.

'Have you given him any encouragement in that direction?' she asked.

'Not encouragement, not exactly,' Lindsay said. 'Have you been reading my post?'

'Only the postmarks,' said Eleanor Runciman. 'Unless Mr Paget's devised a way of doing it by correspondence you and he will have no chance of sharing a cup of tea, let alone a bed until he stops rattling about the country.'

Lindsay laughed. 'Don't you disapprove, Eleanor?'

'It's not my place to disapprove.'

'Aren't you going to me a lecture on fidelity?'

'I read you that lecture years ago,' Miss Runciman said. 'If you had any intention of letting the sailor turn your head, you'd be much less open about it. You're trying to make Forbes take notice, aren't you?'

'Am I that transparent?'

'As glass,' said Eleanor.

'Why hasn't Forbes said anything?'

'Because he's stubborn,' Eleanor said. 'It's a risky strategy, Lindsay. You've got poor Philip quite worried; your father too.'

'Did Papa suggest you talk to me?'

'Yes.'

'Why didn't he talk to me himself?'

'He's embarrassed.'

'Embarrassed? Papa?'

'You know what he thinks of Forbes.'

Lindsay stared through the windows of the dining-room at the trees, a great mass of green that blotted out the harsh landscape of Clydeside. Soon Ross would finish *The Captive Heart* and be ready for her. Then she would have another secret with which to taunt Forbes. Meanwhile, Geoffrey Paget was still a promise, still a possibility.

'Your papa,' Miss Runciman went on, 'loves you far too much to begrudge you a chance at happiness.'

'I don't understand,' said Lindsay.

'He's well aware that in a year or two the boys will have less need of you than they do now.' Eleanor reached across the breakfast table, laid a hand on Lindsay's hand and tapped out the coded little message.

'SOS?' said Lindsay. 'Me, you mean?'

'Don't tell me, as Maeve did, that you're not in distress,' Eleanor Runciman said. 'I've know you too long, my dear, and love you too much not to see what's happening.'

'What is happening?'

'You're unhappy.'

'No, I'm not, not especially.'

'One could hardly blame you for taking a lover.'

'Eleanor!'

'*He* does.'

'Who? Forbes?' said Lindsay. 'Perhaps he does—but I'm not a man; I don't need that sort of thing.'

'We all need to be loved,' Eleanor said. 'Tell me, have you replied to the sailor's letters?'

'No,' Lindsay lied.

'Well,' Eleanor said, with a sigh, 'that's something to be thankful for. At least you haven't compromised yourself.'

214

'Geoffrey Paget may not be the gentleman I supposed him to be,' Lindsay said, 'but I doubt if he'd stoop to blackmail.'

'One never knows with sailors.'

'I do wish you'd show a little consistency, Eleanor. In one breath you're assuring me that you wouldn't turn a hair if I took a lover; in the next you're warning me what will happen if I do.'

'Paget,' Eleanor said, 'is not the man for you.'

'Oh really! Who is the man for me?'

'Not Paget,' Eleanor repeated. 'That's all I have to say.'

'Well, thank you for the advice,' Lindsay said, stiffly.

'Will you heed it?'

'Probably not,' said Lindsay.

*   *   *

Ross had lost confidence. The work was not going well. There was something wrong with *The Captive Heart*, some flaw that he couldn't repair with white spirit and a hogs' hair brush.

He cursed the dazzling spring sunlight for altering his perception, cursed the recalcitrant resins for drying too soon, or not soon enough. He chewed through the stem of his best briar pipe, spilled paint on his best tweed trousers. He snapped at Mrs Ormond, swore at Bobby Shannon and, with difficulty, managed not to blame Maeve for his woes.

The longer he worked on Maeve McCulloch's features, though, the flatter the painting became. Short of scratching out the central figures and starting all over again, he had no choice but to

215

labour manfully on.

'Bugger!' he shouted. 'Bugger and blast!'

Bobby raised an eyebrow.

Maeve poked out the tip of her tongue.

Ross peered around the edge of the canvas, a brush stuck in his mouth like a pirate's cutlass.

'What,' he growled, 'are you doing?'

'Nothing,' Maeve said. 'We're lying here, good as gold.'

'You've done something to yourself. Have you had your hair cut?'

'Nope.'

'Still, lie still.'

'I am lying still.'

'Something's different. Something's changed.'

'I had a bath this morning,' Maeve said. 'Maybe I've gone all wrinkly.'

'Like a prune,' said Bobby.

Maeve laughed, rocking a little.

Ross, exasperated, stalked out from behind the easel and tossed the brush on to the trolley. 'We're getting nowhere,' he said. 'Perhaps you'd better take a breather, though God knows you don't deserve it.'

'It's hot,' Maeve said. 'Bobby's sweating like a pig.'

Bobby stretched an arm above his head and sniffed at his armpit.

'I'm not,' he said.

'Dry yourself, Bobby, if you have to.' Ross headed for the kitchen. 'I suppose we could all do justice to a cup of tea.'

Bobby seated himself on the dais and towelled his calves.

'Do you always sweat like that?' Maeve asked.

'I don't do it deliberately.'

'Bet you're a hazard in the drawing-office.'

'Be more than my job's worth to drip on drawings at the office.'

'My grandfather wouldn't sack you, would he?'

'Tom, old Tom? Nah, old Tom wouldn't dare sack me. Mr Lightbody wouldn't stand for it.'

'Mr Lightbody? Is he your union representative?'

'Aye—only draughtsmen don't have a union.'

'What do draughtsmen have then?'

'An association.'

'Don't you pay dues?'

'Aye, we pay dues.'

'Can you call a strike?'

'What makes you ask that?' Bobby said, suspiciously.

Maeve held up both hands. 'Sorry,' she said. 'I didn't mean to pry.'

Bobby shrugged. 'Aye, we could withdraw our labour if we had a good enough reason.'

'The miners are threatening a strike, so I hear.'

'Now the war's well an' truly over,' Bobby said, 'the coal mines are returnin' to private ownership, so, naturally, wages are bein' cut to the bone.'

Ross appeared with the tea.

He said, 'I trust you're not filling this innocent girl's head with Trotskyist nonsense, Robert?'

'I'm no Trotskyist.'

'Lenin's your man, is he?' Ross said.

'I'm with the Socialist Labour Party, if you must know.'

'Did they run guns to Ireland before the Easter Rising?' Maeve asked.

'Nah, us socialists steered well clear o' the Irish troubles.'

217

'Why?'

'In case we got tarred with the same brush.'

'The same brush?' said Maeve. 'Sure an' what brush would that be?'

'Enough, enough!' Ross said. 'Perhaps we should curtail this controversial debate before you two come to blows.' He sipped tea, then said, 'Tell me, Maeve, how's your Aunt Lindsay?'

'She's fine.'

'Haven't seen much of her since she decided you didn't need a chaperone.'

'I'm thinking she's the one who needs a chaperone these days.'

Ross choked a little, coughed. 'Pardon?'

'We think she's got a sweetheart.'

'A sweetheart?'

'An unknown admirer. He writes to her all the time.'

'He does? Who does?'

'Miss Runciman thinks he's a sailor.'

'Oh!' said Ross, 'What does Forbes—what does your uncle have to say about that?'

'He doesn't know.'

Ross stirred his tea and stared down into the cup. 'Or doesn't care?'

Maeve knew she had been tactless. If Bobby Shannon was a devout socialist he probably had a low enough opinion of the Franklins without her adding to it. She had heard a lot of socialist jabber in Dublin where the Marxists and the Fenians were at loggerheads about using nationalism as a weapon in the workers' struggle for emancipation. As a Protestant in Catholic Dublin, she had rarely felt the lash of bigotry, but she had seen men come to blows on the pavement outside McKinstry's over the true aims of revolutionary nationalism and the vicious sectarianism of the labour movement.

There were too many wars, too many 'revolutions' to keep track of them all, though. Living under her uncle's roof and having a bit of money in her pocket had clouded her views on a lot of things that had seemed very clear back home in Endicott Street.

'I think,' she said, cautiously, 'Uncle Forbes has a lot on his mind right now. He's worried about—about other things.'

'Falling orders, for example?' Ross said.

'Aye.'

Bobby turned his head and stared at her, sullen to the point of surliness. The lock of fair hair bobbed on his brow. He swept it back angrily.

Maeve sucked in a deep breath and said, 'I don't suppose he's the only one.'

'The spectre of mass unemployment haunts us all,' Ross said.

'Not you, but,' said Bobby.

'No, not me,' Ross said. 'I'm lucky in that respect.'

'Aye, money breeds money,' Bobby said. 'It's not you nor your kind who'll suffer if there's a slump, Mr Franklin.'

'I agree with you,' Ross said. 'But that, alas, is the way of the world.'

'It needn't be,' Bobby said. 'The world can be changed.'

'I doubt it,' Maeve heard herself say. 'If you'd seen what I've seen, Bobby Shannon, you wouldn't be so confident about what can and can't be changed.'

'You—what do you know about it?'

219

She knew she was being dragged into an argument that had no possible outcome but she was so annoyed at Bobby's dismissal of her opinions that she blurted out, 'Wait till you've had your house blown out from under you, Bobby Shannon, wait till you've had a copper shoving a gun in your face and you'll think twice about calling for a revolution.'

'Ireland's an occupied country,' Bobby said. 'You're after freedom to govern yourselves. You'll never get it, though, not while it threatens the *status quo*. Anyhow, what've you got to complain about, you with a silver spoon to eat your dinner with an' clean drawers for to wear every mornin'?'

Maeve rounded on him. 'You leave my drawers out o' this,' she said, testily. 'At least we've got *men* in my country, men who are willing to die for what they believe in.'

'Aw, aw!' Bobby snarled. 'So you think we're cowards, do you?'

'I never said that,' Maeve told him. 'But—aye, since you mention it, I don't think you have the gumption to shake off what you call capitalist oppression. I think you've had it too bloody easy for too bloody long.'

'That's a bit harsh, Maeve, is it not?' Ross said.

She swung on her hip, kicking her legs under the ragged blue skirt.

'What right has he got to criticise me, him prancin' about in a fancy kilt pretendin' to be a poor shepherd boy? I'll bet he's never even seen a shepherd boy. I'll bet he's never smelled the stink o' a flock so starved they're chewin' the wool off each other's backs; or tenant farmers so crushed by the landlord's lackeys they haven't a crust o' bread to shove in their kiddies' mouths.'

'I know about the Irish famine,' Bobby said. 'I read my history.'

'History?' Maeve shouted. 'History? You think it's all just history, do you?' She jumped from the dais, tore off the plaid shawl, threw it on the floor and stamped her bare foot upon it. 'That's what I think of *your* country's history, Bobby Shannon. It's all just tartan and tears, all glorious yesterdays and golden tomorrows, with never a thought for the state you're in right now.'

She stormed off into the bathroom, and slammed the door.

Bobby stared blankly after her, then glanced at Ross in bewilderment.

'What's wrong with her?' he asked.

'I believe you insulted her,' Ross said.

'How?'

'You mistook her for a Franklin,' said Ross.

*   *   *

Much of what Eleanor said made sense and Lindsay, chastened, kept Geoffrey's letters to herself now. Stealth seemed to add weight to the paper affair, however, and, within a week, Geoffrey was writing to chide her for fickleness.

The weather turned fair and warm, spring eased into summer and Maeve and she went to theatre matinées, to the pictures, to art exhibitions and, on lovely May afternoons, walked in Kelvingrove or drank coffee at a café table by the side of Bingham's boating lake. For all that, Lindsay remained unsettled, for there were too many things going on in the wings.

221

Forbes had been in an odd mood all evening, indrawn and distracted. Arthur had been unable to lure him into an argument. Even Maeve, in a spanking new Paris-model summer frock, had been unable to coax a word from her uncle, let alone a smile. He had retired to his room shortly after dinner but was still up and moving about long after eleven.

Lindsay turned the knob and went in.

'Forbes, what *are* you doing?'

'For God's sake! Is there no privacy in this bloody house?'

Entangled in a skein of steel springs, he struggled to rise from the carpet. He was clad in an Aertex vest and underpants, black socks and suspenders. His skin was mushroom pale in the lamplight and his stomach wobbled like blancmange as he strove to free himself from the clutches of the exercise device.

Lindsay stood over him, chuckling.

'It's not bloody funny.'

'Oh but it is, Forbes.'

He lay back, panting. 'Well, now you're here—uninvited, I might add—the least you can do is give me a hand.'

She kneeled by his side. 'You really should be more careful, darling. You could do yourself a terrible injury with that thing.'

'The advertisement said—'

'That it would turn you into a fine figure of a man in a fortnight? I'm surprised you, of all people, were taken in by false promises.'

'I refuse to discuss the matter while I'm tied in knots.'

'Didn't the advert warn you not to go in search

222

of eternal youth while wearing suspenders?'
Lindsay said. 'You're snagged, that's all, hoist by
your own petard.' She reached out, released the
clasp that held up one black stocking, separated it
from the wire spring, then detached the handle
from his instep.

'There!'

Springs twanged, snapped and slithered. Forbes
hurled the device across the room, and sat up.
Under roly-poly accumulations of flesh he was still
well muscled. Lindsay could not help but look at
that part of him that nestled under his belly. She
had forgotten that Forbes was unusually well
endowed.

'Stop staring at me, Lindsay. I know—I'm fat.'

'Well, not exactly fat.'

He sat with knees drawn up to his chin like an
ageing cherub in one of Ross's canvases. 'Plump,
portly, chubby. Call it what you like, it comes to the
same damned thing in the end. Fat, that's what I
am—too bloody fat.'

'Haven't you been feeling well?'

'I feel fine.'

'You could try eating less.'

She was still kneeling beside him. She drew her
knees together and tucked in her skirt. She was
taken by a sudden irresponsible urge to touch him,
to test, as it were, the speed of his reaction for,
exhausted or not, fat or not, he was still her
husband and once, long ago, had been her lover
too.

She scrambled quickly to her feet and backed
away.

'You're not doing it for the sake of your health,
Forbes, are you?' she said. 'You're doing it to

223

impress someone.'

'Rubbish!'

'Who is it this time?'

'I might ask you the same question,' Forbes said.

'Are you implying . . .'

'Stop it, Linnet,' Forbes said. 'I've seen the letters. God knows, you haven't been hiding them, have you?'

'You—you of all people have no right to criticise.'

'Fair comment,' he said. 'Who are they from?'

'None of your damned business.'

She waited for his brain to go to work, waited for him to say 'Paget' but it seemed that he had forgotten the lieutenant-commander and her chaste little brush with love all those years ago.

'All right, don't tell me.'

If she had told him there and then she might have averted disaster. Hindsight was all very well, but at the time she had no idea how much, or how little, her husband knew. She had needed a secret of her own, a safe little antidote to Forbes's infidelities.

She said, 'They're from Ross.'

'Ross Franklin? Cousin Ross?'

'Yes.'

'Why's he writing to you when you see him every other Sunday?'

'I don't know. He just is.'

'What does he have to say in these letters?' Forbes asked.

'Nothing of any consequence. Chit-chat, that's all.'

'About his painting?' Forbes paused. 'About Maeve?'

'Yes, that sort of thing.'

'You wanted me to think you had a lover, didn't you?'

'Well—you see, I don't.'

'Old cousin Ross isn't interested in you.'

'What makes you so sure?'

'He isn't interested in women.'

'Are you implying that he's not—not normal?'

'I don't know what Ross is, and I don't much care. If he wants to waste time writing letters to you then fine, let him get on with it, just don't try to exert pressure on me by pretending it's something it's not.' Forbes hoisted himself to his feet and patted his round belly. 'By the by, there's nothing unusual about a chap of my age wanting to be fit. I've the devil of a lot on my plate at the moment and a lot more to come, so if I feel the need to shed a few pounds and get back to my fighting weight that's really no concern of yours.'

He had turned her question aside with a plausible answer. He obviously didn't care whether she believed him or not; their marriage had reached a new low when one lie was used justify another.

'Now,' Forbes said, 'if you'll just hand me those chest expanders, dearest. I'll do a few more turns before bed. I'm not finished yet.'

'Oh yes you are, Forbes,' Lindsay said. 'As far as I'm concerned, you are,' then, kicking the springs across the carpet, hurried out of the room.

*   *   *

It had been a strenuous three-hour session on the dais, for Ross had found his fire again, and Maeve

225

was more stiff than tired. She fancied that walking home to Brunswick Crescent would ease the kinks in her neck and restore a bit of spring to her legs but she had gone no more than a few yards along Flowerhill Drive before she realised that she was being followed.

At first she thought that it might be Bobby but when she swung round there was only a mother pushing a perambulator and a very old man taking an afternoon constitutional to be seen.

She darted round the corner into Bowling Green Road.

And stopped.

He came hurrying round the corner after her, hands in the pockets of his long black raincoat, walking on the balls of his feet with quick, crabbing little steps. Relieved, Maeve planted her hands on her hips and confronted him.

'Ay-hay,' she said, 'now isn't this a coincidence. What are you doing in this neck o' the woods, Ewan Calder?'

'I'm just—just out for a Sunday stroll.'

'Was that you hiding in the hedge?'

'Not me,' he said, not meeting her eye.

'Must've been your double, then.'

'My doppelgänger,' Ewan said.

'I'm not going to ask what a doppelgänger is,' Maeve said, 'but I am going to ask why you're following me.'

The raincoat was made of light waterproof material and seemed quite out of keeping with a warm May day. It was unfashionably long and trailed well below his knees. Beneath it were grey flannels and blazer. He cringed for a moment, twisting into a strange hunched shape before he answered.

'Will you walk out with me?'

'*What?*'

'I'll buy you an ice-cream.'

'For God's sake, Ewan!'

'Bingham's isn't far away.'

'How long have you been lurking outside Mr Ross's house?'

'I wasn't lurking. I just happened to be in the vicinity at what one might call an opportune moment.'

'Sure now, don't be giving me more of your lies, Ewan Calder,' Maeve said. 'Who told you where I'd be today? Harry?'

'You pose for Mr Franklin every Sunday afternoon.' Ewan rearranged his posture, jerking upright by degrees. 'In effect, you told me yourself.'

'Did I?' Maeve said. 'Aye, well, maybe I did.'

'I'll walk with you, if that's all right.'

'And buy me ice-cream?' Maeve said.

'If that's your wish.'

She gave a little snort of amusement. 'Tell you what, I'll stand you an ice-cream if you promise not to go sneaking up on me ever again. You gave me a scare there, you know.'

'This is Glasgow, not Dublin,' Ewan said. 'I'm not going to stick a pistol in your ear.'

Ewan Calder was too well informed for his own good and had made an intelligent stab at the reason for her nervousness. He had been hanging about the house in Brunswick Crescent a lot lately, one of the gang yet not one of the gang. She suspected her grandfather's only son would never be one of the gang.

Ewan said, 'Was the boy with you today?'

'If you mean Bobby Shannon, he's hardly a boy.'

'Was he there?'

'Of course.'

'Is he good-looking?'

It wasn't the sort of question a schoolboy should be asking, Maeve thought; it was a schoolgirl's question, a giggly sort of question. It was beginning to dawn on her that Ewan Calder was courting her.

'Bobby is quite good-looking, I suppose,' she said.

'Is he better looking than Harry?'

'Harry? What's Harry got to do with it?'

'Don't you think Harry's good-looking?'

'I wish you'd stop asking me that,' Maeve told him. 'If you're going to walk out with me then you'd better change your tune.'

'My sisters think Harry's wonderful.'

'Aye, so it's sister talk, is it? Well, I'm older and wiser than your sisters,' Maeve said. 'I'm also your sister, in a manner of speaking, so don't think because I'm walking down the road with you that you can take liberties.'

'Would buying you an ice-cream be construed as a liberty?'

'In a dish?' Maeve said.

'If that's your pleasure.'

'With strawberry syrup?'

'Now that,' Ewan Calder said, 'would be a liberty,' and with a sudden burst of self-confidence reached out and took her hand.

CHAPTER TEN

Pigs and Whistles

Forbes had heard no more from Coffey about the death threat and reckoned he had been played for a fool. His mother had been invited to spend a few days with Donald and Lilias over Easter and, so far, had not returned to her tenement flat in Partick; a week, it seemed, had become a month, a month almost two. Forbes was relieved to have her out of his hair.

Twenty years ago the seasons had been marked by great gatherings when the sons and daughters, wives, husbands and grandchild of the Franklin family were expected to demonstrate unity and declare loyalty to the clan; no such jolly parties took place now, for Johnny was dead, Pansy and Mercy married, Donald retired, and Ross had bowed out of the business. There was no unity and precious little loyalty to call upon when it came to protecting what remained of Owen Franklin's legacy.

The weather was still warm but a fine rain had drifted over the river from the Govan shore early that afternoon, shrouding the shipyard in gloom.

Lights were on in the drawing-office and the drumming of carpenters' hammers from the decking of one of the cargo vessels had given Forbes the beginnings of a headache.

'Are you busy?'

'I'm always busy,' Forbes said, looking up from his desk.

Martin removed his bowler hat and, ominously, hung it on the hat-stand. He closed the door, extracted a handkerchief from his breast pocket and mopped rain freckles from his brow.

'What are you doing?'

'Costing,' Forbes said.

'Costing what?'

'Pitch pine and outfit. We're short on quota.'

'I see,' Martin said.

Forbes closed the catalogue he had brought up from the file room, planted his elbows on the desk and gave his cousin a hard stare. 'Look, if you're going to hand me a lecture, at least have the decency to sit down first.'

'Have you been negotiating contracts behind my back?'

'No.'

'For a tanker, perhaps, a bulk oil-tanker?'

'Oh that,' said Forbes.

'Don't tell me it slipped your mind.'

'We're nowhere near the contract stage, old chap.'

'Don't "old chap" me,' Martin said. 'I'm still chairman of the board of this partnership.'

'Of course you are.'

'In that case, would you be good enough to tell me why every shipwright and apprentice seems to know what's going on, and I don't?' Martin had been an eager fresh-faced young man when he'd first stepped into the boardroom twenty-one years ago but the years had taken their toll. 'The men seem to think that a large order is about to come our way, an order for a bulk tanker.'

'Rumour, wild rumour.'

'Is it?' Martin said. 'If it's no more than wild

rumour why does Tom Calder have a design team working up hull plans? Why have you booked the testing tank and why, pray tell me, has this "rumour" already been allocated a job number?'

'Tom has to keep his men employed somehow.'

'Forbes, for God's sake!'

'All right, all right,' Forbes said, grudgingly. 'Yes, there is a tanker and, yes, she has been given a job number: three-four-three, if you must know.'

'A job without a contract?'

'There is a contract, or will be very soon.'

'Who is the client?' said Martin. 'Will you at least tell me that?'

'Foreign-based company: Gideon Rowe and Spellman.'

'I've never heard of them.'

'I'm not surprised,' said Forbes. 'I suppose I do owe you an explanation, so unless you're rushing off . . .'

'I'm not.' Martin drew out a chair and plonked himself down on it. He hitched up his trousers, spread his knees, and leaned forward. 'I trust you're not going to palm me off with another pack of lies, Forbes.'

'I didn't lie to you, Martin. I just didn't want to raise false hopes.'

'Is this company, this Gibbon . . .'

'Gideon,' Forbes said.

'Yes, Gideon Rowe, is he sound?' Martin asked. 'I assume you have checked out his financial viability.'

'As soon as the designs are approved,' Forbes said, 'and we state a launch price, they'll slap down eight per cent.'

The scowl vanished. 'Eight per cent, you say?'

'Cash down,' Forbes said. 'Naturally they're cagey because we haven't built a tanker before, but their British representative was impressed by Tom's designs. Tank testing was the client's idea.'

'Are we hiring the tank to the ship-owner or are we covering costs?'

'We're covering,' Forbes said.

'How much?'

'I don't know. I haven't completed the calculations. The salient point is that Tom's come through with an advanced design and we have a testing tank lying empty. We're already one up on the competition.'

Reluctantly, Martin nodded.

Forbes went on, 'We'll proceed on receipt of eight per cent down, followed by a ten per cent guarantee and all the usual stage payments. In every respect it's a standard contract; every respect—save one.'

'I knew there'd be a catch,' said Martin.

'I can't tell you the client's name.'

'Gideon Rowe and Spellman, isn't that what you said?'

'The British representative must remain anonymous.'

'Oh, that's fishy, that's awfully fishy,' Martin said. 'Whose name will be on the contract? I mean, who will sign the guarantees?'

'A banker.' Forbes hesitated. 'A French banker.'

'Oh, God, not the French!' Martin said. 'You'll be telling me next it's some Jewish moneylender who wants to invest in shipping.'

Forbes bridled. 'And what's wrong with that?'

'Nothing in principle. I just don't quite trust them, that's all.'

232

'Jews?' said Forbes.

'Frenchmen,' said Martin. 'This tanker proposal is all very well on paper, Forbes, but I'm not convinced it's for us. Is Calder for it?'

'Absolutely.'

'And Arthur?'

'I haven't put it to Arthur yet.'

'What about Lindsay?' Martin said. 'We mustn't forget about Lindsay.'

'As if I ever could,' said Forbes.

* * *

He lay across her, naked. He placed his hands on her flanks and cautiously withdrew. She turned her head on the pillow and peeped at him through damp blonde hair. He eased his hand between her thighs and stroked her for a moment before he pushed away the sheet.

It was still, just, daylight, the window of the ground-floor bedroom sprinkled with raindrops. He moulded his body to hers, kissed her neck and felt her twist beneath him, her hip pressing into his belly. He pulled her round and straddled her, lifting himself up as if he were about to begin again.

'Don't be such an optimist, Forbes,' Stella said.

'I can't get enough of you,' he whispered.

'God knows you try hard enough.'

'Is that a complaint?'

'An observation.' She turned her head. 'What time is it?'

'I have no idea.'

'It must be after seven.'

'I imagine it must be.'

233

'I think'—she pulled him down and kissed him—
'it's time to be sensible and call a halt, don't you?'

'No,' Forbes said. 'I think it would be much more
sensible to stay put.'

'Come along, my lad, hop off.'

He pressed down with his hips and belly. 'See
what you're missing?'

'Now you're just showing off.'

'True,' Forbes said. 'Enough?'

'For today, yes thank you, sir.'

'And tomorrow?'

'Drew will be home tomorrow.'

'All day?'

'I'm afraid so.'

'Can't you get away?'

'I doubt it.'

'I have a place we could meet, in Glasgow.'

'No, Forbes, not when everything's going so
well.' She pushed with both hands. 'Come along,
time to make yourself scarce.'

'Hmm, I suppose you're right.'

He swung his leg over her and rolled to the side
of the bed. He felt soggy suddenly, almost light-
headed. She looped an arm about his waist and
leaned her cheek against his back. 'I don't want you
to go, my darling,' she said. 'I want you to stay here
with me forever,' then gave him a shove.

He staggered to his feet and for a moment felt as
if he might faint. Stella moved behind him,
stripping sheets. He straightened slowly, heart
thumping against his ribs.

'My God, Forbes!' he heard her say. 'It's almost
nine o'clock. You'd better scoot.'

'When's he due in?'

'His train arrives in Glasgow at eight forty-seven.'

'I had better scoot, hadn't I?'

Unlike the rest of the house, this room had a comfortable, cluttered feel to it; Stella's den, her retreat. Like Stella, it was all velvet and silk, all plump and soft and gaudy. He dressed quickly while Stella, a robe floating behind her, changed sheets and pillow-cases and then, going into the bathroom, switched on the electrical light and ran a bath.

'Has Ronnie gone to fetch him?' Forbes called out.

'Yes.'

In the flow of light from the bathroom he caught sight of himself in a half-moon-shaped mirror above the dressing-table and thought how spent he looked. He buttoned his collar and knotted his tie. He would concoct some plausible excuse to keep Lindsay from asking too many questions and head upstairs as soon as he reached home. He would probably have to contend with Arthur too, for Martin was bound to have spilled the beans about the tanker. He was in no fit state to parley with his father-in-law tonight.

'Are you ready, my darling? Do be quick.'

'That's not what you were saying four hours ago.'

She pitched herself against him and gave him a hard, swift kiss while simultaneously edging him to the door.

'I think I might be in love with you,' Forbes said.

'I think I'm falling for you too,' Stella said.

'I'm not sure you really mean it.'

'I do, I do. Oh, but I do.'

They crossed the angle of the living-room. Stella switched on the overhead lights and unlocked the front door, reached up, cupped his face between her hands and kissed him once more.

'I do,' she said again, and pushed him out into the rain.

*   *   *

Harry's features were shaped by strong shadows and in the lamplit room he looked every inch a man.

'Not disturbing you, am I?' Maeve asked.

The boys' room was large and not as untidy as she had expected it to be. Lead soldiers marched along the window ledge and a beautiful model yacht rested on top of a chest of drawers. Books, lots of books, were organised on shelves. Sucking the cap of a fountain pen, Harry was seated at one of two desks, schoolbooks open before him.

'Where's Philip?' he said.

'Playing dominoes with your grandfather.'

'And Mum?'

'Going over menus with Miss Runciman.'

She wondered why he needed to know where everyone was. Perhaps it reassured him to realise that the household was functioning normally while he was studying upstairs.

'Your father hasn't come home yet.'

'That doesn't surprise me,' Harry said.

'I gather there's been some trouble at the shipyard. I heard Mr Arthur talking to your mother about it. I wasn't eavesdropping,' Maeve added quickly. 'I couldn't help it.'

'There's a strike of engineers in the offing,' Harry said.

'And draughtsmen?'

'No, they're a pretty passive bunch on the whole,' Harry said. 'Besides, I don't think they have the funds to sustain a strike for very long. Draughtsmen? Why draughtsmen?'

'It just popped into my head—because of my grandfather.'

'Hmm.' Harry was more alert now. 'You didn't trudge upstairs just to discuss industrial relations, Maeve, did you?'

She approached the desk. 'Tell me a bit about Ewan Calder.'

'Ewan?' Harry said. 'Has he been bothering you?'

'I wouldn't say bothering me, no.'

'He's a twerp,' Harry stated.

'You say that about everyone.'

'Ewan really is a twerp. Has he tried to . . .' Harry got up from the desk and walked to the centre of the room. 'Has he molested you?'

'He held my hand.'

'When?'

'Sunday. He met me outside Mr Franklin's. We went to the café by the boating lake and had ice-cream.'

Harry slapped one fist into the other. 'What else happened?'

'Nothing. We just talked.'

'What about?'

'Mostly about the family.'

Harry seated himself on the end of the bed. 'It's not right.'

'Because he's my—whatever he is—relative?'

'Yes.'

'He's just being nice.'

'No, he's not,' Harry said. 'You don't know him

237

as well as I do. Ewan's a thoroughly nasty piece of work.'

'He wants to take me to the pictures.'

'Don't go.'

'I need a reason not to.'

'For one thing, my father won't let you,' Harry said.

'Because it's a picture house, because it's dark.'

'Because it's Ewan Calder. What was he doing at Ross's?'

'Waiting for me, I suppose.'

'Did he come up into the studio?'

'No.'

'He hopes to catch you without your clothes on.' Harry's cheeks were scarlet. 'He asked me if I—if I had.'

'So that's what you boys talk about, is it now?' Maeve said.

'I don't. I won't. Just once, when Ewan . . . Look, Maeve, perhaps you'd better discuss it with my mother. I'm not the proper person to give advice.'

'Don't you fancy seeing me in the altogether?' Maeve said, adding, 'Not that you're going to, by the way.'

He came to her and put his hands on her upper arms. For a moment she thought he might be going to kiss her. Kissing was the last thing on Harry's mind, though. 'I'll sort the wee beggar out,' he said. 'Ewan won't bother you again, you have my word on that.'

'What are you doing to do?'

A little growl in the back of his throat made him sound like his Uncle Ross. 'I'm going to have quiet word in his ear. Ewan may be a twerp but he's not an idiot. He knows he can't be your sweetheart or

238

your—your man.'

'Too true, he can't,' Maeve said. 'I already have a man.'

'The Irishman, Trotter? I thought you'd forgotten all about him.'

'Well, I haven't,' Maeve said, then ruefully, 'I think he's forgotten about me, though. I haven't heard a chirp out of him in months an' months.'

'Are you sending him money?'

'Not to Turk, to my mam.' She gave herself a shake, tossing her head. 'You're not much used to girls, are you, Harry? Any of you?'

'Ewan is. He has sisters.'

'In the bit of Dublin I come from, the boys know about girls and the girls know what boys want, so it's up to us where to draw the line.'

'The line?' said Harry.

'Half the girls my age are married,' Maeve said. 'It's the only way out, especially for Catholics. Must be terrible for Catholics, it being a mortal sin an' all.' She paused. 'Do you ever wonder what it'll be like?'

'Mortal sin—oh yes, I see what you mean,' Harry mumbled. 'Well, sometimes, I admit, sometimes I do wonder.'

'You'll have to wait another—what, seven or eight years to find out.'

'Nearer ten, probably,' Harry said. 'Different way of doing things. I'm expected to get an education, find a good post, accumulate money, offer the girl a home and prospects before I—you know.'

'Meantime, you have to toe the line and behave. Right?'

'Right,' Harry agreed.

'Ewan Calder doesn't behave.'

'But you do, Maeve, don't you?'

She hesitated, then said, 'No, I don't think I do, really.'

'Do you still want to go home?'

'To Dublin? Aye, of course.'

'Isn't it better here?'

'I don't belong here, Harry.'

'If you stay for a while you'll get used to it.'

'That's what I'm afraid of,' Maeve said.

She sensed his disappointment. Harry might be a sensible young man but in so many ways he was still a boy, hamstrung by expectations and demands. He hadn't learned how to separate what was asked of him from what he wanted for himself and, given the kind of chap he was, she doubted if he ever would.

She stepped close to the bed and patted Harry on the shoulder.

'Thanks for the chat, Harry.'

'Any time,' he said, sadly, and watched her leave.

*　　*　　*

Forbes limped down the driveway and stopped to light a cigarette. If he hadn't stopped when he did he would have walked right into the glare of the bull-frog headlights of Pickering's massive Humber tourer. He dived into the shelter of a laurel bush just as the motor-car entered the gate. Crouching among wet leaves, he thanked his stars that he had parked the Lanchester out of sight in an alley at the bottom of the hill.

The Humber circled the gravel in front of the house, and stopped.

Ronnie hopped out and opened the passenger door.

The welcome light was on over the door but Stella did not appear in the doorway. Two men climbed from the motor-car.

One was Drew Pickering but the other . . . it took Forbes a moment to recognise the man, to fish him from the closet of his memory. 'Paget,' he hissed. 'Bloody Geoffrey Paget,' and as soon as the men had gone indoors set off downhill at the double.

*   *   *

The nightdress wrapped itself around her hips and pinned her beneath the sheets. Forbes tipped the lampshade and light shone straight into her eyes. He pulled her up and jabbed his fingers into her spine. 'You lied to me, Lindsay. Those letters aren't from Ross. They're from Paget, aren't they?'

'Forbes, you're hurting me.'

He backed away and said, 'Get up.'

'Why?'

'Get up, Lindsay.'

It was only a little after ten. She had not been herself all evening and Eleanor had chased her off to bed early. Now she wanted to sleep, to escape the cramp that had nagged her since dinner time. She fluffed her hair with her hands and pressed her knees tightly together.

'I have absolutely no idea what you're talking about, Forbes.'

'Ballocks!' He spat the word out. 'You know perfectly well what I'm talking about: Paget, Geoffrey bloody Paget with bloody Drew Pickering,

241

both of them together, thick as thieves.'

'Where—at the club?'

'No, not at the club.' He rubbed a hand over his face. 'It's Paget who's been writing to you, isn't it?'

'Can't this wait until morning? I've a thumping headache.'

'I'll bet you don't have a thumping headache when Paget's sticking it up you,' Forbes said. 'How long has he been back—or has he never been away?'

'You can be awfully foul-mouthed at times, Forbes,' Lindsay said, 'and awfully stupid. Yes, Geoff's been writing to me for the past couple of months. Before that—well, I hadn't heard from him in years. I was just as surprised as you are to discover that he knew the Pickerings.'

'The party, you saw him at the party?'

'If you hadn't been so occupied snuggling up to that Hussey woman perhaps you would have seen him too.'

'Have you been meeting him on the sly?'

'We had lunch—once.'

'Where?'

'In a hotel, the Central Hotel,' Lindsay said.

At a less inconvenient time she might have told him the truth or, more wounding and damaging, have allowed him to believe his own accusations.

'Did you go upstairs with him?'

'No.'

'Didn't you want to?'

'That's another matter.'

'You knew he knew Pickering, didn't you?'

'Of course I did.'

'Why didn't you tell me?' Forbes said. 'Did Paget ask you not to?'

'Yes.'

'So a promise to this chap whom you haven't seen in twenty years . . .'

'Sixteen.'

'. . . sixteen years, means more than loyalty to me, does it?'

'Yes.'

'Dear God! You *want* to go to bed with him, don't you?'

'Not,' Lindsay said, 'particularly.'

'Is he still in the navy?'

Lindsay nodded.

'Then what's he doing sucking up to Pickering?' Forbes asked.

'He married Stella Pickering's sister.'

'You're joking!' Forbes plucked off his hat and threw it on the floor. She almost expected him to jump on it like a character in a comic cuts. 'Don't tell me he's *related* to Drew Pickering.'

'Used to be,' said Lindsay. 'He and the sister are divorced.'

'So he isn't married to her now?'

'No.'

'For God's sake, Linnet, why didn't you tell me before?'

'Before what, Forbes?'

'Before I . . . Oh, never mind.'

'But I do mind. I mind very much. You can't storm into my room, drag me out of bed and accuse me of being next best thing to a tart and expect me *not* to mind,' Lindsay said. 'Perhaps I should have told you, but I didn't. Geoff asked me not to, and I didn't. Simple as that. Before you start hurling insults think of all the things you've done over the years that you've kept from me.'

243

She opened a box on the bedside table, fished out a cigarette and lit it.

The stuffing had been knocked out of him. He sagged against the dressing-table, oblivious to the fact that his sleeve was trailing in spilled face powder or that he had knocked over two or three perfume bottles. He rubbed his face, his hair, and uttered a series of groans as if he were in pain. It wasn't guilt that tormented him, however, but anxiety.

He sucked in a deep breath. 'I wish you'd told me, Lindsay. I wish to God you'd told me sooner.'

'What difference would it have made?'

'A great deal.'

'To me, or to you?'

'To all of us,' Forbes said. 'Is he back with the Admiralty?'

'Yes, in Contracts and Commissions.'

'Christ!' Forbes shook his head. 'I should have known.'

'Known? Known what, Forbes?'

He came to the bed and for an instant she thought that he was going to kneel at her feet. Instead, he took the cigarette from her fingers, put it to his lips and inhaled smoke. He sat down on the bed and put an arm about her shoulder and handed back the cigarette in a curious gesture of rapport.

'Look,' he said, 'I'm sorry for what I just said—unforgivable, I know—but this is important, Linnet, crucially important. Paget, you have to keep in with Paget, find out all you can about the deal he's cooking up with Drew Pickering.'

'What makes you suppose Geoffrey's involved in any sort of deal?'

'Trust me, trust me, just trust me,' he said. 'This isn't about you and Paget, or me and—and anyone else. There's something big in the wind and I've the queerest feeling that Franklin's might be the target. I need information, as much information as you can get from him. If he wants to see you again, wants to take you to lunch, go.'

'And you, what about you?'

'What about me?'

'What will you be doing while I'm pumping Geoffrey for information?'

'I think I might take a holiday,' Forbes said. 'Might make a little trip.'

'A little trip to where?'

'Morocco,' he said.

And Lindsay, to her credit, didn't laugh.

*   *   *

Tom Calder said, 'It's the best idea you've had in a long time. Do you want me to come with you?'

'Not much point,' Forbes said. 'It's not as if we're trying to sell ourselves to Gideon Rowe and Spellman. I just want to make sure they really do have an office in Rabat and are sufficiently solvent to meet our terms.'

'Might it not be simpler,' Tom said, 'to make a few telephone calls to folk in the Shipowners' Association?'

'I'd rather not let anyone know where I'm going, or why.'

'That won't be easy,' Tom said. 'Especially when everything's going to pig and whistles. The engineering union is girding its loins for strike action and, of course, the arms limitation talks in

Washington will take place soon. I expect our government will back President Harding's call to drastically reduce the number of capital ships we can build.'

'It won't come to that,' Forbes said. 'After a great deal of yaw-yaw they'll reach a compromise. However, if an arms limitation treaty is in the pipeline that's all the more reason not to put our eggs in the navy basket.'

'What will you tell Martin?'

'The truth—that I'm off to North Africa to secure a contract.'

'He'll fight you, you know.'

'If Martin thinks that buttering up the workforce and harbouring resources will see us through a global slump he's got another think coming,' Forbes said. 'In fact, I'm looking forward to seeing how our gallant socialists cope with this dilemma. They're already yelling that there must not be another war, war must be stopped and swords turned into ploughshares. Stirring stuff, indeed. When it dawns on them that they're the very ones who make the swords, they'll change their tune quickly enough.'

'No,' Tom said, with a sigh. 'They'll blame us, the employers. They'll expect us to find a cure for all their woes.'

Forbes nodded. 'Right now I'll settle for securing a single big order. With that in the bag we can face up to arms limitation treaties and howling mobs of Red revolutionaries with a degree of equanimity.'

'When will you leave for North Africa?'

'As soon as I can arrange passage.'

'How long will you be gone?'

'Couple of weeks, I think.'

246

'What if you discover that Gideon Rowe and Spellman is just a back-street firm with only a couple of old rust-buckets to its name?'

'In that case,' Forbes said, 'I may not come home at all.'

*   *   *

Stella was on the point of leaving to join her husband for lunch when a taxi-cab appeared in the driveway of Merriam House and, a moment later, Forbes McCulloch's wife rang the doorbell.

Ronnie had gone around to the garage at the rear of the house to warm up the Humber. Hat in hand and overcoat thrown over her arm, Stella answered the door herself. She knew it couldn't be Forbes. He had called from his office that morning just to tell her how much he loved her, a gesture she found rather touching. Forbes wasn't the conceited fool that Drew and Geoff supposed him to be. He was quite dashing, really, a demanding lover and a romantic at heart.

She was thinking of Forbes when she pulled open the door and found herself face to face with Lindsay McCulloch.

'Oh!' the woman said. 'You're just going out. I won't keep you.'

'No, no, do come in,' Stella said. 'I'm only lunching with my husband and he'll forgive me if I'm late.'

'I should have telephoned first.'

Why didn't you? Stella thought. Did you think you'd find Forbes here? Did you hope to catch us *in flagrante*? She said, 'Would you care for a drink? I'd offer you lunch, but . . .'

247

'Nothing to drink, thank you,' Lindsay said.

Stella hadn't appreciated how delicate Forbes's wife was. She looked as if a puff of wind would blow her away. She was dressed in a coral silk afternoon dress and a straw panama and Stella felt quite lumpy in comparison.

'I'm looking for Geoffrey Paget.'

'Ah!' Stella exclaimed, relieved. 'Geoff? He isn't here, I'm afraid.'

'Do you happen to know when he'll be back in Glasgow again?'

'Soon, I imagine.'

'He's been writing to me, you know.'

'Has he really?' Stella said. 'Can't say I'm surprised.'

'Letters from all over England.'

'He does travel to the most outlandish places, doesn't he?'

'Are you in touch with him?' Lindsay asked.

'Now and then.'

'If you happen to bump into him,' Lindsay said, 'please ask him to telephone me.'

Stella laughed. She had the upper hand again; Lindsay McCulloch had obviously been taken in by Geoff's declarations of devotion, which would make it a great deal easier for all concerned.

'He's very taken with you, you know,' she said.

'Really?'

'Really and truly,' said Stella, smiling. 'I'm sorry he isn't here right now.'

'He does put up with you, though, doesn't he?'

'Put up?'

'Stay with you when he's in Glasgow?' Lindsay said.

'Yes, we have billeted him for a night or two.'

248

'Doesn't your sister object?'

'Jo? Why would Jo object? She still has a soft spot for Geoffrey. It was a perfectly amicable parting on both sides.'

'How nice,' said Lindsay. 'Didn't your sister remarry?'

'She did,' said Stella. 'To a French chap. Very wealthy.'

'How nice,' said Lindsay again. 'Does she live in France?'

'In Paris.' Mrs Forbes McCulloch was becoming just a shade too inquisitive, Stella thought. 'If I do bump into Geoffrey I'll make absolutely sure he gets in touch with you. Are you ever up in London?'

'Rarely,' Lindsay said. 'Is that where Geoffrey lives, in London?'

'Did he not tell you?'

'No.'

'He has a little flat off Marylebone High Street.'

'It might be possible . . .' Lindsay said. 'I mean, perhaps I should go up to London more often. When Forbes—when my husband is away.'

'You could take the boys,' said Stella.

'The boys?'

'Your children.'

'Oh no,' said Lindsay. 'I don't think I'd want to take the boys.'

'Forbes—your husband isn't away at the moment, is he?' Stella asked, though she knew the answer to that question perfectly well.

'He's planning a trip quite soon.'

'Is he?' said Stella. 'To far-flung places?'

'I believe so,' Lindsay said. 'Africa, I think. North Africa.'

'How interesting!'

'Have you ever been to North Africa, Stella?'

Stella nodded and, at almost the same moment, shook her head.

She said, 'When will he be leaving for—for Africa?'

'Soon,' Lindsay said. 'Quite soon.'

'Aren't you tempted to go with him?'

'I think,' Lindsay said, 'that I might find a little jaunt to London more rewarding, don't you?'

'I do, indeed,' said Stella and after exchanging a few more pleasantries, escorted Mrs McCulloch out to the waiting taxi-cab and, five minutes later, was driven off in the Humber to break the good news to Drew.

CHAPTER ELEVEN

A World of a Difference

Wreathed in fairy lights, the organ popped up from the orchestra pit with a deafening fanfare that made Maeve clap her hands to her ears. Slouched in a plush seat beside her, Ewan smirked and patted her knee.

The thousand-seat La Scala cinema was filled for the matinée performance of *The Four Horsemen of the Apocalypse*. The allure of the latest screen sensation, Rudolph Valentino, who did funny things with his eyes and even funnier things with a whip, had brought the crowds out even on a beautiful summer afternoon.

'You didn't tell anyone that you were stepping

250

out with a young man, did you?' Ewan asked.

'I'm not stepping out with a young man. I'm stepping out with you.'

'We are stepping out, though, aren't we?'

'Sure an' I suppose we are,' Maeve admitted.

'Has Harry never asked you out?'

'He doesn't have to,' Maeve said. 'I see Harry every day.'

'He doesn't have the nerve. You're too much for him.'

'Is that supposed to mean I'm not too much for you?' She looked down at him. 'At least you've stopped squirming. I can't stand it when you squirm.'

'I do not squirm.'

'You do, you know; squirm like a blessed worm.'

He sulked for a moment and, not surprisingly, squirmed.

'See,' Maeve said. 'You're doing it now.'

'I am not.'

'Are, too.'

Ewan slid down in the seat, muttering, but when the lights dimmed he placed his hand on her knee again and, reaching up, rubbed something against her lips.

Maeve flinched and jerked her head away.

'Behave yourself,' she said. 'What, what is it?'

'Chocolate,' he said, and dropped a square of Five Boys neatly on to her tongue.

*   *   *

It was too nice a day, Lindsay decided, to mope indoors and soon after lunch she went out for a walk.

The drone of heavy industry had been replaced by music. Bands were out in force. Flutes, bagpipes, bugles and drums punctuated the air with march tunes. On Great Western Road Lindsay was passed by an omnibus crammed with Socialist Workers on their way to an unemployment rally in George Square, all bawling out choruses from *The Merry Widow*. It wouldn't have surprised her to find cousin Ross serenading the neighbours from the studio window, but the leafy street off Cleveden Road was quiet.

She climbed the steps and knocked on the door.

As a concession to summer Ross had replaced his heavy tweed suit with flannels and a linen jacket.

'It's such a lovely day I thought I might take Maeve for ice-cream in the café by the boating lake,' Lindsay said.

'Maeve isn't here.'

'Oh! Where is she?'

'Afternoon off.'

'She said nothing to me about an afternoon off.'

'Not her idea,' said Ross. 'Bobby, the young man, he's off to rail against the government at this rally in the Square.'

'I didn't realise he was a communist.'

'They're all communists at his age,' Ross said. 'They learn sense later.'

'Has Maeve gone with him?'

'Not sure,' Ross said. 'If they are stepping out together they'd hardly confide in an old fogey like me.'

'Stepping out?' said Lindsay. 'Are they stepping out?'

'I doubt it,' Ross said. 'Would you mind if

252

they were?'

'I might,' Lindsay said.

'Surely you can't object to Maeve being wooed by a draughtsman. God knows, there are plenty of them in our family.'

Lindsay decided to change the subject. She walked to the easel and studied the painting. 'It's finished, Ross, at last?'

'Almost.' Ross stood by her. 'Little touch around the outline of the figures and, yes, it's done.'

'Are you pleased with it?'

'Pleased to be rid of it, certainly.'

'When will you deliver?'

'It takes about a month to dry properly, after which I'll invite Lady Mary up to give it her approval and, hopefully, sign a fat cheque.'

'Where will it hang?' Lindsay asked.

'In her Edinburgh house, I imagine.'

'Won't it go on public exhibition?'

'I sincerely hope not.'

'Don't you care what happens to it, Ross?'

He shrugged. 'My paintings are popular with folk who know little or nothing about art and despised by folk who think they know everything. Truly, Lin, it makes no difference to me.'

'Lin?' she said. 'You haven't called me Lin in years.'

'Slip of the tongue. Sorry.' Ross rested his shoulders against the window. His beard looked golden in the afternoon sunshine, like that of a Viking warrior, except that he was too gentle to be a warrior of any sort. 'Those were fine times, those holidays we spent in Strathmore with Grandfather Owen when we were all together, all young.'

'The best of times—if only we'd realised it.'

'I did,' Ross said. 'At least I like to think I did.'

'Is that when you decided to become a painter?'

'I rather think it was,' he said. 'Lindsay, are you happy?'

'I'm not unhappy,' she answered. 'Are you— happy, I mean?'

'I'm better off than most,' Ross said.

'That wasn't what I meant.'

'I know.' He placed a hand flat against the pane, fingers spread. 'I trust,' he said, 'that you haven't forgotten your promise to sit for me.'

'I haven't forgotten,' Lindsay said.

'I'd like to make a start fairly soon.'

'Forbes is going to North Africa on business,' Lindsay said. 'I think I may take a little trip to London while he's gone.'

Ross looked round. 'Any special reason?'

'No,' Lindsay said. 'I haven't been up to town for ages.'

'You'll take Maeve, of course.'

'I doubt it.'

Ross pushed himself away from the window and picked a soft sable brush from the trolley. He stroked the tip with his thumb, thoughtfully.

'Are you meeting a man in London?'

'Yes.'

'I assume Forbes knows nothing of this.'

'On the contrary,' Lindsay said, 'Forbes knows all about it.'

'This man . . .'

'He's a sailor,' Lindsay said. 'He works at the Admiralty.'

'Ah, so it's business, is it?'

'It might be,' Lindsay said, 'then again, it might not.'

'Why are you teasing me?'

'I'm not teasing you,' Lindsay said. 'I'll only be gone three or four days and as soon as I'm back, we'll make a start on the portrait, if you like.'

Ross studied the sleepy reaches of Flowerhill Drive.

'It really is a beautiful day,' he said. 'I think I might go out for a bit of a breather. This place by the boating lake . . .'

'Sells tea as well as ice-cream,' Lindsay said.

'Shall we step out then, Lin,' he said, 'if you've nothing better to do?'

'Nothing that can't wait,' she said.

*   *   *

Horsemen, yachtsmen, soldiers, a slender little aviator had all given her pleasure but she had kept her lovers as one keeps pets and treated them with even less consideration than she treated her children. So, Stella thought, what am I doing in a seedy apartment on a fine summer afternoon, with my dress up and my knickers around my ankles, pandering to an Irish nobody?

He brought her a glass of water from the kitchen and sank down beside her on the bed. She drank. He took the glass from her and drank too. Hairy limbs, a pot belly, the creepy little moustache of which he was so proud; Forbes McCulloch was a weasel compared to her broad-shouldered, flat-bellied husband, yet Forbes had taken her out of herself as no other man had ever done.

'I take it she enquired about Paget?' Forbes said.

'First thing.'

'What did you tell her?'

255

'I suggested she meet him in London.'

'Good,' Forbes said. 'She told you about my trip to Rabat, too?'

'Of course.'

Forbes sighed. 'Bitch!'

'I thought that's what you wanted her to do.'

'What? Betray me?'

'That's harsh, old chum,' Stella said. 'Tell me, what do you hope to find on the Barbary coast, a pot of gold?'

'I might,' Forbes said. 'Do you know where it's buried?'

Stella laughed. 'I could answer that, but I won't.'

'I've booked passage on the *Tara* with the British India Line. It leaves from the Royal Albert Docks on the 17th. Five days direct to Tangier.'

'We could have gone by rail to Marseilles, you know, and saved a day.'

'I'm not in that much of a rush,' Forbes said. 'Are you?'

'No, darling,' she said. 'The longer the better, in fact.'

'I take it your typhoid certificate is up to date?'

'That's not a very romantic thing to say, post *l'amour.*'

'Is it?'

'Yes, and my smallpox certificate too.'

'When were you there last?'

She lifted herself from the damp sheet and kissed him. 'You ask far too many questions, Forbes. In due course all will be revealed. It isn't what you think it is. It's all more or less above board.'

'Except that your husband knows nothing about it.'

256

'Which makes it all the more delicious, don't you think?'

Forbes put the empty water glass on the cabinet and bridged her stomach with his arm. 'I know you think I'm crazy,' he said, 'but I want you where I can keep an eye on you. What excuse have you offered?'

'I've told Drew I'll be visiting with Jo in Paris.'

'Does he believe you?'

'He always believes me.'

'What if he telephones Paris?' Forbes said.

'He won't,' Stella said. 'He won't telephone Paris—just in case.'

'In case what?' said Forbes.

'I'm not there,' said Stella.

*   *   *

It felt odd to be eating dinner in a room filled with sunlight. She had not told them that she had spent the afternoon at the pictures with Ewan Calder. 'In town, window shopping,' she'd said—and they'd believed her.

Ewan had put an arm about her, a hand beneath her breast, his palm warm against her ribs. He had reached over and kissed her and might have gone on kissing her if a woman in the seat behind them hadn't tapped his shoulder and told him to stop his nonsense. Later, he had slipped a hand between her legs; an inch further and she would have slapped him but Ewan Calder knew just where to draw the line. She had felt safe with Turk because she was too young for him. She wasn't too young for Ewan Calder, though, and what they were doing seemed so much like an interesting

257

experiment that she had been sorry when the picture had ended.

They had walked up Sauchiehall Street, blinded by brilliant sunshine. She'd had enough of the devil in her to take big strides, to forge on as if she were mad at him. Finally he had asked her to slow down and, red-faced and gasping, had pressed a hand to his chest.

'I—I—thought you—liked it?'

'Well, I didn't.'

'You—you should—have stopped me.'

'What? An' made a scene?'

'Won't—won't you go—go out with me again?'

'I don't know. I'll have to think about it. Are you all right?'

'Yes, it's the pollen, just—the pollen.'

She had taken his arm and walked him as far as Charing Cross where they had boarded a tram for the remainder of the journey home.

Now she sat, innocent as milk, eating dinner as if nothing of any consequence had happened that afternoon.

'Africa?' she heard Philip say. 'Lions and elephants, Dad?'

'North Africa,' Forbes said. 'Camels, I think.'

'The Sahara?' said Philip. 'Gosh!'

'French or Spanish?' Harry asked.

'French,' Forbes said. 'We land at Tangier.'

'"We"?' said Harry. 'Is Mum going too?'

'We,' said Uncle Forbes, 'as in passengers. Then it's train to Rabat.'

'What's in Rabat?' said Harry.

'The head office of a firm of ship-owners who are interested in commissioning Franklin's to build them an oil-tanker.'

'How much will she cost?' said Phil.

Forbes waved a hand. 'Upwards of three hundred thousand pounds.'

Maeve swallowed a tender piece of meat and tried to concentrate.

Mr Arthur was saying, 'Bellasco's used to run tramp steamers up and down that coast. Offices in Liverpool, branch office in Marseilles. Back in the late nineties we tendered for replacements but the business went to Thorneycroft's. Changed days now, I suppose.'

'What do you mean by "changed days", Grandee?' Phil asked.

'There were still sailing ships in service thirty-five years ago. Some ship-owners weren't convinced that coal was the coming thing.'

'In 1890?' Harry said. 'Surely not?'

Arthur nodded. 'Now it's oil.'

'What's inside your tanker, Dad?' Philip asked.

'Oil-fired engines; three thousand horsepower.'

'Good God!' said Arthur.

'Your grandfather designed them, Maeve,' Forbes said.

'He's a clever old stick, your grandfather,' said Arthur.

'Sure an' I've heard that from a lot of people,' Maeve said, politely.

'Who, for instance?' said Harry. 'From Ewan?'

She darted a glance at her cousin who leaned over his plate and put food into his mouth. Soon his examinations would begin and soon after that he would sit for entry into the Faculty of Law in Glasgow University; a world of a difference from her school chums who thought themselves lucky to find jobs in Guinness's brewery or Jacobs' biscuit

259

factory, for becoming a golden boy in Dublin meant only one thing—taking up the gun.

'From Bobby Shannon, actually,' Maeve said.

'The model chap,' said Philip. 'He's one of our draughtsman, isn't he?'

'He thinks a lot of my grandfather, though he's too stubborn to say it.' Maeve squared her knife and fork. She hoped that pudding would be something cold and sweet. 'Is Bobby Shannon a good draughtsman, Uncle Forbes?'

'No complaints as far as I know,' her uncle answered.

'Why aren't draughtsmen paid more?'

Arthur chuckled. 'I'll leave you to answer that one, Forbes.'

'Uh-oh,' said Philip. 'I think I smell politics coming up.'

'No, you don't,' said Lindsay. 'What you smell is vanilla soufflé.'

'Oh good!' said the brothers, in unison.

*　　　*　　　*

Ross spent the best part of Sunday morning prowling about the studio glowering at the unfinished areas that linked the figures to the landscape. He was reasonably satisfied with his efforts. Maeve's dark good looks chimed well with Bobby Shannon's startled innocence and the composition reflected the romantic theme of the novel, if not its sugary overtones. There was, Ross thought, a wee bit too much sex and not quite enough sentimentality in the painting to satisfy devotees of the late Fiona McWhirter's contribution to popular literature, but the sheep probably made up for it.

Soon he would be free to move on to better things. Better things being a portrait of his cousin Lindsay and Maeve McCulloch posing in summer hats and flowery dresses. He had studied Lindsay carefully while they'd sipped tea at the café table by the boating lake and had known again the peculiar pang of longing he had experienced during his year in Paris and the lonely years of the war. Rowing boats and parasols, a few swans, the green café tables, boys and girls playing by the water's edge; it was hardly the *Regatta at Argenteuil*, hardly Renoir or Berthe Morisot, but just being out and about with his cousin on a lovely summer's afternoon had stirred his creative juices nonetheless.

Maeve arrived promptly at two o'clock, Bobby a few minutes later.

Ross shooed them into their costumes and began painting almost at once.

He was too professional to be slipshod; the habit of uncertainty kept him hard at it. Was the painting really finished? Should he let it go? A highlight misplaced there, a shadow too sombre there, the angle of an arm distorted, the perspective all cock-eyed? He chewed his pipe stem furiously and craned so close to the canvas that, for once, he got paint on his beard.

In due course the linking areas were filled and the brush hung over the canvas with nowhere else to go. Ross peeped around the edge of the easel for one last look at his fictional lovers then, with a sigh, said, 'That's it,' stuck his brush in a jar, wiped his hands on a rag and went into the kitchen.

Bobby sank down on his knees and arched his back.

261

'Does he mean it?' Maeve asked. 'Is he actually finished?'

'Aye, I think he is. Finished with me at any rate,' Bobby said. 'I reckon he'll find more work for you, though.'

Bobby's cheeks were lightly tanned and in the V of the old-fashioned shirt his chest was mottled pink.

'Won't you sit for him again?' Maeve asked.

'If he needs another Highlander or a soldier o' the line, maybe I will. He paints to order and has a lot o' commissions.'

'But the chances are I won't see you again,' said Maeve.

Sunlight blurred Bobby's profile and he looked almost as young as Ewan Calder. She had lain with him in chaste intimacy for weeks and knew little or nothing about him. She wondered what sort of life he returned to when he hurried away from the studio, which of the thousands of tenements that flanked the river he called home. She wondered about the ailing sister and whether he had brothers, a mother alive, a father in work; wondered what he thought about when he sat at his drawing board, if his mind was entirely fixed on machinery, or if he thought of her now and then.

'You might,' Bobby Shannon said, 'if you haven't gone home.'

'Home?' Maeve said. 'Oh, you mean to Dublin.'

'Aye.'

'Well, I will when I'm old enough.'

'Old enough for what?'

'To get married and settle down.'

'What'll old Tom have to say about that?'

'It's not up to "old Tom",' Maeve said.

'I heard you'd been packed off in disgrace.'

'Did you now?' Maeve sat up. 'Who told you that?'

Bobby shrugged. 'Can't remember.'

'It wasn't my grandfather, was it?'

'Heck no,' Bobby said.

'I wasn't packed off in disgrace. I was invited here by my auntie.'

'Aye well, however it came about, you've landed on your feet.' He stood up and stepped from the dais. 'By gum, I tell you if the Franklins ever took me in, they'd never get rid of me. But then'—he shook his head—'you're their kind an' I'm definitely not.'

At that moment Ross returned from the kitchen. He had washed the paint from his beard and the tip of his nose and carried a bottle of champagne in one hand and three fluted glasses in the other. He put the glasses on the dais, popped the champagne cork and poured out the foamy stuff.

'So it is finished, Mr Ross?' Bobby said.

'Indeed it is. Do you want to see what I've made of you?'

'I'm not that curious,' Bobby said.

'Don't you like looking at yourself?' Maeve asked.

'Not if I can avoid it,' Bobby answered.

Ross raised his glass and held it out towards the easel. 'Here's to *The Captive Heart*. Thank you both for all your hard work,' he said, and presented them each with a five pound note.

Soon after, Bobby Shannon took his leave.

'Decent young chap, don't you think?' Ross said.

'I suppose he is,' Maeve said, wistfully, and to disguise her confusion, dipped her nose in the

263

bubbles and pretended to enjoy the champagne.

* * *

Forbes had hoped that he might get away without having to answer any awkward questions from his father-in-law but, late at night, after the house was locked up, Arthur, wrapped in a worn dressing-gown, knocked on his bedroom door and, without waiting to be invited, entered.

'What?' Forbes said.

'A word,' said Arthur.

'I'm just going to bed.'

'No, you're not. You're still dressed.'

'All right,' Forbes said. 'You'd best come in. Brandy?'

'No, no thanks. I'll come straight to the point, if I may.'

'Do, please.'

'I've been active in the shipbuilding business for fifty years and I've never seen anything like the palaver that's going on over this tanker of yours.'

'Palaver?' Forbes said. 'I'm pursuing a contract, that's all.'

'I don't like the way you're going about it.'

'I know you don't,' Forbes said. 'Martin doesn't like what I'm doing either, but he's got enough sense to see that it's necessary.'

'Why is there no record of Gideon Rowe? Why no listed fleet? Why no loading berths, or home offices?'

'That's what I'm going to Rabat to find out.'

'The *Mimosa*,' Arthur said, 'went down with all hands.'

'So did a lot of other ships.'

'Gideon Rowe and Spellman weren't the owners.'

'I know that, too,' said Forbes. 'I've checked *Lloyd's Register*.'

'The Fergusson Line—'

'Sold the *Mimosa* on, yes.'

'I think Gideon Rowe and Spellman are a shell.'

'I'm sure they are,' said Forbes. 'If they are, then somebody with a great deal of money is behind them. If that's the case, slapping down three hundred thousand pounds for an oil-tanker isn't going to bother them one bit.'

'I think Andrew Pickering's behind it.'

'I do, too,' Forbes said.

'In spite of all his honours and positions,' Arthur said, 'I've never quite trusted that fellow.'

'In that,' said Forbes, 'you are not alone.'

'I hear he's made an offer for Bradford Steel.'

'I wouldn't be surprised,' Forbes said. 'Given what we're paying for steel these days owning a steel mill is like owning a gold mine.'

'What does a ship-owner want with a steel mill?'

Forbes said, 'Pickering is a prime example of the new face of capitalism. Nothing's too big for Pickering, nothing's too small. In fifty or sixty years' time, Papa, after we're dead and gone, the world will belong to men like Andrew Pickering.'

'That,' Arthur said, 'is a chilling prospect.'

'Not if Franklin's is part of it.'

Arthur's eyebrows shot up. 'Is that what you're after, Forbes, to become another Andrew Pickering?'

'Not me,' Forbes said. 'My sole concern is to secure new business for Franklin's. If I have to negotiate with Pickering to do it, then I will.'

'So you're going to be a hero and save Franklin's,

265

are you?'

'I am, that I am,' said Forbes. 'By hook or by crook.'

'In that case,' Arthur Franklin said, 'I can only wish you luck.'

'And give me backing if I need it?'

'Financial backing?'

'No,' Forbes said. 'I was thinking more of moral support.'

And Arthur, with a grim little smile said, 'Huh!'

*　　　*　　　*

Night trains were exciting, none more so than the sleeping car express from Glasgow to London. His luggage had gone on ahead. He was burdened by nothing heavier than an overnight bag. Tomorrow afternoon he would be steaming down the Thames on board the *Tara* heading for North Africa and adventures unknown. Tonight's adventures would be less novel but no less thrilling and he found himself waiting in the narrow compartment with all the breathless expectancy of a bridegroom awaiting his bride.

The days were long since gone when Lindsay had brought the boys to see him off, to wave their little hands and weep. There had been too many departures in the intervening years for his wife and sons to be concerned about his safety, and whether he was setting out for Sa˄Σo Paulo, San Francisco or a day in South Shields, he was sent on his way with no more than a peck on the cheek from Lindsay and a hurried 'Goodbye' from the boys.

He could not be sure that Drew Pickering would be quite so casual, however, and hid in the single berth while the locomotive hissed and vibrated and cheerful 'adieus' crept in from the platform.

At length—whistles, shaking, a lurch forward, the grind of iron wheels gathering momentum. It took an effort of will on Forbes's part not to fling open the door and peer out into the corridor. He stood, swaying, one hand on the edge of the wash basin, his twin in the oval mirror beside him, hand out and trousers unbuttoned, while the train limped through outlying signals and then, like a creature unleashed, gathered speed.

Knuckles on the door, gentle, imperious, eager too.

'Yes?' Forbes said. 'Who is it?'

'The lady with the gin,' she whispered.

He opened the door, caught her by the arm and pulled her inside.

Stella dropped the bottle on to the bunk and closed the door with her shoulder. She lifted her skirt and let him unbutton her knickers. He kneeled before her, hugging her thighs. Braced against the swaying of the train, he kissed her, kissed her belly, then rose up into her.

Holding her upright, he swung against the window.

The blind shot up, fluttering like a caged bird.

Forbes saw himself reflected against the darkness outside, house lights rushing through him without shape or singularity.

'Oh, God!' Stella hissed. 'Do me, do me, darling, please.'

He took her first as the train shrieked through Motherwell and again before they crossed the border. And again and again in the days that followed, while the *Tara* steamed south to Tangier.

CHAPTER TWELVE

Helm Orders

If Maeve was disappointed at not being invited to accompany Lindsay to London, she hid it well. In fact, she seemed pleased to be left at home to 'look after' Mr Arthur and the boys.

Arthur, on the other hand, was concerned that the mysterious letters and the trip south were connected, and that the connection might well be a man. 'If there's something you want to tell me, Lindsay,' he said, 'I'm always ready and willing to lend an ear.'

'I think it's better if you don't ask.'

'Lord above, Lindsay!' Arthur said. 'His majesty's halfway to North Africa and you're rushing off to London, and you expect me to ignore—'

'I'm calling on Geoffrey Paget.'

'Ah!'

'I knew you'd be angry.'

'I'm not angry. I thought the Paget thing was over years ago. Has he turned up again?'

'Yes,' said Lindsay, 'he has turned up again,' and went on to explain how the lieutenant-commander had entered her life once more.

'Are you still attracted to him?' Arthur asked. 'I mean, you're not hopping off to London to do anything rash?'

'Dear God, Papa, what do you take me for?'

'Many a girl would be flattered to be pursued by a handsome naval officer, even if he is a shade past his prime. Is he a shade past his prime?'

'Geoffrey's no more past his prime than I am,' Lindsay said. 'I still find him attractive, I admit, but I'm not in love with him.'

'What about the letters, all those letters?'

'Forbes think the letters are a blind.'

'Forbes? So you've told Forbes about Paget?'

'Of course,' Lindsay said. 'Forbes is still at the helm.'

'This is all too much for an old chap. Perhaps it's time I retired.'

'You! What would you do all day?'

'Play tennis, go bowling, walk on the silver strand. Might even move down the coast. A nice little house with a sea view would suit Eleanor and me.'

'Eleanor? You'd take Eleanor with you?'

'If she's willing to go.'

'What about me, what about us?' said Lindsay.

'You'll have to manage without me sooner or later,' Arthur said.

'Oh, Papa, don't talk that way. You're not sick, are you?'

'Heavens, no!' Arthur said. 'I just don't have the stomach for another fight. I've had my fill of slumps and strikes. The glory days are over, Lindsay, my glory days at any rate. I'll see to it that you have the house and I'll sell some of my shares to give me a nest egg.'

'According to the articles, partners have first option to purchase, remember.'

'I'm well aware of that.' He smiled and patted her knee. 'Never fear, I'll still be here on Friday when you get back from London. Where are you staying, by the way?'

'The Billington,' said Lindsay.

The Billington Hotel was situated between Baker Street and Gloucester Place. It was clean, modern and rather austere, and catered mainly for ladies of a certain age. It also had the advantage of being close to Marylebone High Street.

Lindsay unpacked, bathed, changed her frock, put on make-up and took tea in the less than enchanting lounge on the ground floor. Then she went out in search of Geoffrey Paget and a solution to the mystery of what she was doing here at all. She had informed Geoffrey only that she would be in the capital before the end of May. As a serving officer at the beck and call of Sea Lords and secretaries, he might not be in the country, let alone London, and she hoped that her trip wouldn't turn out to be a wild-goose chase. On the other hand, she rather enjoyed playing Geoffrey at his own game by turning up out of the blue.

Coventry Place was just this side of respectable. The door to Geoffrey's flat was tucked between a greengrocer's and a fishmonger's. Small mullioned windows peered down on a public house that was already open for business. Lindsay inhaled the aroma of fish and vegetables, beer, horse manure and petrol fumes and wondered why on earth Geoffrey had settled here in this part of London and not closer to Mayfair or Park Lane. She loitered at the corner, looking up.

The roof of Geoffrey's building was a steep, narrow slope of black tiles topped by far too many chimneys and ornamented not with figureheads or cannon but by a row of dusty pigeons. The windows were curtained with net, the rooms filled with shadow. Naturally, there was no sign of Geoffrey.

Suddenly she felt homesick, dreadfully, appallingly homesick. No one here had ever heard of Franklin's. No one here cared tuppence about Clydeside shipbuilders. She knew no one in London, no one except Geoffrey and, though he might think of himself as her lover, he wasn't even her friend. She turned on her heel and set off up the High Street, but just as she stepped from the pavement a hand closed on her shoulder.

'My God, Lindsay!' Geoffrey said. 'You're here, you came.'

She felt sick with embarrassment, and relief.

She leaned against him when he kissed her and then, without resistance, let him lead her up to his flat.

*   *   *

'Sure and you really are a persistent wee devil, aren't you?' Maeve said. 'Your dad would skin you alive if he knew what was going on.'

'Nothing's going on, more's the pity.'

'For God's sake, Ewan, I'm your half-sister. There's a name for that sort of thing. It's a terrible crime, a hanging offence.'

'You are not my half-sister,' Ewan said. 'Your mother is my half-sister.'

'Aye, well,' said Maeve, 'that makes it even worse.'

'We,' said Ewan, 'are just kissing kin.'

'You don't half come out with the fancy phrases,' Maeve said. 'Try adding this one to your vocabulary—bugger off.'

271

'Oh, you swore. I'll tell my dad you swore,' said Ewan, grinning. 'What are you doing on Saturday afternoon? Shall we go to *The Queen of Sheba*?'

'Seen it.'

'No, you haven't.'

'Have, too. Aunt Lindsay took me.'

'Something else then,' Ewan said. 'Anything you fancy, anything at all.'

'What happened last time will not happen again. My God, Ewan,' said Maeve, 'you're only a kid.'

'And you're what—an old woman?'

'Girls grow up quicker than boys.'

'Anyway,' Ewan said, 'I'll be seventeen next week. I'm having a birthday party. Will you come?'

'Who else will be there?'

'Harry and Philip,' Ewan said, 'and my sisters.'

'Will there be dancing?'

'Dancing? I never thought of that.'

'Booze?' said Maeve.

'Booze? No, I'm not allowed strong drink.'

'Not going to be much of a party then, is it?'

'What sort of parties do you have in Dublin?'

'I thought you knew all about Dublin?' Maeve said.

'I know all about *you*,' Ewan said. 'I know a lot more about you than you know about yourself.'

Ewan had appeared on the doorstep about half past four o'clock. Miss Runciman had been reluctant to let him in but Maeve had suggested that he might accompany her to Partick to see if her grandmother had returned from holiday. Gran McCulloch had not returned from holiday. Ewan had attempted to kiss her in the gloom of the old close but she was not in the mood for his nonsense and had pushed him away. They had walked back uphill to Brunswick Park. Ewan had taken off his school blazer and had spread it on the grass and Maeve sat primly upright, convinced that Miss Runciman was stationed in the drawing-room window, her beady gaze fixed upon them.

Ewan lay back, forearm covering his eyes. He looked harmless, almost pretty lying there like that. If they had been out in the country she might have tickled his ear with a grass stalk.

She said, 'If I give you a kiss, will you tell me what you know about me?'

He shifted his arm and frowned. 'It's worth a lot more than a kiss.'

'Is it now? How much more than a kiss?'

'Come down,' he said, wheezing. 'Come closer, and I'll tell you.'

She glanced up at the windows, tucked in her skirts, and leaned over him, her ear close to his lips while he whispered words that she had heard all too often on the floor of the biscuit factory and around the doors of public houses.

'Ewan Calder!' Maeve exclaimed. 'What a thing to say!'

She should have leaped up, insulted and shocked, but she could not bring herself to do so. It was as if he were casting a spell that revealed not only the ugly side of Ewan Calder but the ugly side of Maeve McCulloch too. If a grown man—Turk Trotter or Bobby Shannon—had spoken to her like that she would have been scared, but in the mouth of a boy as slight and shy as Ewan Calder the words sounded too unnatural to be offensive.

She said, 'You shouldn't be speaking to me, to any girl, like that.'

'Why not?' he said. 'You know what it means.'

273

'If you think I'm going to let you . . .'

He sat up, so slowly and deliberately that he seemed to be detaching himself from the grass, blade by blade.

'You will, Maeve,' he said. 'Some day you will.'

She stared at him for a moment longer, then, knowing that what he said was true, scrambled to her feet and flounced off towards the gate.

*　　*　　*

Arthur said. 'What's she doing now?'

'Coming in,' said Eleanor Runciman. 'Calder has obviously said something to upset her. I'd leave her alone for a bit, Arthur, if I were you.'

'Of course, of course.'

The couple stood at the window, looking down. They made no attempt to hide themselves from the girl in the street below. She was too distraught to notice them. The boy did not follow her out of the park. He lifted his blazer, shook it, slipped it on and stood in an odd twisted position staring after the girl for a second before he set off, walking fast, down the path towards Partick.

'I don't like that young man,' Eleanor said. 'I don't trust him.'

'He's only a boy,' Arthur said. 'I fear Maeve may be leading him on.'

'Do you really think so?' Eleanor asked.

'Don't forget whose daughter she is,' said Arthur.

'Ah yes,' Eleanor said. 'Promiscuity does run in that family.'

'And blood will out in the long run,' said Arthur, with a sigh. 'In the long run, Eleanor, I fear that blood will out.'

*   *   *

The flat was small and cramped, three rooms
linked by low doorways. Furnishings were sparse.
There were no mementoes of Geoffrey's life in
evidence, no model ships, no photographs of
submarines. On top of a cabinet in the living-room,
however, was an unopened box of Cuban cigars
and beside it, almost hidden, an oval portrait of a
beautiful blonde woman whom Lindsay took to be
Stella's sister, Josephine Proctor, the wife that was
no more.

Geoffrey seated her in a wicker armchair by an
unlit gas fire and gave her a glass of sherry. He
asked if she were cold. She said that she was not.
He asked if she'd had a decent journey up. She said
that her journey had been very comfortable. He
asked where she was putting up. She told him that
she was putting up at the Billington.

He asked how long she would be in London.

She answered, 'Three days.'

Geoffrey said, 'Three nights, do you mean?'

'Yes, three nights.'

'On business?'

'Mainly business,' Lindsay said.

He wore a brown double-breasted two-piece suit
that made him look like an insurance clerk. She
was annoyed with herself for cherishing the illusion
of love for so long, for refusing to let it go without a
last wistful nod at the possibility of an affair.

'Didn't you get my letter?' she asked.

'It wasn't awfully informative.'

'I didn't expect to catch you at home.'

275

'Luck,' Geoffrey said. 'Sheer coincidence.' He was drinking too, whisky not sherry. 'Another moment and we'd have missed each other. What would you have done then?'

'Come back later, I imagine,' Lindsay said.

'You look lovely,' he said, matter-of-factly.

'Thank you.' He's no more eager than I am for this thing to begin, she thought. She said, 'How long have you lived here?'

'Three years, give or take.' He remained standing, the mantelshelf over the gas fire too low to lean against. 'It isn't much of a place, as you can see.'

'Will you stay in England when you retire?'

'It's cheaper abroad. One could just about survive on a naval pension in Spain or the south of France.'

'Near the sea?'

'The sea?' he said. 'I've had my fill of the sea, and of stuffy offices, of doing the Admiralty's dirty work.'

'Dirty work?'

'Routine,' he said. 'Dreary routine.' He put the whisky glass on the mantelshelf and hunkered, rather stiffly, before her. He steadied himself with a hand on her knee. 'I've missed you, darling. You've no idea how much I've missed you.'

He expects me to reciprocate, Lindsay thought, to tell him love, true love has brought me to his door. She was not averse to pretending; she had been doing it, one way or another, most of her married life. She could not find the right lie, though, couldn't bring it to her lips. She patted his hand as she might have patted Philip's hand, to placate him.

Geoffrey hoisted himself to his feet.

He said, 'I expect you're hungry.'

'Hmm,' Lindsay said. 'It's a bit early for dinner, though.'

'We could walk,' he said. 'Stretch our legs first.'

'By all means,' Lindsay said.

'If I'd known when to expect you'—Geoffrey polished off the whisky—'I'd have booked tickets for a show.'

'Dinner, a leisurely dinner,' Lindsay said, 'will be fine.'

'And then a nightcap?' Geoffrey said.

'And then a nightcap,' Lindsay agreed, knowing only too well what that innocent euphemism implied.

*   *   *

Only after they had reached Rabat and checked into the Transatlantique did it dawn on Forbes that inviting Stella to join him on the trip had put him at a decided disadvantage. He intended to go directly to the offices of Gideon Rowe and Spellman but Stella would have none of it; he was too tired to argue.

In the morning, after breakfast, she insisted on taking him to see the sights. She wore a white dress that showed every line and curve of her figure. Her blonde hair was covered by a huge sunhat, her eyes protected by sunglasses. Forbes wore sunglasses too but when sweat built up on the bridge of his nose he would take them off and blink, not at the minarets and towers or the crowded streets of the *souk* but at Stella; blink and stare as if she were a fantasy that had popped out of a bottle, a jinn or

277

genie who, if only he could master her tricks and wiles, would bring him untold wealth and happiness.

She led him first to the Mamounia to admire the pictures in the Moorish salon and the mosaics in the music room. Forbes had no interest in art but Stella was so beautiful, so sexual, and he was so much in love that he would have followed her anywhere. She guided him back through the *souk* and uphill to the gardens of the Oudaiya. Forbes was conscious of the colours, smells, the rich, dense texture of the market-place but felt wonderfully detached from it all, as if he were floating on a pastel tide.

In the Oudaiya's Moorish café, amid luxuriant shrubs and flowering plants, Stella finally allowed him to rest.

At a wrought-iron table in the shade of a striped awning, sipping strong coffee and smoking a cigar, Forbes was so at peace with the world that he felt as if he had entered one of those dreamlike moments that come all too rarely in a man's life— and that pass all too swiftly.

'*Stella!*'

The stranger sported a suit of loose cream-coloured material and a natty little hat, like a fez without a tassel. He was small, dainty, dry, his movements as precise as clockwork. The kiss he bestowed on Stella seemed curiously mechanical, the bow he gave to Forbes even more so.

'*Monsieur,*' the stranger said, '*c'est un plaisir de vous accueillir en Maroc. J'espère que vous pourrez joindre l'utile à l'agréable pendant votre séjour ici.*'

'He doesn't speak French,' Stella said. 'English, Giddy, please.'

278

The hand, the little hand of friendship, inimitably French, was offered.

Forbes, rising, shook it.

The Frenchman's grip, he thought, was too limp to be sincere.

'Allow me to introduce my brother-in-law,' Stella said.

And the Frenchman, bowing again, added, 'Gideon Rowe.'

* * *

Pharaoh's was one of several nightclubs that had sprung up in the wake of the war, a far cry from the sombre brown-leather tombs of Pall Mall. The dining-room was cramped and noisy but the food was well cooked and the wine of excellent quality. They certainly drank enough of it, Geoffrey and she, and chuckled like two youngsters while speculating on who was with whom and why such odd pairings no longer gave offence. Dinner suits, lounge suits, evening dresses, outrageously informal afternoon wear; bobbed hair and long hair, almost no hair at all; men with cuff-links shaped like silver dollars, women with earrings larger than their bosoms; in the background, almost lost in monkey-chatter, the sweet strains of an orchestra playing wartime melodies.

Somewhere, Lindsay thought, with a strange weightless feeling about her heart, somewhere couples are dancing to "Mon Homme", "Whispering", "Look for the Silver Lining", "A Thousand Kisses", all the tunes her father played on the piano when he thought nobody was listening; new rhythms, new steps but the same old mordant expressions of loss and longing that had dogged lonely women from time immemorial. She wanted Geoffrey to put his arms about her and sweep her off her feet, to be coaxed into loving him again.

Geoffrey stubbed out his cigarette and finished his brandy.

'Shall we go,' he said, 'upstairs?'

'I'd love to,' Lindsay said.

He seemed surprised. 'Would you, really?'

'Really, I would.'

Geoffrey drew out her chair. He took her by the arm, led her between the tables out into the mock-Egyptian foyer with its black-faced Nubian slaves in short loincloths, its potted palms and a papier-mâché Sphinx that gazed out on Piccadilly, bewildered by the riddle of the times.

The strains of the little orchestra grew faint and were lost.

He guided her to the stairs and pushed her ahead of him.

The staircase was panelled in cedar, daubed with desert scenes. A young man, not much older than Harry, stumbled past Lindsay, bumping her shoulder in his haste. He was pursued by a very young woman, a girl so slender that she seemed to be all bone and no flesh. She clutched a silver lamé purse to her breast and yelled, almost viciously, 'Reggie, Reggie, he *won't* give it to you. You *know* he won't give it to you. There's nothing left.'

Lindsay stepped into an upstairs room, Geoffrey hard behind her.

Crimson carpet, chandeliers, eight or ten card tables shrouded in tobacco smoke; the room crowded but oddly hushed.

'Do you play, Lindsay?' Geoffrey asked.

'Play?'

'Cards,' he said.

'Well, I . . .'

'Are you carrying any spare cash, by the way? I'm a little short.'

'Something,' Lindsay said. 'A few pounds.'

'Good, that'll get us started,' Geoffrey said, and steered her eagerly to the nearest vacant chair.

*　　*　　*

The Frenchman ordered coffee and seated himself in the shade. Forbes had talked shipbuilding business in some odd places, but none odder than the gardens of the Oudaiya. They made a formidable pair, the Frenchman and the English lady; he would have to keep his wits about him.

'Rowe?' Forbes said. 'What did it used to be—Roux?'

'*Oui*,' Gideon told him. 'My family originally came from Alsace.'

'Is coming from Alsace a reason to change your name?' said Forbes.

'It is something you would not understand,' Gideon said.

'Oh, I might,' Forbes said.

'Forbes is very good at understanding things,' Stella said.

'Where's Spellman?' Forbes said. 'Are we waiting for Spellman now?'

'Spellman has been dead many dozen years.'

'So,' Forbes said, 'I have to deal with you, do I?'

'We deal with each other, I think.'

'Why here? Why not at your offices? You do have offices, I take it?'

281

'My offices are in Paris.' Gideon held the coffee cup in both hands the way a squirrel holds a peanut. 'I have a residence here, if you would care to make a visit to it. However, I think it would be much the more sense if we went to view the place where the money is to be made.'

'Where would that be?'

'A pleasant drive to the forest of Mamora. We pass the stone quarries at Sidi Bou Knadel if you wish to see where from the materials for building come.'

'Building materials—for what?'

'Our new town.'

'Does your new town have a name?' Forbes said.

'Port-Lyautey.'

'How far is it from Rabat?'

'Seventy miles,' Stella said.

'What's so special about Port-Lyautey?'

'At the high water,' Gideon Rowe told him, 'the port opens itself to ships that draw deep.'

'How deep?'

'Fifteen to twenty—feet, it is?'

'Yes,' Stella said. 'Feet.'

'I see,' Forbes said. 'Well, that's one up on Rabat.'

'What is wrong with Rabat?'

'It's a rotten place to build an oil port,' Forbes said. 'Safe anchorage in the roads can only be guaranteed in favourable weather. The river throws up a sand bar that needs constant dredging and big loads have to be discharged by lighter. Can this new town accommodate ocean-going tankers?'

'It will have soon that capacity,' said Gideon Rowe.

'How soon?'

'Before the year has ended.'

'Let's go look at it, then,' Forbes said.

'What?' Stella said. 'Now, before lunch?'

'There's no time like the present,' said Forbes.

* * *

Gideon Rowe's Bugatti-designed pre-war Peugeot Bébé looked like a well-preserved antique but, to Forbes's surprise, fairly ate up the miles.

The Frenchman drove without inhibition, taking straights and corners at top speed. In the box-like passenger compartment Stella hugged Forbes as the car swerved past farm labourers and mules and carts piled high with produce. The high-speed ride delighted her. Anchored to Forbes's arm, she leaned from the open window and waved to the villagers through clouds of dust.

After an hour or so they ran into the forest and rippling bands of shadow gave respite from the heat. Then they came out of the trees and the town lay before them, a maze of half-constructed buildings in concrete and stone with cranes, ramps and scaffolding lining the broadways. Gideon proudly pointed out the recently planted trees that would give the boulevards shade, the new bridge across the Sebou, the railway station and the handful of handsome civic buildings that formed the Place de France.

'What was here before you arrived?' Forbes shouted.

'Only the citadel of Muley Hassan, and a few natives' dwellings.'

'Where are the natives now?'

'Safe in the quarters behind the mosque.'

'How long since the French took over?'

'We landed in the year of 1912.'

'Dear God!' said Forbes. 'You have been busy.'

'We are a busy people no?' Gideon shouted.

'When there's money to be made,' said Stella.

'What is wrong with the making of money, *chérie*?'

'Not a thing,' said Stella. 'Absolutely not a thing.'

'Provided you're not a native,' said Forbes.

They ate lunch on the terrace of the half-finished Carthage Hotel, upwind from the stonemasons' dust sheets. The terrace gave fine views of the lighthouse at the mouth of the Sebou and, according to Gideon, the site of the new oil bunkers that would be fed by the tankers that he, Forbes Franklin, would build.

Forbes did not have the gall to tell the Frenchman that he was a McCulloch not a Franklin and that Irishmen were less inclined to change their names than persons who hailed from Alsace. With lunch, he drank light French beer and a single glass of dark local wine then, fighting off drowsiness, let Rowe pay the bill and lead them back to the motor-car.

Twenty minutes later they were parked on a spit of rocky ground pegged with wooden stakes and painted poles. There were no diggers, no surveyors, nothing but stakes and poles to indicate the scale of the project.

'Don't you have a site plan?' Forbes asked.

'It is safe in my offices,' Gideon Rowe answered.

'In Paris, or Rabat?'

'In my offices in Rabat.'

'I'll need to have a look at it,' Forbes said. 'In fact a copy would come in handy. I mean, I have

284

to find out what this place can cope with. No point in building you a tanker that won't fit your requirements.'

'I have been shown your drawings. They are perfect.'

'They're nowhere near perfect,' Forbes said. 'You—Stella and you—are being pretty offhand about this contract. She's told you our terms, I suppose?'

Stella had wandered to the edge of the rock and sat with knees drawn up, staring out to sea. Forbes watched the breeze flick her hair, her skirt, and whisk away the little wisp of cigarette smoke that escaped from her parted lips.

The sea was pancake flat, blue and passive. He found it hard to believe that this was the same ocean that broke the back of cargo ships en route to New York or gobbled up trawlers off Greenland. In the haze that veiled the horizon there was not one ship to be seen, no funnel, no sail, only a few small skiffs close inshore, as if the continent of Africa were still waiting to be discovered.

'We have been quoted an approximate price of three hundred thousand English pounds,' Gideon Rowe said. 'It will be our pleasure to present you with our eight percentage, twenty-four thousand English pounds, as soon as we have approval of design and settle on variety of contract.'

'Type of contract,' Forbes said. 'Arranging the terms of the contract to our mutual satisfaction may not be easy.'

'You would prefer fixed-to-the-price, I think.'

'And you'd rather have it cost-plus, no doubt.'

'For speed and the simplicity, naturally.'

'However we settle it,' Forbes said, 'I'll insist on

a price variation clause to cover the rising cost of steel between tendering and delivery.'

Gideon Rowe hesitated. 'You will buy the steel in England.'

'We'll buy the steel wherever we can negotiate the best quality at the lowest price,' Forbes said.

'You do not understand,' Gideon told him. 'I am saying that you will buy the steel from a manufacturer who is of our choosing.'

'Whoa now!' Forbes said. 'I can't allow you to dictate where we buy our materials. That's the shipbuilder's affair, not the client's.'

'That is a thing not to be negotiated,' Gideon Rowe declared.

'The heck it isn't! How many ships do you have in service?'

'None.'

Forbes nodded, unsurprised. 'How many do you hope to put into service over the next five or six years?'

'It is our intention to have eight tankers in our fleet.'

Forbes popped his lips. 'You're not lacking in ambition, Monsieur Roux,' he said, 'and, I gather, you're not lacking capital either. At a guess we're talking a ten-year project here and an investment in oil-carrying capacity somewhere in the region of—what?'

'Two and one half a million English pounds.'

'Is this private money, or are you going public?'

'Why do you ask such a question?'

'You never know, I might want to buy in.'

Gideon Rowe smiled and shook his head. 'It is not possible to buy in, Mr Franklin. We are a limited company with members already in position to provide all the necessary capital.'

'Is this the same company that's putting up the capital to build a new town on the coast of French Morocco?'

'It is not the same, no.'

'Where does Stella fit into all this?' Forbes asked.

'She is one of the investors.'

'What about her husband? What about Pickering?'

'He has no involvement.'

'I don't think I believe you, Monsieur Roux.'

'Rowe, I am called Rowe.'

'And I'm not Franklin; I'm McCulloch.'

'Why do we argue about names?' Gideon said. 'Do we not have more important matters to talk about than names? We should go back to Rabat before the night falls. I do not wish to be driving on that road in darkness.'

'All right,' Forbes said, 'just one more question before we head back: these steel producers you want to saddle us with—do *they* have a name?'

'Bradford Steel.'

'Bradford's don't manufacture proper steel,' said Forbes. 'They make tin plate.'

'No longer,' Gideon said. 'They will be equipped to produce what you need to build our ships, Mr McCulloch.'

'So you've bought them over, have you?'

'We have,' said Gideon Rowe.

Coming up behind him and slipping her arms about his waist, Stella nuzzled Forbes's cheek. 'You don't know the half of it, darling, not the half.'

'Do I want to?' Forbes said.

Stella said, 'Frankly, I'm not sure that you do.'

Then, in the last of the daylight, they drove back home to Rabat.

*   *   *

Any doubts that Lindsay might have nurtured that Geoffrey Paget was not the man for her vanished in Pharaoh's nightclub shortly before midnight. From the moment the cards began to run his way, she had known that he would abandon her in favour of the game. She had put up with being ignored for the best part of an hour before she had tapped his shoulder and had told him she was leaving.

'No, Lindsay, please don't go. I'm on a jolly good streak right now and you're bringing me luck.'

'I'm not a rabbit's foot, Geoffrey. Will you take me back to my hotel, or will I look for a taxi?'

Seven at the table, five men, two women, the women players of the game, not bystanders. The men had been impatient. One fat man, wearing a deplorable wig, had muttered under his breath and waved his hand as if to shoo her away.

'Geoffrey, what's it to be?'

'Do you mind awfully going back on your own? It would be akin to a crime for me to leave now. You do see that, Lindsay, don't you?' He had turned his attention back to the cards. 'Tomorrow? Same place and time?'

'Yes, tomorrow.'

She had gone back to the Billington on her own in the back of a taxi-cab.

She had gone to bed, had slept soundly and wakened late.

Now someone was knocking on the door of her room. She rolled over and lifted her watch from the

288

bedside table. It was not quite half past eight. She had a fuzzy little headache, and was hungry.

The knocking continued.

She rose, put on her robe and went to the door.

'Who is it?'

'Desk, ma'am.'

She opened the door. A young woman was standing in the corridor with a huge bunch of red roses, wrapped in cellophane, in her arms.

'Mrs Forbes McCulloch?'

'Yes.'

'For you, ma'am, delivered to reception.'

'Thank you.'

Out of habit Lindsay dug into the pocket of her robe for change, then, finding none, accepted the flowers and hastily closed the door.

Twenty-four blood-red roses; Geoffrey's winning streak had obviously not been affected by her departure. She laid the flowers on the carpet and, kneeling, fished out the note: *My darling, Can you forgive me? I'll make it up to you tonight, Promise. All my Love to You, Geoffrey.*

What arrogance! If Lieutenant-Commander Paget thought for one moment that she would be hanging about Marylebone High Street at half past five o'clock on the off-chance that he would be in the mood for love-making then he had another think coming. She tore up the note and tossed the pieces into the basket beneath the dressing-table.

By the time she'd trotted along to the bathroom, combed her hair, dressed and put on her make-up, however, she had calmed down. Leaving the roses on the carpet, she went downstairs for breakfast.

Then, soon after ten, she set off on foot for Whitehall.

The new Admiralty buildings stood north of the Parade Ground, an imposing pile topped by wireless masts and aerials. Long ago, when she wasn't much older than Maeve, Lindsay had been given a tour of the historic old building with its marble staircases and beautiful chimney-pieces. Modern efficiency, however, had replaced respect for tradition and the block that housed the new departments and directorates was no architectural masterpiece. Even so, not unreasonably, the navy were averse to letting strangers wander at will about its corridors. She might, she thought, have been some blowsy wench off the Plymouth dock with an illegitimate child clutched to her bosom for all the respect she was given.

One rating, then another, then a petty officer and finally a tall young lieutenant challenged her.

'Franklin's, madam?'

'Franklin's Shipbuilding Company, Aydon Road, Glasgow.' Like an impudent schoolgirl Lindsay was tempted to add, 'Britain, Europe, the World'.

'Lieutenant-Commander Paget, you say?'

'Lieutenant-Commander Geoffrey Paget, yes.'

'Which department would that be, madam?'

'The department of Contracts and Commissions.'

'The Directorate?'

'No, the department.'

Decisions had to be made and nobody at ground level was willing to make them. 'Perhaps it would be sensible to telephone Lieutenant-Commander Paget and confirm that he's expecting me,' Lindsay suggested.

'Will he know who you are, madam?'

'Given that he arranged the appointment, I imagine he might.'

The tall lieutenant said, 'May I enquire as to the nature of your business with Lieutenant-Commander Paget?'

'Lieutenant-Commander Paget will be able to answer that question better than I can,' Lindsay said, through her teeth. 'I am, however, a partner in Franklin's so it may have something to do with the two torpedo-boat destroyers we have under construction.'

'You're a shipbuilder, are you, ma'am?' the petty officer asked.

'I'm not a caulker or a riveter,' Lindsay said. 'I am, however, on Franklin's board of management.'

'Good Lord!' the petty officer said, not quite under his breath.

Modernisation did not yet apply to attitude, it seemed. The sailors were nothing more than glorified clerks, though, and probably none too pleased at being removed from sea duty in the Navy Board shake-up. They put their heads together once more and discussed what to do with Lindsay, as if she were a mine or an armed torpedo.

At length, the lieutenant said, 'If you care to accompany me, madam, I will escort you to the appropriate floor.'

'How kind,' said Lindsay and, a few minutes later, was shown into a small office on the fourth floor and invited to wait while the lieutenant went off to locate Geoffrey.

Hot sunshine flooded through the window and lit up the notice-board on the wall behind the desk.

Circumstance, negligence or simply the fact that she was a woman and women weren't supposed to understand such matters—for whatever reason she had been left alone in Geoffrey Paget's office with nothing to do but stare at a green baize notice-board on the sunlit wall, a board whose hue and texture reminded her, and Geoffrey too, probably, of a gaming table.

Lindsay stared at it blankly for a moment and then, focusing, stepped round the desk and, without conscience, read the most prominent notice: *New Construction—Contract-Built Ships Cancelled—Contract-Built Ships Transferred to HM Dockyards for Completion—Battleships—Battle Cruisers—Light Cruisers—Submarines—Torpedo-Boat Destroyers*, and a cruel little list of names, typed out and amended in pencil, among them, inevitably, Franklin's.

'Idiot, you blithering idiot!'

She heard Geoffrey's voice in the corridor a moment before he strode into the office, trailed by the tall lieutenant. He looked at her, at the notice-board, and colour drained from his face.

'The lady said . . .' the lieutenant began.

'Fine, fine, fine, Hathaway, yes, yes, yes.'

'The lady is—er—expected then, sir?'

'Yes. Yes. Go away, Hathaway. Close the door behind you.'

'Sir,' the lieutenant said sheepishly, and left.

'You bastard, Geoffrey,' Lindsay said. 'You're not interested in me. You were in Glasgow to survey naval contracts and thought you'd have a bit of fun fanning the old flame. You're a hatchet-man, Geoffrey, a damned hatchet-man.'

'No,' he said. 'No, darling, it isn't like that at all.'

'What is it like, then?' said Lindsay. 'Look, it's here in black and white: Franklin's, two destroyers, contracts cancelled.'

'So far it's only a recommendation.'

'Whose recommendation—yours?'

'For God's sake, Lindsay, I have a job to do, whether I like it or not,' Geoffrey protested. 'The Contracts Directorate is under the thumb of the Finance Department. Have you heard of the Washington Treaty?'

'The arms limitation talks to discuss cuts in warship building and impose controls on the scale of fighting fleets; yes, I've heard of it, Geoffrey, everyone's heard of it. But the talks haven't even started yet.' She moved away from the board. He retreated before her, shifting backward, one long step at a time. 'You didn't show your face at Franklin's, didn't even bother to inspect the work we have on hand. You were snuggled up with your sister-in-law and her husband, weren't you? It was all just an excuse.'

'An excuse?' he said, puzzled. 'An excuse for what?'

'That, Geoffrey, *darling*, is what I'm here to find out.'

There was dust in the room, much dust, lit by sunlight streaming in from the Mall. It stirred and shimmered about him when he moved. He stood over her, stooped, whispering. 'You shouldn't have come here, Lindsay,' he said. 'I implore you to forget what you've seen in this office.'

'When will the cancellation notices go out?'

'As soon as my chief approves the recommendations and presents them to the finance committee. It's not my job to chop individual

293

shipyards, just to ensure that budget estimates are reduced by specified amounts.'

'In other words,' Lindsay interrupted, 'you could take Franklin's destroyers off the list if you wanted to?'

'I could, yes. I mean, yes I probably can.'

'If I keep my mouth shut?'

'It isn't what you think, Lindsay. I love you. I have always loved you.'

The statement was so banal, so ridiculously inappropriate that she wondered if he had learned the language of romance from captions in *Punch*.

'Geoffrey,' Lindsay said, 'what *is* going on, *really* going on?'

He rested his buttocks on the edge of the desk, studied her for a long moment, then said, 'I'm broke, Lindsay. I'm buggered broke. I've no savings, no investments. In eighteen months I'll be out on the street with nothing but a retirement pension to keep me going.'

'You gambled it all away, didn't you?'

'Yes, most of it.'

'Did you marry Jo Proctor to get out of debt?'

'I married her—I don't know. I thought she was in love with me.'

'Were you in love with her?'

'Yes, I was,' he said, 'or thought I was. I was desperate, Lindsay, absolutely desperate. It was a relief when the war started and I was assigned to sea duty, away from Jo and all those temptations. The trouble is that most of the temptations were still here when I surfaced again. I just didn't have enough—enough anything to make Jo happy, that's why she divorced me and married someone else.'

'Someone who isn't a gambler.'

'Gideon Rowe? Oh, God, no, he's a gambler too, a bigger gambler than I am,' Geoffrey said. 'He gambles on a grand scale, and makes millions.'

'Gideon Rowe.' Lindsay frowned. 'My, my, Geoffrey, you are mixed up with a rum crowd. Did they ask you to turn on the charm and to try to talk me into having an affair?'

He shook his head. 'I made an ass of myself, Lindsay, a complete and utter ass. I should never have fallen in with their scheme in the first place. It wasn't my intention to hurt you, not you.'

'Who then? Forbes?'

'It isn't that simple, Lindsay. Pickering isn't interested in revenge. Power and profit, that's all he cares about. He didn't marry Stella Proctor because she was one of the most beautiful young women in the London. He married her because she had money.' He shook his head again. 'I shouldn't be telling you this. If it gets out that I told you then I'm scuttled. Pickering's promised me a job when I retire, a position in one of his companies that'll bring me a decent little income without stretching my limited talents.'

'And what do you have to do for Pickering?' Lindsay asked. 'Feed him advance information about cancelled orders so he can pick up bargains for his fleet by buying out the contracts?'

'It isn't ships he's after.'

'What is it then?'

'Shipyards.'

Lindsay paused. 'Franklin's?'

'Yes.'

'Franklin's isn't for sale,' Lindsay said, 'and two cancelled orders won't bring us to our knees. What does Pickering want with Franklin's, anyway?'

'It's the right size, in the right location, and it's ripe for a takeover.'

'Nonsense!' Lindsay said. 'We may be a family firm but we've enough reserves to ride out a crisis.'

'You haven't moved with the times,' Geoffrey said. 'You haven't bought into a steel mill, for instance. By the year's end you'll be paying through the nose for plate and castings. If I were you, Lindsay—and I say this as a friend, as someone who does care for you, no matter what you think— if I were you I'd get out as soon as possible.'

'How can I?' Lindsay said. 'If I did want to sell my shares, which, incidentally, I do not, I'm obligated to offer them to an existing partner.'

'Forbes,' Geoffrey said, 'being the obvious choice.'

'Forbes?' Lindsay blinked.

Confession, it seemed, had restored Geoffrey's confidence. He was calmer now and some colour had returned to his cheeks.

'Forbes would buy your shares in a trice, Lindsay.'

'Are you seriously suggesting that I cheat my husband?'

'God knows, he's cheated on you often enough.'

Lindsay bit her lip. 'That may be so—but it isn't the same thing.'

'Where is he right now?'

'In Morocco.'

'Alone?'

'Yes, Tom Calder decided not to go.'

'Forbes isn't alone, Lindsay. He's travelling with another man's wife.'

She knew that she shouldn't fall into his trap, shouldn't ask the question, should preserve her tarnished innocence, her ignorance, be loyal to her disloyal husband. She heard herself say, 'Whose wife?'

Geoffrey said, 'Drew Pickering's.'

She stared from the window at a blue sky smeared by a smoky haze, at a corner of the new building, a corner of the old arch, and knew that Geoffrey had told her the truth.

Quietly, soberly, he said, 'I'm sorry.'

'Why should you be sorry?' Lindsay flashed. 'If Forbes is travelling with Stella Pickering and *you* know about it then I'm damned sure Drew Pickering knows about it, too.' She got to her feet and faced him. 'Would you have told me all this if I hadn't seen that blessed list on your notice-board? I do not play tit-for-tat, Geoffrey. I'm not going to become your lover to get back at Forbes, nor am I going to break up Franklin's partnership just for revenge.'

'Lindsay, he'll take you down with him.'

'Forbes isn't going down. And Franklin's isn't going down either. Carry that message back to whoever gives you your orders.' She moved to the door before he could stop her. 'Thank you for the roses, Geoffrey. Goodbye.'

'Does this mean I won't see you again?'

'What do you think?' Lindsay said and, within the hour, was on a train heading north.

*   *   *

They sailed from Tangier on the *Gracchus* and hit heavy weather north of Cape Finisterre. The storm began before daybreak and lasted throughout the day. Stella, like Forbes, had a cast-iron constitution

297

and was never seasick. They spent the afternoon skidding about the deck, watching the blue-grey Atlantic grow darker and wilder. There were no other passengers up top and around four in the afternoon the captain sent down a request that in the interests of safety the couple go below and remain there.

In the cabin they made love while the *Gracchus* pitched and rolled violently. They clung to each other on the bunk, one up one moment, the other the next, then, finally exhausted, lay back, huddled together like orphans.

'God!' Stella said. 'I'd kill for a ham sandwich.'

'Aren't we dining at eight?'

'It's bound to be a shambles in the dining-room and I'm not up to chasing my supper across the deck.'

'All right,' said Forbes. 'Sandwiches it shall be. Ham, you say?'

'Yes.'

'Coffee?'

'Champagne,' she said. 'In this weather it's safer, don't you think?'

'Absolutely,' Forbes agreed.

He dressed and went off in search of a steward.

A half-hour later he reappeared bearing a tray of sandwiches and, tucked under his arm, an ice bucket containing two glasses and a bottle of Taittinger.

Stella was just as he had left her, except that she had put on a robe.

'The dining-room's closed. No one's interested in dinner. The stewards were surprised to see me. They offered to bring something along but I decided to save them the bother.' He placed the tray on the bed between her bare feet and digging into his pocket produced a jar of English mustard. 'Bit basic, dearest, but you can't expect miracles in weather like this.'

'Where are we?'

'Somewhere in the Bay of Biscay.'

Stella smeared mustard on to a sandwich and bit greedily into the meat. She wiped her lips with her fingers and lay back against the headboard. 'Oh, that's good, so good,' she said.

Forbes popped the cork on the champagne bottle and did his best to pour her a glass. Failing, he hauled himself on to the bed and handed her the bottle. She drank, tipping the bottle up. He could see her breasts, her nipples still swollen with love-making. She widened her eyes and smiled. She was happy to be picnicking in the middle of the Bay of Biscay in the midst of a storm, happy to be here with him. She drank again, handed him the bottle and plucked another sandwich from the tray.

She had children, a husband, famous sisters, a fine house on a hilltop overlooking the Clyde, yet she was delighted to be here with him. He was happy too, happier than he had ever been. He wondered if Harry and Phil would ever be as happy as he was now, or if they would find the fine, irresponsible madness that went hand in glove with selfishness too much to bear.

Stella said, 'What would your wife say if she could see you now?'

'She'd be horrified.'

Stella munched away, smiling her wide smile.

She picked a little fleck of ham from her teeth with her fingernail.

'Leave her. Come and live with me.'

'If only I could,' Forbes said.

'What's stopping you?'

'Money, for one thing.'

'Money? That's pish, darling, that's piddle.'

'All very well for you to say. I have to work for a living.'

'Do you?' Stella said. 'You could sell your shares in Franklin's. We could pool our resources, and run off. Wouldn't you like that?'

'I'd love that,' Forbes said.

'Bermuda or Madeira. Venice, Rome or Sicily. Switzerland or Spain. Anywhere where we could be together, for ever and ever.'

Forbes laughed, not taking her seriously.

She said, 'My children are almost grown. They have no need of me.'

'Wouldn't they miss you?' Forbes said.

'I doubt it very much,' said Stella.

'Mine would,' Forbes said. 'At least I think they would.'

'For how long?' Stella said. 'A week, a month? And then they'd get on with living their own lives and forget all about you.'

'My sons depend on me.'

'For what? Support?'

There was an uncomfortable amount of truth in what she said. Harry and Phil would be well taken care of even if he wasn't around. One thing to be said for the Franklins, they would always look after their own.

He swayed with the pitching of the ship and listened to the roar of the wind and the groan of the steel plates under pressure.

'If I did run off with you, dearest,' he said, 'who'd build your tanker?'

'Very well,' Stella said, 'if you insist on being practical, why don't you make *her* an offer and buy *her* out?'

'Lindsay? She'd never sell. In any case, what good would that do?'

'If you were my husband,' Stella said, 'you'd have more financial backing than you ever dreamed of. Giddy would see to it that all the orders for all the ships his company needs come your way. My God, in four or five years you'd be the big cheese on Clydeside; think of that.'

'Bermuda?' Forbes said. 'What happened to Bermuda?'

'Darling,' Stella said, 'I don't need Bermuda. I need you.'

'What's old Drew going to say about it? Will he let you go?'

'I've served my purpose,' Stella said. 'Drew has everything he wants. I even managed to buy him a knighthood, and he was awfully pleased about that. If I ask for a legal separation, he won't put up a fight.'

'Does he have a—you know?'

'How coy of you, Forbes. Yes, Drew has a mistress.'

'Anyone I know?'

'No.'

'Anyone you know?'

'I introduced them.'

'Don't you mind?'

'I did until you came along.'

'Well!' Forbes said. 'I'm flattered.'

'So you should be, my boy,' Stella told him.

With a start he realised that Stella was serious. He was hazy about the precise difference between

301

separation and divorce, but no doubt Stella would be versed in the legal procedure, given that her sister had gone through it. He had never really considered leaving Lindsay before. The fact that his marriage was a sham, sexually at any rate, was Lindsay's fault, of course. Right would be on his side. Scandal, though; whatever terms were negotiated, however discreet, there was bound to be a scandal. He wondered if he had the guts to put his sons through that ordeal and how leaving Lindsay would affect his position in Aydon Road.

Stella tucked the bottle into the side of the mattress and put both arms about him, enveloping him. The *Gracchus* bucked and pitched. Forbes felt the power of the ocean vibrating in the very marrow of his bones.

She pressed her mouth to his ear.

'I thought you loved me,' she whispered. 'Oh, Forbes, don't tell me I'm just another passing fancy, another Marjorie?'

'God, no, dearest. No.'

'Tell me.' She hid her face in his shoulder. 'Tell me. Say it.'

'I love you.'

'More than anyone else?'

'More than anyone else,' said Forbes.

*   *   *

Forbes travelled overnight from London, alone. Stella had gone to visit her mother in Dorset. Missing her, he had slept fitfully, dreaming shallow dreams, and was relieved to arrive in Glasgow. He was eager to learn what Lindsay had discovered in London and nurtured a faint hope that she might even have gone to bed with her sailor boy, for a silly little act of indiscretion on Lindsay's part would in some measure excuse his indiscretions which, of course, were neither little nor silly.

The big oak door was already open when the taxi dumped him on the pavement in Brunswick Crescent. He climbed the steps, lugging his overnight bag. The inner door opened and Eleanor Runciman, disapproving as always, admitted him. Behind her, like an exercise in perspective, Arthur, Lindsay, Maeve and the boys were stationed in the hall. His first thought was that somehow they had discovered that he had spent the last thirteen nights wrapped in Stella Pickering's arms.

'Well, well,' he said, brazenly. 'What a welcoming committee.'

Arthur stepped forward. 'Forbes, we've had some bad news.'

Forbes experienced a lurch of disappointment and, at the same time, reprieve. Bad news didn't bother him. It couldn't be all that tragic, not when everyone he cared about was gathered in plain sight in the hallway.

'It's Kay,' Arthur said. 'It's your mother.'

A little cloud, like a clot, flitted across Forbes's brain. He staggered and held on to the hallstand. Oh, Jesus, he thought, *An Eye for an Eye, a Life for a Life*. I didn't pay them their blood money and they've killed my poor old ma.

Mouth sticky, throat like sandpaper, he said, 'Is she dead?'

'What?' said Arthur. 'No, not dead. Married.'

'Married? Ma?'

'Yes,' Arthur said. 'To another Irishman.'

Forbes listed to one side like a dredger. He

303

knocked his head on the mirror by the hallstand, and laughed. It might have been tears but instead it was laughter, a low chuckle that rose to a high-pitched *Hee-Hee-Hee-Hee*.

'For heaven's sake, man,' Arthur said. 'It's no laughing matter. We're out of our heads with worry and all you can do is laugh.'

'Coffey—Coffey . . .' Forbes gasped.

'Coffee?' Arthur said. 'Are you drunk?'

'No,' Forbes said, 'Coffey's his name. Me old mother has gone off and married a man called Coffey.'

'How do you know that?' said Lindsay.

'I think,' Forbes said, sobering a little, 'I think I paid for the honeymoon.'

* * *

Much to their chagrin Harry and Philip were chased off to school while the rest of the family trooped into the dining-room to join Uncle Forbes for a late breakfast. Now they were at table and, being sensible folk, eating heartily.

'Donald,' Arthur said, 'assumed Kay was with us and we assumed she was with him. She turned up in Largs just before Easter, stayed a week then said she was going home. Donald offered to drive her but she insisted on going by train. He took her to the station, saw her off. She must have banked on the fact that we wouldn't miss her for a day or two. Turns out we didn't miss her at all.'

Forbes nodded. 'Where is she now?'

'In Ireland, apparently, staying with Coffey's daughter in Cork,' Lindsay said. 'It's all there on the postcard.'

The postcard was a giant-sized tinted photograph of a green hill and a bit of sea that some printer in London thought typical of Ireland. Donald had received an identical postcard by the same early morning mail. The card was balanced on Uncle Forbes's tea plate. Shovelling ham and eggs into his mouth, he glanced down at it and shook his head ruefully, as if he still couldn't believe that his mother had put one over on them.

'Is she settling in Cork, then?' Forbes asked.

'Unfortunately not,' said Arthur.

'She's not bringing him back here, is she?'

'That appears to be her intention.'

Maeve wiped marmalade from her fingers, lifted the postcard and held it between her palms. She read aloud. 'Cyrus and I will be home before the end of the month and are looking forward to seeing you.'

'Home?' said Arthur. 'I'm surprised she remembers where home is.'

'Partick,' said Forbes. 'She's coming back to Partick and bringing Coffey with her. I reckon he's a sponger, a cuckoo in her nest. He asked me for money for the brotherhood and, foolishly, I gave it to him.'

'Why?' said Lindsay.

'I honestly don't know.' Forbes mopped up traces of egg with a finger of toast. He popped it into his mouth, dabbed his moustache, and squinted at Maeve. 'Did you know what was going on? Were you part of it?'

'Me?' said Maeve, astonished. 'Not me.'

'This Coffey chap,' said Arthur, 'have you encountered him?'

'Never.' Maeve dropped the giant postcard back

305

on to her uncle's plate. 'I'd remember if I had, him with a name like Coffey.'

'Cyrus Coffey,' said Arthur, sighing. 'Dear God!'

'So, Maeve,' her uncle went on, 'you wouldn't know whether he's an active member of the brotherhood, or just a chancer?'

'I told you, Uncle Forbes, I've never met him.'

'He doesn't run with your crowd, then?'

'My crowd? If you mean Charlie and Peter—*your* brothers, Uncle Forbes—he must have taken up with them after I left Dublin.'

'You know them all, do you?' Forbes said. 'The whole gang?'

'No, I don't know them all.'

'Of course you don't, dear,' said Lindsay. 'Forbes, do stop badgering the girl. It's not her fault that your mother ran off and married another Irishman.'

'What's wrong with Irishmen?' Maeve heard herself say.

'Nothing,' said Forbes. 'Hell, I'm one myself.'

'At her age she probably had to take what she could get,' Eleanor said.

'Maybe she loves him,' Maeve said.

And Forbes, with an odd little smile, said, 'Maybe she does at that.'

*   *   *

As soon as breakfast was over Forbes took Lindsay by the arm, led her into the piano parlour and closed the door to keep the others out. He lit a cigar and began his interrogation at once.

'Did you make contact with Paget?'

'Yes,' Lindsay said. 'He took me to a nightclub.'

'To dance all night, I suppose?'

'To watch him gamble.'

'Gamble?'

'At the card table.'

'Did he win?'

'I didn't stay long enough to find out.'

'So your boyfriend's a gambler, is he?'

'He isn't my boyfriend, Forbes,' Lindsay said.

'Gone off him, have you?'

She had known that he would question her closely and had already decided what she would and would not tell him.

'Yes,' she said. 'I've gone off him.'

'Good,' Forbes said. 'The sailor boy is up to something that may be illegal, in tandem with the Pickerings.'

'I know,' Lindsay said. 'He's providing Pickering with information. Geoffrey's an Admiralty hatchet-man. It's his job to recommend contracts for cancellation. Our destroyers are high on the list, Forbes.'

'Did he tell you this off his own bat?'

'No, I went to the Admiralty, to his office, and saw the notices in black and white. Sheer luck. Good luck for us, bad luck for Geoffrey.'

Forbes pulled on his cigar and blew smoke over her head.

'When will the cancellation notices go out?' he asked.

'Within the month.'

Forbes studied the tip of the cigar. 'The destroyers were ordered under conditions of war. The Admiralty has the power to cancel on fourteen days' notice. Contracts terminated, work stopped, vessels dismantled. We're indemnified against

307

claims by sub-contractors and suppliers but not out-of-pocket expenses and, of course, our profits are blown.'

'Can't we take them to arbitration?'

'What's the point? Even if an arbitration board finds in our favour, war contracts have an overriding provision that the Admiralty isn't liable for any sum that exceeds the contract price. We'd still lose.'

'Why did we sign such a contract?'

'We wanted our share of navy business. However'—he blew more smoke—'every cloud has a silver lining. I met Gideon Rowe in Rabat. He's a shifty little swine but I'm sure he has money behind him. They're building a whole new town out there on the North African coast and an oil depository just over the river. Rowe's the front man. There's no Spellman. They bought out a shipping company that went bust in the middle of the war. Now they're a shell company that hasn't a single vessel on its books.'

'I take it you know who Gideon Rowe is married to?'

'Paget's ex-wife, Pickering's sister-in-law,' Forbes said. 'Obviously we're dealing with an Anglo-French consortium and Pickering is a major stakeholder. In other words, the French are building the town and the British are building the ships. They've already bought a steel works in the Midlands, which is a very shrewd thing to do if you're in for the long haul.'

If she had fallen for Geoffrey, if she had become his lover, she would have kept everything from Forbes. That, perhaps, had been the idea, the plan.

She said, 'I assume they've bought a steel works

308

to reduce primary costs when it comes to building a tanker fleet.'

'Sure,' Forbes said, 'why put money in somebody else's pocket when you can keep it in your own?'

'In that case,' Lindsay said, carefully, 'why not buy a shipyard, too?'

'Precisely what I was thinking,' Forbes said. 'Take over Franklin's, alter the berthing capacity, reduce the workforce and cut wages, forge iron-clad union agreements on the strength of a ten-year order book, and save yourself, what— something close to a couple of million quid in the process.'

'Martin will never sell.'

'I'm not asking Martin to sell. I'm asking Martin to lay out capital from the reserve, to borrow if necessary, to do whatever is necessary to nail this Anglo-French contract.'

'Can we do that, Forbes?'

'If we can build tankers cheaper than they can, yes.'

'And if we can't?'

'We go to the wall,' said Forbes.

CHAPTER THIRTEEN

Seeds of Dissent

The birthday party turned out to be no party at all but, rather, a genteel birthday 'tea', with creams, jellies, tiny triangular sandwiches and a pink iced cake decorated with marzipan flowers and miniature candles.

Maeve reckoned that Ewan had been sold a bill of goods by a mother who was unwilling to acknowledge that seventeen was not the same as seven and that her boy was becoming a man.

Ewan slumped at the head of the table, crowned with a paper hat and surrounded by gift packages which, after cutting the cake and squirming through a half-hearted chorus of 'Happy Birthday', he might actually be permitted to open. His sisters were having more fun than he was. They had brought along two school friends, a snotty pair who had expressed faint romantic interest in Dot and Katy's big brother and had consequently been co-opted to make up numbers.

Four o'clock until seven, so said the invitations, after which, Maeve thought ruefully, our nannies will collect us and take us home to bed.

She caught Harry's eye, and winked.

He pursed his lips and frowned, warning her not to make trouble.

Harry was by far the largest person at table. Her grandfather dotted in and out, trailing his wife and the day-maid, bearing plates of sandwiches and jugs of lemonade and smiling a paternal smile in a studied sort of way that indicated that he too was embarrassed by the juvenile nature of the proceedings.

By five o'clock Maeve was so bored that she had scoffed a dozen of the tiny sandwiches and couldn't get the taste of tinned salmon out of her mouth. Two platefuls of strawberry jelly helped only a little. The lemonade was sickly sweet and she was amazed by the ability of Dot and Katy and their snotty chums to knock the stuff back by the gallon, and at the greed of Martin's children, who ate like poorhouse orphans who hadn't seen food in a week.

Encouraged by Cissie, the younger cousins exchanged paper hats, messed about with jelly and grappled in an obstreperous manner while Ewan sat in solemn state, saying little. When instructed, he blew out the candles on his birthday cake then, wheezing a little, thanked everyone for coming and, flanked by his mother and father and armed with a pair of kitchen scissors, began to open his presents. Three copies of *Treasure Island*, a copy of *King Solomon's Mines*, a stamp album, several compendiums of games, a penknife the size of a vegetable marrow, and an assortment of sensible garments piled up on the table. Philip's choice of a hand-charging pocket torch went down well, though, and Harry turned up trumps with a cravat so garish that no self-respecting cad would be seen dead in it.

Eyes down, squirming just a little, Ewan intoned the required responses. 'Thank you so much, just what I always wanted. How nice. How handy. How terribly good of you to go to all that bother.'

In a state of excitement Maeve waited for Ewan to reach for the big square-shaped parcel that she had wrapped with her own fair hand. She had no idea why her heart was beating so rapidly or why she wanted to impress a boy she didn't really like. She watched him cut the string neatly with scissors and unwrap the book. It was bound in black morocco, gilt-edged, and weighed a ton. It had cost her the best part of a month's modelling but she knew, just knew, it would give Ewan Calder pleasure.

He shed the brown paper and, intrigued, peered

at the volume.

His mouth opened and his brows shot up.

'My God!' he exclaimed, to his mother's dismay. 'Oh, my God! Maeve, it's—it's wonderful.'

He opened the book reverently and studied the plates.

'Ewan,' his mother said, 'do not be rude. Show everyone what Maeve has been kind enough to . . .' She leaned forward, peeped over her son's shoulder and, with an involuntary gasp of horror, stepped hastily back.

Ewan held up the hefty tome, open at a grisly steel engraving, and announced, 'It's the *Egyptian Book of the Dead*.'

Dorothy, Katy and their snotty friends shrieked and buried their pretty faces in their napkins, and the very youngest Franklin shrank back, whimpering, '*Muuum-mmmy*.'

'That's right, Alistair,' Ewan said, 'it's a mummy, or will be once it's been disembowelled and had the blood drained and the organs replaced with—'

'Ewan!' Tom Calder said, sharply.

'Sorry,' Ewan said. 'I'm forgetting my manners.'

Tucking the book carefully under one arm, he stepped away from the table and, in full view of everyone, planted a kiss on Maeve's lips.

'Thank you,' he whispered. 'Thank you a million times.'

'I thought you'd like it,' Maeve said, smugly.

'I do, I do,' said Ewan. 'You know I do,' and kissed her once more.

Harry, red-cheeked and furious, flung himself away from the table.

And Aunt Cissie shouted, 'Charades.'

When the doorbell rang Forbes put down his fork and glanced at his watch.

'Is that the kiddies? They're early. Will they want dinner?'

'I doubt it,' Arthur said. 'Cissie will have done them proud.'

Eleanor rose and went out into the hallway to open the front door. A moment later the thump of heavy footsteps sounded and a moment after that a door slammed upstairs. Eleanor returned to the dining-room.

'Not happy, either of them,' she said.

'What about Maeve?'

'Maeve isn't with them.'

'Where is she?' said Forbes.

'I didn't dare ask,' said Eleanor.

The housekeeper had dealt with innumerable fits of childish pique over the years and calmly seated herself at the dining table and resumed eating.

From the parlour came the unmusical *plink-plink-plink* of someone hammering on the piano keys.

Lindsay sighed. 'I'll go.'

Pushing her plate away, she left the dining-room, crossed the hall and opened the parlour door. She stuck her head around it and peeped into the room. Her younger son was seated at the piano, thumping out a tune with two stiff fingers. Lindsay cleared her throat. 'How—how was the party?'

'Rotten.'

'Oh!' Lindsay said. 'Where's Maeve? Isn't she with you?'

'She stayed behind.'

'Where's Harry then?'

'Upstairs.'

'Phillip . . .'

'I don't want to talk about it.'

Lindsay closed the parlour door, climbed the stairs and knocked on the door of Harry's room. She could feel the hurt, the sulk, emanating from the room like a bad smell. She turned the handle and went in. Harry lay on top of the bed, hands behind his head, staring at the ceiling.

'Was it that bad?' Lindsay said.

'Yes.'

'Why is Philip so angry?'

'We quarrelled,' Harry said, gruffly.

'What did you quarrel about?'

'Nothing.'

She felt a sudden wave of compassion for her first-born. He was so tall, so manly that it was all too easy to forget that he was still, really, a boy. She went to the bed and, moving his feet, seated herself.

Harry continued to stare at the ceiling.

'Is it Maeve?' Lindsay said. 'Has Maeve done something to upset you?'

He pursed his lips, fighting tears, and sat up.

'She stayed behind at Tom's house.'

'What's wrong with that?' said Lindsay.

'She stayed behind with—with *him*.'

'Ewan?'

'Yes.'

Lindsay tidied the lock of hair that hung over his forehead.

'You don't like Ewan, do you?' she said.

'I *hate* him,' Harry answered. 'He's a rotter,

314

Mum, a rotter.'

'Well, he is rather strange,' Lindsay said. 'But . . .'

'He wants her all to himself.'

'I see.'

'No, you don't see, you don't see at all.'

'Harry, Harry.' Lindsay tried not to sound patronising. 'Are you annoyed because Maeve pays more attention to Ewan than she does to you?'

'I don't care. No, really, I don't.'

'She's a very pretty girl and pretty girls can be flighty.'

'She kissed him.'

'Well, it is his birthday.'

'She kissed him when she didn't have to.'

'What did Tom have to say about it?'

'He didn't do anything to stop her.'

Lindsay was tempted to put her arms about her lovelorn son and offer comfort in the old-fashioned way but instinct told her that he would only put up with so much mothering.

'Perhaps it was just a friendly kiss, Harry.'

'No, it wasn't. It wasn't, Mum.' He fixed her intently, his cheeks and brow scarlet with hostility. 'He talks about her—Ewan—he says things about her that aren't—aren't right.'

'What sort of things?'

'Nasty things,' Harry confided in a hoarse whisper.

'I didn't know Ewan was like that.'

'He is, he is, believe me. He isn't in love with her. He just wants . . .' Harry lowered his head to his arms. 'He isn't in love with her, that's what I mean.'

Lindsay strove to keep all trace of alarm out of her voice.

'Are you in love with her, Harry?'

'What if I am?' Harry said. 'It's all right if I am. I'm her cousin. Ewan's her—well, I don't know what he is, but it still isn't right, is it?'

'No,' Lindsay said, evenly. 'No, Harry, it isn't.'

'Ewan can't marry her, but it's all right with cousins, like you and Dad.' He caught her hand. 'You have to tell her it isn't all right, not with Ewan Calder. You have to put a stop to it, Mum.'

She experienced a sudden dislike of Sylvie Calder's daughter, the girl who was causing her son so much heartache. And a loathing of Forbes: Forbes for the sly and selfish charm that had wooed her into his arms, into his bed and had blinded her to his many vices all those years ago. Now, it seemed, the legacy of deception and betrayal was being passed down through the generations, carried in the blood like a rare disease.

Perhaps it wasn't just Forbes, though, perhaps it wasn't just the hereditary characteristics of the McCullochs she had to fear, for young Ewan Calder was a Franklin through and through, and Harry, her poor, lovely, innocent Harry, was her son too.

'Leave it with me,' she said, brusquely. 'I'll see what I can do.'

'You won't tell Dad, will you?'

'Why not?'

'He likes Maeve and won't hear a word against her.'

'No,' said Lindsay, lying, 'I promise I won't tell Dad.'

*   *   *

316

Two days before the crucial board meeting, Forbes had a lot more on his mind than young love or, for that matter, love between folk who were old enough to know better. He was relieved that Lindsay had not found out that Stella Pickering had been with him in Morocco. He had provided Arthur with an account of what had occurred in Rabat without mentioning Stella's part in it. If it hadn't been for the damned birthday party, he would have briefed Tom over the weekend too.

Soon after dinner he went up to his room and fished from his shelves several books on contracts to bolster his lack of aptitude with figures and plug the little gaps in his knowledge of company law.

He was not best pleased when, around ten, Lindsay interrupted him.

'What's wrong?' he said. 'Isn't Maeve back yet?'

'She came in about half an hour ago.'

'Is she all right?'

'Yes,' Lindsay said. 'She at least appears to have enjoyed herself. It isn't Maeve I'm worried about. It's Harry.'

'Harry?' Forbes swivelled his chair round. 'What's biting Harry?'

'He thinks he's in love with Maeve McCulloch.'

Forbes snorted. 'Of course he thinks he's in love with Maeve. For God's sake, Linnet, he's a normal healthy young man.'

'She's playing fast and loose with Ewan Calder, and Harry hates it.'

'It's only the hormones,' Forbes said. 'Isn't that the fashionable word for it—the hormones? In my day there were no such things as hormones.'

'Forbes, you're going to have to tell Harry.'

'Tell Harry what?'

'That Maeve may be your daughter.'

'Even her mother, Sylvie, doesn't know for sure who Maeve's father is.'

'You think she's your child, Forbes, don't you?' Lindsay said. 'That's why you sent Sylvie money and set her up in a hotel in Dublin.'

'Call it guilt or call it responsibility, I wasn't willing to take the chance that the girl wasn't mine. Yes, I sent Sylvie money when she asked for it.'

'Now you've met Maeve, do you *feel* she might be your daughter?'

He rubbed a hand over his face. 'What difference does it make?'

'An enormous difference if Harry and she fall in love.'

'They're far too young to contemplate marriage.'

'But not to fall in love,' Lindsay said. 'I will *not* see Harry hurt, Forbes. I will *not* stand by and see his life ruined because you're too cowardly to tell him Maeve may very well be his half-sister.'

Forbes hesitated. 'There is an alternative.'

'What alternative?'

'You could tell Maeve.'

'What a heartless devil you are, Forbes,' Lindsay said.

'Did it not occur to you that perhaps Gowry brought her to Glasgow because she was becoming too difficult to cope with. Maeve's a lovely girl, but the one thing that's not in doubt is that she's Sylvie Calder's daughter and that—that streak is in her, too.'

'Streak?' Lindsay said. 'What streak?'

'She needs a man.'

'That isn't a sin, Forbes, that isn't a streak.'

'It is if you're Sylvie Calder's daughter.'

'Or your daughter.'

'Now it's my fault, is it?'

'Of course it's your fault, Forbes. My God, if it isn't your fault whose fault is it? Are you going to tell Harry?'

'No.'

'Then I will.'

She felt a little welling of contempt for him. Even after twenty years of marriage Forbes did not know her well enough to realise that she would never take it upon herself to destroy his son's faith in him.

'Look,' Forbes said, 'I don't want to see the boy hurt any more than you do, but it isn't up to me to tell Harry. If you suspect there's something going on I'll write to Gowry and he can come and take her away.'

'First Sylvie, now Maeve. You'd ruin her life to save your own neck.'

'My neck's got nothing to do with it.'

'Your reputation, then.'

Pride and ambition ran in the Franklins, but not the petty, pitiless strain of McCulloch selfishness that smothered love at its source. She was tempted to throw his affair with Stella Pickering into the conversation just to see how he would react. For a man with the moral scruples of an alleycat, Forbes had no right to put his reputation before the happiness of his children, not just Harry and Philip, but Maeve, too.

Forbes eyed her as if he were contemplating murder.

He said, 'Would you be happier if I went away?'

'Went away?'

'Would it be better for all of you if I left? I know

319

you wouldn't miss me, Linnet, but what about the boys?'

'That's not a solution,' Lindsay said. 'That's a threat.'

He shrugged. 'You could sell me your shares in Franklin's. I'd give you the best possible price for your voting stock and then we would quietly separate.'

'Separate?'

'You go your way. I go mine.'

'To where—to whom would your way lead?'

'About as far as Aydon Road,' Forbes said. 'If you think so little of me, Lindsay, perhaps you'd be better off without me.'

'Are you suggesting that we divorce?'

'Separate,' Forbes said. 'There'd be no scandal. You'd have the house, the boys and a great deal of money—and I'd have the business.'

'Only yesterday,' Lindsay said, 'you told me that the only way we could survive is by sticking together. Why have you changed your tune?'

'It's you who've changed your tune, Linnet,' he said. 'In any case, this isn't an opportune time to discuss our future. What's important right now is to secure Franklin's future, and that's what I'm trying to do.'

'In other words,' said Lindsay, 'you're not going to do a thing about Maeve and Harry? You want to brush it under the carpet with all your other responsibilities and use Franklin's as an excuse? Do you really want to buy me out, or are you just trying to scare me?'

'No,' Forbes said, 'I'm not trying to scare you.'

'Then why did you suggest it?'

'To put you in your place, that's all.'

320

'My place?'

'My mother marries some scrounging Irish tinker, my son's gone all moony about my niece; next thing you'll be telling me that Enid's put too much starch in my collars and expect me to sort it out. I appreciate what you did in London, what you found out from Paget, but you must leave the rest of it to me now. For ten years you've taken little interest in what goes on in Franklin's boardroom, let alone the yard. You've reaped the benefits, shared in the profits and done nothing to help. That's fine, that's as it should be, perhaps, but now my back's to the wall, Lindsay, and I do not expect you to plague me with matters that are not my concern.'

'Your son's welfare . . .'

'The girl will go back to Dublin as soon as she's good and ready. Harry will forget all about her. It's—what do they call it these days—calf love?'

'What if Maeve decides not to go back to Ireland? What if she decides she likes it here and wants to stay? God knows, she's been given every encouragement to do so by you, by all of us.'

'Keep your eye on her by all means but otherwise leave it alone.'

'Is that your last word, Forbes?'

'It is.'

'And the other thing?'

'What other thing?'

'Separation.'

'Oh that! It was just a passing thought, dearest, just a passing thought,' Forbes said and with a gesture that was all too conclusive, lit a fresh cigarette and turned once more to his books.

Ross seated himself beside her on the divan and put an arm about her shoulders. She turned into him and allowed herself to weep. It had been years since she had wept in front of another person but her embarrassment was secondary to her need to be comforted.

'There,' Ross said, patting her with one huge paw. 'There, there.'

The trail to church that morning had been more like a wake than a family outing, the atmosphere over lunch fraught with tensions that Forbes's forced cheerfulness had served only to increase. She hadn't planned on baring her soul to her painter cousin. She'd called on him that Sunday afternoon only to see *The Captive Heart* finished at last—or so she'd told herself.

The painting was still on the easel, the easel turned to face into the room so that Maeve and the young man, even the sheep, all seemed to be staring at her. She had politely admired the painting, had politely congratulated Ross on capturing Maeve's stormy beauty on canvas and then, almost without being aware of it, had found herself telling him her troubles and, seated on the divan, had suddenly begun to cry.

'There, there,' he said, and hugged her to him.

He smelled not of turpentine and walnut oil but of shaving soap and tobacco, a smell that reminded her just a little—just enough—of her grandfather and, thinking of Owen, of her youth, she wept all the more.

Ross had the sense to say nothing. He held her loosely and let her snivel into the lapels of his summer jacket, blubbing until the weight had gone from her heart and, gradually, her tears dried up.

She looked up at him, her nose and eyes red as rowan berries, two fat teardrops still clinging to her lashes, her underlip pushed out as if she were pouting. He fished a clean handkerchief from his breast pocket and dabbed her eyes with it. She almost expected him to spit on the cloth and give her face a wipe the way Grandfather Owen had done when they were all small and grubby.

'I'm—I'm sorry,' she said.

'No need to be,' Ross said.

'I don't know what came over me.' She took the handkerchief and blew her nose, then, drawing away from him a little, looked up. 'I should go, shouldn't I? I've taken up far too much of your time.'

'I've all the time in the world,' Ross said, gently. 'Besides, you're in no fit state to be seen in public. I'll make tea in a minute. I could certainly do with a cup, I don't know about you.'

He made no move to quit the divan, to leave her, as it were, in the lurch.

She leaned against his shoulder, still shaky. She could feel the edge of his beard, silky soft, brushing her brow.

'You're very good,' she said. 'I mean, it's not as if we've been close, Ross. I mean, I hardly know you well enough to tell you all these things.'

'Cousins have what I believe they call a shared history, even if you've never been to Paris or fought in the war.'

Lindsay managed a watery smile.

Ross said, 'I hadn't realised that things were so bad between you and Forbes. Has he never mentioned the possibility of—ah—of separation before?'

'No, never.'

'It's not something you've thought of either, I take it.'

'Oh, I've thought of it, thought of leaving him . . .'

'For the chap in London?'

'Geoff Paget? Lord, no.' She sat up. 'Once, years ago, I was tempted to run off with Geoffrey, when things were very bad at home with Forbes.'

'Yes,' Ross put in. 'I remember the rumours.'

'True, most of them,' said Lindsay. 'I didn't run off with Geoffrey, though, and I'm jolly glad I didn't, given the way he's turned out.'

'Not the man you thought he was?'

'Few men are,' Lindsay said. 'I didn't stay out of loyalty to Forbes, though. I suppose I stayed out of loyalty to Franklin's.'

'The family?'

'No, the firm.'

'More or less one and the same thing,' said Ross.

'I thought I would cut a fine figure in the boardroom,' Lindsay said. 'I imagined myself becoming very rich and famous as the chairman of Franklin's shipyard, the only female chairman on the whole of Clydeside. Silly.'

'Hmm,' Ross agreed. 'Rather.'

'It didn't take me long to realise that being Owen Franklin's granddaughter and having voting shares in the company wasn't nearly enough to equip me to understand, let alone manage, a shipbuilding yard. It's something that men do well, that men understand; it's in their blood.'

'Are you saying you no longer care about Franklin's?'

'I care very much about Franklin's, but not—it's not mine, not really. I support it through Forbes. I support Forbes, and he supports Franklin's.'

'And now he wants to buy you out?'

'I don't think he's serious. I think he was just—well, testing the waters.'

'This woman you mentioned, is she Sir Andrew Pickering's wife?'

Lindsay nodded.

'How much influence does she have over Forbes?' Ross asked.

'I don't know.'

'Are you sure they're having an affair?'

'They travelled to Morocco together.'

'And yet you're still willing to support him?'

It was a question she hadn't put to herself, not in so many words. She thought about it for a moment, then said, 'Yes.' She hesitated. 'Does that seem strange to you?'

'A little,' Ross said, 'but then I'm not a woman.'

'I'm glad of that,' said Lindsay and, before she made a fool of herself again, got quickly up from the divan. 'Now, enough nonsense for one day. How about that cup of tea?'

'Darjeeling or Earl Grey?'

'Earl Grey, I think,' said Lindsay.

*   *   *

It was after five before she returned to Brunswick Crescent. A sympathetic ear and a shoulder to cry on had restored her spirits. The evening was warm but cloudy and there was a coppery tint in the air that might, she thought, presage thunder. Lights were on in the drawing-room and as she climbed the steps, she saw her father, Forbes and Harry standing with their backs to the window.

She wondered if Cissie or Tom had called round to make a fuss about the friendship between Maeve and Ewan. The prospect of stepping into another squabble held no appeal. She had already decided to heed Forbes's advice and let well alone, at least for the time being.

She didn't ring the doorbell but let herself in with her key. She lingered in the hallway, straining her ears to catch the drift of the argument in the drawing-room but heard instead a great booming, unfamiliar laugh, so hearty that it seemed almost theatrical.

Puzzled, she took off her hat and hurried into the room.

The whole family was gathered there, Eleanor and Maeve included, all staring at the old woman and the stout man who were seated on the sofa, holding hands. For a split second she almost didn't recognise her mother-in-law, for Kay was cherry-cheeked with laughter and Lindsay couldn't recall ever having seen the woman laugh before.

'And then, by Gad,' the groom was saying, 'her ladyship here draws herself up to her full five feet and, filled to the brim with pith and Guinness, filled to overflowing she was, she says, "Offisher, offisher, you won't be findin' any rebels here since they've all gone down to the shithouse at the bottom o' the garden an' I'm tellin' you to do the same."'

The bride, blushing, dug a sharp elbow into her beloved's well-padded ribs and, giggling, declared, 'I never said any such thing, Cyrus.'

He pulled Kay to him, tucked her under his

enormous arm, and chafed her head with his knuckles. 'Ay-hay, my sweetheart, but those were your thoughts, were they not now? Those were the very thoughts that was swimmin' in your pretty head. I can read her mind, see, read her mind like it was an open book. We're two peas in the one pod, my lovely Kay and me.' He looked up, saw Lindsay in the doorway and his expression hardened. 'And who might you be, then?' he demanded, as if she not he were the intruder.

'That's her, that's the one I told you about,' Kay answered before Lindsay could open her mouth. 'She's married to my Forbes.'

Cyrus Coffey did not rise. He shifted his weight forward on the sofa and stuck out a hand. He looked, Lindsay thought, more like a Biblical potentate than an Irish farmer. She ignored the proffered fist.

'Sure and will you not shake my hand then,' Cyrus Coffey said. 'Since we're family now and will soon be neighbours, I'm thinking it would be better if we were also friends.'

'Is that what you think, Mr Coffey?' Lindsay said.

'Snippy,' Kay said. 'Snippy, like I told you, Cyrus.'

'Aye, I can see that,' Cyrus Coffey said, and sat back.

*　　　*　　　*

Dinner was late; mutton chops in onion gravy, a little bit dry and overcooked, for which Cook was not to blame.

'Why didn't you ask them to stay to dinner?' said

327

Forbes.

'Why didn't you?' said Lindsay. 'She's your mother.'

'She's my sister,' Arthur put in, 'and I wouldn't have asked them to stay for all the tea in China.'

'Coffey obviously expected to be fed,' Forbes said. 'I thought we'd never get rid of him.'

'What on earth does she see in him?' said Arthur.

'He's young,' said Eleanor.

'He's not young,' said Forbes. 'He's sixty if he's a day.'

'He's young by your mother's lights,' said Lindsay.

'Another Irish gigolo,' said Arthur, shaking his head. 'Dear God!'

'What's a gigolo?' Philip said.

'A man who a woman pays to—to marry her,' said Maeve.

'Did Gran McCulloch pay Mr Coffey to marry her?' Philip asked.

'No,' Lindsay answered. 'Of course not.'

'Why did Grandee say . . .'

'Philip—enough!' said Eleanor Runciman.

'I'm only asking.'

'Well, don't,' said Harry.

They ate in silence for half a minute.

'Is Mr Coffey after Gran's money?' Philip said.

'Gran doesn't have any money,' Harry told him.

'If Mr Coffey's a farmer,' Philip persisted, 'why isn't he in Ireland, farming?'

Maeve had received help from the old woman at the time of the Easter Rising but she was well aware that since then her grandmother had followed some plan or purpose of her own. Maeve was sure that Charlie and Peter meant more to her grandmother than Uncle Forbes. She didn't know why she was so certain but her instincts had been honed by an upbringing on the streets of Dublin where secrecy, suspicion and a promiscuous awareness of death were part of your education, whether you liked it or not. Her mother's friend Fran Haggarty had been shot in cold blood in the yard of the police station while her mother had been forced to watch. She had lost her own friend, Jansis, to a bullet, had seen the Shamrock, her home and her mother's livelihood, reduced to rubble by an English shell while her dad was off fighting in Flanders with and for the English. Perhaps she had earned the right to hold opinions.

She said, 'Mr Coffey's no more a farmer than I am. You saw the boots, you saw the leggings. They're not what farmers wear. They're what officers in the brotherhood wear these days.'

'If he's an officer in the brotherhood,' Harry asked, 'what's he doing in Glasgow?'

Maeve answered, 'He'll be after money to purchase guns.'

'Guns,' said Philip. 'My goodness!'

'Who'd be daft enough to give him money?' Harry said.

'Who do you think, son?' said Forbes. 'He got some out of me once and I'm sure he'll try again. However, if that is his game he's in for a big disappointment.'

'I wouldn't be so sure,' said Maeve. 'They can squeeze blood out of a stone when they set their minds to it.'

'Not this stone, sweetheart,' said Forbes. 'This stone is going to need every penny he can muster.

Last year Franklin's made a nice profit but this year it looks as if we'll be running at a loss.'

Arthur nodded. 'By the year's end the ship-owners will have us at their mercy, and if the government signs the American treaty to limit warship building then the pressure will become even greater.'

'You mean we'll be broke, Grandee?' Philip said.

'Unless we tender competitively for any work that comes up,' Arthur said, 'we'll have seven empty berths on our hands.'

'But,' said Forbes, 'that isn't going to happen.'

'Why, Dad?' said Harry.

'Because I'm not going to let it,' said Forbes.

*   *   *

The board met at ten o'clock on Monday morning. In addition to the partners and company secretary, Forbes had summoned Hugh Latimer, the firm's accountant, and Eustace James, its legal adviser.

By lunchtime Martin was willing to concede that a policy of expansion and refurbishment, paid for out of capital, might be required if Franklin's hoped to ride out the downturn in trade. He was less happy about the 'shady' nature of Forbes's bid for tanker contracts and reluctant to accept Forbes's assurance that Gideon Rowe and Spellman were backed by an Anglo-French consortium of unlimited financial resource.

Hot soup, cold meats and salad were served at half past twelve.

By a quarter past one Forbes had everyone back round the table to discuss cost estimates and demands. Nobody was happy with the notion of buying steel from Bradford's and it was agreed that Arthur would accompany Eustace James to the negotiation and do his best to talk Gideon Rowe and Spellman out of that contentious clause.

Lindsay had followed the arguments back and forth all morning without saying much. She was all too aware that tea-table chat was no substitute for the knowledge that Forbes, Tom and Martin had gained by a lifetime of experience. While the men discussed the fine points of contract law, her attention wandered to the window where rain had given way to watery sunshine and the hills beyond the Clyde were dappled, fresh and green.

For a time there in the spring she had supposed that she might find love again. Geoffrey had turned out to be a sad disappointment but at least he had taught her that her history could not be altered or reshaped by love alone. She thought of Maeve with her dark good looks and lively nature and wondered how history might shape Maeve's future. She thought, too, of Ross and where he might be at this moment, wondered if he had ventured out of doors, if, with *The Captive Heart* complete, he had quit the studio in Flowerhill Drive for the country or the park, or if he had already applied himself to his next commission and, like the draughtsmen in Tom's office, was stooped over a sheet of graph paper labouring to find a form that would encompass a requirement and a vision, one within the other and, in the long run, both the same.

'Is that agreed then, Lindsay?' she heard Forbes say.

And, though she had no idea what he was talking about, she answered crisply and obediently, 'Yes.'

In spite of her better judgement, Maeve was drawn to her grandmother's house like a moth to a candle flame. She had no liking for the man her gran had married. She knew the type too well to be fooled by his garrulousness and mock jollity. He was one of those thundering Irishmen whose noisy charm hid slyness and opportunism.

She ran upstairs and knocked on the door of the flat.

It was mid-afternoon now. All morning, she had mooched about the house in Brunswick Crescent, drinking tea, chatting to Cook and Enid, trying to avoid the eye of Miss Runciman who seemed to know what she was planning to do and who, of course, was morally bound to disapprove.

She knocked again, heard laughter, a false booming laugh that signified nothing. He called out, 'Patience, my sweetheart, patience,' and opened the door.

He looked, she thought, like her grandfather in his dog days, except that he was younger and not quite so stout. He held a glass of beer in one hand and a newspaper, an Irish newspaper, was tucked under his arm. He wore a collarless shirt, and military-style trousers with the braces hanging down. The buttons of his fly were undone, the fly wide open as if—Maeve shuddered—he intended to pull his new bride into the tiny hall and have his way with her there and then.

'Ay-hay,' Cyrus Coffey said. 'So it's yourself, is it?'

'Where's my gran?'

'Gone to the butcher's.'

332

'I'll come back another time,' said Maeve, promptly.

He transferred the newspaper from one armpit to the other and showing no haste or embarrassment buttoned himself up.

'No,' he said. 'Come in.'

'What for?'

'A chat, that's all; a chat.'

Reluctantly Maeve let him lead her into the kitchen.

She noticed at once that the walls had been papered, the doors scraped and varnished, the sink and window surrounds painted a clean bright green. The old gas fittings had been replaced too and a glass globe hid the naked light bulb overhead.

'Did you do all this yourself?'

'I did, I did, lass. Do you like it?'

'Aye,' Maeve said. 'It's very nice. Must've taken a while to do.'

He stuffed the newspaper behind a cushion, finished his beer and rinsed the glass under the tap at the sink. He swung round, folded his arms and leaned against the sink. 'No time at all for an expert like me.'

'Is that what you are—an expert?'

'In the trade, I'm the best.'

'Trade?'

'Painter an' house decorator.'

'Oh!' Maeve said, nonplussed.

'What did you think I was?'

'I thought you said you were a farmer.'

'I never said no such thing,' Cyrus Coffey told her.

'My uncle had the impression . . .'

'Aye, well, your uncle has the impression I'm a leadin' light in the Brotherhood of Erin. He's wrong on both counts.'

'What are you then?'

'I told you, I'm a house painter. In a week or two, I'll stick notices in shop windows and see if I can earn a bit of spare cash.'

'For the cause, for the brotherhood?'

'For to stock the larder,' Cyrus Coffey said.

Maeve seated herself on the arm of one of the chairs by the fire. The grate and the range surrounding it had been leaded and polished to a high coal-black gloss; even the brass fender shone like gold.

Cyrus Coffey waited patiently for her next question.

Maeve said, 'So you're not with the brotherhood after all?'

'Sure an' I didn't say that. I said I'm no leadin' light in the organisation, and I'm not. I'm Cork, an' the brotherhood's mostly Wexford now.'

'So you don't know my Uncle Charlie?'

'Everybody knows Charlie McCulloch. He's a good man, a hard worker on the political front. Sure an' I've met him often.'

'My Uncle Peter?'

'On the run.'

Whether it was the buttery accent or the man's bluff features she felt as if she were back in Dublin, lurking in somebody's back kitchen, waiting for the rap on the door that would have everybody looking up.

'Is there a price on Peter's head?' she asked.

'Aye, lass, there is.'

'How much?'

'Five hundred pounds.'

'You wouldn't turn him in, would you?'

'Even if I knew where he was—never.'

'Gran—your new wife, she always knows where he is,' said Maeve.

'You're askin' to see if I'm an informer, are you not now?'

'Maybe I am, maybe I'm not.'

'I've marched with them,' Cyrus Coffey said, 'shoulder to shoulder. Have I not had my head bashed a few times by the same sticks as was bashin' the heads of your uncles? No, no, I'm no damnable informer.'

'What did you do with the money my Uncle Forbes gave you?'

'Spent it on a marriage licence, boat fares an' a honeymoon.'

'You told him it was for the brotherhood, didn't you?'

'Another mistook impression,' Cyrus Coffey said.

'If I'd given my money to Gran would you have spent it, too?'

'Like as not,' he said. 'Is it to give her money you've come here today?'

'No, it is not,' said Maeve, stiffly. 'You're a trickster, Mr Coffey, that's what you are. You're just tradin' on those fancy trousers and boots.'

'Gifts,' Cyrus Coffey said, 'from a dear, good friend.'

'Aye,' Maeve said, sceptically, 'an' who might that be?'

'Trotter's his name,' Mr Coffey told her. 'Turk Trotter.'

*　　　*　　　*

335

Slender ribs of clouds lay over the Govan shore but the sky to the west was clear and blue and the tenements that faced Aydon Road so clean and pink that they might have been built that very afternoon.

The whistle had sounded, loud and piercing. Berths, shops and sheds had cleared and Franklin's employees had poured out through the gates, heading for the pubs in nearby Whiteinch, or for home. When Forbes, Lindsay and Arthur left the office block, however, only a few stragglers remained and the yard was uncannily quiet. No late shift now, no night shift, no overtime. Up and down Clydeside stoppages were taking their toll. Soon there would be pay-offs at Franklin's too. An order for one tanker wouldn't save them; the workforce would have to be whittled down.

The Lanchester was parked in what had once been stables. Taking Lindsay's arm, Forbes led the way along a path behind the testing tank and across an angle of the almost-deserted yard to the motor-car, Arthur following on behind. Lindsay seated herself up front next to Forbes. She watched him tug on his driving gloves and work the tight leather down into the roots of his fingers and wondered if he had taken Stella Pickering for a fast ride in his new machine yet, and if the woman had been suitably impressed.

Forbes fired the engine and drove out of the main gate into Aydon Road.

There were children playing on the cobbles, little girls skipping rope, boys kicking a tin about as if it were a proper football. There was a heavy smell of cooking in the evening air.

Over his shoulder, Forbes said, 'If we can solve the problem of where we buy our steel, Arthur, I think we might pull this thing off, don't you?'

'How long will it take to alter and extend the existing berths?'

'We'll bring the yard managers in tomorrow to work out an estimate.'

'We can't even begin until we have the destroyers out of the way.'

'I'm tempted to start dismantling the blasted things immediately.'

'I wouldn't be too hasty, Forbes,' her father said. 'We don't know for certain that the navy will cancel, though I admit it does seem likely. However, the moment we take one bolt out of one hull we'll have the shop stewards jumping all over us, demanding reassurances about job security.'

'That's true,' Forbes said.

'When will Tom have a model ready for testing?'

'July, probably.'

'Quick,' said Arthur. 'Not too quick, I trust.'

'We won't go until we're absolutely ready,' Forbes said, shouting to make himself heard above the roar of the engine. 'I'm looking to the future, Arthur, as you may have gathered, not for one tanker order but two or even three.'

'Hah!' her father said. 'You're dreaming, Forbes. It isn't as it was in the good old days when Frank Traynor would send us a postcard saying, "Two more of the same, please." Do you remember?'

'I remember,' Forbes said, and laughed.

Her husband was enjoying himself, Lindsay realised. His old bounce and thrust were back with a vengeance. She wondered if Martin and Tom realised just what Forbes had put on the table, that

337

he was gambling the whole future of Franklin's on his ability to outwit a consortium of faceless financiers.

Forbes nosed the Lanchester across Dumbarton Road and on to the hill that took them away from the river routes into the heights of Brunswick Park.

Five minutes later, Lindsay stepped on to the pavement and climbed the steps to the door of the house in which she had been born and raised.

She wanted a bath, a change of clothing, a gin and tonic, and dinner. She was suddenly tired, tired of all the squabbling and negotiating, of the handshakes and back-stabbing, the promises and betrayals, of her husband's reckless optimism. In the months ahead there would be talk of little else. Even thinking about it bored her. She needed something else, something new, something that had not been engineered by Forbes, something in which her husband had no hand and over which he held no sway.

She opened the door of the parlour and looked in.

The boys were seated close together on the fender, legs stretched out, backs to the fire that burned in the grate even on summer evenings. Philip steadied himself with a hand on the post of the mantel. Harry's arms were folded and he was talking in a low voice. Phil nodded. They looked, both of them, very serious and grave and very grown up.

'Hello, chaps,' Lindsay said, rather too breezily. 'Dinner in half an hour.'

Her sons stared at her as if she were a stranger. The topic that engaged them was apparently more interesting than the prospect of dinner.

338

She made to close the door and head upstairs.

Harry rose quickly, and called out, 'Mother, wait.'

Lindsay came back into the parlour. 'What is it now?'

'It's Maeve,' Harry said.

'Maeve? What's wrong with Maeve?'

'Dunno,' Harry said. 'She's locked herself in her room . . .'

'And won't come out,' Philip said.

'In her room? What's she doing in her room?'

'Weeping buckets, I think,' said Phil.

*　　　*　　　*

'Married?' Lindsay said. 'Are you sure, dearest?'

'Aye, Mr Coffey told me. Turk married a girl from Kildare. I don't know what he was doing in Kildare. Hiding from the coppers, maybe. They made him do it. I'm sure they made him do it. He doesn't love her. He can't love her. He always loved me. I was always his girl. She's going to have a baby.'

'Mr Coffey may have been misinformed.'

'Turk's been married for half a year. He's back in Wexford with his wife waiting for the baby to arrive. Gran knew all the time and never said a word.'

'Does he still have a price on his head?'

'Aye.'

'If what you've heard is true,' Lindsay said, cautiously, 'perhaps you're better off . . .'

Maeve was heavy and soggy, like a bag filled with sand. Her weight caused Lindsay to rock on the edge of the bed. She had been comforting the girl as best she could but there was more anger than misery in Maeve's attitude.

'Better off without him? Aye. The pig, not tellin' me himself.'

'Did Mr Coffey meet Turk?'

'He says he did. Gran too. Met him when they went to see Peter. Peter's on the run with Turk. They were both in Wexford but when Gran left to go back to Cork with Mr Coffey, Peter was already on the move.' Maeve wrapped an arm around Lindsay's shoulder as if her aunt were the victim and she the comforter. 'Everybody knew what Turk was doin', what he was up to. I heard stories, but I chose not to listen. God, but I should have listened, should I not?'

'If he had been the man for you—'

'The man for me? He was always the man for me.'

'No,' Lindsay said, 'you only thought he was.'

'I did. I thought he was. He said he was.'

'How long since you last saw him?'

'Near two years.'

'And he didn't write?'

'Not him, not that ignorant pig. He was too busy—too busy dandlin' that tart from Kildare. Well'—a shuddering sigh—'good bloody luck to him.'

'What else did your grandmother tell you?'

'Is that not enough for one day?'

'Did she say anything about your father?'

'Da? No, why would she?'

'Maeve, wouldn't you like to go home?'

'Home?'

'To see your mother and father.'

'Why?'

'I just thought that under the circumstances you

340

might like to go back home for a visit,' Lindsay said, 'just a visit.'

'What's the bloody point in goin' back to Dublin now the horse, you might say, has bolted?' Maeve scowled. 'Are you tryin' to get rid of me?'

'Of course not.'

'If you are, all you have to do is say the word.'

'I wouldn't dream of it,' said Lindsay. 'Stay as long as you want, Maeve. We're pleased to have you here with us. Besides, Ross has it in mind to paint your portrait.'

Maeve wiped the corner of her eye with her knuckle.

'Another picture?' she said. 'Another picture with Bobby?'

'No,' Lindsay said. 'A double portrait with me, I think.'

Lindsay was just enough of a snob to be relieved that Maeve would not become the wife of a wild Irish rebel and that with childish infatuation put away she might settle in Glasgow and in due course find a nice young man to marry her, though it would not, could not be Harry. Odd, Lindsay thought, how feelings merged and changed, like the colours on Ross's palette.

'Oh!' Maeve said, without conviction. 'That'll be lovely.'

'I'm sure it will,' Lindsay said. 'Now, if you're up to it, why don't you wash and change, put on a brave face and come down and join us for dinner. Do you think you could manage to eat something?'

'Aye,' Maeve said, with one last sigh, 'I think I probably could.'

CHAPTER FOURTEEN

The Long Weekend

The hiring of chauffeur-driven limousines for anything other than weddings or funerals was considered the height of extravagance and when a Rolls-Royce Silver Ghost collected them at half past ten on a blazingly hot Saturday morning, it occurred to Lindsay that her painter cousin must either be very rich or very foolish. Ross had decreed that they would travel to Edinburgh in style, however, and he was already on board, all trim and tailored in a hand-cut suit of cream-coloured linen that looked cool and comfortable in comparison with her father's formal frock coat and grey waistcoat.

They had barely left Brunswick Crescent—Miss Runciman, Enid and the boys all waving from the steps—before Arthur said, 'I thought we were lunching with a lord and lady?'

'We are,' said Ross.

'Then why are you wearing linen?'

'Because,' Ross said, 'because, my dear old uncle, I am an artist and we artists are expected to be disreputable.'

'You don't look disreputable,' Lindsay said.

'I will become more so as the day wears on,' Ross promised.

'Will Lord Faid be at the lunch, too?' Maeve piped up.

'I expect so,' Ross said. 'I gather Lady Faid rules the roost even if it's the old boy who foots the bill.'

'I've never met a lord before,' said Maeve, wistfully.

'I've met a few in my day,' said Arthur. 'All very disappointing. I was under the impression you didn't attend social functions, Ross. What's coaxed you out of your lair today?'

'Lady Faid is paying me a great deal of money.'

'Oh, you liar.' Lindsay gave his knee a slap. 'You've already been paid.'

'True,' Ross admitted. 'I suppose I'm just showing off.'

'Showing off?' said Maeve. 'Showing off what?'

'My talent,' said Ross. 'My wardrobe. My family.'

'You mean us?' said Maeve.

'Of course I mean you,' said Ross.

'Do you usually take your models to hangings?' Maeve said.

'No, but then I've never had a relative as a model before.'

Shopping, and spending Uncle Forbes's money, had taken Maeve's mind off Turk Trotter's marriage but she was, understandably, still prickly.

'I see,' she said. 'I'm respectable enough to be introduced to this Edinburgh lady but poor old Bobby Shannon isn't? Is that what you're saying?'

Ross had taken the least comfortable seat and was braced against the motion of the motor-car as it nosed through traffic on the way across Glasgow.

'Bobby,' he said, '*was* invited.'

'I don't believe you.'

'But,' Ross went on, 'he refused.'

'Did you really ask him to come to Edinburgh with us?'

'I did,' and Ross, 'and he wouldn't.'

'Did you tell him I'd be there?'

'I made a point of telling him,' Ross said. 'I suggested you might like to have him along for a bit of company, but—no, poor old Bobby just wasn't up to hobnobbing with a real live lord. I think he prefers to keep the enemy at a safe distance in case he discovers that aristocrats aren't all ogres.'

'You asked him for my sake?'

Ross nodded.

'That was nice of you, jolly nice,' Maeve said and then to Lindsay's surprise—and Ross's too—kissed him on the cheek.

*   *   *

At first sight Ann Street was a small, charming by-way with narrow gardens fronting the houses and modest Georgian pediments peeping through the trees. It did not seem like the sort of street in which a peer of the realm would choose to have a residence but as the Ghost bumped over the cobbles to the gate, Ross explained that the house was only a *pied-à-terre* and that the Faids' estate in Ayrshire was much more impressive.

The door was opened by a maid, not a butler. Arthur was relieved of his topper and gloves before they were ushered into a long room on the ground floor where, to Lindsay's surprise, *The Captive Heart* was already on display. Somehow she had imagined that the painting would be ceremoniously unveiled. The painting was too large for the room and a line of guests were pressed against the interior wall, like victims of a firing-squad, struggling to obtain an overall view of Lady Faid's expensive acquisition.

Ross slipped his arm into Lindsay's. 'I don't

know much about art,' he murmured, 'but I do know what I *don't* like.'

'Who are they?'

'Friends of the Faids, plus agents, dealers and journalists. Lady Faid is not one to pass up an opportunity to advertise her mother's literary legacy. You can't blame her. You pays your money and . . .' He detached himself suddenly from Lindsay and held out his hand, wrist arched like that of a Restoration fop. 'Lady Faid, how good of you to put on a show.'

The woman had the craggy features of a fishwife and sharp, observant brown eyes. Her hair was silver, tightly curled, and she wore a dress of dark plum-coloured velvet that Lindsay thought more suited to a night at the opera than an informal summer's day luncheon. Hovering behind her was a timid little man in a grey lounge suit and an unstarched shirt who seemed content to do nothing but smile and smile and, now and then, cock his head to indicate a vague sort of interest in what his wife was saying.

'My husband,' said Lady Faid, nonchalantly.

'Sir,' said Ross.

'Your lordship,' said Lindsay.

Arthur bowed, Maeve dropped a curtsey and Lord Faid smiled and smiled and, like a wisp of grey smoke, drifted away on the trail of his wife as she dragged Ross off to meet people of importance.

'Well,' Arthur said, *sotto voce*, 'wasn't that a thrill? Question is, where's the champers and the grub—and how soon can we get out of here?'

Flanking Ross's painting on the long wall were two deal tables upon which were arranged many of

345

the late Fiona McWhirter's sentimental romances, some in cheap gaudy editions, others in the plain, faded cloth bindings that had been fashionable fifty years ago. Four glass-fronted bookcases at the rear of the room contained what Lindsay took to be the complete *oeuvre*, all uniformly bound in rich tooled morocco. Between the cases and a French door that opened to the garden below, was a portrait of Fiona herself, a portrait that had clearly not been painted by Ross Franklin.

'Dear God!' said Arthur. 'Is that Fiona? Do you suppose she always went around with her eyeballs turned up to heaven?'

'I doubt if it's an accurate likeness,' Lindsay said. 'On the other hand, Papa, if you'd written several million words in purple ink on green paper perhaps your eyes would roll upwards, too. It's a Chubb, unless I'm mistaken. He was a lot better at painting prize cattle than minor literary figures.'

'Minor literary figures!' said Arthur. 'Wash your mouth out with soap, child. Are we not in the proximity of greatness?'

'Actually, no, I don't believe we are,' said Lindsay.

The din from the nave, as it were, had grown hectic. It seemed that Ross was being lionised or, if not lionised, at least patronised which, in an Edinburgh context, amounted to much the same thing.

Set against hazy sunshine from the window, he was taller and hairer than anyone in the room and looked almost saintly in his linen suit. Lindsay gave him a little wave, waggling her fingers.

He smiled and ruefully raised his brows.

'And you? You are?'

Lindsay and Arthur promptly turned around, but the speaker's attention was focused exclusively on Maeve or, more accurately, on Maeve's bosom.

'Sure, sorr, an' I'm nobody,' Maeve replied, affecting a rustic Irish brogue. 'Might I be askin' now who you might be yourself?'

'You're a very pretty nobody,' the man said. 'I'm Gillis.'

'Gills,' said Maeve, wide-eyed, 'like in fish?'

He laughed mirthlessly and, continuing to ignore Lindsay and Arthur, edged closer to his quarry.

'Gillis,' he said. 'Gillis Graham. Have we, perchance, encountered each other before? I rarely forget a pretty face.'

He had slick pomaded grey hair, a nose that lay on the wrong side of bulbous and, Lindsay thought, the most avaricious eyes she had ever seen, eyes that weighed and calculated every chance to enhance his own reputation, whatever that reputation might be.

'Now, sorr,' said Maeve, simpering, 'if I was to be wearin' a plaidie an' a ragged skirt an' showin' you my legs, you'd know me quick enough.'

The possibility that Maeve and he had engaged in a commercial transaction that he, in the honourable tradition of Edinburgh gentlemen, had been too drunk to recall, gave Gillis Graham pause.

Reluctantly he raised his gaze from Maeve's bosom.

'Oh!' he said. 'How, yes, how are you?'

'Very well, thank you,' Lindsay replied.

'And you are?'

'Friends of the artist,' Lindsay answered.

'Ross, jolly old Ross, what a card!'

Screened by Gillis Graham's shoulder Maeve puffed out her cheeks, arched her eyebrows and wrinkled her pretty little nose.

'Know Ross well, do you, Mr Graham?' said Arthur.

'Gave him his first review, first mention. He was frightfully pleased.'

'He would be, I'm sure,' said Lindsay. 'How long ago was that?'

'Ages ago, simply ages.'

'An' what, sorr,' Maeve put in, 'will you be sayin' about his latest masterpiece, that one on the wall there?'

'I will say that once more Ross Franklin has done his patron proud by holding up a mirror to nature. I do not favour his traditional approach to composition or his obsessive use of glazes but as an example of *faux* French classicism, though somewhat less than *à la mode*, it fulfils its intentions.'

'In another words,' said Maeve, 'you don't like it?'

'Subjectively, no, it runs counter to my interpretation of what legitimately constitutes art.'

'I take it,' said Lindsay, 'you've studied the painting.'

'Thoroughly,' Mr Graham said, without a blush. 'Absolutely thoroughly.'

'An' he didn't even recognise me,' said Maeve. 'What a shame.'

'Recognise you?' Gillis Graham said. 'What on earth do you mean?'

'She means,' Arthur put in, 'that we aren't here to look at the painting either. We're only here for a free lunch. Which way, sir, to the buffet?'

And Gillis Graham, temporarily flummoxed, pointed to the stairs.

*　　　*　　　*

Stella wore a bathing suit and mermaid slippers that Forbes, for some odd reason, found erotic. In fact he found almost everything about Stella Pickering erotic, for the old saw about absence making the heart grow fonder applied in equal measure to other parts of his anatomy, too.

Ronnie and the servants had been given the day off. Forbes and Stella were alone in the house and she had been equally eager to quit the goldfish-bowl living-room for the bedroom. Afterwards, she had showered and donned the floral bathing suit and, with factory whistles sounding noon, had poured two very large gin and tonics at the bar upstairs and had led Forbes out to the sunlit balcony.

The unseasonable heat reminded him of Morocco. If it hadn't been for the drone of traffic and the occasional squeal of a passing railway train, he might have imagined himself back in the garden of the Oudaiya, trapped in the dreamlike moment before the Frenchman made his appearance.

A brownish haze blanked out the tenements and tall cranes of Clydebank. He could see nothing but the tops of trees and the vague outline of hills— and Stella; Stella curled on the deck lounger like a gigantic pussycat, sunglasses perched on her brow. A tall glass of gin and tonic, tinkling icily, printed a prism of colour on her bare thigh. She had volunteered no information about her husband's whereabouts and Forbes had been too preoccupied to enquire where Drew might be and when he would return. He sipped gin and smoked a cigarette in a silence so companionable that it was almost uxorious.

Stella's eyes were closed, the cold glass resting against her chest.

'Another one?' Forbes enquired.

She opened an eye. 'Another what?'

'G and T, of course. Are we lunching in, or out?'

'In.' Stella drew up her legs. 'I take it you've no objection to spending an afternoon with me?'

'None whatsoever.'

'Grosvenor pie and pickles, salad, fruit compote to follow. I've chilled a bottle of hock that Drew's been hoarding for a special occasion.'

'I doubt,' Forbes said, 'if Drew would consider this a special occasion.'

Stella smiled and held up her empty glass.

Forbes rose and took it from her. A few shards of ice and a curl of lemon peel were still in the glass. On impulse he drank the dregs, then, with the lemon peel tucked into his cheek, leaned down and kissed her.

'Same again?'

'Please.'

He turned to head into the living-room, to the bar.

'Forbes,' Stella said, 'why haven't you asked about Drew?'

He stopped and leaned against the warm glass doors.

'I trust you, dearest,' he said.

'What time is it?'

He could just make out the tower of Singer's factory hanging in the heat haze, but couldn't see the hands on the clock face.

'Twelve thirty, or thereabouts,' he said. 'Does it matter?'

'Just about now my dear husband will be conversing with your wife.'

Forbes swallowed the curl of lemon peel.

'My wife's in Edinburgh.'

'I know.'

'In Edinburgh with her father and my niece. Our cousin's painting is being unveiled. Buffet lunch thing at some lord's house. Faid, Lord Faid. Surely Drew won't be there.'

'He will, you know,' Stella said. 'Faid's a governor of the Bank of Caledonia who, as it happens, has agreed to finance certain purchases that my husband's company is about to conclude.'

'Bradford Steel, for instance?'

'Yes, darling, a sound investment, don't you think?'

The burning sensation in Forbes's throat wasn't entirely due to lemon peel.

He said, 'Are Faid and the Caledonia bank tied to the tanker business?'

'Forbes.' She sat up. 'I love you. If you don't know it by now then you never will. I'm asking you to trust me, darling, trust me an awful lot.'

'He's after Franklin's, isn't he? All that stuff and nonsense about you protecting your private financial interests behind your husband's back ...'

'I told them you wouldn't fall for it.'

'Them? Who else is involved?'

'Mitchell Hussey.'

'Good God!' Forbes snapped. 'If you think I'm selling Franklin's to a man who makes his living from tinned mutton ...' He peered down at Stella

351

from what seemed like a very great height. She looked smaller now, fatter, almost shabby. 'Are you telling me Hussey knows about Marjorie and me?'

'How do you think my husband persuaded him to join the consortium?'

'And Paget?'

'Geoff? Nothing, a cog in the wheel. He's up to his ears in debt and now he's lost his good looks he's not much use to anyone. Drew will find him a job somewhere or other just to keep him out of mischief but, candidly, our Geoffrey is heading for the breaker's yard.'

The acid rising in Forbes's throat diminished.

He said, 'Whose idea was it to have Paget seduce my wife?'

'Geoffrey dreamed that up himself. He always had a soft spot for your missus, darling. I believe the general intention was to ruin your marriage as well as your business.'

'Lindsay's too sensible to fall for that trick.'

Stella lay back, arms behind her head, breasts swelling against the tight elasticated top of the bathing suit. She kicked her feet in their rubber slippers as if she were treading water. She seemed very pleased with herself.

'God, yes,' she said. 'I could have told them that right at the start. It's all so ridiculously devious, though there is a very, *very* great deal of money involved, one way or another.'

'How many investors in the oil consortium?'

'Drew, of course, Giddy, Mitchell Hussey and two French backers, in addition to the straightforward loans the Bank of Caledonia have agreed to put up against my husband's floating assets.'

'Hold on,' said Forbes. 'Are you telling me Drew's willing to mortgage his cargo fleet to finance the Moroccan scheme?'

'Seed corn,' Stella said. 'He calls it seed corn.'

'He's gambling everything on oil, then?'

'With Drew nothing is ever a gamble,' said Stella. 'It's a competition, rather like a rugby football match; head down and charge. He's set his mind on Franklin's and if he can't persuade the partnership to sell then he'll nibble away until he owns a controlling interest. He has experts in company law behind him and can, I believe, steal Franklin's out from under your nose. Unless . . .'

'Unless?'

'You beat him to it.'

'How do I do that?' said Forbes.

'Buy up shares from the other partners, trade fifty-one per cent to Drew in exchange for a stake in the consortium's profits and chairmanship of Franklin's board. You'll have what you want and Drew will have what he wants, with a minimum of compromise on either side.'

'Whose idea is *this*, Stella? Yours, or your hubby's?'

'Mine, darling, all mine, all my own work.'

'What about Hussey? I thought he wanted revenge.'

'Mitchell Hussey is a bitter old man but greed will get the better of him in the long run,' Stella said. 'By the way, you made an enormous impression on my French brother-in-law. Giddy thinks you and he are birds of a feather. He'll stand up for you if and when it comes to it.'

'Lindsay will never sell. No more will Martin. I reckon they'd rather go public than let Franklin's fall into your husband's hands.'

'In six or eight months' time,' Stella said, 'shares in shipbuilding will be a drug on the stock market. By Christmas, going public may not be a viable option, Forbes. Amalgamation? Possibly—but who'd want to amalgamate with a firm that has nothing to offer but empty berths and a blank order book?'

'If I use the articles of partnership that Owen Franklin imposed all those years ago to acquire majority shares then trade them to your husband none of the Franklins will never speak to me again.'

'Would that bother you, Forbes?'

'No,' Forbes admitted. 'Probably not.'

'There's one other thing you'll get out of it, something my husband doesn't own and will never control.'

'What would that be?' Forbes asked.

And Stella Pickering answered, 'Me.'

*   *   *

Strips of warm chicken on a bed of lettuce and red cabbage leaves kept Arthur happy. He was on to his second helping before most of the guests detached themselves from the wine table and tottered down to the buffet in the kitchen.

By that time Arthur, Maeve and Lindsay had found sanctuary on a rustic bench under a mimosa tree at the far end of the back garden and were keeping themselves to themselves for, as Maeve put it, 'one dose of Gillis bloody Graham is enough for one day,' a sentiment Lindsay heartily endorsed.

It was not unpleasant in the garden, for the

drone of Edinburgh's busy bees airing their opinions was carried aloft on the thermal currents that the hot afternoon had generated. Later, as soon as Ross had freed himself from the Faids, the limousine would drive them up to the Old Town and Maeve would be treated to a tour of Edinburgh Castle and a stroll down the Royal Mile before they set off home.

Lindsay stooped to put her empty plate on the flagstones.

Her father said, 'Dear God! Is that who I think it is?'

Lindsay looked up. Andrew Pickering, grinning like an ape, was striding up the length of the garden towards them. He hadn't gone the whole hog with frock coat and grey waistcoat but looked uncomfortable in blazer and flannels, as if he had somehow failed to judge the tenor of the luncheon and was all too well aware of it. His coarse, swarthy face was tinted crimson and he carried a glass in one hand and a balled-up handkerchief in the other. He mopped his brow, stuffed the handkerchief into a breast pocket, and held out his hand.

'Arthur,' he said.

Arthur juggled plate and glass and, rising, shook hands.

'My daughter, Lindsay,' Arthur said. 'Her niece, Maeve.'

'The lassie from the picture?' said Drew Pickering.

'Aye, sir,' said Maeve.

'A fine likeness,' Drew Pickering said. 'He's very handy with the brush, your uncle. Shipbuilding's loss was art's gain.'

'Would you care to join us?' Lindsay enquired, politely.

'No, no, not at all, thank you. I'll have to be off soon. I've an appointment at two. I just popped in to please Harry Faid. Couldn't leave without saying "Hello," however.' He swayed on the balls of his feet and peered down at Lindsay with strange, unflattering intensity. 'I believe you've been a guest in my house, Mrs McCulloch. Unfortunately I was too occupied on that occasion to introduce myself. Perhaps you'll come to Merriam House again—for dinner.'

'That would be delightful,' Lindsay heard herself say.

She could well imagine this coarse-featured man covering the plump blonde woman as a stallion covers a mare; the image slithered unbidden into her mind as her eyes met his. She wondered what Stella Pickering could possibly have seen in Forbes that had induced her to cheat on her husband.

'With your husband, of course,' Drew Pickering said. 'Forbes and I have so much in common now that I can guarantee you an interesting evening.'

'I'll look forward to it,' Lindsay said.

The dinner invitation would never materialise, of course; the threat was enough to indicate that he knew what was going on between Forbes and his wife. Pickering was too cunning a negotiator to come straight out and tell her the truth. He was probing to discover if she knew of Forbes's affair and if, separately or together, they might make capital out of it. She remained amiable, hiding the anger in her heart, anger at Forbes, at Pickering, at the plump blonde wife; not blind anger, though, not destructive, for her mind was already racing with all sorts of plans and possibilities.

The hand again, no soft paw like Ross's, but big, leathery and hard; 'Goodbye, Mrs McCulloch, for the time being,' Drew Pickering said. 'Young lady, Arthur—enjoy your lunch. So nice to have met you.'

'Likewise, I'm sure,' said Maeve.

But Sir Andrew Pickering had already gone striding off down the garden path towards the kitchen, mopping his brow as he went.

* * *

Squabbling was not uncommon on the tennis courts that snuggled under the shadow of the handsome sandstone terraces of Brunswick Park South.

Gentlemen in white flannels and ladies in long skirts often bickered over a line call or argued about the score and, in the heat of battle, an uncouth junior had been known to hurl his racquet to the ground or batter a ball out into Madison Street, the latter offence punishable by one month's suspension in a season that was already all too short for true devotees of the game.

Philip was a true devotee. He would have spent every waking hour on the courts if that had been possible. He longed for the day when, like Harry, he would graduate from being a junior member, attain all the rights and privileges of tennis citizenship and could no longer be kicked off the beautiful red clay in the middle of a set just because four old dears fancied a half-hour of push and slap or some autocratic team player felt compelled to practise serving.

357

With Grandee in Edinburgh, and not a cloud in the sky, Phil fumed and fretted all morning long and, already dressed in smart white flannels and an open-necked shirt, walloped through lunch at a rate that Harry could not match.

Harry was no longer merely a brother; Harry was the key that would unlock the gate of Brunswick Park South's tennis courts, for club rules stated that junior members could not play on Saturdays unless accompanied by an adult, which exalted status Harry had recently attained.

It was after two o'clock before Phil managed to drag his brother over the hill to Madison Street, clutching a net of balls, his racquet, a brand-new celluloid sunshade and a bottle of barley water. All that was now required was for Harry to scribble their names on the waiting list for the next free court and, in a half-hour or so, he would be out there, lunging and plunging, wrestling not with life's minor problems but with ground strokes and smashes.

Philip lounged on a patch of scratchy grass adjacent to the steps of the pavilion and scowled at the four players who occupied the end court, willing them to wind up their set.

He heard the gate behind him squeak but did not turn round.

He watched Mrs Sampson miss a simple volley and giggle as if she'd done something awfully clever. Then Ewan Calder slithered on to the grass beside him and, without any preamble whatsoever, demanded, 'Where is she?'

'Uh!' said Philip. 'What are you doing here?'

'Where is she?'

'You're not a member, Ewan. Go away.'

'I said, where is she?'

'Maeve? In Edinburgh.'

'What's she doing in Edinburgh?'

'Gone to look at a painting.'

'She said nothing to me about going to Edinburgh.'

'Why would she?' Philip said. 'Look, Maeve isn't here, old chap, and since you aren't a member . . .'

'We were supposed to be going to the pictures.'

'Pictures?' Philip darted a glance at his cousin. 'What pictures?'

'The cinema,' said Ewan. 'Any cinema.'

'Are you telling me you've taken Maeve to the pictures?'

'She should have had the decency to tell me,' Ewan said, wheezing. 'Least she could do would be to tell me she was out of town. Yes, often.'

'How often?'

Ewan smiled. 'Often enough.'

'She never said a word to Harry about it.'

'Of course not. She's having too much fun with me.'

'Fun? What does that mean—fun?'

Ewan glanced at the crowd on the steps of the pavilion, elegant athletes and slender ladies leaning on the rail, smoking and laughing.

Harry was not among them. Harry was nowhere to be seen.

Ewan Calder leaned towards Philip and, cupping a hand to his mouth, whispered a triumphant definition of 'fun' into his naïve young cousin's ear.

'*Madge*,' Mrs Sampson shouted. '*Madge, I say, look out.*'

The boys came rolling down the slope, squealing like stoats, and crashed into the netting behind the court. Mr Sampson shook his fist and dumpy little Mrs Sampson jumped up and down in a state of agitation as the boys—one of them a stranger— grappled in the gravel trough and shook the netting so violently that it sagged against the uprights and discharged a fine rain of rust all over the unfortunate Madge.

'*Stop it, stop it this instant.*'

Deaf to all entreaties, Philip grasped his cousin by the throat, pinned him against the netting, then, with a motion akin to a well-executed backhand, punched Ewan's simpering smile and brought blood spurting from Ewan's mouth and nose.

'*McCulloch? Where's Harry McCulloch? Someone fetch the brother.*'

Blood sprinkled Ewan's shirt and stained his smart grey flannels. Blood flew about in all directions and all you could see, so Madge claimed forever after, was the poor boy's tongue flapping in a pool of blood while the McCulloch creature went on hitting him without an ounce of pity or reserve.

Philip was still punching when Harry and three other stalwarts from the Academy hauled him off, still trying to kick his cousin who lay huddled in a foetal position in the gravel trough with his hands over his head.

They dragged Phil away—it took four of them to do it—dumped him on the grass and held him there until all the fight went out of him.

Phil stared up at the blue sky, at Harry's chin and upside-down mouth, and with a soft, shuddering sob, his only sign of remorse, said, 'Did I kill him?'

'Unfortunately not,' said Harry.

*   *   *

The Ghost whisked Maeve and Arthur off up the steep cobbled dog-leg of the Mound and left Ross and Lindsay on the corner of Princes Street Gardens.

Ross had declared that he'd had enough of history and that the Old Town of Edinburgh held no charms for him. It had been agreed that Lindsay and he would spend a couple of hours in the gardens while Arthur conducted Maeve on a lightning tour of the castle. They would rendezvous at five o'clock on the steps of the National Gallery and drive home together.

Lindsay was relieved to step down from the bustle of Princes Street. The gardens were busy too but no one seemed to be in a hurry. On the paths, mothers pushed babies in perambulators or restrained small toddling children, girls flirted, weary wives gave their feet a rest and old men dozed on the benches; bold squirrels and timid pigeons begged to be fed and a band played Scotch airs in the stand by the tearoom near the gilded fountain.

She took Ross's arm and adapted her step to his. He lit his pipe and puffed along at no great pace, looking up at the wall of rock that dominated the gardens. She wondered again how her cousin's view of the world differed from her own, what shapes and hues he saw that she did not.

He took the pipe from his mouth, and said, 'I'm glad that's over with.'

'It wasn't so bad, was it?'

'Bad enough,' Ross said.

'At least the lady appreciated the picture.'

'She liked it well enough, I suppose. Said I'd

361

caught the essence of her mother's vision—whatever that means. Back-handed compliment, perhaps.'

'Why do you pretend to be a cynic? I think it's all pose.'

Ross gave her arm a squeeze. 'Some of it, not all.'

'What's next on your agenda?'

'A commission from Sir James Gloag. He requires a rousing scene from *Tam o' Shanter*. Gloag's President of the Burns' Society and is determined to present the society with one of my masterpieces before he retires in January.'

'Sonsy young witches prancing around a bonfire in a kirkyard?'

'Possibly, or Tam's old mare sacrificing her tail on the brig, perhaps,' Ross said. 'I'm really rather good at painting horses.'

'Maeve would make a wonderful "sonsy" witch, would she not?'

'She would, indeed,' Ross agreed. 'However she might not be too keen on being draped in a short shirt and hung from a rope pulley every Sunday afternoon for months on end. Flying is essential for witches, you see.'

'I assume that Bobby Shannon's too young to model for Tam?'

'Not necessarily. Why do you ask?'

'Maeve likes him.'

'I gathered as much.'

'He's a decent young chap, by all reports.'

'Seems to be,' said Ross.

'Tom Calder thinks highly of him.'

'Lin, are you match-making?'

'Of course not.'

362

'You are. You're match-making. Why?'

She told him about Maeve's jilting by the Irishman, and the havoc caused in the household.

She concluded, 'Forbes says she needs a man.'

'Forbes would, wouldn't he?'

'Maeve isn't wicked, but she is—I don't know—restless. She has no restraint, no self-discipline, no patience. She isn't like us in that respect.'

'I should hope not,' Ross said. 'I wouldn't wish that on anyone.'

'She isn't right for Harry, and never will be.'

'Snob!'

'No, it isn't that at all.'

'Are you afraid of her, Lindsay?' Ross said.

'Not afraid, not exactly afraid. Afraid *for* her, perhaps.'

'Pack her off home to Dublin.'

'That wouldn't be fair,' Lindsay said.

'To you, or to Maeve?'

'To both of us,' Lindsay said. 'Besides, she doesn't want to go.'

Ross knocked the dottle from the bowl and put the pipe into his pocket.

'Match-making,' he said, 'isn't an exact science, you know. Bobby Shannon may give every appearance of being a diamond in the rough but, like the rest of us, he might be hiding his true nature. He looks after a crippled sister, I believe, so he doesn't come unencumbered.'

'In any case,' Lindsay said, 'he may not care for Maeve.'

'I think he does, at least a little bit.'

'Do you care for Maeve?' Lindsay asked.

'Of course, but I don't—what's the fashionable word?—I don't "fancy" her. She's very pretty, intelligent and lively, but I'm old enough to be her father.'

'When did age ever stop a man making a fool of himself?'

'If I decide to make a fool of myself it won't be with Maeve.'

'Oh, so there is someone in your closet, is there?'

He nodded. 'Yes, there is. However, to return to the question of my commission: I won't begin laying out the Burns' painting until September and if Maeve hasn't run off with the milkman in the interim, I'll make a stab at transforming Bobby Shannon into a tipsy middle-aged farmer and Maeve into a witch—but only on one condition.'

'Which is?'

'That you keep your promise to sit for me this summer.'

'Together with Maeve?'

'A double portrait, not done in the studio.'

'Really? Where then?'

'Somewhere,' Ross said, 'in the great outdoors.'

'With sheep?'

'Cattle, I think,' said Ross, 'lots and lots of cattle.'

'Good Lord, is that how you see me, like a country loon?'

'How I see you, my dear cousin, is my secret. Rest assured, though, I'll pick an appropriate setting, and do you full justice.'

'By holding up a mirror to nature?'

'Certainly not,' said Ross. 'After all, a promise is a promise, is it not?'

And Lindsay soberly agreed.

*   *   *

The boys were seated on the sofa in the parlour. They looked clean, almost shiny. Eleanor had insisted that they bathe and change before she doctored Philip's wounds with Pond's cold cream and iodine. His right hand was bandaged, a bruise on his cheek was the colour of a damson and his upper lip was swollen. He did not meet his grandfather's eye and let Harry to do the talking.

Arthur, hands on hips, shouted, 'Banned?'

'For life.'

'Both of you?'

Harry nodded. He was too decent to lay all the blame on his brother's shoulders or declare himself hard done by. 'I think the committee wants a word with you, too.'

'Good God, they're not kicking *me* out, are they?' Arthur said. 'Come to think of it, I'll just save the beggars the trouble, and resign.'

'I'm sorry, Grandee,' Phil said, thickly.

'Does your father know about this?' Lindsay asked.

'Not yet,' Harry answered.

'Where is your father?'

'Not home,' said Harry.

'What in God's name were you fighting about?' said Arthur.

Philip peeped up at Maeve. 'Nothing.'

'Nothing, you say! You and your cousin Ewan knock lumps out of each other in full public view and you have the gall to tell me it was nothing,' Arthur said. 'What happened to Ewan in the wake of the slaughter?'

'They took him home,' said Harry.

'Is he hurt?' Maeve asked.

The boys, both of them, squinted up at her.

'Who took him home?' said Lindsay.

'Some of my friends,' said Harry.

'I'd better go round there,' said Arthur. 'Straighten it out.'

'No,' Maeve said. 'Please don't.'

'It's not up to you, young lady,' Arthur told her. 'Harry, who started it? Did Ewan Calder start it? What was he doing at the tennis club, anyway? He isn't a member. He doesn't even play.'

'We—we had words,' said Harry.

'Words?' said Arthur.

Harry licked his bottom lip and pushed the lock of hair back from his brow. His caution and perplexity were all too apparent.

'He insulted me,' Harry said.

'So you stuck him first, did you?'

'Harry didn't touch him,' said Philip. 'It was my fight.'

'What on earth did Ewan say that was so terrible?' Arthur asked. Philip glanced at Harry who gave an almost imperceptible shake of the head. 'You're not going to tell me, are you?'

'It—it was a—a personal matter, sir,' Harry said.

'Personal matter, was it? Well, I'm going round to Calder's house right now to get to the bottom of it. If you won't tell me perhaps Ewan will.'

Lindsay put a hand on her father's arm. 'I don't think that's a good idea, Papa. If Tom wants an explanation then he'll come round here. No point in making matters worse.'

'Banned for life,' said Arthur. 'Isn't that bad enough?'

'It's only a tennis club,' Lindsay said.

'My tennis,' Philip mumbled, dolefully. 'Oh, dear!'

Maeve kneeled at her cousin's feet and whispered, 'Does it hurt?'

Harry rose immediately. Philip followed suit.

'If you want us,' said Harry, 'we'll be upstairs.'

They walked out, leaving Maeve kneeling before the sofa, her brow pressed down on the cushion.

'Now do you understand?' Lindsay whispered to her father.

'Uh-huh!' said Arthur, nodding. 'I think I've got the picture.'

*　　*　　*

Forbes flung open the office door and greeted Tom with a jovial wag of the head that was so inappropriate that it was almost insulting.

'Didn't see you at church yesterday, old man.'

'We decided not to attend,' Tom said.

'Arthur was looking out for you.'

'Was he, indeed?' said Tom.

Forbes pulled out a chair. 'How is your boy?'

'His nose isn't broken but he has two loose teeth.'

'Really!' Forbes said, showing surprise.

'Did you punish him?' Tom said.

'Punish Phil? Why should I? By all accounts, it was a fair fight.'

'Cissie wouldn't agree with you, Forbes.'

'No,' Forbes said. 'I don't suppose she would.'

'She's been waiting all weekend for you to call round and apologise.'

'Look, Tom, you and I both know who caused the bad blood between our lads. It's not Maeve's fault, of course. If anyone's to blame, it's you.'

'Me?'

'I take it you've had a word with the young Lothario.'

'I don't know what you're talking about, Forbes.'

'Ewan—he's fallen hook, line and sinker for your granddaughter.'

'Is that what Philip told you?'

'He didn't tell me. He didn't have to. It's as plain as a pikestaff what the squabble was about. I don't know what was said to trigger it, but it certainly got Philip's dander up and Ewan, I suspect, was spoiling for a fight when he showed up at the tennis courts.'

'Ewan isn't a fighter. His asthma . . .'

'Sure now,' said Forbes, 'there's his asthma.'

'Ewan was only protecting Maeve's honour.'

Forbes laughed aloud. 'Her honour?'

'Ewan's too embarrassed by the whole episode to say any more.'

Tom was less sure of his son's integrity than he pretended to be. He had been shocked when Dorothy had come running round to the bowling green late on Saturday afternoon to fetch him. By that time the doctor had been and gone and Ewan was propped up in bed, with Cissie spoon-feeding him a milky drink and his sisters fawning over him as if he were a war hero. It had been late into the evening before he had screwed up sufficient courage to go into the bedroom and confront his son, man-to-man. He was too old to cope with the passionate nature of youthful emotion now and felt separated from Ewan, not by the boy's eccentricities but by his arrogance.

'My lot won't talk either,' Forbes said. 'If it's any consolation, Tom, they've been chucked out of the tennis club. I don't suppose that'll cut much ice

368

with Cissie but it means a lot to them.'

'I don't think Cissie's going to forgive you that easily.'

'Oh well,' said Forbes with a sigh. 'That's women for you, women all over. They create so much trouble and then blame us for it. I just hope this isn't going to affect our friendship, that's all.'

'Our friendship?' said Tom.

'Our good working relationship, I mean,' said Forbes. 'I'm counting on your support, Tom, and it would be daft to let a squabble spoil what's shaping up to be a wonderful opportunity.' He paused, then said, 'So—I don't want to hear any nonsense about Cissie persuading you to throw in the towel.'

'Throw in the . . .'

'Retire.'

'Cissie doesn't want me to retire.'

'Oh, sorry. It seems I've spoken out of turn,' said Forbes.

'What's Cissie been saying?'

'I've probably caught the wrong end of the stick. Put it out of your mind, entirely,' Forbes said. 'I thought—I mean, I had the impression that now you're nearing sixty . . .'

'What does my age have to do with the boys?'

'They're the future, Tom. What happened at the weekend proves it.'

'Proves what?'

'They're flexing their muscles, aren't they? Squabbling about girls and shaping up to a future in which you and me will have very little say? I take it Ewan isn't interested in becoming a naval architect?'

'It's not something we've really discussed.'

'You never bring him to the yard.'

'No, I admit he hasn't shown any interest in what I do.'

'You see,' Forbes said, spreading his hands.

'Actually,' Tom said, 'I don't see.'

'We're the last of our generation, Tom. Once we've secured the future of Franklin's shipyard—well, it might be time for us to bow out.'

'You'll never bow out, Forbes,' Tom said. 'You're barely forty. You've years and years ahead of you, a lot more productive years than I have. What are you trying to tell me? Come on, out with it.'

'There's never been any bad blood between us, Tom,' said Forbes, 'so all I'm saying is, don't do anything hasty. Franklin's needs you. You're the best designer of ships on Clydeside. It would be almost impossible to replace you.'

'Replace me?' Tom said. 'I'm not going anywhere.'

'I know, I know,' Forbes said. 'I get tired of it too, so damned tired.'

'Forbes . . .'

'However, we must struggle on, mustn't we? For the sake of the children, if nothing else, we do have to struggle on.' He tapped both hands on the desk and got briskly to his feet. 'Right. I've had my say. I hope it's cleared the air a bit. You have my apologies, if any are necessary, for what happened at the weekend. No point in trying to fathom what's behind it. They're sensible fellows, our sons. I'm sure it'll all blow over.' He laughed. 'Sure and if Maeve wasn't a blood relative, we could just stand back, you and me, and watch the fun.'

'Actually, I don't think they are having much fun,' Tom said. 'But I take your point, Forbes. At least I think I do.'

'Good,' said Forbes. 'Jolly good. We're not done yet, what?'

'No,' Tom said, uncertainly. 'No, we're not done yet,' and, more bewildered than ever, watched Forbes breeze through the drawing-office and head downstairs to the yard.

CHAPTER FIFTEEN

A Mirror to Nature

Ross wasted no time in assembling a travel kit, not just paints, brushes, a folding easel and the flimsy canvas stool that insisted on collapsing under him at inopportune moments, but a motor-car too, a sturdy second-hand Morris Oxford that he'd purchased for cash from a garage in Kelvindale.

The Oxford was noted more for reliability than style and the dealer assured him that the model was very popular with general medical practitioners because of its cork-lined clutch. Ross couldn't quite see the connection but he was willing to take the dealer's word for it. It was five years since he'd last been behind the wheel of a motorised vehicle, ferrying patients to and from the railway station at Bramwell. To his amazement he found the blessed machine very easy to drive and was, in fact, so taken with the 'Doctor's Coupé' that he rented a wooden garage a few minutes' walk from the studio house just to give the thing a proper home.

'New car?'

'Hmm, almost.'

'Are we going far?' Maeve asked.

'Far enough,' said Ross.

'To the seaside?'

'Nope.'

'You're not going to tell us, are you?' Lindsay said.

'It's meant to be a surprise.'

'My dad,' said Maeve, 'used take folk on mystery tours. That's what he did before he went away to the war. He drove a charabanc for a man named Flanagan. They had a falling out, though, and when Dad came back from the war he couldn't drive because of his bad hand.'

'Your father's had a very interesting life,' said Ross.

'Not really,' said Maeve. 'Unfortunate might be a better word for it.'

'Ross,' said Lindsay, 'where *are* we going?'

'You'll see when we get there,' her cousin said, smugly.

The Oxford ate up the miles of metalled road that led east and north; a bright day, not as warm as it had been earlier in the summer, with great swags of cloud trailing over moor and mountain. The glens trapped sunshine, though, and lochs glittered and the rivers that followed the car glistened like brown silk until the forest swallowed them up again.

Curled up in the back seat, Maeve sang to herself—and asked questions. She was too vivacious to sulk now that Brunswick Park was behind her and she had shaken off the atmosphere of accusation that had pervaded the house for the past fortnight. Harry and Philip had hardly addressed a civil word to her in that time and even Mr Arthur had been uncharacteristically guarded, as if the fight at the tennis club had been her fault—which, in a way, it was.

Of Ewan she had seen neither hilt nor hide. She had been far too cautious to enquire after his welfare or mention his name, even to Uncle Forbes, although he still seemed to be more amused than offended by the whole incident. In any case, she didn't see much of the Great Unmentionable except at breakfast. He was seldom home for dinner for, she gathered, he was very, very busy drawing up plans to alter and expand the shipyard.

The news of Turk's marriage had come almost as a relief. Deep within she had known all along that Turk had cast her aside, that her daddy had acted with great shrewdness and—what was the word?—perspicacity in bringing her to Glasgow to sample a taste of the high life. Even so, on several rainy afternoons she had slipped out of the house to drop in on Mr Coffey and catch up on the Dublin gossip that seemed to float Mr Coffey's way, despite the fact that he was a house-painter and paper-hanger in Glasgow now and no longer active in the brotherhood.

'There's not much life around here, is there?' Maeve said. 'It's even worse than Wexford.'

'Do you know where we are, Lindsay?' Ross asked.

Her aunt was seated on the edge of the front seat, bobbing up and down like an excited child, though it was just the roughness of the road that did it.

'Oh, you devil, Ross,' Aunt Lindsay said, suddenly. 'We're on the old road to Kelkemmit. You're taking us to Strathmore, aren't you?' She sat back. 'It always seemed so very far away when we were young.'

'In those days it was,' Ross told her. 'Train to Perth, then that wonderful grinding ride across the hill in the carrier's cart, all of us bundled together with the luggage.'

'Now we can be there by motor-car in a couple of hours.'

'That's progress for you,' Ross said. 'May God, and Mr Ford, be praised for inventing the internal combustion engine.'

'Strathmore?' said Maeve.

'Grandfather Owen's country retreat,' Lindsay explained.

'Do the Franklins still own the place?' Maeve asked.

'Alas, no,' Aunt Lindsay told her. 'It was sold off years ago.'

'Why are we going there then?'

'For old times' sake, I think,' said Lindsay.

*   *   *

They were working like demons to dismantle the second of the destroyers and save the parts that still had value. The berth where the first boat had stood was empty save for a team of surveyors marking out entrenchments for the new diagonal slipways.

Motor lorries stood by, a jib-crane was working overtime, for once the navy contract had been officially cancelled, Martin had conceded that there was no other road for Franklin's to travel but the route that Forbes had mapped out for them. Designs for the tanker's hull were almost ready to hand over to the modellers and in a week or so, before the Glasgow trades holiday cleared the Clydeside yards, Forbes's mysterious client would be invited to send experts to observe the tank testing and, hopefully, approve the results.

Martin was more than willing to leave the design side of things to Tom Calder. He was sleeping badly and his digestion, always delicate, had gone completely to the dogs. Aurora had insisted that he visit a medical consultant but the specialist had discovered nothing untoward and had cheerfully prescribed a nerve tonic and a long holiday, preferably in the sun; a holiday was impossible, however. He had his hands full coping with union leaders who, led by vociferous Jack Burgoyne of the Amalgamated Engineers, viewed cancelled navy contracts and so-called 'modernisation' as direct attacks on hard-won working practices and another ruse on the part of the employers to put one over on the men.

'Lay-offs,' Forbes said. 'Threaten them with lay-offs, Martin. If you won't do it, I will. Send Jack bloody Burgoyne to me and I'll kick his arse for him. Why is he ranting about working practices in any case? Good God, if he draws any more lines of demarcation we'll be paying small boys to stir the bloody teacans for his precious bloody engineers.'

'He wants four engineers in on the tank testing.'

'Himself included, I suppose?'

'He is the senior man in—'

'I don't care if he's a direct descendent of George Stephenson, we're treading thin ice with the client as it is and having Burgoyne breathing down our necks isn't going to help matters,' Forbes said, not quite snarling. 'He wants to find out how much the job's worth so he can screw us for double

375

time on weekend and evening shifts. If we give the engineers an inch, they'll take a mile, then we'll have every snot-nosed shop steward stepping forward with his hand out. Tell him—no, I'll tell him—he's lucky to have a full packet of employment when half the yards in the country are on short time. Tell him he'd better brace himself for a round of wage cuts.'

'Wage cuts?'

'Come on, Martin, you know we can't deliver the tanker without reducing the wage bill. It's either a wee bit less in everyone's pocket or men out on the street. Do you think because Burgoyne and his cronies wear boiler suits they can't read small print? Do you imagine that when big Jack puts his feet up on a Sunday morning he dives for the *Sunday Post* and the *Racing Pink*? I'll bet you a pound to a penny Jack's weekend reading consists of the *Economist* and the *Financial Times*. He might get up on his hind legs at TUC conferences and shout the odds but he's squealing quietly inside, just like the rest of us.'

'Nonetheless, if we push him too far he'll call for strike action and have the whole yard out.'

'Let him bring them out,' Forbes said. 'The ball's in our court right now. Unemployment's rising faster than a spring tide at Gourock. We're in for a long, costly struggle, however you look at it.'

'A class struggle,' said Martin, with a sigh. 'Another one.'

'Same one,' said Forbes. 'Same old song of sixpence, Martin. I beg you to bear in mind just whose side you're on when the fighting starts. The unions won't stand together. Look what happened during the miners' lockout. Sympathy strikes by transport and railway workers didn't materialise, the miners were left high and dry and Hodges had to eat humble pie and sign a series of temporary wage settlements. We'll start with the draughtsmen, with, let's say, fifteen per cent knocked off the basic wage. Lightbody will counter with a campaign for observance of minimum wage rates; we'll agree to a ten per cent reduction; they'll accept—and we'll be in control. And, by God, old son, we'll need to be in control when it comes to negotiating with Burgoyne and the engineers, to say nothing of platers, boilermakers and the other allied trades.'

'I do not enjoy seeing the men starve.'

'They won't starve,' said Forbes. 'They'll scrape by somehow. They always do. If you need balm for your bleeding heart, Martin, I suggest you poke your nose into the public houses along Dumbarton Road and count the number of pints being served. There may not be money for bread, but, by God, there's always money for booze.'

'You're a hard man, Forbes, very, very hard.'

'Someone has to stand up to them, otherwise they'll skin us alive.' He got to his feet and placed a soothing hand on his cousin's shoulder. 'Are you up to this, Martin? You don't look too chipper these days. Is the belly acting up?'

'No, I'm fine.'

'Good,' Forbes said. 'Now what I need you to do is open the reserve fund and transfer it to the working capital account.'

'All of it?'

'Sixty per cent will do for a start.'

'We'll need partnership approval.'

'It'll be nodded through at Tuesday's meeting, I promise. I mean, you won't oppose it, will you? I know you think of the reserve fund as rainy day money, Martin, but this *is* a rainy day.'

'What else do you want me to do?'

'Atta boy,' Forbes said, winking. 'Now you're getting into the spirit of the thing. Right, broach Burgoyne and suggest that Lightbody and he come up with a fair proposal for overtime rates. Mention of overtime always sets their pulses racing. They fought hard for their precious forty-seven-hour week and if they think we're solvent enough to pay them an increased rate for the nine hours they drummed out of us they'll be less inclined to agitate about the details of the tanker contract which, after all, is none of their damned business.'

'Anything else?'

'Arthur will meet with Rowe and Spellman's lawyers on Wednesday to iron out unfavourable clauses in the draft contract.'

'Like having to buy our plate from Bradford Steel?'

'That, and several other sticking points.'

'Where's the meeting taking place? Here?'

'Neutral ground: the boardroom of the Shipowners' Association in St Vincent Street.'

Martin nodded meekly.

He wasn't thinking clearly; much of what Forbes had said had gone in one ear and out the other. His stomach ached. He had a rancid taste in his mouth that neither tobacco nor sweet tea could alleviate. He wanted to be out in the fresh air, out in the yard, talking to the employees, whose welfare was still his prime concern. He looked at his cousin and business partner, at Owen Forbes McCulloch, the Irish interloper, who seemed to be in full command of everyone and everything now.

'Forbes,' he said, 'are you actually enjoying yourself?'

'Too true, old son. I'm having the time of my life. Aren't you?'

'Yes,' Martin murmured, obediently. 'Yes, of course I am,' and limped out into the corridor, clutching his bowler to his chest.

*   *   *

The picnic hamper had been delivered by the caterer early that morning. The lettuce was slightly wilted but everything else was daisy fresh and ten minutes immersed in the icy waters of the loch chilled the bottles of Sancerre.

Smoked salmon, roast chicken, a salad bowl, cheeses, bread rolls and a thick whisky-flavoured pudding were duly unpacked and laid out upon the chequered cloth, together with plates, silver cutlery, crystal glasses and stiff white linen napkins.

Cloud had gone from the heights of the hill, the water gleamed like a fresh-caught salmon and only in the shadow line under the trees on the Kelkemmit shore did the loch show its darker depths. Pine and fir, spruce and slender birches stirred in the faint breeze and on the pastures above the hamlet sheep had stopped grazing and the cattle had lain down. Nothing seemed to be moving but a pair of buzzards floating in great lazy spirals against the sky.

Maeve sat back on the grass and sank her fangs into a bread roll.

'Is this how you're going to paint us, Ross, pigging away like this?'

'Tempting though it is,' Ross said, 'no.'

'There's lots of famous pictures of folk eatin' outdoors.' Maeve chewed and swallowed. 'I've seen them in books. The French ones are a bit naughty, though, aren't they?'

'One or two,' Ross conceded.

'There's that one with two chaps in frock coats and a girl with—'

'Maeve,' Ross said, 'it's not my intention to produce a copy of *Le Déjeuner sur l'herbe* but if you feel a desperate need to gallop about in the altogether at least wait until we've finished eating.'

Maeve slid a silver of smoked salmon into her mouth.

'I wonder,' she said, 'what I'd look like with my clothes off?'

Ross snorted. 'Well, if you don't know, no one does.'

'Aye, that's true,' said Maeve, and finally reached for a plate.

They had settled on the loch shore at the foot of the meadow that fronted the big house of Strathmore. Lindsay could see the house clearly through the trees. It too looked smaller than it had done twenty-five years ago. She wondered if, as she became older, everything would become miniaturised. There were no signs of life at the house. No smoke issued from the chimneys.

'Who lives here now, Ross?' she asked.

'Nobody,' Ross said. 'A couple named Carter rented it from the duke but didn't stay long, a year or two at most, then it was leased to an English family who spent every summer here until the outbreak of war. I don't know if it's true, but I heard they lost all four sons on the Western Front and couldn't bear to come back to Scotland afterwards.'

'At least our memories are happy ones,' said Lindsay.

'And remain so, by and large,' said Ross.

'Do you miss Johnny?'

'I do,' said Ross. 'He was a jovial wee soul, wasn't he? I don't think it occurred to him that he wouldn't have a jolly time fighting the Germans, and come back a hero. He loved boats, do you remember? I wonder if he thought of us, and of Strathmore, as he stood watch on freezing winter nights in the Baltic.'

'I'm sure he did,' said Lindsay.

Ross concentrated on extracting the cork from a bottle of Sancerre. 'Perhaps we should eat up and do a bit of work before the sun disappears.'

'Work?' said Maeve.

'I didn't bring you all the way out here to enjoy yourself,' said Ross. 'I do have to earn my gingerbread, you know.'

'What are you going to do with us?' Maeve said. 'I mean, where do you want us to pose?'

'Up by the house,' said Ross.

*　　　*　　　*

Strathmore was not as it had been in Grandfather Owen's day. Moss smeared the walls, weeds sprouted from cracks, the doors were peeling and the window frames rotting. Mounds of brown leaves were piled against the ornamental pillars of the terrace, the handsome French doors to the drawing-room were warped and the lawns hip-high with thistles and tall poppies.

Lindsay felt as if she were floating in a sea of

381

neglect. She almost expected Forbes—Forbes as he was now—to appear from the drawing-room. She shivered, and backed away from the French doors.

'What's wrong, Lindsay?' Ross asked. 'Seeing ghosts?'

'Yes, of a sort,' she admitted.

With Maeve's help, Ross had lugged his materials across the meadow and with uncharacteristic enthusiasm had planted the easel and canvas stool on the gravel below the terrace.

He stripped off his jacket and rolled up his sleeves. He had been here recently, Lindsay felt sure, had selected the spot on the terrace in which he wanted Maeve and her to pose. She was not in the least self-conscious and the position Ross had chosen for them was comfortable. He had brought along three stretched canvases. He propped the smallest one on the easel, locked it tightly, and seated himself on the stool. He opened the huge japanned box that housed his paints and brushes and dainty little bottles of oil and thinners.

She leaned on the pocked and lichened stonework that fronted the terrace—Maeve was a few feet to her right—and watched her cousin squeeze a blob of viridian paint on to the lid of the box. He opened another tube and another, picked up a brush, dabbed at the lid then, lo and behold, without any preliminary measuring or drawing, began to paint.

Until that moment Lindsay had supposed that Ross would compose the portrait in the studio from sketches, and that the finished product would be as stiff and formal as all his other canvases. Now she realised that he intended to render them with swift flowing strokes, direct and dashing and bold, as if

Maeve and she might suddenly vanish into the forest, like deer.

Ross dipped and splashed and stroked the brush on the canvas and in forty minutes or so had completed the painting to his satisfaction. He unlocked it from the easel, brought it on to the terrace and propped it against the wall. It was much more than an oil sketch, an impression. He had caught their attitude of ease, the house leaning over them, amber shadows in the room behind them; all pale greens and dusky blues with the faint warm fall of granite supporting and encompassing them. He had turned Maeve's shoulders a little, inclined her head into a three-quarter profile so that the girl seemed to be looking at Lindsay, critical and admiring at one and the same time.

They might, Lindsay thought, have been mother and daughter, separated by different needs but bound together by love.

Maeve cadged a cigarette and, holding it inexpertly, puffed and blew smoke. 'Never saw you go at it like that before, Ross. What's got into you?'

'*Alla prima*,' he said. 'Haven't tried my hand at that technique since the—in years.' He took the cigarette from Maeve's fingers, put it to his lips and inhaled deeply. 'Spontaneity makes me nervous.'

'It's beautiful, Ross,' said Lindsay. 'It's—it's us.'

Pleased, he growled softly into his beard, handed the cigarette back to Maeve and fished a watch from his trouser pocket. He read the time and glanced up at the position of the sun.

'Game for one more?'

'Aren't you tired?' Lindsay asked.

'Not in the slightest,' he said. 'Maeve, take off your bonnet and stand at the corner of the terrace,

383

lean casually against the wall and look out across the lawn. Lindsay, against the half pillar, the third one along, looking towards me. If you lift your head just a touch . . .'

'As if I'm surprised?'

'Hmm,' Ross said. 'Hmm, exactly.'

In less than five minutes he was seated at the easel again with the sun behind him and the shadow of the gable of Strathmore lying across him. Lindsay looked at him. She had been instructed to look at him, to look at him as if he had stepped through the French doors and surprised her just as Forbes had done all those long, empty years ago.

She watched him paint, watched him lay down colour and adjust areas of tone and, with a strange melting sensation in the region of her heart, realised that he was no longer simply pursuing his craft, that what he was engaged in now was not an act of creation but of love.

*   *   *

Forbes said, 'I'm not paying three hundred quid . . .'

'Guineas.'

'. . . three hundred anything for *that*. Look at it, looks as if you'd knocked it off in a couple of hours. I thought you said it would take until Christmas.'

'No,' Ross said. '*You* said it would take until Christmas.'

'It doesn't even look like Maeve. And, while we're at it, why did you put Lindsay in the picture? I didn't want Lindsay in the picture. Our contract was for Maeve, just Maeve.' He swept a hand

384

under the tail of his jacket and leaned forward, scowling. 'Where is that? Is that supposed to be the place where we all went on those miserable wet holidays together?'

'Strathmore,' Ross said.

'Looks nothing like Strathmore.'

'If you don't like it,' Ross said, 'you don't have to buy it.'

'I don't like it. But I do want one, a proper one.'

'Without Lindsay?'

'That's what I asked for in the first place.'

'Didn't you court Lindsay during one of those miserable holidays at Strathmore?' Ross said.

'Who told you that? Did she tell you that?'

'I expect she did,' said Ross.

Forbes glowered at his bearded cousin.

'You took them up there, didn't you?'

'Of course,' Ross said. 'I only work from nature.'

Forbes hesitated, troubled by a stray thought, then with a little snort, he said, 'Funny how women remember these things.'

'Isn't it, though,' said Ross.

'How did you get there?'

'We motored.'

'You don't have a car, do you?'

'Hmm, a Morris Oxford.'

'By gum,' said Forbes, 'must be money in paint after all.'

'Second-hand,' said Ross, humbly.

'She didn't say anything to me about it, either of them.'

'Perhaps you haven't been seeing enough of them lately.'

'Are you being sarcastic, Ross?'

'Certainly not.'

'It's no joke running a shipyard these days.'

'I'll bet it's not.'

In fact, it had been a good day for Forbes, and it wasn't over yet. He had called another board meeting that afternoon and had at last persuaded the partners to approve his plan and release reserve funds. Profits would be non-existent for the next financial year, every red cent ploughed back into expansion. Tomorrow Arthur would have a second meeting with Rowe and Spellman's legal representatives to thrash out a final contract. Bradford Steel would supply plate and castings, but a rider allowed Franklin's an out if quality wasn't up to scratch.

Forbes congratulated himself on having steered clear of the contract negotiations. Gideon Rowe hadn't shown his face so far and there was no official hint that Franklin's had climbed into bed with Far East Oil.

He glanced at his wristlet watch.

Ross said, 'I take it you're hastening off.'

'I am.'

'All work and no play, Forbes. However, if you really don't want my picture that's perfectly all right with me.'

'What'll you do with it?'

'Paint over it, probably.'

'Give you a tenner for it.'

'Somehow,' Ross said, 'I'd a feeling you'd say that.' He lifted the canvas from the easel. 'My agent will manage to sell it to some benighted fool, I expect.'

'And Maeve?'

Ross nodded. 'I'll do you a "proper" portrait on the same terms.'

386

'By Christmas?'

'If not before.'

They shook hands and a moment later Ross ushered his cousin out of the studio and watched him hurry off, on foot, down Flowerhill Drive.

He returned to the studio, lifted the painting and studied it. He was not in the least offended by Forbes's refusal to purchase; quite the contrary, in fact. He carried the picture into the bedroom and hung it on the wall by its companion piece, then, lighting up his pipe, lay back against the pillow with his long legs dangling and contemplated his handiwork.

'Forbes,' he said softly, releasing a little ball of smoke, 'Forbes, you really are a fool,' then he laughed, heaved himself from the bed and went to pour a whisky and soda before he settled down to work once more.

PART THREE

PART THREE

CHAPTER SIXTEEN

The Horse's Mouth

By mid-summer it was obvious that predictions of a massive slump were coming to pass. Ratification of the Washington Treaty was followed by a spate of cancelled orders, and lay-offs galore. Those pacifists, socialists and communists who had called for an end to all wars by limiting arms production were finally paying the price for their idealism. Early in the year there had been some room for hope but by July even the most optimistic analysts had to concede that things were going from bad to worse. With two cargo vessels nearing completion and an order for a bulk oil-carrier almost sealed, it appeared that Franklin's would survive, however, that Forbes McCulloch had finally earned his spurs and the bragging rights that went with them.

Tank testing of the twelve-foot scale model had thrown up a resistance problem that Tom Calder's team had not foreseen. The fault was found at last not in hull design but in the calibration equipment and the second run went well enough to satisfy the three gentlemen, two of whom were French, who had been appointed to liaise with Franklin's managers.

Franklin's management wined and dined the visitors at the Ashton and Forbes discreetly interrogated them as to who had handed out their brief and to whom they were ultimately answerable. The Frenchmen were charming, affable, witty, but gave nothing away, and the English expert, Miles

Bennett, seemed unwilling to open his mouth at all except to shovel food into it; yet it was he who at the end of the evening shook Forbes's hand and declared that he would recommend an immediate signature of the contract.

At this announcement the Frenchmen smiled and flapped their hands about and, to his considerable embarrassment, hugged Martin and would have kissed Arthur on both cheeks if he hadn't ducked in time.

'Who the heck are they, Forbes?' Arthur asked as he and his son-in-law drove home late that night.

'I have no idea,' Forbes said, 'but I do intend to find out.'

'How will you do that?'

'By going straight to the horse's mouth,' said Forbes.

*   *   *

Early the following morning Forbes arrived unannounced at Merriam House.

It was raining hard and views of Clydebank were bleached out by lowering cloud. Forbes skipped from the shelter of the Lanchester and pounded on the door like a fugitive from justice or, more appropriately perhaps, a police officer. Ronnie opened the door. Forbes pushed past him and, trailing drops of rainwater across the polished parquet floor, rounded the angle of the living-room into the breakfast bar.

To his relief there was no sign of Stella.

'Good morning, Giddy,' he said. 'I trust you slept well.'

At the glass-topped table the dapper little

Frenchman toyed with a bowl of porridge. He was flanked by Drew Pickering and Miles Bennett, the stony-faced Englishman. Clad in pyjamas and a ratty old dressing-gown, Geoff Paget was propping up the bar.

'Geoffrey, old chum,' Forbes said, 'what a surprise!'

Drew Pickering was half out of his chair, fists clenched. He had a napkin tucked into his collar and was unshaven.

Forbes slipped off his overcoat and dumped it, with his hat, on the bar. He turned to Ronnie, and said, 'I'll have the grilled kidneys and a little dollop of scrambled eggs. Coffee. Black.' Rain poured down across the side window in a torrent. Forbes said, 'The builder cheated you on the exterior plumbing, Andrew. Your pipes are too narrow.'

'Is that why you're here, McCulloch, to discuss my pipes?'

'Come now'—Forbes drew out a chair—'you know why I'm here. If you and your cohorts expect me to hand you Franklin's on a plate then I have to be sure who I'm dealing with and, more importantly, what I'll get out of it.'

'Is an order for a bulk oil-carrier not sufficient?' Pickering said.

'Nope,' Forbes said. 'I'm no faded naval officer with a gambling habit to be palmed off with the promise of a sinecure in one of your regional offices.'

'I say,' Geoffrey complained, 'that's a bit below the belt.'

Forbes held up a hand. 'Be careful, sonny boy. I don't know what you're doing back in Scotland but if I catch you within half a mile of my wife you'll be

393

retiring early on an invalid pension.' He leaned on the glass-topped table and grinned at Gideon Rowe. 'Not too keen on Scotch porridge, Giddy?' he said. 'Can't say I blame you. Now, tell me, who's your pal here? He claims to have worked for Thorneycroft's, but I don't think that's accurate.'

'Why do you not invite him to speak for himself?' Gideon said.

'Because I've no chance of getting a straight answer,' Forbes said. 'He's not a naval architect, is he? I reckon he's a bigwig from Far East Oil.'

'Has my wife been talking out of turn?' Pickering said.

'Stella?' Forbes shook his head. 'No. I did my level best to open her up but she's tighter than a clam.' He glanced round. 'Is the lady not joining us for breakfast?'

'Late night,' Pickering said. 'She isn't as young as she used to be. What makes you suppose Mr Bennett is associated with Far East Oil?'

'The fact that he's seated at your breakfast table,' Forbes said. 'The fact that for four days he's hardly opened his trap. The fact that he doesn't seem to know the two Frenchies and that he, unlike them, isn't putting up at the Ashton.'

'So you think you know who I represent, Mr McCulloch?' Bennett said in a well-pressed English voice. 'Believe me, you have no idea who I represent. You have your tanker order; be satisfied with that.'

'According to his wife,' said Geoff Paget, 'he's never satisfied.'

Still without turning, Forbes said, 'If you mention my wife again, Geoffrey, you'll be counting what's left of your teeth.'

'Why is it,' said Gideon Rowe, 'that you are so much hostile?'

'Because,' Forbes said, 'I have something you want and you're trying to winkle me out of it without paying the going rate.'

'What is it you believe that we want?' said Gideon.

'Franklin's shipyard.'

Pickering laughed, curtly. 'You're dreaming, Forbes.'

'Is that what you told poor old Mitchell Hussey when you bought out Bradford Steel?' Forbes said. 'What did you offer him by way of inducement? My head on a silver platter?'

'You have only yourself to blame for antagonising—' Geoff Paget began.

'Be quiet, Geoffrey,' Pickering snapped.

'John Brown's and Fairfields are out of your reach, and you probably can't afford to buy into Scott's, Yarrow's or Denny's,' Forbes continued. 'Franklin's is about the right size and in the right location for your purposes, so you dangle a single order—albeit it a big one—in the expectation that we'll be so desperate for work that we'll lay out the capital to modernise the yard to secure it, which, by the by, is exactly what we are doing.'

'May I remind you,' Pickering said, 'that in a matter of weeks you'll be twenty-eight thousand pounds in pocket.'

'The first payment,' Forbes said, 'is so ringed around with clauses that you already have us by the short hairs. Franklin's operates under Scots law, which is rather different from English law, as I think you're well aware, but Franklin's is no longer the same firm that old Owen left behind.'

'Make your point, Forbes,' Pickering said.

'I will,' Forbes said, 'just as soon as you tell me the truth. Do you, or do you not, intend to take control of Franklin's shipyard and pump in enough capital to build a fleet of tankers?'

Without hesitation, Miles Bennett answered, 'Yes, we do.'

'Right,' Forbes said. 'At last, we're getting somewhere.'

'Can you get it for us?' Pickering said. 'Franklin's, I mean.'

'Probably,' Forbes said.

'Probably?'

'There are conditions.'

'I guessed there would be,' Miles Bennett said. 'What are they?'

'If I acquire a majority of existing shares in accordance with the Articles set down in the Deeds of Partnership I'm then at liberty to introduce new partners—anyone I, or you, choose.'

'Who holds the majority shares at the moment?' Bennett asked.

'My cousin Martin, my father-in-law, and my wife,' Forbes said. 'I hold twenty-one sixty-fourths.'

'How much is this liable to cost us?' Bennett said.

'You'll have to pay the premiums each partner originally subscribed, plus a portion of capital assets. You will not, however, be responsible for existing debts. New broom, clean sweep, in other words. Given that we're currently eating into our reserves to improve the yard, and given that you gentlemen have reasonably deep pockets, I reckon you can acquire fifty-one per cent of Franklin's without too much bother.'

'What about the other forty-nine per cent?' said Pickering.

'That's my fee.'

'Ouch!' Miles Bennett exclaimed, softly.

'Our capital, your shares?' said Gideon Rowe.

'Franklin's isn't an assembly line,' Forbes said. 'We can't run off bulk oil-tankers like Ford Model Ts. You're looking at a long-term project for which you'll need continuity in the shape of a fully equipped, modern shipyard, a trained workforce, and an experienced shipbuilder who knows precisely what you're up to; that, Gideon, is what you'll get for your money.'

'Take it or leave it?' said Sir Andrew Pickering.

'Take it or leave it,' said Forbes.

*   *   *

It was the fourth day of the Glasgow holiday, and still raining. Rain or no rain, Maeve was too energetic to mope about the house like Philip and Harry. On afternoons when she wasn't sitting for Ross, she took herself off to visit her grandmother and listen to Mr Coffey's endless stories of wild Irish rebels, past and present. She had seen nothing of Ewan Calder since the disastrous birthday party but at least Harry and Phil were speaking to her again. There had been talk of spending the holiday in a hotel down the coast but Uncle Forbes had said that he was far too busy and Aunt Lindsay had let the matter drop.

It was raining that Tuesday afternoon. Mr Coffey had gone out on a paper-hanging job and she had been left alone with Gran. She had taken her leave about half past three and had gone down into Partick to buy five cigarettes from a little newsagent's shop on Dumbarton Road.

The sky above the tenements was oppressively dark for a summer's afternoon in holiday time. Rain bounced off the pavements and the gutters were full of dirty water. She draped the shawl that Enid had lent her over her head and splashed downhill to Dumbarton Road.

Boys lounged in close mouths, men hung about outside the pubs, though the pubs wouldn't open for another hour or so. What else had they to do, Maeve supposed, but wait? Half of them were on holiday with a bit of change in their pockets and the other half were out of work and stony broke. Then she saw Bobby Shannon navigating a careful path along the pavement, pushing the big, ramshackle perambulator before him. He passed Maeve without a second glance. With the shawl over her hat and a pair of rubber galoshes over her shoes, it wasn't surprising that he'd failed to recognise her.

Trams rattled past, lorries, a cart with a drenched and dejected horse between the shafts, a high-sided motorised van bringing live sheep up from Finnieston Docks. Four young louts leaned against the shutters of the Wine Vaults. They smoked cigarettes cupped in the palms of their hands, and spat. Rain dripped from their caps and their boots were soaked. They jeered Bobby Shannon for pushing the big, ungainly perambulator. Bobby turned his head and stared at them, took a hand from the pram's long wooden handle, stuck up two fingers and yelled back.

Giggles emerged from under the hood of the pram. Maeve hastened past the idlers and put a hand on Bobby Shannon's arm. He swung round as if he were about to strike her, then, reaching under the metal frame, hauled on the handbrake and stopped the pram an inch from the pavement's edge.

'So it's yourself, is it?' he said. 'Where did you get the shawl?'

'Borrowed it,' Maeve answered.

'I knew it couldn't be yours.'

'I've a worse one at home, smarty.'

'In Dublin?'

'Aye,' Maeve said. 'In Dublin.'

He edged round so that the pram was behind him.

Maeve said, 'Is that your sister you've got in there?'

'What if it is?'

'Aren't you going to introduce me?'

'She isn't much of a one for introductions.'

'What's wrong with her?'

'She's crippled.'

'How? An accident?'

'Born crippled,' Bobby said, tight-lipped.

'Can't she talk?'

He uttered an indignant *phah* and flicked wet hair from his brow with a toss of the head. ' 'Course she can bloody talk. It's her spine that's damaged, not her brain.'

'Bobby?' A tiny voice, sharp as a chisel blade. 'Who're you talkin' to back there, Bobby?'

'Nobody, sweetheart, just a—a lady.'

'What lady? You gotta lady friend, then—'sides me?'

'Nah,' Bobby said over his shoulder. 'It's just a woman I used to know.'

'Introduce me,' Maeve said again.

He shook his head.

'At least tell me her name?' said Maeve.

'Alice,' came the voice from under the hood. 'My name's Alice.'

'See.' Maeve leaned so close that she could feel rain dripping from his hair. She whispered, 'Are you ashamed of her, then?' and walked around the pram and peered into the swaddle of blankets and oilskin sheets.

The girl wasn't small, delicate or sweet. She had a large, round face, pitted with acne, a straggle of wispy fair hair and a pair of blue eyes as icy and acute as any that Maeve had ever seen.

'I'm Maeve,' she said. 'Him an' me do the modelling together.'

'You're her, then?' Alice said.

'Aye, I'm her.'

Alice Shannon's head and shoulders were in proportion but there was only a narrow wedge where her torso and legs should be and, propping up the sheet in the basin of the pram, two feet, small as tent pegs.

Maeve experienced a strange insufficient compassion for Bobby Shannon's sister, a compassion that she did not dare express.

'Did he tell you about me?' Alice Shannon asked, eagerly.

'Sure an' he did,' said Maeve. 'He's never done talking about you. Bores the drawers off all of us, so he does.'

The girl giggled. 'He's a beggar, ain't he? A cheeky beggar.'

'Where's he—where are you going?' Maeve asked.

'Ciggies,' the girl said. 'Dixon's shop for ten Player's Weights.'

'Five Woodbine does me.' Maeve coughed theatrically. 'It's me chest, doctor. It's me tubes. Five ciggies a day an' me bellows conk out.'

Alice laughed and rocked against the straw-filled bolster that kept her upright. Looking up over the hood, Maeve detected love in Bobby Shannon's eyes, and at that precise moment sensed that he might be the man for her.

*　　　*　　　*

Ross tapped the end of the pencil against his teeth and rubbed his beard with his free hand. 'What's got into you today? You seem uncommonly cheerful.'

'Am I not usually cheerful?'

'Well, yes,' Ross said, 'but not so—so smug about it.'

'Smug?'

'Pleased with yourself.'

'I'm just happy it's finally stopped raining,' Maeve said. 'Do you want me to look solemn?'

'Not particularly,' Ross said. 'I would, however, prefer it if you didn't sit there grinning like a Cheshire cat.'

'Paint the smile,' Maeve said. 'That Italian did a good job on a smile.'

Ross let out a bark of laughter. 'The *Mona Lisa*, you mean. There's a theory that the reason she was smiling was because she was pregnant.'

'Oh! Well, you can put your mind at rest, Ross. I'm not pregnant.'

'That would be a turn-up for the book, though,

wouldn't it?'

'What do you mean by that?'

'Forbes would have a purple fit.'

'Never mind Uncle Forbes,' Maeve said. *'I'd
have a purple fit.'*

Ross had positioned her on a gilded chair
against a background of blue velvet draped from a
plaster urn. He had provided her with a simple,
full-length dress to wear, no cap or hat. He had
already completed a series of preliminary drawings
on graph paper and, with the canvas tilted on a pile
of books on the table top, was patiently building up
the composition.

Maeve said, 'Why don't you do me the other
way?'

'Other way?'

'Straight into paint; Ali Baba?'

'Alla prima,' Ross said. 'My client doesn't fancy
anything too modern.'

'Client? You mean somebody wants a picture of
me?'

Ross lowered his head and diligently pencilled in
another line or two. 'Not specifically you, Maeve.
He's—he's a gallery owner, and pictures of pretty
young ladies do tend to sell rather well.'

'How much is he paying you?'

'Three hundred guineas.'

'Is that all?'

'What?' Ross said. 'Do you think you're worth
more?'

'Lots more,' said Maeve, and laughed.

She was quiet for a while, then she said, 'I met
Bobby yesterday.'

'Did you now?'

'He was shoving his sister down Dumbarton

Road in a sort of pram thing he and his old man built. His old man's a brass finisher. What is that, anyway?'

'I have no idea,' said Ross.

'She's really sick, his sister. She's got a crooked spine and her legs are wasted. She can't sit up, can't walk, can't—'

'Did Bobby tell you this?'

'No, she did; the sister did. She talks a lot— mostly about herself.'

'Perhaps she doesn't have much else to talk about,' Ross suggested.

'Aye, that's true,' Maeve said. 'She's lucky she has Bobby to look after her. The mother's dead. There's just him and his old man. They live in a tenement in Riverside Street. It doesn't sound very nice. In fact, it sounds to me a bit like Endicott Street.'

'Riverside's a tough neighbourhood,' said Ross. 'Personally, I'd think twice about venturing down there.'

'I'd only go if I was invited, and that's not liable to happen,' Maeve said. 'They have to pay a woman to come in and look after the girl when they're at work. Costs a lot, that sort of thing. They've paid umpteen doctors, too, but nothing can be done to cure her. That's why he needs the money you give him.'

'Maeve . . .'

'What?'

'Nothing, nothing.'

'If he loses his job, they'll be in queer street,' she said. 'Can't you find more work for him, Ross?'

He put down the pencil. 'Maeve,' he said, 'you mustn't let your heart rule your head. Bobby

403

Shannon is not a lost cause. Promise me you'll be careful.'

'Me? I'm always careful,' Maeve said, bridling. 'Too damned careful sometimes. I asked you a simple question, Ross. How about an answer?'

'Yes, of course I'd do my best to help him out.'

'Not charity—work.'

To hide his anxiety, he tried to make light of it. 'The Charge of the Light Brigade, the Retreat from Caporetto, the Hospital at Scutari, with all the soldiers looking like wee Bobby Shannon? I think someone might notice.'

'He's not wee, and it's not funny.'

'No, it isn't,' Ross said. 'I'm sorry.'

She shifted position, dipping her head into the band of shadow that cut across the corner of the big bow window. She wondered why he needed light. He wasn't doing anything with colour, with paint. He was drawing, just drawing, the way Bobby would draw at his desk in the office in Aydon Road, and draughtsmen didn't need light, not natural light.

'How long is this stupid portrait goin' to take, anyway?'

'If you sit still,' Ross said, 'about ten weeks.'

'Then you'll need Bobby again, won't you?'

'I might,' Ross said. 'Yes, I probably will.'

She moved her head back into the sunlight and corrected her pose.

Ross went on drawing. 'Have you told anyone at home about your chance encounter with Bobby Shannon?'

'No.'

'I wouldn't if I were you.'

'Why not?'

'I just wouldn't, that's all,' said Ross.

* * *

They were alone in the kitchen. The old man had gone to Macafee's to spend what was left of his holiday pay. It was still broad daylight. Bobby hadn't lit the lamp over the mantel. There was a fire in the grate. He heated water in a kettle on the range in the old-fashioned way. He poured the water into a pudding basin and brought the basin and a towel to the bed in the alcove, for yesterday he had promised he would wash her hair.

She had been bad yesterday. He wouldn't have taken her out if she hadn't insisted. She was, he supposed, making the most of his holiday. He couldn't blame her, cooped up all day, every day, when Pa and he were at work, cooped up night after night because it was too risky to take her out in the cold. She loved fresh air. She loved sunshine. She even liked the rain on her face and to paddle her hands in the puddle in the hollow of the oilskin.

When they got home yesterday she had been struck by pains, terrible racking pains in her neck and head. She had moaned with the pain, always a bad sign, and he had sent Pa to the late-night chemist's along Dumbarton Road where the pharmacist dispensed the oily green sedative that Dr Macdonald had prescribed. Pa had stopped for a drink on the way back. It had been after midnight before the syrup had been administered. Eventually Alice had fallen asleep, head nodding on her breast. Though he knew the rules of hygiene only too well, he hadn't the heart to undress her. He had slipped the bedpan under her and had left

405

the nappy pinned about her hips.

She had slept far into the morning. He had managed to rouse Pa before he went out to buy eggs, sausage and back bacon. When she finally came to, he had made her breakfast, like a Sunday breakfast. Mrs Molloy had gone on holiday for the week so he was obliged to wash and dress his sister. The pains had eased, thanks to God, and she had been chatty and flirty all day. He had risked taking her out in the afternoon, bumping the pram downstairs then climbing up to the top floor again to carry Alice down on his back, her hands about his throat, her lank fair hair tickling his ear.

He had walked her along the muddy path by the water. How quiet everything was in the sunshine, everything steeped in rain, the yards silent for the holiday. He had taken her down Sword Street and had bought her a tot of banana rum in Macafee's. He had sat with her in the stinking snug while she sipped it, sipped it slowly, like a bee imbibing nectar. He had wheeled her home via Dumbarton Road, half hoping he'd bump into Maeve McCulloch again, without the borrowed shawl, her hair loose, bobbing and bouncing. He hadn't thought of anyone that way for a long, long time, not since Ma had died trying to give birth to another baby, not one like Alice.

Pa had made French toast and boiled peas. They had eaten together, Alice in bed, the table heaved over near to the hole in the wall. Then, about eight, Pa had gone out, and he had warmed water and filled the pudding basin and had taken down the bottle of liquid soap he'd bought at a church bazaar, had put two drops into the water and, with a towel about her neck and her breast supported by a cushion, had begun to wash her hair.

'Has she got money?'

'Who?' Bobby said.

'That girl we met yesterday.'

'What makes you think she's got money?'

'You told me she was a lady.'

He worked the soapy water in drop by drop. She didn't like being touched about the head, though she enjoyed the rinsing. He curled a wisp of hair about his finger and rubbed it with his thumb. He could see the high, crooked curve of her spine, the bones prominent beneath the skin.

'She's a relative of the Franklins,' he said. 'Forbes McCulloch's her uncle and Tom Calder's her grandfather.'

'I've heard terrible stories about that family.'

'Have you,' Bobby said.

'Tom Calder's daughter ran off wi' somebody's brother, years ago.'

'Who told you that?'

'Mrs Molloy. How much money have they got?'

'I don't know, Alice.'

'Enough to make me better?'

He watched the bones on the top of her spine swell until it seemed they might burst through her skin. She was nodding, nodding into the cushion, urging him to answer, '*Yes*.'

He said, 'Wheesh now. I'm gonna do your ears.'

She put a hand behind her, palm open, ordering him to stop, telling him that she had something to say, something that wouldn't wait.

'If you married that girl we'd have enough money to make me better. We'd live in a big house and she'd cook the dinners for you an' Pa while I'm gettin' better.'

'It's not her money,' Bobby said. 'If it was her money she'd hardly be modelling for old Ross, would she?'

'They'd give her the money.'

'Not them,' said Bobby. 'Not if she married the likes o' me.'

'You're lovely.'

'Aye, but not lovely enough for the Franklins.'

'Would you not like to have her in your bed?'

'What, her an' me an' Pa?'

'In the big house she'd buy for us we'd all have beds.' Alice lifted her chin from the cushion to make herself heard. 'If you married her, the Franklins would give us a house with a garden. I'd have a room with windows lookin' out, a great big room to lie in while I was gettin' better.'

'Aye, Alice,' Bobby said, sighing, 'wouldn't that be grand?'

'Marry her then. Get the money. Get the money for me.'

'Close your eyes.'

'What for?'

'I'm gonna rinse you now,' Bobby Shannon said, and, rising quickly from the bed, went to refill the basin from the kettle on the hob.

*   *   *

Martin's illness came as a bonus. On Wednesday of fair week he was lugged off to the Western Infirmary, bleeding profusely. Aurora, in panic, sent for Lindsay and Lindsay in turn summoned Donald. Forbes, as it happened, could not be found. Before Forbes received the news, Martin had been given three pints of somebody else's

408

blood and by the time Forbes arrived in the evening the patient was propped up in bed.

Aurora and one of her sons were at the bedside. Donald had taken the younger boy back to Largs with him to keep him out of harm's way.

'It's you,' Aurora said, furiously. 'It's all your fault, Forbes.'

'Me? What have I got to do with it?'

'Aurora, please,' Martin whispered.

'It has to be said and I may as well say it.'

'Before you do, do you mind telling me what's wrong with him?'

'I'm here, you know, I'm still here,' Martin whispered.

'He has an ulcer in the peritoneum.'

'Isn't that dangerous?' said Forbes.

The boy, Colin, was seated on the other side of the bed. The ward was criss-crossed with bars of sunlight and a faint haze of cigarette smoke hung over the communal table in the middle of the room where the walking wounded banded together. The boy was bored. When Forbes asked his question, he sighed and raised his eyes to heaven.

'Of course it's dangerous,' Aurora hissed.

She had clad herself in black, heavy black, as if she were already a widow. Her flame-red hair had prominent grey streaks in it and she was no longer the desirable piece she'd been when Martin had married her. There was money behind her, though, a great deal of money. She was in for a fair share of the Swann family fortune when her old man finally gave up the ghost.

'He could die at any time,' Aurora went on.

'What are they going to do about it?' Forbes asked.

'The knife,' said Martin, almost inaudibly.

'Nonsense!' Aurora told him. 'Surgery is not the answer. Nursing is the answer, good nursing and freedom from worry. I hope you're satisfied, Forbes.'

'I don't like to see him like this,' Forbes said, lamely. 'I'll admit he doesn't look too well. He can't be in mortal peril, though, or Donald wouldn't have gone back to Largs.'

'That is not relevant,' said Aurora. 'Donald is doing his best.'

'Where's Lindsay?'

'Ross came this afternoon and he took her home.'

Forbes made eye contact with Martin for the first time since he'd arrived in the ward. 'I see Ross has bought himself a motor-car, one of those Oxford jobs. Did he tell you about it, old chap?'

Martin managed a shake of the head.

Aurora said, 'Overwork and far, far too much responsibility, that's the root cause of the tragic situation in which we find ourselves. I will, of course, be seeking a second opinion.'

'Of course,' said Forbes. 'How long?'

'How long?'

'How long will he be out of the office?'

'Great God! How can you—how *dare* you ask me that. You—you and Franklin's together—have all but wrung the life out of my poor husband and now you're demanding yet another pound of his flesh.'

'Well, I'd hardly put it like that, Aurora,' said Forbes.

'I know not and care not how you would put it, Forbes. Martin will be "out of the office" for as

410

long as it takes to restore his health and strength. I will not allow him to set foot inside Aydon Road until he is fully recovered. When he is and when he does I shall expect you to shoulder somewhat more of the burden of management than you have done in the past.'

'I understand that,' said Forbes. 'What length of time are we talking about here? A month, six months—a year, perhaps?'

'You are *incorrigible*,' Aurora snapped. 'You will not be happy until you have worked my poor husband into an early grave, like, like . . .'

'McGillicuddy's donkey,' Colin suggested, helpfully.

Aurora ignored him and moved on. 'Where *were* you this afternoon?'

Forbes had been studying his cousin throughout Rora's little rant, trying to decide whether Martin really was at death's door or if, as was her wont, his wife was exaggerating.

'Pardon?'

'I asked where you were this afternoon. You were not in the office.'

'Aurora, dearest, it's the middle of the fair holiday. Aydon Road's like a graveyard, except for some clean-up and maintenance crews.'

'You weren't at home either.'

Forbes manufactured a sigh to precede the lie. 'I was with the accountants, if you must know. I was closeted in a boiling-hot office in Blythswood Square endeavouring to make sense of our latest set of figures. In case you haven't heard, we—'

'Oh, I've heard, I've heard. I've heard nothing else for months,' Aurora interjected. 'You're bent on squandering all our money on some harebrained scheme to build oil-tankers for the French. Great God—the French!'

With dignity and gentlemanly aplomb, Forbes got to his feet. He buttoned his overcoat and put on his hat. He looked down on Aurora from as much height as he could muster, then across at the boy.

'Take care of your mother, Colin,' he said, then, leaning, patted Martin lightly on the cheek. 'And you, old son, take care of yourself. I'll drop by tomorrow and bring you some grapes.'

'No,' Aurora snapped. 'No grapes.'

'Jelly, then,' said Forbes.

With a wink and a final nod to poor old Martin, he turned and walked from the ward, doing his best not to skip with delight until he was out of sight of the patient and the patient's formidable wife.

*   *   *

Dust coated the kitchen table and the tea tasted rusty. He had intended to replenish the stock of gin but somehow it had slipped his mind. They were seated in the dingy kitchen of the flat in Flowerhill Drive, sipping tea without milk. Stella had been tetchy all evening and rather less passionate than usual.

'You really should do something about this place, Forbes. It's disgusting.'

'I'll bring in a woman.'

'Now there's a phrase to conjure with,' Stella said.

'You know what I mean—a cleaner.'

'All things considered it's probably not worth the bother.'

412

'All things considered?' said Forbes, anxiously.

'We won't have to put up with these furtive meetings much longer.'

'Oh,' said Forbes, relieved. 'No, of course we won't.'

'How is Martin?'

'Not well, not well at all.'

'I assume you visited again today?'

'First in when the bell rang this afternoon. Lindsay will take the evening shift. Aurora's there constantly, of course, monitoring visitors. He's going to be in dock for at least another week, then there's talk of them all decamping to Donald's house for the rest of the summer. Sea air, invalid menus, lots of rest. Aurora and her mother-in-law rub along quite well, actually.'

'Birds of a feather?'

'Pretty much,' said Forbes. 'Point is, if we play our cards right I'm fairly certain I can persuade Martin to sell his share in the partnership. It's highly fortuitous from our point of view, though not so jolly dusty for Martin, of course. Anyhow, if Martin goes then I think Arthur will follow, particularly if I peddle the idea that Franklin's is a sinking ship. Lindsay may be more of a problem.'

'What about Calder? We want to hang on to Calder, do we not?'

'If possible,' Forbes said, 'though he's not a major stakeholder and he is knocking on in years.'

'Why *did* you turn up at Merriam House for breakfast?'

Forbes shrugged. 'I reckoned it was time to put some of my cards on the table. Simple as that. I had a feeling that the little Frenchman wouldn't be too far away, though I hadn't anticipated bumping into Paget.'

'Geoffrey,' Stella said, 'is becoming rather a nuisance.'

'He's not still after my wife, is he?'

'He's still gambling.'

'Oh dear!'

'Drew was rather admiring of the way you handled things.'

'Good, that's good.' Forbes covered her plump hand with his. 'I can't wait for it all to be settled so that we can be together. I assume your hubby will want to hang on to the place in Dalmuir after you separate?'

'I'm not sure,' Stella said. 'I'll get nothing out of it, of course. One can hardly blame Drew if he cuts me off without a penny.'

'But you do have interests of your own, don't you?'

'Some, a few,' Stella said.

'Never mind,' Forbes said. 'I've a bit tucked away, and we'll have my salary, plus dividends. With Far East Oil behind us I don't suppose there'll be any quibble about payment. Perhaps we should buy a nice little summer place in Morocco, you and I, in Port-Lyautey, say. I hear it's bidding fair to become the Athens of the North African coast.'

'I much prefer the south of France.'

'I thought the world was our oyster.'

'Travelling will hardly be a practical proposition if you're still managing Franklin's, will it?'

'You're right, darling. Of course you are,' Forbes said. 'Still, in ten years or so we'll be able to retire and do what the hell we like. One huge advantage of living in Glasgow meanwhile is that we'll be able to keep in touch with the children.'

'Frankly, Forbes, I couldn't care less about the children.' She leaned across the dusty table and chastely kissed his cheek. 'I just want to be with *you*, so hurry, my darling, please hurry and make it happen.'

'I will,' Forbes promised. 'By Christmas Franklin's will be ours and you, my sweet'—he put on a plummy voice—'will be mine, all mine.'

CHAPTER SEVENTEEN

The Best-Laid Plans

As soon as the holiday was over, and Martin out of the way, Forbes wasted no time in bringing the workforce to its knees. There was fear in the ranks, and resentment too. The only folk who seemed to think that they still held the balance of power were the shop stewards. Word went down to the accounts department in the form of a memorandum bearing Forbes McCulloch's signature. Within ten minutes of the memo being received the news was all over the yard and Jack Burgoyne was heading for the manager's office.

'What, Mr Forbes, is the meaning of this?' Burgoyne slapped a copy of the memo down on Forbes's desk.

Forbes rose and quietly closed the office door.

'Precisely what it looks like, Jack,' he said, 'a list of wage reductions.'

'When will these cuts be brought into effect?'

'Friday,' Forbes said. 'I don't like it any more

415

than you do, but if we can't cost we can't build.'

'There are two ships in the ways and you're spending money hand over fist on an expansion programme. How, sir, do you square that with wage cuts?'

'The cargo boats are due for launch in September. After they sail off into the sunset, Jack, what then?'

'This tanker . . .'

'Uh-huh,' Forbes said. 'What about this tanker?'

Burgoyne blinked and frowned. 'We were led to believe the order had been confirmed.'

'Well,' Forbes said, 'it hasn't.'

'The testing . . .'

'The clients were very impressed with the tank tests. What they are not impressed with is our quoted price. By the by, in case you're under the impression that the clients are paying for the expansion, let me assure you that they are not. The money's coming out of our capital reserves and, whatever you may think to the contrary, my family doesn't hold a key to the Royal Mint.'

'When's Mr Martin coming back?'

'Mr Martin is a very sick man and may not be coming back at all,' Forbes said. 'From now on you'll be dealing with me, Jack, and I sincerely hope you'll persuade your members to accept a bit of tightening of the belt.'

'This is not right,' Jack Burgoyne said. 'We should have been consulted.'

'You're being consulted now,' Forbes said. 'For all our sakes, Jack, I'm asking you to have due regard to the situation and not do anything drastic.'

'Like what, Mr Forbes?'

'Like strike,' said Forbes.

Against his better judgement Tom had taken the family on holiday. It was the usual thing, a fortnight in the Bruce Hotel in Rothesay, on the Isle of Bute. But not quite the usual thing, for buckets, spades, beach balls and water wings no longer amused his children who mooched about the hotel or slunk along the Esplanade in search of entertainment, and shelter from the teeming rain.

Ewan spent hours closeted in his room, smoking cigarettes and poring over copies of *Tit-Bits* and the *News of the World* or, when that brush with debauchery palled, lolled in an armchair in the residents' lounge studying back issues of the *Tablet*.

Tom and Cissie did what all rain-bound parents do on holiday: they drank too much tea, ate too many scones, attended too many unmusical concerts and speculated on what their incomprehensible offspring were up to. In fact, Dorothy and Katy had discovered a café with an absolutely gorgeous Italian boy behind the counter, and hung coyly about the door or, once seated at a marble-topped table inside, acted all cosmopolitan and consumed too much ice-cream.

Ewan, meanwhile, lined up with the kiddies for *Summer Follies* matinées and moodily appraised the buxom young chorines in their scanty costumes or took himself to the town's one and only picture house and sat, smoking furiously, through flickering old cowboy films while brooding over the half-sister who wasn't really his half-sister but who, through fate or ill-luck, *was* a blood relative and whose body was therefore taboo.

On the steamer, going home, the sun came out to cheer Tom's children as they bade farewell to rousing Rothesay and vowed in their hearts that they would never be dragged back there again.

* * *

On Sunday at St Anne's three little darlings were being baptised and the church was almost full. Cooing and crying drowned out the choir and if he hadn't managed to find a seat directly behind Maeve, Ewan would have risked opprobrium and crept away up the long aisle to steal a smoke in the lavatory.

As it was, he had a perfect view of the fine dark hairs that curled over Maeve's collar and her perfect pink ears and when they rose to sing hymns he could make out the line of her cheek and throat and the swell of her bosom under her coat. An uneasy truce had been declared between Calders and McCullochs. Egged on by his mother, Philip even went so far as to enquire if Ewan had had a good time in Rothesay, to which Ewan replied, 'No, rotten.'

He didn't care about making up with his male cousins, didn't care if they thought ill of him or if he never saw them again. He had eyes only for Maeve and she, he thought, had eyes only for him. She blushed when he asked her how she was, blushed again when he murmured that he'd missed her.

Then Harry, bloody Harry, strode up behind them and led the girl away.

* * *

418

Harry sipped a third cup of coffee and said, 'It's going to feel very odd not to be going to school with Phil next week.'

'Make the most of it,' Forbes said. 'In six weeks you probably won't know what hit you. You'll be a new boy again—a fresher, isn't that what they call it?—and, unless I'm much mistaken, you'll hardly have time to blow your nose.'

'Thank you, Dad,' Harry said. 'Most encouraging.'

'Ah, you'll be fine. Sure you've a head on your shoulders, which is more than I had at your age.' Forbes wiped his moustache with a napkin and got up from the breakfast table. 'Right, must push. Arthur, are you coming?'

'We're off to call on Martin. Didn't anyone tell you?' Arthur said.

'Nobody tells me anything,' said Forbes. 'Who's off to see Martin?'

'All of us,' Lindsay said. 'Eleanor and the boys included.'

'Everyone except me,' said Maeve. 'I'm sitting for Ross this afternoon.'

'Hmm!' Forbes said. 'I do think you might have said something, Papa. I've slated a meeting with the shop stewards for noon.'

'I'm sure you'll manage without me,' Arthur said, stretching. 'It's a fine day and a breath of sea air will do us all good. Donald's expecting us. He'll pick us up at the railway station. Martin, I gather, is not making much headway. We'll cheer the poor beggar up, won't we, Eleanor?'

'Without doubt,' said Eleanor Runciman, gloomily.

'Do let Cook know when you'll be home for dinner, Forbes,' said Lindsay.

'I'll probably dine at the club,' said Forbes.

'Pity you're promised to Uncle Ross, Maeve,' Philip said. 'Largs can be very bracing at this time of year, and Aunt Lilias always puts up a good lunch.'

'What time's your train?' Forbes asked.

'Ten thirty,' Lindsay answered.

'Give my best to Martin,' Forbes said, 'and please assure him that I have everything under control.'

'Have you?' Arthur said.

'No, I haven't,' Forbes said, 'but don't tell Martin that.'

*   *   *

The noon meeting in the spar shed went off with less acrimony than Forbes had anticipated. He was well aware, though, that it was no more than an opening skirmish in the battle between the workers and the swine who employed them.

Swine number one was Owen Forbes McCulloch who was still regarded by the greybeards in the ranks as an upstart, a role that Forbes rather enjoyed. He perched on the temporary platform and listened to Jack Burgoyne put the case for arbitration, to Lightbody complain about the employers' high-handed attitude in slashing wages without consultation—all the usual clichéd rhetoric. At length the shop stewards yielded the floor to Forbes. He sauntered to the front of the platform, lit a cigarette, blew out smoke and, with his Irish brogue turned up full blast, cursed the shop stewards for their short-sightedness.

He knew that the hoi polloi were disconcerted by bad language coming out of the mouth of a man in a hand-tailored suit and he cursed them roundly for several seconds, then, stepping to the edge of the platform, he explained just how seriously Britain's economic position had been assailed by the disorganisation of the European and Asiatic markets in the wake of the war and how former customers for Clyde-built ships were now rivals in the world market-place. For fifteen minutes or so, he laid out the facts of the employers' case, and when that was done, he invited questions.

The tanker? Ah, yes, the tanker. Has the contract been signed? No, the contract has not been signed. Why not? Price is the sticking point. Price might yet sink the order and leave Franklin's cupboard bare.

'What are the partners doing about it?'

'No,' Forbes shouted, 'what are *you* doing about it?'

'What we're not doing, Mr McCulloch, is taking it lying down.'

'All right,' Forbes said. 'Put it to your membership.'

'I will,' said Jack Burgoyne. 'We all will.'

'I need your agreement soon, Jack,' Forbes said. 'But I warn you if there's any stoppage of work, we'll lose the order and, with it, any hope of securing future orders from that source.' He paused, then shouted, 'And I'm not going to stand by and see you cut your own bloody throats. I've given as much of my life to this firm as you have and, by the Holy Jesus, I'll do anything I can to save it from closure.' Forbes chopped a hand across

421

his throat. 'I'm not above taking drastic action, be damned clear about that.'

'Lockout, you mean?' somebody yelled.

'If the cap fits,' Forbes said, then, followed by Tom and Archie Robb, turned abruptly and left the spar shed, well satisfied with his morning's work.

*   *   *

As soon as they were alone in Forbes's office, Tom said, 'I thought the contract *was* secure?'

Forbes said, 'It is.'

'Then why are you goading the shop stewards?'

'There's nothing Burgoyne would like better than to force a strike. If they do strike then the engineers will call the tune. On the other hand if we lock the gates, we'll have the thing under our control and the unions will be at each other's throats before the week's out. Solidarity? Fat chance.'

'Have you discussed a lockout with Arthur?'

'Nope.'

'With Lindsay?'

'Lindsay couldn't care less.'

'I wouldn't be too sure of that,' said Tom.

'Oh, I'm sure of it,' Forbes said. 'To tell you the truth it's on her mind to sell her shares in Franklin's before the price drops through the floor.'

'Has she said as much?'

'Arthur definitely wants out,' Forbes said. 'In fact, they've gone off this very day to talk it over with Martin, and seek Donald's advice.'

'Tradition, family tradition—'

'Matters not a damn any more. The Franklins

422

aren't like you and me, Tom. None of them, not even Martin, have shipbuilding in their bones. Look at Ross, he sold out first chance he got. Look at Donald, he took early retirement as soon as his profits showed signs of dropping.'

'He lost his son, Forbes, that might have had something to do with it.'

'Johnny gave his life for the nation and, in my humble opinion, Donald did Johnny's memory a disservice by quitting when he did.'

'I'm not convinced.'

'I want this firm to survive, Tom, and I'll do whatever's necessary to ride out the storm. I'll even put myself in hock to soak up the partners' shares if they aren't wholeheartedly behind me. I don't want this firm to fall into the hands of some money-grubber who'll strip the assets and sell the ground to a developer. I'm proud of what I do, Tom, and I've no wish to see my life's work flushed down the lavatory pan.'

'I had no idea you felt so strongly, Forbes.'

'Well, I do. By God, I do.' Forbes held up a hand, finger and thumb an inch apart. 'All I need is *this* much support, old son, *this* much, and I'll move in and save Franklin's from the hammer, even if it puts me up to my ears in debt.'

'Will there be a place for me in all this, Forbes?'

'There will always be a place for you, Tom.'

'I—I have some savings . . .'

'No,' said Forbes hastily. 'Hang on to your savings. You've a boy to educate and two girls to marry off and you and Cissie have earned a comfortable retirement, when that day comes. I appreciate your offer, but no, this is something I have to do on my own.' He shook his head, sighed and glanced at his watch. 'We've missed lunch. Tell you what, give me a couple of hours to clear up here and we'll drive back to Brunswick Crescent, pick up Maeve and take her out for an early dinner.'

'Didn't Maeve go to Largs with the others?'

'Ah, no.' Forbes tapped his nose with his forefinger. 'She isn't one of them, you see, isn't a true-blue Franklin and it's very hush-hush stuff that'll be discussed round Donald's table. Besides, I think she's sitting for Ross this afternoon. So, what do you say to a bite of dinner somewhere nice, just you, me and Maeve?'

Tom smiled. 'I'll give Cissie a call and tell her not to expect me home.'

'You do that,' Forbes said. 'See you at five thirty?'

'Five thirty it is,' said Tom.

*　　　*　　　*

Ross told her that the sitting would be shorter than usual as he had to pop into Glasgow on business at half past three o'clock. He sent her into the bathroom to put on the white dress while he secured the canvas to an easel and as soon as Maeve was settled in her pose began to apply paint.

He worked quietly, saying little. Maeve was glad of his reticence. She had a great deal on her mind and needed an opportunity to think. Last night she had dreamed in turn of Bobby Shannon and Ewan Calder. She wished she could ask her mother to explain her confusion and tell her what she should do for the best. It wasn't the sort of question she could put in a letter, though, and she wasn't even

424

sure that Mam's advice would help, for her mother's letters were filled with trivial gossip about the characters in Endicott Street and vague hints of longing for days that were gone, for the dashing and deceitful Fran Haggarty who had become the love of her mother's life now that he was dead and buried and had left her nothing but memories— and Sean, of course, and Sean.

Ross worked for an hour and then, rising, told her to make herself scarce.

By the time Maeve had slipped out of the flowing white dress and put on her outdoor clothes, Ross had donned a smart dark blue suit and a hard-collar shirt with a sober necktie.

'Must be important business for you to dress up like a toff.'

'I'm seeing my bank manager first,' Ross said, 'then my solicitor.'

'You're not going broke, are you?'

'No.' Ross smiled. 'I'm not going broke. I'm thinking of buying a house, if you must know.'

'Any particular house?'

'Not really. I've just started sniffing around.'

'Good luck then,' said Maeve. 'Same time tomorrow?'

'Please.'

He offered to drive her home but she knew that he was pressed for time and said that she would walk. It was a dry afternoon, sunny but cool. She had no reason to hurry back to Brunswick Crescent and even considered taking a tram into Glasgow to do a little window-shopping. Why she changed her mind was a mystery. Instinct, perhaps, drew her back to Brunswick Park where, on a bench under the shabby trees, Ewan Calder lay in wait.

She spotted him at precisely the same moment that he spotted her.

She crossed the road and leaned on the railings.

'What do you think you're doin' down there?' she called out.

'Give you three guesses,' Ewan called back.

He climbed the path to the gate. He wore a shirt with the sleeves rolled up, the collar open, grey flannel trousers and tennis shoes, and looked, Maeve thought, almost sporty.

He leaned over the gate and kissed her.

'They told me where you were,' he said, 'but they wouldn't let me wait indoors.'

Maeve opened the gate. 'Who wouldn't?'

'That bitch of a servant.'

'Enid?'

'The other one.'

'Cook. She probably thought you were after stealing the silver.'

'Where is everyone?'

'Gone to visit Uncle Martin in Largs.'

Ewan pulled her to him and kissed her again. He pushed his thigh against her stomach, crushing her dress. He spread his hand across her chest and for one breathless moment she could feel her heart beating against his palm.

He said, 'They won't be home for hours, will they?'

'No,' Maeve said, 'not for hours.'

'Are we going inside?'

And Maeve said, 'I don't see why not.'

*   *   *

The Franklins trooped out along the promenade,

heading in the direction of the pier. All roads in the little town led to the pier.

In the height of the season steamers came and went constantly, ploughing from the mouth of the Clyde, gliding round the tail of the Isle of Cumbrae or up from the Mull of Kintyre, sleek beautiful steamers with names like *Waverley, Talisman* and *Jeanie Deans*, names that linked literature with industry; the *Marchioness* of this or the *Duchess* of that, too, just to remind you that ships were vassals of a system that was at root still feudal.

Men and boys gathered on the pier to watch the steamers and, given half a chance, the old men would tell you proudly that they had smelted the iron, shaped the steel, bolted the boilers, raised the masts or painted the funnels of that fine fast vessel there, that whatever name was emblazoned on the hull she was 'their' ship and always would be till rust or progress sent her to the breaker's yard.

The strains of the deck bands didn't chime with Largs. Unlike Rothesay, across the firth, the town was neat, sedate and elegant.

Floral beds, gardens and stately mansions adorned the front and two tall churches gave you points to steer by when you hired a rowing boat and sculled the family out on the salty breast of the Clyde and looked back at the town nestled in an amphitheatre of green hills.

If he had been alone, which he rarely was these days, Arthur would have gravitated to the pier like so many others of his ilk and spent a happy afternoon watching the steamers come and go. But Eleanor had taken his arm and, thus hobbled, he strolled with genteel gravity along the promenade between the flowerbeds and the pebble beach.

Arthur was happy, though. Arthur was at peace. He loved the Clyde coast, loved being with his family, and most of all he loved being out and about with Eleanor. Up ahead were Donald and Lilias, arm-in-arm; ahead of them Rora and Lindsay pushed poor Martin along in a bath chair, though Martin declared that he was quite fit enough to walk, thank you, and that it was only his wife who insisted that he was still an invalid. Where Phil and Harry had got to Arthur had no idea. They would turn up, no doubt, when the procession reached the pier and turned to head back to Donald's mansion in time for afternoon tea.

She was slow now, was Eleanor, but he owed her a debt and a duty and did not resent having to adjust his pace. She had looked after him for too many years to count; now he must look after her. He had been married once, happily married, but his wife had died so long ago that he could hardly recall what she looked like and what feelings he'd had for her. What remained of those distant days were Lindsay and Eleanor, the remnant of a life that had given him joy.

He patted Eleanor's hand affectionately and surprised himself by saying, 'If I sold my interest in Franklin's and came here to live, would you still keep house for me?'

'Of course.'

'If I asked you to marry me, would you do that too?'

'Of course.'

'I take it,' Arthur said, 'that a quiet little wedding would suit us best?'

'It would.'

'In September, say?'

'September would not be too soon,' said Eleanor.

'Is it settled then, my dear?'

'I do believe it is,' Eleanor Runciman said.

'Shall we tell the others?'

'Not yet.'

'Our secret?' Arthur said, grinning.

'For a little while longer, yes.'

*   *   *

They were lying on the carpet in front of the fireplace in the piano parlour, his son on top of his granddaughter, both with enough flesh showing to shock Tom to the core. His first thought was that Maeve had fainted and Ewan was trying to revive her, but the boy's panic-stricken reaction to his appearance swiftly put paid to that notion.

Maeve's skirts were thrown up around her middle, her frock was unbuttoned, her breasts and thighs exposed. It was the sight of his son's skinny buttocks that horrified Tom, though, and he let out a yelp that brought Forbes hurrying from the hall. By that time Ewan had crawled behind the sofa and was trying in vain to button himself into his trousers.

Glassy-eyed and unsteady, Maeve flopped against the fender.

Forbes shouted, 'What the hell is going on here?'

Doubled over, fumbling, Ewan was sober enough to answer, 'Nothing, nothing. We had a little drink, that's all, and . . .'

Forbes scrambled over the sofa, grabbed Ewan by the arm and cuffed him about the ears, shouting,

'Drink, was it? Drink! You have the gall to tell me it was the drink put you in that state. God, I'll have the skin off your back, you bugger, if you've harmed one hair of her head.'

On the carpet stood a whisky decanter and a bottle of Arthur's special French brandy. There were glasses in the hearth, a cigarette smouldered on the rug and Maeve's underwear—brassiere, lacy drawers and stockings—was strewn in all directions. Forbes caught Ewan by the neck and forced him to his knees.

'Did you do it?' he hissed. 'Did you put your thing inside her?'

'Dad?' Ewan whimpered. 'Dad, he's hurting me.'

'Did you, did you do it? Answer me.'

Ewan began to weep. 'I tried but—but I—I couldn't.'

Forbes released his grip on the boy's neck. 'See to him, Tom,' he said. 'I'll deal with her.' Kneeling, he cupped Maeve's chin and lifted her head. 'Did he hurt you, sweetheart?'

Maeve's eyes struggled to focus, and managed to shake her head.

'Good Christ!' said Forbes. 'She's as drunk as a lord.'

When he put an arm around her to help her to her feet the front of her frock fell open. He groped behind him, pulled a cushion from the sofa and pressed it against her nakedness. Ewan stood by his father's side, whimpering like a child. Gingerly, Forbes helped Maeve to her feet and put her down, more or less upright, on the sofa, the cushion still clasped in her arms. He tugged down her skirt, picked her underwear from the carpet and placed it by her.

430

He looked at Tom, and the weeping boy, and growled, 'Goddamn it!' Then he strode into the hall and bellowed for Enid to come up at once; no answer from below, no hasty tap of feet on the stairs. He returned to the parlour.

'Where are Enid and Cook?'

'I—I don't know,' Ewan said. 'They went out, I think.'

'And left you alone, you little bugger. And you thought you had your chance at last, did you? You thought you'd take advantage of an innocent—'

'Forbes, that's enough,' Tom said. 'Can't you see he's upset?'

'Jesus Christ!' Forbes exploded. 'What's got into *you*, Tom Calder? She's your granddaughter, for God's sake! He could go to jail for this. If this ever gets out—if she happens to be—I mean, it's a crime, a heinous crime, even if he is only seventeen years old.'

'She made me do it. She—she asked for it.'

'You lying little bastard,' Forbes snarled. 'She wouldn't, she isn't . . .' He threw his hands in the air. 'Get him out of here, Tom, get him out of my sight before I break his bloody neck.'

Sniffing and tear-stained, Ewan glanced up at his father.

'You—you don't have to tell Mama, do you, Dad?'

'We aren't going to tell anyone,' Tom said. 'Are we, Forbes?'

Forbes plucked the brandy bottle from the carpet, wiped the neck with the flat of his hand and took a long pull. He blew out his cheeks.

Maeve sagged and sprawled across the sofa and, still clutching the cushion, appeared to be falling asleep.

'Are we, Forbes?' Tom Calder repeated.

'No,' Forbes said. 'No, we're not going to tell anyone. But keep him away from her, from me, from all of us. I don't care what excuses you make to Cissie, I never want to see his nasty little mug in this house again. And you'—he pointed the bottle at Ewan—'if you so much as breathe a word about what happened here, or if I ever—*ever*—catch you near my daughter again, by God next time I will have the law down on you.'

It was out before he could help it, the sharp, rat-a-tat, quick-as-a-flash retort. 'Your daughter?' Ewan said. '*Your* daughter?'

'Get him out of here,' Forbes said.

And Tom, very quickly, led his son away.

*   *   *

The curtain was closed but there were soft splinters of light around the edges, a subdued sort of light that might signify dusk, or possibly dawn. She moved her head on the pillow and groaned. Her head hurt and her eyes felt as if they had been poked with a sharp stick. She had a sour taste in her mouth that stretched all the way down her throat and burned in her chest. For a moment she felt as if she might be sick. She sat up. The room spun like a merry-go-round. She stuck out an arm to steady herself and saw the shape in the chair in the corner and, thinking it was Ewan, let out a shuddering cry, '*Noooooo.*'

He was with her in an instant, holding an enamel basin under her chin.

'Uh—Uncle Forbes?'

'Are you going to be sick?'

She gulped and swallowed. 'I—no, I don't think so.'

He had taken off his jacket and loosened his collar. He looked, she thought, like one of those kindly old-fashioned doctors, but there was a rasp in his voice that brought out the Irish. He pressed the rim of the basin against her tummy and kept it there, taking no chances. She was in her nightgown. The clothes she had been wearing downstairs were folded neatly over a chair. The lamp had been taken from the table and placed on the floor. She could see only the shape of him against the low light from the lamp.

'My head hurts.'

'I'm not surprised,' Forbes said. 'Listen, it's almost half past ten ...'

'Night?'

'Yes. The family will be back at any moment. I'm going to tell them you're unwell. Do you understand what I'm saying?' Maeve nodded, and felt as if her head might fall into the basin. Forbes went on, 'You've a hangover—and it serves you right. What you allowed Ewan Calder to do was very, very stupid. I have to ask you—did he—I mean, what *did* he do? Do you remember?'

She squeezed her eyes shut. 'Are you goin' to send me home?'

'No, I'm not going to send you home, not unless you want me to.'

'I don't know what I want.'

He put the basin on to the floor by the bed and took her hand.

In the half light, he looked very like her father.

She recalled something, something that Ewan

433

had said. It lay in the sump of her memory along with all the things she wanted to forget. Uncle Forbes was right, though; she had been stupid, very, very stupid, to get carried away. It hadn't all been Ewan's fault. She had wanted it too, wanted to see what it was like to be touched, what a man would look like down there. Once the brandy had soothed her apprehension, she had found the things that Ewan did exciting.

'You know what I'm asking,' Forbes said. 'Did he go inside you?'

'No.'

'Did he try?'

'Yes, but something went wrong with—with his thing before he could—you know. Where is Ewan?'

'That's no concern of yours, Maeve. You won't be seeing Ewan Calder again, that I promise you.'

'He said something.'

'He said a lot of things,' Forbes said, 'Now, if you're sure, absolutely sure, that he didn't—you know, then I'm willing to keep quiet about the whole sorry affair, and let it go at that.'

'Tom, Grandpa Tom . . .'

'He's very angry and very disappointed in both of you.'

'It wasn't Ewan's fault.'

'Yes, it was,' said Forbes. 'Whatever Ewan might have told you, whatever you may think, Maeve, it *was* his fault. Dear God, even at seventeen he should know better. What he tried to do to you could land him in prison.'

The pulses in her head beat like a kettle drum. She felt as if her eyes were about to pop out at any second. She groped to make sense of what her uncle was telling her, but that half-remembered

434

thing kept nagging away at her brain. She was far from being tearful, though. She felt too awful to be remorseful. Her only serious regret was that she had been found out.

'Listen,' Forbes said again, 'I'm going downstairs to make a pot of tea. I'll bring it up. As far as Cook's concerned you were taken ill. If she does make a shrewd guess at the truth of it she'll keep it to herself. When the family comes home I'll tell them you felt sick. Lindsay will probably come to see you. Tell her—tell her anything you like; tummy upset, woman's trouble, anything except the truth. All right?'

'Aye.'

Forbes got to his feet. 'Get yourself into the bathroom, Maeve. Give yourself a wash. It'll make you feel better.'

She was not so naïve that she didn't know what he meant. Male juice hadn't touched her there. She remembered Ewan cursing, remembered laughing at him. She shouldn't have laughed at him. Ewan didn't know what was happening any more than she did. He had thrown himself on top of her. If she hadn't been tipsy she would have shoved him off. Then the door had opened and her grandfather had appeared in the parlour.

Forbes said, 'You'll feel better once you've had tea.'

'I could do with some toast, too,' Maeve said, 'if that's all right.'

Forbes gave a rueful little snort.

'Toast,' he said, 'it shall be,' and hurried off downstairs.

*　　　*　　　*

435

The pain had returned. He lay with her on the bed in the hole in the wall and covered her eyes with the flat of his hand. The old man was at the sink under the window, staring at the rooftops of the Riverside. Bobby had no idea whether the old man was dying for a drink or grieving because Alice was suffering so much and he could do nothing to help her.

The old man wore a creased and shiny three-piece suit. He hadn't removed the jacket and looked, Bobby thought, as if he were still deciding whether or not to stay. In the window glass he could make out the reflection of the old man's face defined by a lick of sparse white hair and the drooping walrus moustache; he braced himself against the sink, arms spread, as if he were preaching to an unseen host in the court below.

Alice whimpered and clung to him. He had given her as much medicine as she could stomach. Besides, the bottle was almost empty. He would have to keep a spoonful or two in case she started screaming again, for her screaming wakened the neighbours and they would hammer on the wall and yell at him to keep her quiet. She had been warped from birth, a misshapen wee wretch lying in a shoe-box, given up for dead. Perhaps it would have been better for all of them if she had gone straight back to her Maker.

Nearly midnight now: neither the old man nor he was able to sleep when Alice was this bad. He clung to her, holding her so tightly that he might have been trying to absorb her pain through his pores.

'Paw,' he said. 'Go on to your bed.'

The old man didn't move.

436

Bobby put his brow against her cheek. He could feel the rotation of her bones under his hands, a strange grinding, like intricate gears. The doctors claimed it was a blood disease that had affected the cells that affected the joints. They could do nothing to cure it.

Marry that girl, Alice had told him, *marry that girl and make me well*.

God, he would marry the girl in half a second if he thought it would cure Alice. He would marry that girl even if Alice were removed to a happier place than Partick and was safe, supple and well.

Maeve McCulloch offered everything he had missed in his apprentice years, a verve, a vitality rare in Riverside Street, big brown, shining eyes and a smile that seemed to be verging on laughter. He prayed there'd be more modelling work, more opportunities to be close to Maeve again, especially now that she had met Alice and knew how it was with him.

'Paw,' he said. 'For God's sake, go to bed. If you're not going to bed put the kettle on the gas and brew us some tea.'

'I hear,' his old man said, 'they're strikin', your place.'

'It's not settled. There's been no call-out as yet.'

'There's no extra, our place neither.' His father addressed his own ghostly presence in the glass. 'No overtime. No Sunday work. What'll we do about the rent if there's a strike?'

'No point in worryin' about it till it happens,' Bobby said. 'Mr Burgoyne won't do anythin' rash. Mr Lightbody won't let him. If the worst comes to the worst we'll have some sort o' strike pay.'

'Hah!' his father said. 'Maybe.'

For a big man he had a soft voice and a remarkably gentle disposition. There were times when Bobby wished his old man had been tough and hard. Hardness of character might have served them better than his tearful retreat from the unyielding reality of Alice.

Bobby said, 'Are you listenin' to me? Put on the kettle.'

'What about her?'

'I'll look after her.'

'Does she want tea?'

'Make some anyway.'

'She'll only boke it up.'

Alice had stopped whimpering. Her eyes were wide open. He could tell by her eyes how bad it was. He smiled down at her, and winked.

'I know what she wants,' he said.

He fished behind him and plucked a packet of five *Player's Weights* from the edge of the mantelshelf. There was one cigarette left in the packet. He tapped it out, sniffed the tobacco, then struck a match and lit the cigarette.

Alice scowled up at him from under the crook of his arm, her little monkey-face alive with desire. Bobby took a long drag on the cigarette, then, propping her up, held it to her lips and let her puff and inhale and blow out tiny curls of grey smoke as she tried in vain to make a smoke ring hover in the air. She coughed and craned forward, a small sign that the pain was at last receding.

'Better,' she said. 'Better. Puff, puff.'

He held the cigarette to her lips and let her smoke it down to the last, wet shred and when at length she fell asleep in his arms, Bobby dozed off, too, and left it to the old man to turn out the light.

438

CHAPTER EIGHTEEN

Riding out the Storm

At half past ten on Thursday forenoon Franklin's management met with representatives of the Employers' Federation and announced their intention to lock the gates at Aydon Road. There were questions but no dissent around the boardroom table for, like Forbes, the members of the Employers' Federation were of the opinion that talk of 'organised labour' was a contradiction in terms. Arthur was unhappy, Tom Calder depressed. Forbes would not be dissuaded. As soon as the meeting closed he drove straight to Merriam House to lunch with Andrew Pickering and Stella.

He left Pickering's at half past three o'clock with Stella's whispered promise that they would soon be together ringing in his ears. He drove back to Aydon Road and issued emergency instructions to the managers.

Chains and padlocks were produced from storerooms and, soon after the shipwrights wended off home for the night, defences were set up. It was the dirtiest of dirty tricks to shut the yard on pay-day but Forbes justified his actions by claiming that Jack Burgoyne and the minority unions were only biding their time until the national council pledged support and financial assistance.

At dinner that evening Arthur and Eleanor announced their intention to marry. Subdued celebrations followed and later, when they were alone, Arthur informed Forbes that he planned to sell his shares in the partnership. Forbes was canny enough to indicate that he was willing to bid. His father-in-law nodded. 'There's no stopping you, Forbes, is there?' he said. 'I just hope the outcome makes you happy.'

'Happy?' Forbes said. 'I'm happy for you and Miss Runciman. It's high time you made an honest woman out of her. God knows, you've earned your retirement. Nobody, past or present, living or dead, can grudge it to you.'

'If only I were twenty years younger, Forbes,' Arthur said, 'I wouldn't let you off with it.'

'Off with what?' said Forbes, feigning surprise.

But Arthur just shrugged and went downstairs to the parlour to play a few wistful tunes on the piano.

*　　　*　　　*

'Good God!' Ross said. 'You're the last person I expected. I take it Maeve's not coming?'

'She insisted on going to Aydon Road with Forbes,' Lindsay said. 'The prospect of witnessing a mass demonstration seems to appeal to her.'

'She's Irish, of course,' Ross said. 'Militant gatherings are in her blood. Is it because of the lockout she's been out of sorts lately?'

'I doubt it. There's some chap involved. Could it be your young man from the drawing-office?'

'Bobby? Perhaps,' Ross said. 'I'm not Maeve's confidant, you know.'

Lindsay had arrived soon after one. Ross had been enjoying a leisurely lunch. The remains of a ham sandwich and a glass of beer were still on the table, the *Glasgow Herald* lying open on the floor. He produced a bottle of red wine, already uncorked, poured a glass for Lindsay, and drew out a chair.

'Why aren't you manning the barricades,' he said, 'shoulder to shoulder with your man?'

'Forbes regards me as more of a liability than an asset. It's partly my own fault,' Lindsay said. 'I let him off with too much for too long. I was afraid of losing him, I think.'

'To another woman, you mean?'

She nodded and sipped the strong red wine. 'I convinced myself that living with my mistake was the right thing to do.'

'You're not the martyr type,' Ross told her.

'I think that's something one has to find out for oneself. My father's retiring to the coast. He finally got around to proposing to Miss Runciman. They'll look for a property almost immediately.' Lindsay managed a smile and raised her glass. 'Good luck to them.'

'Is Arthur selling his share of the partnership?'

'Yes.'

'To Forbes?'

'I think so.'

'What's the quoted price?'

'That hasn't been decided. Why do you ask?'

'I might be interested in buying in again—' Ross stroked his beard and chuckled—'just to spite old Forbes. He'd have a blue fit if I topped the bidding.'

'You're wicked,' Lindsay said. 'What do you know about shipbuilding?'

'Not a dashed thing,' Ross admitted. 'Shipbuilding was never for me; not in my blood, you might say. Besides, I've other little pots on the boil.'

'More commissions?'

'Oh, plenty of those. Far too many of those. It isn't Forbes's hold on Franklin's that I covet.'

'What is it then?' Lindsay asked.

It was very still in the studio, the sounds of tramcars on the Great Western Road muffled by the sullen heat of the August afternoon. He was so relaxed that his answer seemed almost casual.

'His wife,' Ross said.

'I see,' Lindsay said.

It dawned on her that he must have been in love with her for a very long time and that only an innate sense of decency had prevented him declaring himself before now.

'I'm telling you this,' he went on, 'only because I think we're heading for a family crisis and I want you to know that I'm here if you need me.'

'Ross, are you saying that you love me?'

'I do believe I am.'

She set her glass on the floor and got up. She walked around the table, took him by the hand and pulled him to his feet.

'Now what?' he grumbled.

'Now this,' said Lindsay, and kissed him.

*   *   *

At first the protest was embarrassingly tame. More newspaper reporters than shipwrights gathered in Aydon Road. A selection of the more trustworthy members of the press were admitted to the inner sanctum to hear the employers' side of the story from Owen Forbes McCulloch. He was hot on tradition was Owen Forbes and if he mentioned 'pride' once he mentioned it a dozen times. He was also exceedingly complacent was Owen Forbes

McCulloch, too bloody complacent for the acting chairman of a company that had five empty berths and not a rivet being hammered or a bolt tightened.

While Forbes rambled on in the boardroom, the crowd outside grew restless and fell to lobbing stones over the walls and rattling the padlocked gates. Eventually Jack Burgoyne took it upon himself to address the multitude. He urged them to 'stand firm', though quite what they were standing firm for was anybody's guess.

In the middle of Jack's harangue, a nondescript motor van hove into Aydon Road and a dozen or so burly gentlemen armed with clubs and iron bars bundled out, gentlemen who represented a less passive arm of the revolutionary left than Mr John Burgoyne. At almost exactly the same moment as the van disgorged its squad of militants, a dozen mounted policemen appeared at the corner of Fairhaven Street and spurred their horses to a gallop.

The racket was clearly audible in the offices upstairs.

The press crew rushed to the windows, then poured downstairs.

Forbes grabbed his hat to follow them, then, realising that his daughter was not in the room, shouted, 'Maeve? Where the devil are you, Maeve?'

*   *   *

The mounted copper galloped past, baton raised. She could feel the wind of it, smell the horse smell. She wished she'd a stout length of wood to hand.

443

According to Turk nothing was more effective against a galloping horse than a plank thrust between the forelegs. She had seen it done in the square in Wexford one wild Saturday afternoon last summer and recalled how the horse had come down on its belly, slithering and squealing, and had rolled on top of the copper and how the boys had fallen on it with their sticks.

She shook her fist, and screamed, *'Bugger you, you bastards,'* and ran after the horse. *'Leave them alone, you stinkin' pigs.'*

Another mounted copper clattered towards her. Maeve swore at him too. He leaned from the saddle, grinning, and neatly swiped her hat off with his baton. She ducked and fell to her knees and, with heat rising in her like steam in a boiler, lifted both hands to heaven and cursed the forces of capitalist oppression. Bobby dug his hands under her armpits and hoisted her to her feet.

'Come on,' he yelled. 'Time we got outta here.'

Maeve struggled. He lifted her off her feet, an arm wrapped around her waist, a hand perilously close to her breast. She kicked her legs, leaned back against him, breathing hard.

Horsemen, a dozen mounted constables was all it took to put Franklin's employees to flight. The militants had more guts, more gumption. She saw one of the horses rear up, the copper hanging on for grim death, saw one of the militants crack a steel bar against the copper's thigh, the horse brought down, the copper lurching and falling, his helmet rolling away.

Bobby flung her to the ground and covered her as two mounted constables rode furiously past, missing them by inches, then he had her on her feet

444

again and they were running, running like the wind, for the lane between the tenements. She was wet, her skirts wet, her knees bleeding, but she felt wonderful, flying away with Bobby Shannon.

She was aware of women leaning from the windows, shouting abuse, children prancing about the puddles, small boys on the roofs of the wash-houses, the shrill urgent sound of police whistles. Bobby dragged her across the backs into a close and familiar tenement smells enveloped her.

'Stop,' she cried. 'Bobby, stop.'

She sank back against the wall of the close. He caught her again around the waist as if he thought that she were about to swoon. His hair was sticking up and sweat glistened on his face.

'What?' he said, panting. 'What, Maeve, are you hurt?'

Her stockings were torn, her knees grazed. She rested against the wall, feet spread wide. Bobby hunkered at her feet, spat on his fingers and rubbed at her dirty knees until blood oozed out, clear and red. He ran his hands under the hem of her skirt, spreading her legs apart. She clasped his head and pushed his face into her skirts and felt his breath through the fabric, warm against her skin.

He got up slowly, pulling himself against her.

'Look at the state of you,' he said. 'You can't go home like that.'

'No,' she said, hardly daring to breathe. 'I can't, can I?'

'We'll need to patch you up,' he said. 'Come on.'

'Come where?'

'To my house,' Bobby Shannon said.

* * *

445

Bully boys were ten a penny if you knew where to look for them. Some were men of principle whose mission was to destroy an unjust social system; most were just in it for the drink.

Forbes had no idea where the men came from or who they represented. He had tipped the wink to a disaffected journalist, shelled out twenty quid and the journalist had done the rest. He would have been satisfied with the morning's work if he hadn't lost Maeve. He had brought her down to Aydon Road over Lindsay's protests, for it was no bad thing to have a pretty young girl with you to give reporters something to think about while little wheels were whirring behind the scenes. He had last seen Maeve in the office chatting to her grandfather and had assumed that she had come into the boardroom with him. It was only when trouble broke out at the main gate that he missed her; nobody, it seemed, had noticed her leave the building.

The pitched battle in Aydon Road did not last long. The bully boys were back in the van and away before the mounted police could summon reinforcements. There would be an inquiry, of course, but the employers would come out of it smelling of roses, and poor old honest Jack would spend a frustrating weekend trying to rally support for an action that had now been tainted by violence.

Forbes loitered by the gatehouse wall and watched the road empty.

Soon there was nothing to be seen but tattered handbills blowing about and placards discarded in the gutter. Still no sign of Maeve. The girl had

446

been reared in a vicious neighbourhood in Dublin and had probably witnessed more violence than he had. Common sense informed him that she taken herself out of harm's way and gone home.

Aydon Road was not quite deserted. Three or four reporters still hung about outside, and one photographer with a big box camera.

Forbes straightened his hat, buttoned his coat and had the side gate unlocked. He stepped out into the road, then, without Burgoyne to set matters straight, strode forward to tell the press precisely what he thought of his workers, who, it seemed, had chosen anarchy over arbitration.

*　　*　　*

'Nice knees,' the sister said. 'Not as nice as mine, but, are they, Bobby?'

'Not near as nice,' Bobby said. 'Your stockings are ruined.'

'I'll buy another pair on the way home,' Maeve said.

'Buy another pair?' said Alice Shannon. 'As easy as that, eh?'

Maeve was propped against the draining board, holding up her skirt. She had loosened her garters and allowed Bobby to peel off her torn stockings to sponge her bruises with milky disinfectant from a big brown bowl. He crouched now on a stool, her foot in his lap, and gently bathed the cuts.

'Wisht I could buy stockin's when it suited me.' Alice was seated in a low chair directly before the range. She looked more robust today, more mobile and attentive. She wore a long cotton skirt that covered her legs and her boots were fashionably

447

petite. 'You givin' her a wee tickle then, Bobby Shannon, you dirty dog?'

'I'll give you a wee skelp on the ear if you don't hold your wheesh.'

Alice said, 'He gives me a wee tickle when he thinks I'm not lookin'.'

Bobby glanced up at Maeve and shook his head.

He dabbed at the last of the grazes, wrung out the sponge and dropped it into the bowl, reached for a clean towel and dried her off.

'I won't need a bandage, will I?' Maeve said.

'Nah,' Bobby said. 'You'll be able to hide the cuts with stockings.'

'Silk,' Alice said. 'It'll be silk stockin's for you, I suppose.'

'Aye,' Maeve said, thinly. 'Scarlet silk all the way through—except my knickers; they're made of ostrich feathers.'

'Eh?'

'She's just jokin', Alice,' Bobby said.

'Her kind, you never know.'

'Bugger off, Alice,' Bobby said. 'Leave Maeve alone.'

The sister's bed was inset into the inner wall. The outer wall was dominated by the window and sink. An ugly iron range peered across the room at a wooden coal bunker. Bits and pieces of clothing hung from a pulley overhead. Linoleum covered the floor, and a wafer-thin strip of carpet. Everything was worn but spotless, unlike the flat in Endicott Street which was always a bit of a mess.

Bobby slipped Maeve's foot from his lap and got up. He poured away the milky fluid and washed the bowl under the cold water tap. Maeve was aware of the sister's eyes upon them, her jealous gaze

448

unnerving.

She had hoped that by some miracle the sister would not be at home. She'd longed for Bobby to take her in his arms again, to spend time kissing her. But he was still timid. Perhaps he had brought her to his house not to make love but just to entertain Alice.

Through the half-open door she could make out the cramped hall that linked the kitchen to the bedroom. She wanted to see the bedroom, the bed where Bobby slept. She wanted him to take her in there and to lie with her on the bed. Bobby wasn't like Ewan Calder. Bobby wasn't a boy angling for what he could get without knowing what to do when he got it.

'That'll see you home,' he said.

'Home?'

'You'll not want them to know where you've been,' said Alice.

'No, of course not,' Maeve said.

'Your uncle wouldn't like it if he knew you'd been visitin' the enemy.'

'You're not the enemy,' Maeve said, quickly, 'not my enemy.'

'Aye, but you're not our friend, neither,' Alice said.

'I thought we were,' Maeve said, 'friends.'

'If we was friends you'd stay for your dinner.'

'Alice,' Bobby warned.

'You'd go out an' buy us pies for our dinner.'

There was a lot more to Bobby Shannon than good looks and a tender nature. He wouldn't have earned himself a board in Franklin's drawing-office if he'd been a dunderhead. He didn't deserve to be imprisoned in the world of his sister's fantasies,

449

trapped by responsibility. She had thought of him as the lover, the swain, the wide-eyed shepherd boy whose heart she had made captive, but that was an illusion, a fiction; Bobby Shannon's heart was not his to give away.

Alice said, 'I'd love a juicy mutton pie for m' dinner.'

'I'll get you a pie,' Bobby said, through his teeth.

Maeve draped an arm about Bobby's shoulders.

Alice's eyes hardened.

'Tell you what, Alice,' Maeve said, 'I'll give you a couple of shillings and you go out an' buy the pies while I stay here and keep Bobby company.'

It was cruel thing to say but, for Bobby's sake, she felt she must assert herself or yield the upper hand to his sister.

'Me?' Alice said. 'How can I buy pies, you daft bitch?'

'If it's the money, I've got money,' Maeve said.

Bobby had taken his hands from the water in the sink and had stretched out an arm in search of a towel. He was frozen in that pose, as motionless as if he were modelling for some drab depiction of life in the tenements of Clydeside.

'I can't go out,' Alice said. 'I can't get of out this bloody chair.'

'So it isn't just money?' Maeve said.

She swayed slightly, nudging Bobby's hip. She could tell by the little wrinkle at the corner of his eye that he understood what was going on.

'Bitch!' Alice raised both fists and thumped them down. 'Bitch,' she said again, then laughed. 'Nah, it's just me, ain't it? Just me.'

'Right,' Maeve said, brusquely. 'If it's just you, we'll take you out and you can eat as many pies as you like, with gravy and mushy peas. I'm inviting you to a sit-down dinner in the City Bakeries tea-room.' She performed a little folderol and affected a posh voice. 'Luncheon we call it up in the Park. I would have you up to the Park for luncheon, Miss Shannon, but since Robert and I have just been waging war on the forces of capitalism the chances of a warm welcome from Uncle Forbes are nil. In fact, it would not be above him to have us thrown out on our arses.'

Bobby said, 'We can't take your money, Maeve.'

'Oh, aye, we can,' said Alice.

* * *

'Did I mention that my father's getting married?'

'Yes, when's the wedding?'

'Soon,' Lindsay said. 'The end of September, I think. Eleanor will have to acquire a trousseau first and, as I told you, Papa's scouting for a villa on the coast to be close to your dear mater and pater.'

'Rather him than me,' Ross said. 'Strange, isn't it, how each generation gravitates towards its own as it ages. Eventually I suppose I'll make peace with Martin and Rora and start spending time with Pansy and Mercy. What a sobering prospect.'

'We could run off to Strathmore and ignore the lot of them, of course.'

'Easier said than done.' Ross propped himself on an elbow and looked down at her with a frown. 'Has someone been talking out of turn?'

'What do you mean?'

'It so happens I've been making enquiries about Strathmore,' Ross said. 'It's still owned by the Duke of Perth but the Forestry Commission have an eye on the entire estate and would, I think, simply blow the house up.'

'No!'

'The duke's factor is appalled at the notion of such vandalism but the old boy needs the money to renovate the family seat and may be forced to part with Strathmore, including the house, to pay for it.'

'Would it cost much to buy the house and few acres by the loch?'

'One could pick them up for a song, I imagine.'

'Wouldn't it be fun to buy the place, if only for old times sake?'

'And live there, you mean?' said Ross.

'In summer, certainly: Christmas, too.'

'Forbes would never stand for it.'

'It has nothing to do with Forbes,' Lindsay said. 'If I sold my shares in Franklin's I would have more than enough money of my own to spend how I please.'

'What about the boys?' Ross asked.

'They'd love having a country seat to go to during the holidays. We could build Phil a tennis court at the top of the meadow.'

'We could,' Ross said. 'We could indeed.'

Lindsay lay back against the pillow and pulled him down upon her.

'It's a lovely thought, dearest,' she said. 'Isn't it?'

He touched her breast with his forefinger, brushing her nipple, then kissed it, tasting her with his tongue. He drew back a little and, fearing that he intended to leave, Lindsay wound a leg about his thigh. She had thought that he would be portly, the way Forbes was, but Ross was surprisingly muscular.

He said, 'I didn't mean this to happen, Lindsay. I

didn't plan it.'

'I know. It took us both by surprise.'

'I'm sorry.'

'Sorry for what, for heaven's sake?'

'It's not—I mean, you're not just . . .'

'What—a bit of fluff, a passing fancy?'

'I've been in love with you for an awfully long time, you know.'

'Since we were children?'

'Just about.'

'Children at Strathmore?'

'This,' Ross said, 'is becoming too sentimental for words.'

'Stop talking then,' Lindsay said and, reaching under the bedclothes, cupped his buttocks with both hands and drew him down on top of her again.

*   *   *

Arthur was in the dining-room with Eleanor when Forbes returned home. They had cleared an end of the long table and were seated side by side, heads together, compiling an invitation list for the wedding.

Forbes barged in, saying, 'Where is she? Isn't she here?'

'Who?' said Arthur, looking up. 'Lindsay?'

'No, not Lindsay—Maeve.'

'Isn't she with you?' Arthur said.

'Would I be asking you if—no, she isn't with me.'

'Last I saw of her,' Arthur said, 'she was chatting to that boy.'

'Boy? What boy? You don't mean Ewan Calder?'

'No, the draughtsman.'

'Shannon's his name, as I recall,' Eleanor put in.

'Yes, Bobby Shannon,' Arthur said. 'They were listening to Jack Burgoyne shouting the odds. I say, you don't think she got caught in the fighting, do you?'

'I don't know what to think right now,' Forbes said. 'Why did you abandon ship?'

Arthur shrugged. 'I've no stomach for it any longer, Forbes.'

It was now mid-afternoon. Forbes had left Archie Robb in charge of the empty yard. There were two burly constables on duty at the main gate but further demonstrations were not on the cards. A meeting of all trades had been called for Saturday afternoon in Partick Burgh Hall but the first matches in the football league season were being played and Forbes was cynical enough to suppose that Burgoyne would be addressing a great many empty seats. The pitched battle, the injured copper and, more especially, the dead horse would drain public sympathy for Franklin's workers and the national unions would be unlikely to come out in support.

By Wednesday, Thursday at the latest, it would all be over.

Arthur said, 'I wouldn't worry about her, Forbes. She's a sensible girl.'

'I'm not so sure about that,' Forbes said. 'Besides, I promised Gowry I'd look after her and I don't want to let him down.'

'It isn't your brother you're letting down.'

'What's that supposed to mean?'

'You've let us all down.'

'What?'

454

'Oh, don't play innocent with me, Forbes,' Arthur said. 'I know you arranged that bloody fracas in Aydon Road. Wage cuts, the unannounced lockout, police intervention in a peaceful demonstration—you orchestrated everything from the word "go".'

'What if I did?' Forbes said, defiantly. 'Sure and it isn't how it would have been done in the old days. It isn't how mealy-mouthed Martin would have handled it. He'd run us into the ground before he'd challenge the unions. In a month we'll be laying keel on a tanker ship, Papa, and won't have to scrounge for naval contracts or trail round the shipping agents begging for a crust of work. We'll be solvent. With a reduced wage bill and a reduced workforce, we'll be in the best possible position to ride out the storm. Isn't that enough?'

'Do you really believe that the end justifies the means, Forbes?'

'I do,' Forbes said. 'Yes, Arthur, I really and truly do.'

'That's what I thought,' said Arthur curtly and, turning his back on his son-in-law, returned to compiling his wedding list.

*   *   *

After she had paid for three lunches, including a round of fizzy drinks, eight shillings and ten pennies remained in Maeve's purse. It would be pointless, not to say tactless, to offer the money to Bobby so she slipped seven shillings into Alice's hand while Bobby was visiting the gents.

She couldn't honestly say that she liked the crippled sister. She felt sorry for Bobby, though.

455

Pride was something she understood.

God knows, she'd seen enough of it in the back streets of Dublin and was well aware of the damage it could cause. Bobby Shannon's pride was stuffy and stubborn, not ferocious. Few men would open themselves to ridicule by posing for an artist; few men of Bobby's age would boldly push a perambulator through the streets of Partick. He had earned the right to be proud and she, by inference, would be proud to call herself his sweetheart.

She walked towards the corner of Riverside with a hand on Bobby's arm. The sister was almost asleep, head lolling, seven shillings clasped in her fist, hidden under the blankets.

Late editions of the *Evening Times* and *Citizen* had been rushed out and vendors' hoardings shouted the news about a bloody riot at Franklin's shipyard. There would be no serious comment on the incident until morning, though, and neither she nor Bobby spared more than a glance at the headlines.

'I thought you were gonna buy new stockings?' Bobby said.

'I am. I'll pop into Hoey's for a cheap pair to cover me up.'

'We passed Hoey's a while back. Where are you goin'?'

'I thought I might come back with you.'

'Nah,' he said, not sharply. 'You've done enough for one day, Maeve.'

'I haven't done much,' she said. 'Not as much as you've done for me.'

He glanced at her, frowning slightly. 'My old man will be home soon.'

'I'd like to meet him,' Maeve said.

Bobby shook his head. 'Best not,' he said. 'Best leave it the way it is.'

'What way is that, then?'

They reached the corner. A bank and a pub glared each at the other across the width of Riverside Street. Men gathered outside the Kelvin Vaults a full hour before opening time. Further down the street knots of boys and men lounged about the close mouths, as if idleness had already become a habit. A paper boy barked news of the latest *sen-say-shun* and claimed a dozen dead in shipyard slaughter; no one showed much interest.

Bobby applied the brake and leaned against the pram.

Maeve kept her hand on his arm and when he moved, moved with him, performing a queer tight little dance on the dusty corner.

'Listen,' he said, 'I'm not for you.'

'Don't you like me? I thought you liked me?'

'I like you well enough, Maeve—but it's not right.'

'I'm not what you think I am.'

'You're Tom Calder's granddaughter. You live in McCulloch's house,' Bobby said. 'Maybe you think that doesn't matter, but it does.' He stepped closer. For a fleeting instant she thought he was about to wrap an arm about her waist and pull her to him. He went on, soft-voiced, 'I'm not for you, Maeve. I'm not for anyone. I can't ask any woman to look after Alice. She's my sister and . . .'

'You're stuck with her?'

'I'm all she's got, all she'll ever have,' he said. 'Look, if there's work, if Ross needs me, I'll see you up there, but don't come to our house again,

457

Maeve. Please, don't do that.'

'I was invited, you know.'

'I know. I know. But . . .'

'You're afraid you'll get to like me too much, aren't you?'

'Maybe I like you too much already.'

'So,' she said, trying to be flippant, 'so, this is goodbye, is it?'

'Aye,' Bobby said. 'I reckon it is.'

'And not even a goodbye kiss?'

She could not believe what happened next, what Bobby Shannon did.

He kissed the tips of two fingers and touched them, like a priest's blessing, to her lips. She felt them press against her, feather-light, then, with a nod, he jerked the brake and was gone, trundling his sister, unself-consciously, down the long road to the river and his tenement retreat.

* * *

Would he know, Lindsay wondered, would Forbes take one look at her and sense that she had been unfaithful to him? Unfaithful? How ridiculously inappropriate the word seemed in the context of a marriage riddled with hypocrisy and lies.

Now *she* had a lover, and she'd be damned if she'd allow guilt to ruin it for her. She hadn't even realised that she had fallen in love until that afternoon, that wonderful, magical moment when Ross had picked her up—literally picked her up— and carried her into the bedroom. She had yielded willingly, of course, had laughed when he'd swept her into his arms. He was so strong, so unexpectedly strong that she'd felt like a child in

458

his arms and had clung to him even after he'd set her down on the bed.

Ross, being Ross, had asked for no more than she was willing to give.

'Are you . . . is this . . . will it be all right?'

'Yes,' she'd said, 'yes, dearest, yes, yes.'

Tomorrow: Ross would be waiting for her tomorrow. They would make love again, and no one, certainly not Forbes, would be one whit the wiser. She would hold the secret, cherish the secret, and learn all the tricks of the adulterer's trade, though when her father and Eleanor decamped to live on the coast secrecy would hardly be necessary, for Forbes neither knew nor cared what she did with her time or how she filled her days.

Ross had driven her to the corner of Madison Street in his motor-car and they had kissed, not at all furtively, before parting.

He was just as he had been before, just as he had always been, except now he seemed more sure of himself, not cocky, not arrogant, but confident enough to let her see how much he loved her. Tomorrow: yes, Lindsay thought, now there would be a tomorrow, an infinity of tomorrows, for Ross, her dear, darling cousin Ross, would never let her go.

She walked around the corner, climbed the steps to the big front door. She rang the doorbell. Enid opened the door. Lindsay took off her hat and her summer coat and handed them to the maid, then, fluffing out her hair, went directly into the piano parlour in search of her husband.

He was lying full length on the sofa with a cigarette in his mouth and a glass in his hand. He had, she saw, been drinking for some time. He looked up at her blearily, not rising, not even lifting his head.

She stood by the door, staring at him as if she had never seen him in her life before, as if they were total strangers.

'Well,' he said, thickly, 'aren't you going to ask me how it went?'

'No,' Lindsay heard herself say, 'I don't believe I am.'

'Where the heck have you been anyway?'

'With Ross,' Lindsay said. 'All afternoon, with Ross.'

'While I'm working my backside off you're out enjoying yourself.' Forbes sipped whisky from the glass. 'Women,' he said, shaking his head. 'Bloody women. What an easy time you have of it.'

'Where's Maeve?'

'Upstairs, I think,' said Forbes. 'Sulking.'

'What's wrong with her?'

'How the heck do I know,' Forbes said. 'She won't talk to me either.'

Lindsay sighed and left the parlour.

Eleanor was waiting by the drawing-room door.

'Have you spoken to Maeve?' she said. 'She came in just before you and went straight to her room. She's upset about something.'

'And the boys, where are they?' Lindsay asked.

'Playing tennis in the park, I believe.'

Lindsay was suddenly weary of other people's problems. She wanted to be lying snug and secure in Ross's arms.

'I'd better go up and talk to her, I suppose.'

'I think that might be wise,' said Eleanor.

Lindsay climbed the stairs to the top floor and entered Maeve's room.

The girl was sitting dolefully on the end of the bed, her hands in her lap. She had, it seemed, been crying but there was also a faint whiff of pleasurable self-pity in her pose. Lindsay went to the bed and sat down beside her.

'What is it?' she said. 'What's wrong?'

'Oh, Auntie Lindsay,' Maeve wailed, 'I think I've fallen in love.'

'Well, dearest,' Lindsay said, trying very hard not to smile, 'that's hardly the end of the world.'

CHAPTER NINETEEN

A Measure of Forgiveness

In spite of Rora's attentions, Martin's health continued to decline. Early in September lawyers were summoned to Harper's Hill not to redraft his will—the chap was poorly but not at death's door— but to discuss the dissolution of the partnership, for, like Arthur, Martin had decided to retire.

Accounts were prepared, valuations agreed and settlements duly signed. When it was done Arthur heaved a sigh of relief, and Martin wept. Lindsay kept silent. She was well aware that Forbes wanted her share of the partnership too and that he would be willing to bargain to get it.

With Forbes hardly ever at home Lindsay and Maeve went house-hunting with Arthur and Eleanor or drove north with Ross to prowl about the big, gaunt house of Strathmore. It did not take Arthur long to find a suitable villa on the outskirts of Largs and preparations for the wedding went ahead, full steam. The launch of the cargo ships and the extension of the slipways took up more time, and in Aydon Road as well as Brunswick Park it was all, as Arthur put it, 'go'.

Maeve had no opportunity to mope over Bobby Shannon. She thought about him now and then but for the most part threw herself gaily into the doings in Brunswick Park and, on those rare afternoons when Ross felt like painting, sat for him in the studio in Flowerhill Drive while Aunt Lindsay smoked cigarettes, sipped tea and observed the bearded artist at work as if every brush stroke was a masterpiece.

In the midst of all the excitement, leaves turned brown, the days grew shorter and the wind that whistled through the closes of the Riverside acquired a wintry edge. Unknown to Maeve, little Alice Shannon's condition deteriorated, she became very sick and in the early hours of a Tuesday morning, clasped in her brother's arms, she finally passed away.

*   *   *

Forbes said, 'At the risk of blowing my own trumpet, it's all going really rather well. We'll lay keel as soon as Bradford's deliver the steel.'

'Jolly good,' said Stella. 'What about the missus?'

'The missus?'

'Your wife, darling, your wife.'

'Oh, Lindsay! She'll come around eventually.'

'Eventually? What precisely does that mean?'

She had her back to him, cocktail glass in hand. She wore a woollen outfit that clung to her body like red lead. Forbes had no idea where her

462

husband was. At the back of his mind, he nurtured a suspicion that Pickering knew about the affair but what, if anything, that implied for the future Forbes did not enquire.

'Lindsay has a lot on her mind right now,' he said. 'Once the wedding's over and her father moves out, I'll put together an offer she'll won't dare reject. Patience, sweetheart, patience. We'll be together soon.'

It was after one o'clock and there was still no sign of lunch.

They had made love for a half-hour downstairs. Stella had seemed distracted, not her usual eager self. She had satisfied him, of course, but with more efficiency than enthusiasm and he was left with the uncomfortable feeling that he had somehow failed to please her.

He glanced at his wristlet watch. He had slated a meeting with Franklin's accountants at two thirty. He assumed that Stella would serve lunch and had worked it into his schedule; otherwise he wouldn't have time to eat at all.

He put down his glass and twined an arm about Stella's waist.

'What's wrong, darling?' he said.

'It's this damned weather. I hate this climate.'

She shivered, pulled in her elbows, swallowed her cocktail and, reaching over her shoulder, handed him the empty glass.

'More?' said Forbes, cautiously.

'Yes. It's in the shaker.'

'Perhaps we should have some lunch first.'

She stared out of the plate-glass window at the drizzling rain that shrouded the river valley, and did not rise to the bait.

Forbes cleared his throat. 'Are we having lunch?'

'I thought you were busy.'

'I am, I am. I'm up to the eyes.'

'Then I'll excuse you.'

'Excuse me?'

'Let you go,' Stella said.

'I'm not in that much of a rush.'

'In that case, pour me another cocktail.'

He hurried across the parquet to the bar and unscrewed the top of the shaker. He poured the liquid carefully into the glass, added an olive, and carried the cocktail to her. She took it and drank it.

'Is—er—is Ronnie making lunch?' Forbes asked.

'It's Ronnie's day off.'

'Odd, I never think of Ronnie as having days off.'

The olive lay neglected in the throat of the glass. For a moment Forbes thought she was going to hurl the glass against the window. He had no idea what he had done to offend her, or that she was close to tears.

'I think you should go now, Forbes.'

'Why?'

'Haven't you things to do?'

'Yes, but . . .'

'Please,' she said, struggling to find her smile. 'Please, darling, just go.'

'When will I see you again?'

'Soon,' she promised, kissing him. 'Very soon.'

He collected his hat, opened the front door and left, still blissfully unaware that the affair was over and that he would never see Stella again.

*　　　*　　　*

464

Miss Runciman had no kin of her own. There was, perhaps, a distant cousin, last heard of in Kent, but for all intents and purposes Arthur's family was her family too. She had been in the Franklin fold for as long as anyone could remember and, in spite of her severity, everyone was fond of her.

The wedding was set for Saturday, the first of October.

Banns were read in St Anne's. Forbes would give Miss Runciman away, Ross would be groomsman, Lindsay matron of honour, Maeve a bridesmaid. The reception would be held in the ballroom of the Ashton Hotel, after which the happy couple would stay with Donald and Lilias until their villa was ready.

If Arthur had intended to slip quietly into retirement he was doomed to disappointment. The West of Scotland Shipbuilders' Association honoured him with a dinner, and the Society of Naval Architects with a somewhat more rambunctious 'smoker'. Presentations were made, compliments heaped upon him, toasts drunk, songs sung. Arthur was moved. Even Forbes had a tear in his eye when the back-slapping and hand-shaking ended and Arthur, Tom Calder and he crammed into the back seat of a taxi-cab to drive home and Arthur, staring out at the rain-wet pavements, said in a soft breaking voice, 'Sixty years, sixty years. Dear God, where did they go, chaps, where *did* they go?'

New clothes hung in every bedroom in Brunswick Crescent. The boys were dragged to the barber's, hairdressing appointments were lined up for the ladies. At Lindsay's insistence, Ross had his beard trimmed. Gifts arrived, gifts by the dozen,

465

gifts by the score. Canteens of cutlery, Chinese vases, bits and pieces of furniture, rugs and ornate silverware piled everywhere until Arthur took a stand and, gathering the cards into one big file, borrowed a lorry and four hands from Aydon Road and had everything transported to Donald's house for safe-keeping. Eleanor continued to go about her duties, full of little *tsks* and *tuts* at the fuss being made over two aged people finally tying the knot.

On Wednesday evening, three days before the wedding, the family assembled for dinner in Brunswick Crescent. Donald and Lilias cried off at the last moment. Donald was 'chesty' and felt he should save himself for the wedding proper. Rora sent round a note of apology on Martin's behalf. He too was under the weather and wanted to be 'right' for Saturday.

Cook and Lindsay devised a menu between them. Aided by two of her sisters, hired for the occasion, Enid pulled out the extensions on the dining-room table and, under Miss Runciman's eagle eye, unpacked the very best linen and the very best dinner service and, in late morning, began to dress the table.

Sixteen settings: sixteen chairs.

Arthur assumed that Lindsay had done the arithmetic, Lindsay thought that her father had made the calculation.

Neither noticed that, in addition to Calders, Franklins, Maeve, and the new Mrs Coffey and her husband, there was one extra place.

Forbes's contribution; Forbes's big surprise.

* * *

466

'Daddy!' Maeve shouted. 'Ay-hay, it's me da!'

She had been kneeling on the carpet playing cards with Harry and Philip, whiling away the dreary hours of a wet afternoon before it was time to dress.

She leaped to her feet, ran to the door and threw her arms round Gowry who, it transpired, had arrived off the Irish boat after a rough crossing and had not quite gathered his wits. Eleanor had relieved him of his raincoat and hat but his trousers were sodden and his shoes squelched. He clutched a parcel, wrapped in wet brown paper, under his arm and staggered a bit at Maeve's delighted onslaught. She punched his shoulder. 'You sneaky old devil,' she said, 'why didn't you tell me you were coming?'

'Forbes put the kibosh on it,' Gowry said. 'He wanted it to be a surprise.'

'It's that all right,' Maeve said, 'a lovely surprise. Did Uncle Forbes send you the ticket?'

'Aye, he did,' Gowry said. 'I had the heck of a job gettin' time off and I'll have to be away home on the night boat on Saturday but'—he smiled at last—'at least I'm here to see you all dolled up in your pretty stuff.' He pushed her off a little way and looked at her admiringly. 'By Gar, you've grown. You're not a wee slip of a thing any more.'

She punched him again. 'Get away with you, Da. I was never a wee slip of a thing.' She turned. 'You remember Harry and Philip, don't you?'

'Of course.'

He propped the parcel carefully against the piano stool and solemnly shook hands with each of the boys in turn, not with the gloved wooden hand,

467

that reminder—that relic—of the war but left hand to right, like a secret sign between men of similar persuasion.

In the six months since he had dragged her up the steps and into the hallway so much had changed. She was not the same person that she had been then. Harry and Philip had changed, too, had become more manly and mature. Only her dad seemed unaltered, shabby, scarred, guarded and utterly, utterly dependable. He had been right to bring her to Scotland, to get her out of Dublin when he did. She wondered, as she hugged him once more, if she was grown up enough to admit it. For sure, she was grown up enough not to ask why Mam hadn't come with him.

'How's Mam?'

'She's well. She's fine. She sends her love.'

'And Sean?'

'Oh, he's a wild one, he is. Keeps us all on our toes.'

'Does Grandee know you're here?' Philip said. 'My grandfather, I mean.'

'Arthur's gone out,' Harry said. 'Mother and Dad, too. One or all of them will be back very shortly, I expect. Meanwhile, sir'—he placed a hospitable hand on Gowry's sleeve—'I imagine you might wish to change and have something warming to drink. Afternoon tea may or may not appear. Everything's in rather a muddle in the kitchen, as you may imagine.'

'Is there a room?' Philip said. 'If not, do feel free to use mine, sir.'

Gowry laughed, and just hearing that soft back-of-the-throat sound made Maeve wish that she was at home again in Dublin town. The pang of homesickness passed off almost at once and she heard her father say, 'Sure, an' I'm thinkin' you're far too big now to be callin' me "sir". I'd be much obliged if you'd call me Gowry.'

'Gowry it is then, sir,' said Harry. 'Thank you.'

Eleanor put her head around the door and, in a slightly less than welcoming manner, informed Gowry that he would have to make do with the small guest bedroom on the second floor and she would see to it that sheets and blankets were laid out as soon as she could spare one of the maids.

She went away, closing the door with just a shade too much force.

'What's wrong with her?' Phil asked.

'She doesn't like surprises,' Harry said.

'Well, I do,' Maeve said. ' 'Specially this sort o' surprise,' and wrapped her arms around her father once more.

*   *   *

Miss Runciman was finally persuaded to leave the finishing touches to Cook and Enid and join the rest of the family in the drawing-room.

She wore a brand-new dress and was, Arthur declared, the belle of the ball or, to paraphrase our American cousins, an absolute knock-out. He was certainly knocked out, he said, and poured her a glass of champagne.

It was all so civilised and warm that Maeve wondered why she had ever dreamed of going back to Dublin. She thanked Uncle Forbes for bringing her father over for the wedding, thanked Aunt Lindsay, too, though for no particular reason except that she was in a very grateful mood tonight.

469

'Now,' Arthur said, after the bride-to-be had been toasted, not once but twice, 'now, this mysterious parcel, Gowry? May I open it?'

'Sure an' that's why I brought it,' Gowry said. 'It's your wedding gift.'

Philip produced a penknife from his pocket. Arthur proceeded to cut the twine and peel the wrapping paper from the package to reveal a smoky aquatint, beautifully framed and glazed. He held the picture up to the light, squinted at it and, to everyone's amazement, his eyes filled with tears.

'Dear God, Gowry,' he snuffled, 'where did you find it?'

Gowry shrugged. 'In a bookshop—on a book barrow, actually—in Dublin. I had it framed by a feller who lodges upstairs in Endicott Street. Made a decent job of it, didn't he?'

'Look, Eleanor, look,' Arthur said, holding the picture towards her.

'Hmm,' Eleanor said. 'Not awfully pretty, is it?'

Arthur wiped his eyes with a knuckle. 'No, it certainly isn't pretty. Don't you know where it is, though?'

'I do not,' Eleanor said.

'I do,' Arthur said. 'It's Cardiff, seventy or eighty years ago. That's the Glamorganshire canal and that, I'll swear, is Hugh Pemberton's little forge where my father served his apprenticeship before he came to Scotland. What a remarkable find, Gowry, remarkable. I wasn't even aware that you knew anything of our family's history.'

'History's his speciality, ain't it, Daddy?' Maeve said.

'It used to be,' said Gowry, and everyone laughed.

'It's a wonderful present,' Arthur said. 'I—Eleanor and I will treasure it and make sure it has pride of place in our new home. Ah,' he sighed, 'how simple things were in my father's day. He was an orphan, you know, reared in a foundlings' home. He wasn't ashamed of it, not him. He knew where he was going, knew what he would do with his life. Steam saved him, he often told me, steam and steel. And now'—another sigh—'now it's all become so complicated. Still, still, I'll hang this picture on my wall and think back to the way it used to be. Meanwhile, I'll leave it here on the table and you can all have a good look at it and ponder on Owen Franklin, and how much energy, how much honest toil it cost him to put us where we are today.'

'Hear, hear, Grandee,' Philip said.

Then the doorbell chimed and, a minute or so later, young Ewan Calder sidled into the room.

*   *   *

Success, sex and the prospect of change had mellowed Forbes sufficiently to acknowledge that Tom Calder had a problem on his hands. How could Tom explain to Cissie that Ewan was *persona non grata* in Brunswick Park and that accepting Arthur's invitation to join the family for dinner would be impossible?

After due consideration Forbes climbed down and gave Tom permission to bring the boy along—a decision that would haunt him for the rest of his life.

'Forbes.' Ewan deliberately dropped the 'uncle', and shook hands with a slimy sort of fervour that

471

should have put Forbes on his guard.

'Maeve.' Ewan kissed her hand with all the formality of a Bavarian count, and moved on, as if to pollinate the room with his affected charm. 'Aunt Lindsay, Mr Arthur, Miss Runciman—and you,' he said, pausing at Gowry, 'you must be the Irish gentleman, the *pater innominabilis*.'

'The what?' said Gowry.

'He's showing off his Latin,' said Harry. 'He means Maeve's father.'

'Do I?' said Ewan. 'Yes, of course I do.'

He gripped Gowry's hands, wood and flesh, and pumped away, smiling that sinister, affable smile, and squirming not at all. He might have drawn Gowry off to one side right there and then for a confidential exchange of views if Tom hadn't dragged him away and planted him on the horse-hair sofa between his giggling sisters.

The faint air of tension, almost of alarm, that had entered the drawing-room with Ewan Calder was dispelled by Ross's arrival. He had kitted himself out in full Highland dress, complete with kilt, hairy sporran and a silver-hilted dagger stuck into his stocking top. It said much for her bearded cousin, Lindsay thought, that he did not appear ridiculous.

'Good God!' said Arthur. 'What's come over you all of a sudden?'

'Found it while rooting in the closet,' Ross said. 'I'm not going to waste my hard-earned cash purchasing a new suit just for your nuptials, old chap. It was either this or a mitre and crozier. Lindsay, what do you think?'

'I think it's very fetching,' Lindsay said.

'Me, too,' said Maeve and taking her painter by

the arm whirled him round and round in the centre of the room, until they both ran out of breath.

* * *

Candlelight created an atmosphere of mystery and romance that reminded Lindsay of dinner parties in the huge dining-room in Harper's Hill long ago. Arthur was at one end of the long table, with Eleanor on his right. Forbes, at the other end, had Lindsay on his left. Ross was directly opposite her, Tom on her left, and Maeve, facing Ewan. Below them were Kay and her husband, Gowry, Cissie, her girls, Harry and Phil, dipping in and out of the golden light of the fat wax candles in the Georgian candlesticks.

Subtle shadows and flickering candlelight: what better way to survey her friends and family? The only fly in the ointment was Cyrus Coffey who seemed to have taken it upon himself to be the life and soul of the party and roared with laughter, and kissed his wife demonstratively, and all in all displayed the worst traits of Irish character. He would even have led conversation round to politics if Gowry hadn't forestalled him.

Laughter, the rise and fall of conversation, a plenitude of nourishing food and quantities of good wine, the youngsters all rosy, lively, and lovely in their finery; Lindsay glanced across the table at Ross who was gazing at her as if she were the only person in the room and all the others mere distraction.

She lifted her glass and toasted their shared secret. What did it matter if Forbes saw her? She had already decided that once the wedding was

473

over, she would detach herself from Forbes once and for all. In a year's time Philip would go up to university, and share rooms with Harry. They would love that, the pair of them, a flat of their own in the West End; gentlemen of independent means and independent spirit.

She had few concerns about her boys, fewer still about Forbes.

Ross raised his glass and winked, as if he knew what she was thinking.

Enid and her sister bustled to clear away plates and bring in the puddings and cheeses. Eleanor watched them critically.

Mr Coffey leaned over the table, talking with Gowry while Harry listened and now and then put in a word or two. Phil was flirting inexpertly with Dorothy Calder who had already learned to trade on character rather than looks.

Then Ewan Calder said, 'I'm going away, you know; or, to be absolutely accurate, I am being sent away. Packed off, Maeve, packed off, bag and baggage. I trust that will make you happy.' His voice sounded strange, not strained but crimped, as if he had rehearsed not just the words but the manner of delivery. Lindsay turned her head, listening but not yet comprehending. 'Dartmouth wouldn't take me because of my chest.' He gave a theatrical cough, fingers spread over his heart. 'Not fit to hang from the yardarm or whatever it is they do to midshipmen these days. Dartmouth, what a stupid idea that was. My father's idea, of course, probably hoping I'd be lost at sea, what?' He laughed—*haw, haw, haw*—and gave a twitch of the shoulders, a jerk of the head. 'No, no, not the rollicking life of a sailor boy for me. I've decided to seek refuge in religion.'

'What twaddle you do talk.' Philip had abandoned his flirtation with the elder Miss Calder and, like everyone else, was listening to Ewan now as if to a parliamentary speech or a pulpit sermon.

'Tell them, Dad,' Ewan said. 'Tell them what an evil little boy I turned out to be and why you have to be rid of me.'

'Ewan, please,' Tom said, 'this isn't the time or place . . .'

Harry said, 'Where?'

Ewan said, 'Wreeford's Academy.'

Arthur said, 'Isn't that in Dumfries?'

'The very depths of Dumfries, sir, yes,' Ewan said. 'After that—Durham, St Andrews, Edinburgh; anywhere but here, anywhere but home.'

'Are you sending him away, Tom?' Forbes said.

'It—it was Ewan's idea, Ewan's choice,' Tom said.

'No, Dad, it was your choice,' Ewan said. 'And your fault, Maeve.'

'What's he talking about, Tom?' said Cissie.

Cyrus Coffey said, 'Well, if I'd been give an education when I was your age, son, I wouldn't be hangin' wallpaper now.'

Maeve said, 'My fault!'

Ewan said, 'Like mother, like daughter.'

'*What?*' Maeve exploded. '*What did you just say?*'

'She was a tart, too,' Ewan said. 'God, Maeve, you don't even know which one of them is really your father.'

Forbes and Gowry rose as one.

'Shut your mouth,' Forbes roared, 'just shut your bloody mouth.'

Ewan and Tom got to their feet and, at the far

end of the table, Harry too.

Enid paused in the doorway, a bowl of creamy Scotch trifle in her hands.

'Go on,' Ewan said. 'Ask them, ask them. It's the family secret, the family scandal. Everybody here knows she slept with both of them.'

Maeve looked first at Forbes, then at Gowry.

'Daddy?' she said, in a tiny voice. 'Daddy?'

Tom hustled his son from the dining-room before Forbes could beat the boy to the ground. Cissie and the girls followed, Cissie sobbing, the girls frightened. Maeve sat quite still, hand covering her mouth, but when Forbes came to her and, crouching, tried to put an arm about her, she shook him off, craned her neck, raised herself and, leaning on her hands, peered down the length of the table into the golden candlelight.

'You,' she said. 'Gran, is it the truth he's tellin' me? Is the story true?'

Without a second's hesitation, Kay McCulloch Coffey answered, 'Yes.'

Maeve fled.

*   *   *

The men were in the parlour when Lindsay came downstairs again. Through the open door of the dining-room she glimpsed Eleanor and Enid snuffing out candles, the remains of the dinner party strewn across the table, the bowl of Scotch trifle standing untouched, like a reprimand.

She opened the front door, stepped outside and peered along the crescent. Light rain was falling. There were haloes around the streetlamps. No point in calling Maeve's name. If, as seemed likely,

Maeve had rushed out of the house in tears, she would not be lurking in the vicinity of the house.

Lindsay returned to the parlour.

Arthur sat slumped on the piano stool. Sheet music was spread on top of the instrument, for he had hoped that his special evening would end with a sing-song. The lid of the piano remained closed. He looked so old and defeated that Lindsay experienced a sudden wave of anger at the trouble Maeve had brought to the house: no, not Maeve— Forbes. Everything was Forbes's fault. She would do well to bear that in mind in the days that lay ahead.

Forbes had taken off his dinner jacket and planted one foot on the fender like some dissolute laird. He sipped from a glass of whisky and soda. He had been handsome once, but his looks had faded, eroded by selfishness, charred by ambition. Gowry at least had dignity, a shabby, indefinable dignity.

Lindsay crossed the carpet and linked arms with Ross.

'Where are the boys?' she asked.

'I sent them to bed,' Forbes answered.

'Why?'

'It isn't for them, this—this thing,' Forbes said. 'Is she in her room?'

'No,' Lindsay said. 'I think she's gone.'

'Gone where?' said Forbes.

'I've no idea,' Lindsay said.

'Vicious little bastard.' Forbes spat the words out. 'Why did he do it? Why did he tell her? Did he want her so badly he couldn't bear to see her happy if he couldn't have her?'

'Want her?' Gowry said. 'Physically, you mean?'

477

'Yes, he's twisted,' Forbes said. 'He's been warped since the day he was born. He probably thought it was a great game to chase his half-sister, or whatever the hell she is.'

'Did he—did he try to have her?' Gowry said.

Arthur said, 'I'm sure he did. Something the boys said—that fight at the tennis courts—it all adds up to a very unpleasant picture.'

'Maeve isn't blameless,' Kay said.

'Enough out of you, Ma,' Forbes said. 'Why didn't you lie to her?'

'She's been lied to once too often,' Kay said. 'It's you I blame, Gowry, you and that whore you married. I know what went on in your house, her with her fancy man and her bastard son while you were off fighting the war for the English. You took her, you should've known how to keep her.'

'I kept Maeve, didn't I?' Gowry said.

'Well, you've lost her now,' Kay said. 'You've hurt her, both of you, and she'll not be quick to forgive either of you. She won't come whimpering home in a hurry with her tail between her legs.'

'Nonsense!' Forbes said. 'Maeve knows what side her bread's buttered on. She's happy here. She'll come back as soon as she's calmed down.'

'Come back to what?' Lindsay said. 'Back to you, Forbes, to you, Gowry, when you've both let her down.'

'What about the wedding?' Arthur said. 'Under the circumstances perhaps we should call it off.'

'Absolutely not,' said Lindsay.

'Poor girl, poor girl.' Arthur shook his head. 'Shouldn't we at least be out looking for her?'

'Looking where?' said Forbes.

'On the streets,' Kay Coffey said, 'where she and

478

her mother belong.'

*　　　*　　　*

The old man was gutted with drink. He wore an under vest, baggy flannels stained with vomit, and was barefoot. He squinted at her out of the gloom.

'Bobby?' she said. 'Is Bobby at home?'

'Nae money, hen. Naw, we've gived it all a'ready.'

'Who is it, Pa?'

'Naethin' left, naethin'.'

The old man made to close the door but Bobby pushed him gently aside.

'Maeve?' Bobby said. 'I thought I told you—'

'Please,' she said. 'Please let me in.'

He stepped back and Maeve moved uncertainly into the tiny hall.

Losing interest in the visitor, the old man shuffled into the bedroom and closed the door. In the faint light from the kitchen she saw how haggard Bobby was and wondered if he, too, had been drinking.

'You've heard then?' Bobby said.

'Heard what?'

Frantic in her need to escape, she had flown from the house in Brunswick Crescent without pausing to snatch an overcoat from the cloakroom. Her dress was wet through, her hair plastered to her brow. She shivered a little, for there was no fire in the kitchen and the room was cold.

Bobby wore tight black trousers and a pure white shirt fastened at the collar with a steel stud. In the dismal light of the tenement kitchen he looked like a young priest. There was no food

479

on the table, no cloth. The room reeked of disinfectant. The padded wooden armchair was nowhere to be seen. The bed in the alcove had been stripped to bare boards. She knew even before Bobby told her that her suffering was nothing compared to his.

He said, 'Alice died last week, last Tuesday.'

'Bobby, Bobby,' Maeve said. 'I didn't know.'

'Why would you?' he said.

'I thought—I mean, my grandfather didn't say anything.'

'I never told him. Never told anyone. I just took a day off.'

'One day, just one day?'

'For the funeral, aye,' he said. 'She's buried up at Cadder cemetery, where she can see the hills.'

She longed to smother him with the love that had been smothered in her that night, to link her loss with his, but she could not equate the unprotected bleakness of his life with the lives that she had led in Dublin, Wexford, and in Brunswick Park. She knew nothing of grinding despair and such a weight of grief as this.

'If you didn't know about Alice, why did you come here tonight?'

'I—I—just wanted to see you again, to see . . .'

'Alice?'

'Yes, Alice.'

'Too late.' He whistled through his teeth. 'I'll say, too late.'

'I'll go,' Maeve said. 'I'd better.'

'She slipped away quick at the end,' he said. 'She was never gonna be an old woman—I was ready for that—but you think to yourself everything will just stay as it is, however bad. But it never does,

480

does it?'

He groped behind him, felt for the bare boards of the bed, seated himself. He thrust his hands between his knees, fingers locked into fists. The steel stud in his shirt collar glinted in the shadows. Maeve couldn't see his face properly, only his knees and hands and the glint of steel at his throat.

'She'd been bad all day. Come nightfall it got worse. Something upstairs in her head just blew. There was no pain at the very end. She was smiling up at me when she . . . Aye, it's a blessing, so the doctor said. The minister said she would be better off in the next world. Better off? Huh! What can be better than what you have, what you love?' He pursed his lips again. 'I was all Alice really had, all she ever wanted.'

'Why didn't you tell me?'

He looked up, frowning. 'What could you have done?'

She had been tricked by her father, had channelled her childish passions into causes that were not childish at all. She had thought herself grown up because she had breasts and the boys chased after her, because she had the spirit to go with it, but spirit was something that had to be proved and the rest, like little Alice Shannon, would in time dwindle and die.

'Nothing,' she admitted. 'I could have done nothing.'

'Go back,' he said, quietly. 'Go on, Maeve, go back where you belong.'

'I would,' she said. 'If I knew where that was, I would.'

She stroked her hair from her brow, tugged down the damp dress and went to him. Giving him

481

a nudge with her hip, she forced him to move over. She sat down beside him, the pair of them perched on the planed wooden planks as if on top of a coffin. She fished for his hands and unlocked his fingers.

'How can you be sure,' she said, 'that I don't belong here with you?'

'Because'—he darted her a sideways glance— 'because you're rich.'

'Not rich enough. Oh no,' Maeve said, 'not nearly rich enough.'

*   *   *

The pubs had emptied well over an hour ago and the last drunk had staggered off home. The rain had eased away. The streets were deserted. Ross, still in full Highland dress, leaned against the bonnet of the Oxford, puffing his pipe.

Somehow she wasn't surprised to see him.

She paused in the close mouth.

Ross folded his arms, waiting patiently.

She said, 'How did you know I'd be here?'

'Where else were you going to go?' Ross said.

Bobby was with her. He had buttoned a coat over his shirt and put on shoes. Maeve had a raincoat thrown over her shoulders. The night was cold after rain but the air smelled sweet and clean.

'Good evening, Bobby,' Ross said, nodding.

'Good evenin', Mr Ross.'

Ross knocked out his pipe and climbed into the motor-car. He looked away, studying the blank wall of the coal merchant's yard that bordered the railway line. There was nothing for him to do now but wait. He had been waiting all his life, it seemed,

482

and was well used to it.

'Will you go with him? Do you want to?' Bobby said.

'Yes,' Maeve said. 'I have to face up to them some time.'

'I'll—I'll see you again, will I?'

'Sure an' you will,' Maeve said. 'Soon, too.'

He kissed her, first on the brow and then on the lips. She slipped out of the raincoat and handed it back to him.

'I'll be all right, Bobby. Really, I will. What about you?'

'Better now,' he said. 'Much better now.'

'Are you sure?'

'Aye, I'm sure.'

He kissed her once more then released her. She walked to the edge of the pavement and paused, looking back at the young man in the close mouth.

'Thank you,' she said, softly, then slid into the passenger seat.

Ross started the engine, engaged gear and drove off, slowly, up Riverside Street. He said nothing for a while, just driving.

'His sister died,' Maeve said. 'I didn't know that when I went there. She died last week. He didn't tell anyone, no one at all. There was just him and his father at the grave, him and his old man and a minister. I don't think the minister even knew who she was: Alice.'

Ross said, 'Do you want me to take you home?'

'Uh!' she said. 'Uh-huh.'

'They don't know what to do with you, Maeve.'

'I don't know what to do with myself.'

The motor-car rumbled on to the cobbles of Dumbarton Road.

Ross said, 'Two dads, two fathers; what a lucky girl you are.'

'Which one is the real one?'

'Nobody knows,' Ross said. 'Not even your mother.'

'She—she loved them both, you mean?'

'So it would seem,' Ross said.

'Brothers?'

'Yes.'

'What will happen to me now, Ross? What will become of me?'

'That's up to you,' he said. 'But if I were you, Maeve, I wouldn't do anything rash. Let Arthur and Eleanor celebrate their wedding as best they can. The Calder boy won't be there, you can bet on that. Once the wedding's over, then you must choose what you want to do.'

'Uncle Forbes will want me to stay here and Daddy will want me to go back to Dublin with him.'

'I was thinking more of you, what *you* want to do,' Ross said. 'You're not a child any longer, Maeve. You don't belong to either of them. In fact, they can ask no more of you than a measure of forgiveness.'

'Forgiveness?' Maeve said. 'What do I have to forgive them for?'

'Precisely,' Ross said and, fisting the wheel, turned the car into Madison Street and headed up the long steep hill that led to Brunswick Park.

CHAPTER TWENTY

Sleeping Partners

On Friday, the day before the wedding, Lindsay brought Maeve down to the parlour soon after lunch. Ross had volunteered to drive Arthur, Eleanor and the boys to Largs to check on the decorator's progress, and, Lindsay suspected, to have a quiet word in Arthur's ear about the future—her future, not Maeve's.

Ross had assured her that they would be home in ample time for dinner, Arthur and Eleanor's last in Brunswick Crescent.

Tomorrow, of course, there would hardly be time to breathe, for, whether you were old or young, a wedding day belonged to the bride and groom. Gowry was due back on duty at the Dublin docks on Sunday evening and would slip away from the reception to catch the night boat. It was still uncertain whether or not Maeve would accompany him. So far she had steadfastly refused to discuss Ewan Calder's outburst and its implications, and no one had been sufficiently rash to press for answers. Now the time had come for the girl to make decisions, though nothing in life, Lindsay assured her, was irrevocable, not motherhood or marriage or the mockery that men call success, not even the bonds of a family that had once seemed so strong and secure.

Forbes was absorbed in the legal complexities required to dissolve the partnership and looked somewhat crushed by the sheer weight of paperwork. He lay in the big leather armchair, pretending to be asleep, hands folded neatly over his stomach, legs stretched out. Gowry had opened the sash window and was puffing nervously at one of his smelly little cigars and fanning smoke into the raw autumn air. They were less like brothers, Lindsay thought, than a couple of decrepit prize-fighters too nervous of each other to exchange even threats.

She ushered Maeve into the room.

Gowry tossed the cigar from the window to burn itself out on the pavement, and Forbes, with a hoarse little grunt, sat up and opened his eyes.

In spite of the chill, Maeve had put on her best summer frock. She had brushed her hair and bound it with a blue ribbon and looked more beautiful than ever. She seated herself on the sofa, as prim and formal as if she were posing for a photograph.

'Well, there's no point in pretending,' Lindsay began. 'We know what happened all those years ago. I'm not going to rant on about the sins of the fathers. However, I think it's only fair to Maeve that you tell her the truth and let her decide what she wants to do. Now,' Lindsay went on, 'which of you is brave enough to begin?'

'Forbes,' Gowry said.

'Gowry,' said Forbes.

Lindsay said, 'Oh, I see. You're afraid, are you? Gowry, the brave soldier, and Forbes the terror of the trade unions, afraid to open your mouths. You weren't so reticent twenty years ago, Forbes, were you? You weren't at all bashful when it came to—'

'All right, all right,' Forbes blurted out. 'I'll tell her.'

Maeve said, 'Do you know what she calls you,

486

my mam? She calls you the Great Unmentionable.'

'Well, I suppose I deserve it,' Forbes said. 'Your mother, sweetheart, was once my sweetheart.'

'Your mistress, you mean?'

'Yes, my mistress. I loved her. I did. You don't have to believe me if you don't want to, but I loved her. By God, though, she was difficult.'

'Sylvie was sixteen, Forbes,' Gowry said. 'Tom Calder had abandoned her and she'd been brought up by a pair of religious rogues. She had every right to be "difficult". Besides, she assumed you were going to marry her.'

'How could I marry her when I was already—' Forbes bit off the end of the sentence and sat for a moment, brooding. 'Oh, bugger!' he said, at length. 'It's true. I deceived her. I thought she understood the situation, but apparently she didn't. I don't know what she's like now, sweetheart, but take my word for it, back in those days Sylvie wasn't exactly rational.'

'She was in love with *you*, Forbes,' Gowry said. 'You can't get more irrational than that.'

Forbes swung round. 'In love with me? Aye, so in love with me that she let you into her bed at first asking.'

'Not quite first asking,' said Gowry.

'Did it give you a thrill to steal my girl, Gowry?' Forbes said. 'Was it your way of getting back at me because I'd made a good life for myself in Glasgow and you were just my bloody chauffeur?'

'I didn't marry a Franklin, of course,' Gowry said. 'I didn't follow dear old Ma's plan for advancement and marry into money.' He came forward from the window and, pulling out a chair, seated himself in Maeve's line of sight. 'The long

487

and the short of it, Maeve, is that your mother got pregnant.'

'With you,' Forbes put in.

'She thought that would do the trick,' Gowry said. 'Aye, I know that's a harsh thing to say, but she was young and didn't understand either of us, *any* of us. She was under the impression that because she was carrying a child my brother would do the decent thing, divorce Lindsay and marry her. That was never going to happen, was it, Forbes?'

'Of course it wasn't,' Forbes said.

'You had far too much to lose by that time.'

Forbes dabbed his brow with the back of his hand. 'Look, Maeve,' he said, 'I behaved badly, very badly. I wasn't much older than your mother, remember, and I really didn't know what to do when I found out she was—'

'You liar, Forbes,' Lindsay chimed. 'You always know what to do.'

'I stuck with you, Linnet, kept my promise to you,' Forbes said. 'I sent Sylvie money when she needed it to lease that blasted hotel, the Shamrock. I didn't abandon her completely.'

'No,' Maeve said, 'but you abandoned me.'

'I knew Gowry would look after you,' Forbes said, 'and I had word of you from your grandmother.'

'Sure an' what sort of word was that?' Maeve said. 'Gran hated my mam then and hates her now. She hates my mam because she stopped Dad marrying another cousin and getting a share of all that Franklin money.' She looked at Gowry, unflinchingly. 'Is that not the truth of it, Dad? I know about Gran. I know that when she ran off

488

with Grandpa McCulloch the Franklins wouldn't forgive her and I think she's been looking for revenge ever since.'

'Everything might have been all right if it hadn't been for the war.'

'What war, Uncle Forbes?' Maeve said. 'Your war, or ours? Our war has always been there. It didn't come as a surprise.' She drew in a breath. 'What Ewan Calder said is fact: you really don't know who I belong to.'

Lindsay said, 'But you know, Maeve, don't you?'

'Oh, aye,' Maeve said. 'I know.'

'Who?' Forbes said.

'Not you, Uncle Forbes, not you,' Maeve said, quietly. 'You've been kind to me since I came here and you did give Mam money, but it wasn't you who hugged me in the dark nights when I was frightened. It wasn't you took me out to look at the warships at the mouth of the Liffey, or came back to find me after the war when you didn't have to. That wasn't you, Uncle Forbes. That was my daddy. That was my *real* daddy.'

Forbes lay back and rubbed a hand over his thinning hair. 'I see.'

'I doubt if you do,' said Lindsay.

'You'll go back to Dublin now, I suppose,' Forbes said. 'And I'll never see you again.'

'Oh no,' Maeve said. 'I don't have to go back to Dublin. I know my daddy loves me. He'll always be there for me. It doesn't matter who Mam—who was there when I happened. I'd like to stay here in Scotland, if that's all right. Daddy, is that all right?'

But Gowry couldn't answer through his tears.

*　　　*　　　*

489

The wedding went off without a hitch. Miss Runciman was as beautiful a bride as ever graced the aisle of St Anne's, so Arthur said. Forbes performed his duties admirably and, as surrogate father to the bride, even made a touching speech at the reception. There were several witty speeches, of course, but no toast to 'absent friends', for the Calders were conspicuous by their absence. Rumours flew about that Cissie had fallen out with Lindsay, that Tom had had a barney with Forbes, but those who knew the whole story kept it to themselves.

It would have been much more difficult to pretend that all was sweetness and light if Kay Coffey had failed to put in an appearance. Cyrus dragged her along to church, though, and to the reception afterwards. There were no apologies from Kay, no congratulations, no words crossed with either of her brothers. She did what Cyrus told her to do and sat throughout dinner and, later, in the ballroom, with pursed lips and an embittered scowl. Only when Cyrus plucked her from her chair in the corner and whirled her into a waltz did her stiff old limbs loosen and the scowl fade away. Arthur did not remark the transformation in his sister, for he was steering his bride gingerly around the dance floor and had eyes for no one but her.

The Ashton's resident band was hardly up to ragtime but it did manage a fair rendering of 'Whispering' that brought Lindsay an unwelcome reminder of that night in the Pharaoh Club when she had almost allowed herself to fall for Geoffrey Paget. She thanked her lucky stars that he had revealed his true colours before she'd made a

490

complete ass of herself.

For a large man, Ross danced like an angel. He partnered her through strathspeys, slow fox-trots and even, to much applause, a version of the latest craze, the tango. Rora and Lilias cheered and called out, rather vulgarly, for glimpses of his underwear. Ross did not oblige, and when the band changed tune, chose to dance with Maeve to restore some much needed dignity.

'Where did you learn to dance like that?' Maeve asked him.

'In the war.'

'You danced in the war?'

'In the nut-hatch,' Ross said. 'Our Saturday night dances were very popular even with poor souls who could hardly stand up without shaking. There's something in men as well as women that just can't resist a sentimental tune, something Jerry shells can't quite blow out of our brains.'

'You never talk about the war.'

'No, and I'm not going to start now.' Ross executed a series of steps so intricate that it was all Maeve could do to keep up. 'I'm abandoning your portrait, by the way.'

'Are you?' Maeve said. 'Why?'

'Commercial logic.'

'I thought your dealer liked pictures of pretty young ladies.'

'Everyone likes pretty young ladies,' Ross said. 'I've a commission I must get finished before the client loses interest: a large painting, with a horse in it.'

'What else?'

'A girl—and a young man.'

'Oh,' Maeve said, bright-eyed. 'A young man?'

'I thought you might know of a suitable model?'

'Oh, I do,' Maeve said. 'I know just the chap.' She paused. 'He won't have to take his clothes off, will he?'

'Absolutely not,' said Ross.

And Maeve, with a fruity chuckle, said, 'Sure an' isn't that a shame.'

*   *   *

Following tradition, Forbes danced a few steps with the bride, then with Rora because she insisted, then with Maeve because he wanted to. But he had no inclination to dance with anyone else, not even Lindsay. He loitered by the door in a cool draught from the corridor and smoked a cigar that Gowry had given him. The cigar was strong and tasted foul but that somehow suited his mood. He glowered disconsolately out at the dancers and longed for it all to be over, not just Arthur's wedding but this whole drastic period of upheaval.

By the end of next week he would have new partners, sleeping partners. He was anxious to meet the men that Pickering had chosen to make sure he toed the line. He would be head of the firm, however, a new firm under an old name. He would have to learn new tricks and take on new responsibilities, but in exchange he would be 'it'. He would have fulfilled his destiny and his old ma would have her revenge on the family that had cast her out.

He watched Linnet dancing with her bearded cousin and thought how lovely she looked in her evening gown. He wondered if it might be possible to hold on to her, to separate her from the partnership but keep her as his wife. And still have Stella too.

'Penny for them, Forbes,' Gowry said.

'Penny for what?'

'Your thoughts,' Gowry said.

'Huh!' Forbes said. 'I'm not sure they're worth anything right now.'

'Don't you have what you've always wanted?'

Forbes glanced at his brother and wondered if there was enough rapport between them to enable Gowry to deduce what he'd been thinking. Long ago they had been a fighting team, in cahoots on all sorts of mischief. He had always been the golden boy, though, Ma's chosen one, and by the time they'd reached manhood they had become rivals, not friends.

'And what's that, then?' Forbes said.

'From what I hear you're about to own the firm.'

'Who told you that?'

'Lindsay, I think, or it might have been Arthur.'

'It's true,' Forbes said. 'Well, nearly true.' He drew closer to Gowry. 'I'm throwing my hand in with the oil men. If the future pans out the way I think it will then I'll be a very rich feller indeed.'

'I'm glad one of us lived up to Ma's expectations,' Gowry said.

'About Maeve . . .'

'What about her?'

'I know I only have her on loan,' Forbes said. 'She's yours, Gowry. Always has been, always will be.'

'I sincerely hope not.' Forbes cocked an eyebrow in surprise. 'I let her go once,' Gowry explained, 'and she came back. But now—well, it's not up to us what she does with her life. You can only protect them for so long, Forbes. After that they must spread their wings and learn to fly.'

'The way I did, the way you did?'

'Aye,' said Gowry. 'We were damned lucky to escape from the cage. We might be on the run like Peter or stuck with the lost causes that Charlie's attached to. Come to think of it, we might very well be dead.'

Forbes nodded. 'Do you love her?'

'Who? Maeve. Of course I—'

'Sylvie, I mean.'

'Aye, I love her.'

'After all she did to you?'

'After all we did to her, you mean,' Gowry said. 'Still, still, if you have to believe in something, I reckon it might as well be love.' He fished his watch from his pocket. 'God, will you look at the hour. I'll have to go soon.'

'I'll drive you to the quay.'

'No,' Gowry said, 'but you can shell out for a taxi, if you like.'

'Damned if I will,' said Forbes, grinning.

'Damned if you won't,' said Gowry.

*　　　*　　　*

No tears this time, no wailing and lamentation, certainly no wrestling on the pavement. She hugged him, kissed him, and sent him on his way with gratitude. She stood out in the rain waving until the taxi-cab vanished into the haze then, with just a little sigh, returned to the foyer.

Forbes would have come down with her, Lindsay too, but she'd asked for a few moments alone with her daddy. She had nothing much to say to him, though, apart from the usual platitudes, reminders to deliver her love to her mother and brother and come back to see her as soon as he could. She let him go, as once he had let her go, only there was no sadness in her, no reluctance now that she had finally learned the truth.

The strange concatenation of circumstances that had brought her to Brunswick Park seemed to have a pattern as precise as a draughtsman's drawing but whether you called it history or destiny mattered not to Maeve as she loped up the carpeted staircase to the ballroom.

Kilt tucked modestly between his knees, Ross was seated on the top step, smoking his pipe. Aunt Lindsay stood behind him, a hand resting on his broad shoulder.

Maeve stared up at them.

'Ay-hay,' she said. 'What's this then?'

'We're taking a breather,' said Ross.

'A very long breather,' said Lindsay.

'I think there's something you should know, Maeve,' Ross said, gravely. 'Your aunt and I have— well, we've fallen in love.'

Maeve seated herself at Ross's feet, propped an elbow on his knee, looked up at her aunt. 'Well, Auntie Lindsay,' she said, with a wink, 'that's hardly the end of the world.'

*   *   *

The morning church parade had not been the same without Arthur and Eleanor, and Forbes had elected to stay in bed. There had been no sign of the Calders in kirk and, after Saturday night's excitement, the service had seemed even more

495

dreary than usual. A shower of rain had chased the McCullochs up Madison Street. Cook had turned her ankle and had to be helped over the last hump, and luncheon was late because of it.

As soon as the last plate had been cleared away, Aunt Lindsay took herself off to call on Ross, Uncle Forbes retired to his room to work on a pile of paperwork, and Maeve and the boys were left alone in the parlour.

Maeve was no longer at ease with her cousins, cousins who might in fact be half-brothers. No doubt Harry had explained the situation to Philip, for although he had been a law student for less than a week, Harry had already acquired the pontificating manner of a high court judge.

'I suppose you're aware, Maeve,' he said, 'that my father has purchased both Arthur and Martin's share of our firm.'

'I did hear something of the sort,' said Maeve.

'Dad is now effectively in control.'

'Really?' Maeve tried not to appear nosy. 'I thought your mam had a big stake in it, too?'

'A stake, but no say.' Harry reached out and tipped cigarette ash into an ashtray on the fender. 'However, there's something else going on and I— ah—I wondered if you had information you'd care to share with us.'

'Information—about what?'

Philip, sitting cross-legged on the carpet, said, 'She talks to you, Mum does. She doesn't talk to us much any more.'

'Where did Uncle Forbes find the money to buy all those extra shares?'

'You're beggaring my question,' Harry said. 'However, given the changed circumstances, it's not unreasonable for you to be interested in our finances.'

'What's that supposed to mean?' Maeve said.

'It's patently obvious that you'll be included in any disbursements that my father may make in future.'

'Plain English, please,' said Maeve.

'You'll be in his will,' said Philip.

'Will I?' said Maeve. 'I mean, why?'

'Because my father will wish to avoid the embarrassment of a court case.'

'How can he be embarrassed if he's dead?' said Maeve.

'He's looking to the future,' Harry said. 'Our future.'

'Come on, Harry, your dad's a long way from popping off—and you're a long way from qualifying as a proper lawyer, so stop acting like one.'

'Be that as it may,' said Harry, undaunted, 'you will be a nominated heir in addition to Philip and myself, although I receive the impression that none of the participants is entirely certain from whom you are descended.'

'You've looked all this up in a book, haven't you?'

'I'm protecting my interests, that's all.'

'And mine,' Philip reminded him.

'I thought you liked me?' Maeve said.

'That's got nothing to do with it,' said Harry, flushing. 'If you must know, Maeve, I think you're quite selfish.'

'Me?' said Maeve, sitting bolt upright. 'What've I done?'

'Ewan Calder,' said Philip, 'has been packed off to a monastery, practically, because of you.'

'I'm not the one who tried to knock Ewan's block off.'

'You were the cause of it,' said Harry.

'You warned me about him in the first place.'

'A warning you didn't heed, apparently,' said Harry. 'Nonetheless, you obviously intend to settle here and ingratiate yourself into my father's favour. Therefore we must face up to the possibility, however remote, that if my father dies before his time, your mother . . .'

'Leave my mother out of this.'

'. . . your mother will claim that you're entitled to share—'

Maeve shot to her feet. 'I thought you were different, Harry McCulloch. You're not. You're just like the rest of them—a snob, a mercenary snob. If you're bent on fretting about the future, fret about this then: what if none of us are here? What if there's another war, and we're all killed?'

'There won't be another war,' said Harry.

'There'll never be another war,' said Phil.

'How do you know?'

'Dad says there won't be another war.'

'The League of Nations will see to it,' Harry stated.

'Sod the League of Nations,' Maeve snapped. 'I've seen what useless things leagues are. Answer me this, Harry, where did your dad get the money to buy up all those spare shares?'

Harry hesitated. 'I expect he borrowed it.'

'From a bank?' said Maeve.

'Yes, I would imagine so.'

'Never mind a war, then,' said Maeve. 'What if there's a slump? I may not have your brains, Harry, but, by Gar, I know what a slump means. What if your old man can't pay back what he's borrowed? What if he goes broke?'

'Mum has lots of money,' said Phil, disingenuously. 'She'll have a lot more too when Grandee passes away. He told us as much, though Miss Runciman will have to be taken care of now, I suppose.'

'Shut up, Phil, for heaven's sake,' said Harry, sourly.

'Ay-hay,' said Maeve. 'Now I've given you something to think about, sure an' I have. Anyway' —she could not resist—'you might have a lot more to worry you than my mam stealing your money before much longer.'

'What?' said Harry. 'What, for instance?'

'Nothing, for instance,' Maeve said, and headed hastily for the door.

*   *   *

After they made love, they talked, and talked, as if all the words saved in lonely hours in lonely years could safely be spent at last; not just words of love but promises of a practical nature that Lindsay found almost as satisfying.

Clad in one of Ross's dressing-gowns, she sat before the fire in the living-room next to the studio and made notes on a pad, jotting down figures that Ross read out to her. Bank statements, tax liabilities and insurance policies lay upon the table and with the same sort of thoroughness that he applied to painting, Ross drew a picture of his exact financial worth which, as it turned out, was considerable. For the wife of a man who had been reluctant to tell her the time of day, such

499

confidences were doubly reassuring.

Ross wasn't boasting or preening but simply sharing with her a record of his success in pounds, shillings and pence, as if he were telling her that he did not need her capital to make a go of things, that he, an artist not a businessman, had done just as well as her husband and was more than capable of taking care of her in, as it were, the style to which she had become accustomed.

'How much?' Ross asked. 'Grand total.'

She told him.

He whistled. 'I say, that's rather jolly.'

'Jolly is not the word for it,' Lindsay said.

'Enough, isn't it?'

'Enough for what?'

'To make an offer for Strathmore.'

'No,' Lindsay said.

'No?' said Ross. 'Not enough?'

'Oh yes, more than enough to offer for *half* Strathmore,' Lindsay said. 'The other half— split fifty to fifty—is mine, including repairs and renovations.'

'I don't want your money, Lin.'

'I know,' Lindsay said. 'It's my body you want.'

Ross chuckled and, leaning over her, slipped a hand beneath the dressing-gown and lightly cupped her breast. She laughed and shook him off, not roughly.

'Behave yourself,' she said. 'You already have my body—you can have it any time you wish—but I won't allow you to buy it.'

'Ah!' Ross exclaimed, taking his hand away. 'I'm sorry, Lin. I'm not trying to set you up as a kept woman.'

'I'm that already,' Lindsay said. 'Have been for

years. Fifty to fifty, old chap, or we kiss and part.'

'Are you absolutely sure you can afford it?'

Lindsay drew two firm lines under her calculations and, licking the point of the pencil, added a figure of her own. She slanted the pad to show him what she had written.

'Good God!' Ross said. 'What's *that*?'

'What Forbes will have to pay to be rid of me.'

'Rid of you? Are you sure he wants rid of you?'

'I'm sure,' said Lindsay. 'Forbes doesn't know it yet but he can't have both of us. I intend to leave him free to do as he likes.'

'Which is?' said Ross.

'To marry his blonde tart,' said Lindsay.

*　　　*　　　*

Tom Calder's resignation arrived on Forbes's desk first thing on Monday morning. Flinging the letter aside, Forbes hurried to the drawing-office only to find Tom's cubicle stripped of all personal items: books, pens, photographs, calendars and diaries, even the little wooden monkey that he, Tom, had brought back from the Niger umpteen years ago. It looked as if the office had been wiped clean and every trace of the occupant removed, like fingerprints from the scene of a crime.

Forbes tramped into the drawing-office and cornered Bob Lightbody.

'Where,' Forbes said, 'is Mr Calder?'

'Gone, Mr Forbes. Took his stuff out in a box first thing this morning, then shook hands with all of us and left. I thought you knew about it.'

'Well,' Forbes spluttered, 'well, yes, of course I knew. I just hadn't realised—I mean, I'd forgotten he was leaving today.' He forced a laugh. 'Typical, what? Typical of our Tom just to slip away. Never was much of a one for making a fuss, what?'

'I take it, Mr Forbes,' Bob Lightbody said, 'you've appointed his replacement. Anybody we happen to know, sir?'

'No,' Forbes said. 'No, nobody you—we—I mean, I haven't sorted out the applications yet, and there will have to be interviews.'

'We've lost a good man there, sir.'

'The best,' Forbes said, automatically. 'The best.'

'Who'll manage the office meantime, if you don't mind me asking?'

Forbes closed his eyes. For an instant, he felt dizzy, the bright overhead lights spinning around his head. 'You will, Bob,' he heard himself say. 'You'll stand in as office manager—temporarily.'

'A responsible job, given what we have in the ledgers.'

'There'll be a salary increase, of course.'

'I thought there might be, Mr Forbes,' Bob Lightbody said. 'I can manage the office fine but I'm no chief designer, sir, so who'll issue the job specifications and approve the patterns?'

And Forbes, still one remove from reality, answered, 'I will.'

*   *   *

It was there in black and white, the essence of all partnership agreements: *Power of Single Partner to Bind the Firm: Each partner has full authority to act as agent for the firm in all matters of business: Each partner is capable of making a contract that will be binding on his co-partners.* The deeds were a page and a half long, typed out in full with spaces for the partners' names. Funds had been funnelled through Gideon Rowe and Spellman to pay Martin and Arthur, and tomorrow Franklin's Shipbuilding would cease to be a family firm and would pass into the hands of an oil consortium.

Forbes had used all his powers of persuasion to get Tom to withdraw his resignation but Tom, who blamed himself for what had happened between his son and his granddaughter, remained adamant. There would be no familiar faces at the boardroom table tomorrow, no Arthur, no Martin, no Tom Calder, only accountants and lawyers. Of the 'old gang' only Lindsay remained, but the last person Forbes wanted in the boardroom was his wife.

Late night in Brunswick Crescent: most of Arthur's furniture had been removed to the villa on the coast and in a week or so the piano would be gone from the parlour and the old photographs from the hallway. Lindsay would have to purchase suitable pieces to replace them. Forbes leaned over the desk, hands cupped to his ears, and stared at the documents that would bind him to a future that had precious few links with the past.

'Forbes?'

He glanced up.

'Oh, it's you,' he said, wearily. 'I thought you'd gone to bed.'

'Not just yet,' Lindsay said. 'What are you doing?'

He shrugged. 'Attending to business.'

'In that case,' Lindsay said, 'perhaps you might care to attend to a little bit of business on my behalf.'

'Your behalf? What's that supposed to mean?'

He swung round in the captain's chair and peered up at her. She seemed younger tonight, light-hearted, almost gay. From behind her back she brought out a piece of plain white card and placed it on the desk before him.

'I'm selling out, Forbes. Have Mr James draft an agreement of transfer, and I'll sign it.'

'Lindsay, are you—'

'Sure? Of course I'm sure. It's what you want, isn't it? Do you recall how angry you were when Grandfather Owen left me two sixty-fourths of the business and how furious you were when I bought another four sixty-fourths from you? It seems like a very long time ago, however, and I've practically lost track of who owns what.'

'You don't have to do this, Linnet.'

'Oh, but I do,' she said. 'Indeed, I do. The boys aren't going to follow in your footsteps, are they? I mean, what will be left for them by the time your friends in the oil business have gobbled up everything they can lay hands on?'

'You're exaggerating, my love,' Forbes said. 'I'm only protecting our interests. I'm not selling them the River Clyde, you know, only one small failing shipyard. I'll still be in charge of everything.'

'Not everything,' Lindsay said.

Forbes touched the plain white card with his forefinger, edged it towards him and peered at it. 'What's this?'

'My price,' Lindsay said.

'It's too much.'

'I don't think so.'

'You're taking out the capital, too?'

'Yes, everything.'

He felt sick, just a little bit sick, at the ease with

which she had capitulated. There would be no problem about payment. The consortium would meet her price, stiff though it was, without a qualm. She had never been a fool, his wife, never dull and dim-witted like, say, Cissie Calder. She had been passive, though, a quiet, careful sort of woman who had swallowed all his nonsense, looked after him dutifully, and kept her nose out of his business. In all respects—save one—she had been the perfect wife.

He felt quite sick at the thought that when trade boomed and Pickering's Anglo-French associates brought home the bacon, he would be sharing it with Stella, not Lindsay.

'All right,' he said. 'I'll see to it. Might take a week or two, though.'

'If you want to keep the house,' she said, 'you'll have to pay for it out of your own pocket, of course, unless you can persuade your lady friend to—'

'The house? What house?'

'This house,' Lindsay said. 'My father's house.'

Forbes got slowly to his feet, holding on to the edge of the desk.

'There's absolutely no rush,' Lindsay went on. 'In fact, it would be much better for the children if one of us stayed on, at least until Phil goes up to university. I suggest you advertise for a housekeeper to replace—'

'Who told you?' Forbes said.

'Told me? Told me what?'

'About—about . . .'

'Stella, you mean? Come now, darling, surely you didn't think you could keep that one a secret?' Lindsay frowned. 'You weren't planning on installing her here, I trust? Not even you would be that crass. Think of the scandal, apart from anything else. If we're patient, there will be almost no scandal at all, just a little bit of gossip. In a year or so we'll be at liberty to separate.'

'Separate?'

'Isn't that what you want?'

'No. No.'

'Well,' Lindsay said, 'it's what I want.'

'Where are you—what are you . . . ?'

'What am I going to do with all the money your friends will pay me?' Lindsay said. 'I'll put out some of it to buy Strathmore.'

'Strath . . .'

'Ross and I,' Lindsay said, 'together.'

'Ross?' Forbes said. 'So it's bloody Ross, is it?'

'Well, you didn't think it was bloody Paget, did you?'

'I didn't think it was anyone,' Forbes said. 'I didn't think anyone would be interested in you. Dear God! Why Ross?'

'Because he loves me.'

'Because he's a bloody Franklin, you mean.'

'That too, perhaps,' Lindsay admitted.

'Does your father know what's in the wind?'

'Ross told him.'

'And does he approve of what you're doing?'

'Well, he never approved of you, Forbes. I can't imagine why.'

Still holding on to the desk, Forbes drew himself up. 'By selling me your shares in Franklin's,' he said, 'do you hope to purchase your freedom?'

'Don't be such a prig, Forbes,' Lindsay said. 'And do stop being so melodramatic. I'm not walking out with a shawl over my head and my boots tied

506

around my neck. I'm making you an offer of my shares without capital attachments. If you want them, buy them. If you don't, I'll be happy enough to leave them where they are and receive my annual dividends. Freedom doesn't come with a price ticket; that's just another figment of your imagination.'

'It's all about Stella, isn't it?'

'No, it's not about Stella, or Marjorie, or Sylvie Calder for that matter. It's not about you at all, Forbes. For once, it's about me, what I want. If you wish to marry Stella Pickering, that's your business. I really don't care.'

He picked up the card and stroked his chin with it.

'Have you slept with him yet?' he asked.

'Of course.'

'All right'—Forbes nodded—'if this is how you want our marriage to end, I've no choice but to accept your terms.'

'And buy my shares?'

'And buy your shares,' said Forbes.

*   *   *

They arrived through the rain in two shiny black motor-cars, each driven by a uniformed chauffeur. Work on the gantries that overlooked the gatehouse stopped and men crowded to the rails to catch a glimpse of the new owners. In the drawing-office, too, boards were abandoned and draughtsmen and tracers rushed to the windows to see what their new masters looked like. In fact, they looked much the same as their old masters. They sported the same sort of hats, the same sombre black overcoats, and walked with the same swagger. In the long run it didn't matter whether they were worth one million or ten, provided they kept the order books full and paid out punctual every Friday afternoon.

Forbes did not go out to greet his faceless partners. He continued to sit in his grandfather's big carved chair at the head of the boardroom table, Meg Connors at his side, her notebook open and her little quiver of pencils at the ready. Franklin's lawyers were assembled around him, a mass of papers spread upon the polished mahogany. He had never felt more alone. He looked down at Mrs Connors, at the strands of grey that showed in her fair hair, and wondered what she thought of it all, wondered if she cared about him, or any of them.

Outside, the men had gone back to work. The familiar sound of hammering drifted up from the slipways. The familiar smell of tar and coke smoke hung in the damp air like the very breath of industry.

On the wall behind Forbes the big clock ticked relentlessly. At five minutes to noon, the sergeant from the gatehouse knocked on the door and opened it, and the new partners and their retinue trooped in.

Forbes rose and walked the length of the room and shook hands.

Shook hands with Gideon Rowe, Sir Andrew Pickering and, to his dismay, with Mitchell Hussey who, it seemed, had elected to replace his wife, Marjorie, as Forbes's sleeping partner.

508

CHAPTER TWENTY-ONE

The River in the Rain

The first delivery of steel plate from Bradford's proved to be well below standard. Forbes shipped it back. He despatched Archie Robb to Sheffield to inspect the works and was dismayed by the manager's poor report. He interviewed three applicants for the post of chief designer; none was suitable. He made one last attempt to persuade Tom Calder to return but Tom claimed that he was enjoying retirement, and would not relent.

The intricacy of Tom's designs confused Forbes and he relied on Bob Lightbody to keep things ticking over in the drawing-office, a situation that was less than ideal. Jack Burgoyne had recovered from his August defeat and was reorganising the unions to resist the next round of pay-offs. Pressure also came from Forbes's new partners by letter and telephone, a constant cold-blooded hectoring by Mitchell Hussey, whose interference contributed nothing to managerial efficiency or confidence.

Matters were no better in Brunswick Crescent.

Cook had been lured to Largs to work for Arthur and Eleanor. Enid had taken over the kitchen and had brought in one of her sisters as a day-maid. Without Eleanor Runciman's firm hand on the helm the girls rapidly became insolent and lazy. Breakfast was often late, dinner a disaster, Sunday lunch little more than a bowl of soup and a plate of cold mutton. Lindsay did not seem to care. She was spending more and more time with Ross, and Forbes was too preoccupied to advertise for domestic staff and, as autumn edged into winter, he gradually came to accept that he was no longer master in his own household.

He saw even less of Maeve than he did of Lindsay. When the girl wasn't sitting for Ross, she was out 'visiting' her friend Bobby Shannon. Harry had discovered the joys of the Students' Union and spent more time there, drinking beer and arguing politics, than he did at home. Philip, bored, ignored and disgruntled, joined St Anne's Youth Fellowship and passed his evenings playing badminton in the church hall and, though Forbes knew it not, embarked on a tentative, well-mannered courtship of Dorothy Calder.

November was a dismal month. All that kept Forbes going was the thought that he would soon be with Stella and that she would offer ample compensation for all the ills that an unjust world had heaped upon him.

He waited three weeks, and heard not a word.

He waited another week, then telephoned Merriam House.

No one answered the call.

Friday, he rang in the morning, quite early. No answer. He rang again just after lunch. Still no answer. He rang again on Monday, several times. No one, not Pickering, not Stella, not Ronnie or any of the invisible servants deigned to lift the receiver from its hook.

Forbes was worried now. He wanted her. He wanted her as he had wanted no other woman. He brooded about her silence. He knew that she wasn't cautious and, therefore, chose to interpret her lack of response as another of her wiles, her wonderful little tricks for keeping him on the boil.

He wrote her a personal note, inviting her to lunch at the Cardross Arms. He drove downriver in drizzling rain early on Wednesday afternoon, and drank a solitary glass of wine at the bar, watching the table by the window, watching the door, waiting for Stella to sweep in wearing her swagger overcoat and the tight little hat that made her look like an aviatrix, to flash him her wide-mouthed smile and demand that he buy her a cocktail.

Stella did not sweep in. Stella did not show at all.

Finally, well after two, he ate alone—soup, fish, lemon tart, washed down with too much wine. He ate unhurriedly, staring out at the rain falling on the river, contained and insular and filled with a thin gruel of despair.

He sat in the Lanchester for ten minutes, smoking a cigarette, then, with dusk just beginning to drift over the Clyde, drove back along the twisting country roads to Dalmuir and up the track to Merriam House, knowing in his heart what he would find there.

The *For Sale* notice was prominently displayed on a large board wired to the wrought-iron gate. Forbes climbed out of the car and approached the gate. Helplessly, he shook the chains and padlock. Leaves littered the driveway. The rectangles of the house were grey and foreboding in the half dark, not a light to be seen, not a solitary light.

He returned to the motor-car, leaned on the bonnet and stared up into the rain-drenched sky. He heard the whack of steam hammers, the soft, ineluctable roar from yards and factories drifting up from the river in the rain.

And he knew it was over, that all he had was all

he had ever wanted, and the one thing he had wanted, he had lost forever.

* * *

The shawl was an affectation. She didn't think Bobby would mind. She trotted down Riverside Street along with the crowd of shipyard workers who, now that night came early, spilled through the gates at five. She had the shawl over her head, no hat, and had dug out the heavy shoes she'd been wearing when she'd arrived in Glasgow all those months ago. She felt comfortable in them, though the woollen skirt and blouse were new and the outfit—the *ensemble* Aunt Lindsay would call it— did not altogether fit the image of a working-man's wife.

She had borrowed a canvas shopping bag from Enid and had raided not only the larder but Uncle Forbes's cabinet as well. She had lugged the bag down the hill from Brunswick Park with a half-bottle of whisky clinking against a big tin of pears. Eggs, bacon, butter, bread and the thick slices of sausage meat that she'd cut from the round in the larder were padded in newspaper, and safe.

She felt different now, more at home in the canyon-like streets that bordered the river than she had ever done up on the hill.

Having two fathers had been a lot less advantageous than Ross had predicted. While she was perfectly willing to forgive her daddy, and her mother too, for those long-ago indiscretions, she could not allow them to spoil her life. In Dublin she had been a rebel, precocious and headstrong, encouraged in her wild ways by her mother's affair

512

with a gun-runner, by her father's refusal to fight for causes in which he did not believe, by her Irish uncles, her first love, Turk, and the harum-scarum gang that hung out in the Shamrock Hotel.

She had seen all that go *pop* and, as a consequence, had tumbled into womanhood rather too quickly for her own good.

Now, thanks to her daddy, she had been forced to experience the gilded, repressive, protected life that her poor Scottish cousins had to endure. And it was not for her. She did not want to become a piece of someone else's story, a figment of someone else's imagination, like the girl in *The Captive Heart*.

She wasn't daft enough to believe in happy endings. She already had an inkling that life goes rolling on, that you cling to it, take what happiness comes your way and pay for it as best you can.

She would model for Ross when he needed her. She would call at the house in Brunswick Park when invited. She would be a loyal niece to Uncle Forbes, and Aunt Lindsay's friend. She would even put up with Harry once he fell off his high horse. She would go home now and then to Dublin and take Bobby with her, leading him forth and back across enemy lines. She would soften his anger, soothe his grief, and feed him well. She would look after his old man, too, and make a home in the tenement in Riverside, a fine rough little fortress from which to look out at what might have been.

And, if luck were on her side, she would have no regrets.

He was waiting for her, watching out for her, at the close mouth.

The collar and tie made him seem smart,

different from the men in greasy boiler suits and flat caps. He wasn't different, though—except that he was the man she had fallen in love with, and *that* was what made him different.

He took her hand, would have taken the shopping bag too if she'd allowed it, and led her up the dank, gas-lit staircase, past the lavatories on the landings, led her up to the top of the tenement, and, with his key, unlocked the brown-painted door and ushered her into the hall.

She swung the shopping bag carefully on to the top of the coal bunker and let him take her into his arms. He kissed her, fondled her, pressed her against the edge of the bunker, the wet shawl hanging from her shoulders, her hair loose.

She had watched him with his sister, with Alice. She knew how much love was in him. But it was the other thing, that strange wilful thing that came on you whether you liked it or not that she had fallen for, the swift, trusting giving away of yourself that has no label and no name.

Bobby pulled away. He blew out his cheeks.

'Have you told them about us yet?' he asked, huskily.

'Not yet,' said Maeve.

'You'll have to tell them soon,' said Bobby.

'Or what?' said Maeve.

'I might forget I'm a gentleman.'

'All right,' Maeve said. 'I'll tell them very soon.'

'When?'

'Just as soon as you ask me properly.'

'Properly?'

'I want to hear you say it.'

'Uh-huh,' the draughtsman said. 'Miss Maeve McCulloch, I'm fair daft about you, so will you, for

God's sake, marry me?'

Maeve, quite naturally flattered, answered, 'Yes.'

*   *   *

It had taken Ross weeks to find the ideal beast, a passive dappled grey mare pastured not more than a half-mile from the big house of Strathmore.

He had spent days out in the field, drawing board propped on the dyke, with carrots and a pocket full of sugar lumps to coax the plump old pet to him. He had filled six or eight pads with sketches and, in the evenings, crouched before the fire in the drawing-room sorting them out and working them up.

He had also purchased several large books on the anatomy of the horse and, to Lindsay's delight, had even painted, *alla prima*, a picture of the mare at full gallop, cleverly turning the canvas to catch the animal from several different angles so that it seemed that Tam o' Shanter's faithful nag was part of a herd, thundering, wild-eyed, over the outline of the Brig o' Doon.

Ross worked boldly, in chalk as well as pencil, and there was, Lindsay felt, a new dimension to his work, a vigour that had not been there before. In a week or ten days he would fetch Maeve and Bobby to the studio and set up the strenuous poses. He had no intention of buying the blessed mare and installing her in his garage in Flowerhill Drive, Ross said, for however talented he might be in other directions, Bobby Shannon was probably not a horseman, any more than Maeve was really a witch.

'I think, however,' Ross said, 'that I'd better not

515

tarry too long in putting this picture together for, by the look of it, Mr Shannon and your dear niece may be contemplating a union of some sort and I've no wish to wind up painting variations on the Madonna and Child.'

'Maeve's too sensible to allow that to happen,' Lindsay said.

'Maeve's old enough—and ripe.'

'Ripe!' said Lindsay. 'What a horrid word.'

'Accurate, though,' Ross said. 'In a peasant community Maeve would be regarded as a valuable and fertile property.'

'Brunswick Park is not a peasant community.'

'I wasn't thinking of Brunswick Park.'

'Where then? Riverside?'

Ross rolled on to an elbow and peeped at Lindsay over his shoulder. He wore heavy tweed trousers that made his bottom look broad. The heavy cable-knit pullover suited him, though, and seemed to match his beard. He looked, Lindsay thought, like a woodsman, not an artist. She had no doubt that in two or three years' time, when they finally set up home in the big, rambling country house, he—and she too—would go swiftly and wonderfully to seed.

Ross said, 'What about you?'

'What about me?'

'Are you—I mean, do you think you might still be young enough?'

'Ross!' Lindsay said. 'I'm forty years old.'

She was lying on the moth-eaten leather sofa that they had wheeled through from the hall. The pine log fire in the old stone fireplace blazed and sizzled and the wind beat against the French doors that Ross had roped shut with baling twine. Water

516

and electricity had been restored and a few urgent repairs done to the roof but the main work of renovation would not begin until spring.

In the meantime it was quite an adventure to rough it, to cook huge meals in the cavernous smoke-filled kitchen, to snuggle down in the canopied bed in the big, beamed room on the first floor and watch the firelight flicker on the walls and hear the house growl contentedly around them.

One neglected old mansion house and thirteen acres of land shared jointly between cousins, a folly, a caprice, a bolt-hole from the tedium of middle age; Lindsay felt no guilt at what she was doing. She had cheated no one of any consequence, not even her sons. She would ease herself out of Brunswick Crescent, detach herself gently from the boys, from Forbes. She would not abandon them entirely as Tom Calder had abandoned Sylvie, and Forbes had abandoned Maeve. She would draw Philip and Harry back to her as soon as they were mature enough to forgive her which, she thought, might be all too soon.

As for the rest, she was relieved to be shot of her share of the partnership, that inappropriate burden that her grandfather, out of kindness, had hung around her neck all those years ago: Forbes, Forbes and the shipyard, Forbes and Sylvie Calder—and Maeve; the dark secrets that men have that meek, obedient women are not supposed to share, those strange universal longings that, like childhood trinkets, are supposed to remain hidden under the marriage bed.

She slipped from the sofa and lay by her cousin on the worn hearth-rug.

She reached out and teased his beard with her fingertips.

'Do you really want babies, Ross?' she asked.

'Babies?' Ross said. 'Well, one would do for a start.'

'I don't know if it's possible.'

'I think I'd make rather a good father, don't you?'

'You'd make a wonderful father,' Lindsay said. 'That isn't the problem. The problem is that I may be too old.'

'Are you sure? I mean—Oh, you know what I mean.'

She sat up, pixie-like, hugged her knees and stared into the fire.

'I've always wanted a daughter,' she said, wistfully. 'I love my sons dearly, but a girl—you wouldn't mind if it were a girl, Ross, would you?'

'A daughter would suit me very well indeed.'

'Actually,' Lindsay said, 'I'm probably not too old, not yet. But we'll have to be quick, Ross, and if we do—if something lovely happens, then a legal separation won't be enough. How long do divorces take?'

'I have no idea,' said Ross.

'Oh,' Lindsay said, 'what a scandal that would be, what a dreadful, gossipy family scandal.' She laughed. 'Harry would have a fit.'

'Forbes, too, I imagine.'

For a moment she *almost* thought of Forbes, *almost* wondered what he was doing right now, then the thought went floating out of her head.

She had given too much to Forbes already, too much time, too much attention, too much of herself. She must cherish every moment of what was left, every precious moment, and not spoil her happiness by worrying, out of habit, about her husband who, no matter what she said or did, would survive.

'A baby,' she said, serenely. 'Well, why not? Why ever not?'

Then, glancing towards the French doors, she gasped in surprise.

'Look, dearest,' she said. 'I do believe it's beginning to snow.'

'So it is,' Ross said. 'My, my, my!'

He scrambled to his feet, hoisted her up and drew her to the door. She looked out through the cracked glass into a darkness that was dark no longer.

'Shall we step outside for a minute?' Ross said.

'Yes,' Lindsay said. 'Yes, darling, let's do that.'

And Ross untied the baling twine, pushed open the door and, taking Lindsay by the hand, led her out on to the terrace into the lightly falling snow.